MOBILE
Must Fall

A Novel from the deMelilla Chronicles

D1522402

STEPHEN ESTOPINAL

LIBROS

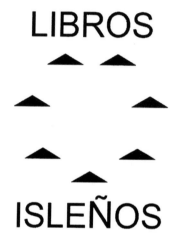

ISLEÑOS

Libros Isleños Publishing

Gonzales, Louisiana 70737

ISBN-10: 1480188816

ISBN-13: 978-1480188815

Dedication

*A special thanks to my sisters,
Catherine and Virginia for
their continuing love,
support and assistance.*

*And, as always,
To the Love of my Life
Marie Elaine Russell*

CHAPTER *1*

D iego led three men along a wooden walkway fronting a row of alehouses. The buildings were to his left, as was his habit. Buildings to the left would require an assailant coming out of an alley or doorway to confront his left side, leaving his right arm free to draw his sword or pummel the assailant. He glanced down each alley they reached before crossing it and scanned both the walkway ahead and the street to his right.

It was a clear, cool December morning and the sun was just beginning to paint the mast heads of ships and keel boats docked along the Mississippi River a bright orange. The street to their right was officially named *Calle de Rey*, but was called *Rue Levée* by the locals. Soon the muddy, rutted plank and ballast roadway would be out of the shadows. Even at this early hour stevedores, wagons, mules and ox sleds were busy moving freight across the shallow mound of a levee to and from the river vessels. The noise of creaking axles, hooves, and men shouting, cursing in a dozen languages covered the sound of the four men as they moved along the walkway, quietly nearing their destination.

The men wore the uniforms of *El Regimiento Fijo de Infantería de la Luisiana* (The Fixed Infantry Regiment of Louisiana) – Governor General Gálvez's core regiment. Instead of the regulation white-trimmed tricorns, however, the men wore white wool garrison caps lined in blue. The pointed tip of each cap was folded over until it nearly touched the wearer's right ear and the bottom turned up at the forehead to form a blue bill decorated with a brass fleur-de-lis, symbol of Charles III, the Borbón King of Spain. Their white, long-tailed wool coats were lined and trimmed in the same shade of blue as the lining of their caps. Beneath their coats were blue waistcoats, shirts and trousers. They wore tall white canvas gaiters buttoned over their trousers from the ankle to the thigh, held in place by thin, black leather straps under the knee and covering their heavy, buckled shoes. All wore infantry short swords and, except for Diego, carried axe handles.

Diego's uniform coat included matching blue epaulets on both shoulders for he was *Sargento* Diego deMelilla y Tupinar, first sergeant – *Primero* – of the regiment's first company, the Tiger Company. Diego was thirty-one years old, tall –five feet, ten inches – wide shouldered and heavily muscled. His height had earned his recruiter an enlistment bonus of forty-five *reales*. His hair was light brown, nearly blond and his eyes were sparkling blue. These traits were commonly found among the natives of Diego's birthplace, Gran Canaria of the Canary Islands. Diego was an *Isleño*. Throughout Spain and all of her colonies, only natives of the seven islands known as the Canaries were called *Isleños*, literally "Islanders." The ranks of Spain's army and navy, as well as her world-wide colonies, were heavily populated with *Isleños*.

Diego stopped his men at the corner of an alehouse named *Le Pot de Rois* (the King's chamber pot). He smoothed his wide moustache with his left hand, then rubbed his closely shaven chin.

"Pook, take Nieves and bracket that window," Diego said as he gestured down the alley separating the alehouse from the neighboring warehouse. He waited until Pook Gonzales and Nieves were in place.

"Follow me," he said to the remaining man, a youngster named Martin who could not have been older than sixteen. Martin had been a civilian sixty days ago, now he was a new *soldado* and thoroughly awed by the big, burly Sergeant deMelilla. "When we get in there," Diego continued, "turn around and cover my back. Anybody, I mean anybody, tries to come up behind me, you hit them right here," Diego pushed on Martin's collarbone, "as hard as you can, just like I taught you. Understand?"

"*Sí, Primero,*" Martin squeaked.

Diego shouldered his way through the unlatched alehouse doors (few such establishments in New Orleans even had latches). He advanced into the center of the dingy room and paused to allow his eyes to adjust. Martin scurried in behind Diego, turned around and almost backed into the sergeant.

Two men appeared to be asleep at a table to Diego's right and a fat, filthy, greasy bearded man was sitting behind a long set of planks set atop two barrels across the back of the room.

"Where is he?" Diego said in his heavily Spanish-accented French.

"Qui voulez-vous (who do you want)?" the man with the greasy beard said with a German accent. It seemed that every second person in New Orleans who spoke French did so with one accent or another. As Greasy Beard spoke the man's eyes briefly flicked toward a door on Diego's left. Diego checked the sleepers, who had not moved, and strode to the door. He tried that latch, but it had been locked.

"You can't go in there," Greasy Beard said.

Ignoring him, Diego pounded on the door and yelled, "Plata, you in there?" He could hear scurrying on the other side of the door followed by the sound of shutters opening. Diego threw his shoulder against the door which gave easily, throwing splinters and pieces of the cast-iron latch plate flying into the room. A pair of bare feet disappeared through an open window.

A woman lay on the bed, naked. She cursed in French, spat and rolled toward the wall, pulling a pillow over her head. A pair of shoes, clearly Spanish army issue, lay next to the bed along with two earthenware jugs. One was on its side, evidently empty. The other was upright, but uncorked.

There was the sound of a brief scuffle from beyond the open window before Pook's voice could be clearly heard. "Good morning, Plata," he said. "Put these on." The sound of chains was mixed with Plata's pleading voice. "You would not shackle a brother soldier, would you, Pook? Have a heart. I will not run, I swear, on my mother's eyes."

"Your mother is dead. Give me your other hand."

"I said you can't go in there," Greasy Beard was yelling and Diego could hear the man's feet as he worked his way around the end of the make-shift bar before heading toward the room.

"I said —." Then there was a thumping sound and Greasy Beard screamed.

Diego went to the window and leaned out to see the shoeless Plata Pérez, wearing only his underclothes, a dirty cotton shirt and ragged trousers. He was shackled.

"Bring him to the street and wait for me," Diego said as he pulled his head back into the room. He picked up the shoes and kicked the jugs. They were empty. He searched the room for the rest of Plata's uniform. There was no closet or armoire, just pegs along the wall. A chamber pot decorated one corner of the room. A small table holding a wash bowl was next to the bed. The woman's dress hung from one peg above cloth slippers. Diego flipped the sheets about, but there was no uniform.

"Get away," the woman commanded. She held the pillow over her face, but made no other move to cover herself.

"*Primero*," Martin said in a shaky voice from the doorway. "The others are awake."

Diego went to the doorway. Greasy Beard was sitting in a corner, holding his left arm against his chest with his right and cursing in German. He was out of the fight. The two sleepers had awakened and were coming toward Martin with drawn knives. They were hairy, rough looking men dressed in buckskin jackets, leather gaiters and moccasins. Diego picked up Martin under the arms and repositioned him to his left.

"Draw," he snarled to Martin out of the corner of his mouth as he slowly drew his own short sword. Both of the ruffians stopped at the sound of steel scraping out of a scabbard. Martin had shifted his stave to his left hand and fumbled for his short sword, finally managing to pull it out and position it at the ready.

"*Messieurs*," Diego said. "I think you should tend to your friend in the corner."

One of the men straightened up. "He's nothing to me," the man said in crude French as he slipped the knife into his belt. He spoke to his companion in English, a language that Diego was only beginning to learn. "Come on, Hank," the man said and his friend put his knife away as well. They both walked to the alehouse entrance without turning their backs on Diego. As they opened the door to go into the street, a blinding light flooded into the room. The sun had fully risen.

"I think I broke his arm," Martin said as he looked at Greasy Beard huddled in the corner.

"Next time he will not interfere with a soldier's duty. See how he cradles his left arm against his chest? You only broke his collarbone. He will live."

Martin's face was pale and he swallowed hard.

"You did well," Diego said. "Keep your sword out until we are into the street and we are certain those two Kentuckians are gone."

The traffic along Levee Street had swallowed up the Kentuckians. Pook and Nieves came up with Plata between them as Diego and Martin stepped cautiously out of the alehouse. Pook led the prisoner along by a short rope tied to the middle link of the shackles.

"Those two took off downriver," Pook said. "Want to get them?"

"No," Diego said as he slipped his sword in its scabbard. Martin followed suit. He had to shift the stave to hold it under his arm and hold the mouth of his scabbard with his left hand as he clumsily guided the sword home. When he finished, he looked up to see the other four men watching him and his face reddened.

Diego took the rope from Pook and pulled Plata until the man had to crane his neck to look up at the tall sergeant.

"Where is your uniform, Pérez?" Diego growled. The fact that he said "Pérez," the man's surname instead of "Plata" an *apodo* (nickname) was not lost on the prisoner. Private Alejandro Pérez was a wiry man of average height, maybe five foot four inches tall, about thirty-five with a full head of white, almost silvery hair which earned him the name "Plata" (silver).

"Where is your uniform?" Diego's face was inches from the ashen prisoner. "Who did you sell it to?" Soldiers on a drunk often sold everything they had, including the clothes off of their backs, just to buy another bottle with no thought of the consequences. Plata shrugged.

"Speak, man."

"I don't know, *Primero*, just some woman. She said she liked the wool."

There was little chance the coat, waistcoat and gaiters would be found. The wool would have been turned into several shirts or gloves or caps and the three dozen or so buttons from the garments used like coinage in the back alleys. Plata would be placed in the labor platoon and set to back-breaking labors until his petty private's pay accumulated enough to buy a replacement uniform. The loss of Plata on the line infuriated Diego. The man was a good soldier, steady under fire, dependable in a scrape and now he would be digging latrines and hauling night soil for three months while the regiment trained for the assault on Mobile.

"Damn fool," Diego exclaimed and he handed the lead back to Pook. "Let's get him home."

They formed a prisoner detail around Plata and led him along the walk-way. They turned at the next street leading away from the river. There was no freight being trucked along this side street so Diego directed them along the center of the roadway rather than having them squeeze along the narrow wooden walkway and forcing pedestrians aside. It had not rained for several days, so the horse manure and dirt that covered the roadway had been packed into a hard surface.

Two officers in red coats dripping with gold trim and wearing feathered bicorn hats were coming the other way. They squinted as they watched the Spanish soldiers approach out of the glare of the rising sun. The officers shuffled to the side of the road to make room for Diego's detail to pass unimpeded. Diego saluted as they passed the officers and said in his best English, "Good morning, Sirs."

One of the officers returned the salute and said, *"Buenos días, Sargento."*

"Primero," Martin whispered after the pair had passed beyond earshot. "Those men were British officers."

"That is correct."

"But, we are at war with Britain!"

"That is also correct."

"What are those officers doing here in New Orleans? Why did you speak to them as if they were friends?"

"Those officers are prisoners of war," Diego explained. "General Gálvez has paroled them. They are allowed to go about the city during the day and must report to their quarters before night fall."

"The General trusts those men?"

"It is not a matter of trust. They are being followed, discreetly. The General has a problem. So far in this war with Britain, we have captured over five hundred regulars. There are not enough soldiers to guard so many and mount a campaign against East Florida at the same time. The General also paroled most of the British militia to their farms, otherwise there would have been thousands to guard and feed. Local planters have been allowed to house British prisoners and work them in the fields. In this way many prisoners have been separated and spread around Louisiana, one or two to a plantation, relatively well fed, well housed. I have heard it said some of the prisoners sent to plantations are finding their new lot in life preferable to being soldiers in the British army. Some may not return when this war is done. The General is planning for the future. If Spain is going to gain control of the Floridas again, it will not do to have a population that has been abused by our army. It is a strange kind of war."

Martin looked back at the two British officers who were well away by this time. *They looked like regular folks,* he thought. *At a word from Primero, I would be expected to kill such men.* Martin was not certain he was going to like being a soldier.

"Eyes front, Martin," Diego snapped. "You are not on a Sunday stroll."

"He's just trying to take it all in, *Primero,*" Plata said.

"Silence, prisoner," Diego ordered. "If either of those two were your commanding officer, you would have the hide lashed from your back for what you have done. It may still happen." Lashing, a common practice in the British army, was not so frequently ordered in Spain's colonial army, particularly under Gálvez. Plata had failed to return from leave, not deserted. A few months in the penalty platoon was likely, though the company commander could request of Gálvez to have him whipped. Once away from the city and on campaign, Plata was a good, dependable soldier. In a city where whores and rum were available, he was useless.

They reached the upper end of the road leading to the magazine and the temporary bivouac area for Tiger Company. Diego halted the detail before the command tent and noted a single guard. A pennant on a staff at the entrance indicated an officer was on duty. When he had assembled his small arrest detail that morning he had been the ranking man at the regimental command tent. It was well before sunrise when Diego sent the night watch to wake the men he had selected for the excursion.

"Who is on duty, Búho?" Diego asked quietly of the guard. The guard, Private Francisco Franco y Madána, was instantly given the *apodo* "Búho" (owl) by his messmates because of the man's wide, round eyes and tiny, beak-like nose.

"Ensign Piernas is the duty officer, *Primero*," Búho said, rolling his giant eyes. Ensign Piernas was the son of a high official in New Orleans. His father had purchased the commission although the Ensign was nearly the identical age of Private Martin, maybe sixteen years.

"Private Franco," Diego said in a louder and official sounding voice, "Please advise Ensign Piernas that Private Pérez has been arrested and is here for –" Diego paused, searching for the right word, "– discipline."

"Bring him in, Sergeant," said a youthful voice within the tent.

Búho pulled the tent flap aside for Diego who pushed the disheveled Plata before him into the command tent.

"Come to attention," Diego growled to Plata out of the corner of his mouth before snapping to attention himself.

Diego saluted, "Sir, Sergeant deMelilla reporting with the prisoner Private Alejandro Pérez."

Piernas' lip curled up. "Why is he dressed only in his underclothes?"

"The prisoner sold his uniform, sir, to buy rum, sir."

"Sold his uniform! Find out where it is, Sergeant. We can't have a uniform of this regiment in the hands of the enemy."

"Most likely, sir, it has been reduced to cloth to make other garments and the buttons distributed around the city, sir."

"And what am I expected to do with this deserter?"

"If I might suggest, sir," Diego lowered his voice slightly so that the many ears listening outside of the tent could not hear. "Place him in the penalty platoon until we leave on campaign, sir."

"I should put him in the penalty platoon for the rest of his miserable life."

"Do that, sir, and he will not be in the line for the next campaign."

Diego wanted Plata in the battle line because he was a good fighter. Piernas took Diego's statement to mean the penalty platoon would give Plata an opportunity to escape battle.

"Sergeant, subject to the approval of Captain Herrera, you will place this man in the penalty platoon until such time as we begin the campaign to take Mobile." Captain Herrera was the company commander of Tiger Company. Technically, a mere Ensign did not have the authority to sentence a man to the penalty platoon, but it was unlikely the Captain would rescind the order. Normally, such a sentence would be followed by a blistering tongue-lashing, but the Ensign had no idea of what should be said.

"Dismissed," was all he could think to say.

"Sir," Diego saluted and unceremoniously pulled Plata out of the tent before the private could open his mouth and make matters worse.

Once clear of the command tent, Diego handed Plata over to Pook. "Take him to his tent and have him put on his garrison uniform, if he hasn't sold that as well. Then bring him to Sergeant Ortega." The garrison uniform was a heavy brown cotton jacket and trousers worn for work details. Ortega was the penalty platoon sergeant. Once officially under Ortega's control, Plata would be ordered to wear his jacket inside-out so all could see he was on penalty detail.

Diego left the regimental command area and walked to the Tiger Company command tent. Second Sergeant Juan Gusman had conducted the morning formation for Tiger Company. Diego had to laugh to himself. Tiger Company was a company in name only. He could not remember a time when there were more than fifty men assigned to the company. Indeed, he could not remember when the Fixed Regiment of Louisiana numbered more than two hundred men present and ready for duty.

Gusman was working on a uniform coat. His head was down as he concentrated on sewing buttons on one of the cuffs. This morning was a "maintenance" morning during which soldiers cleaned and repaired weapons, uniforms and other equipment. The training had been constant for several weeks. Drills, volleys, road marches and bayonet exercises along with the daily need to provide meals, latrines, shelters, and a thousand other things necessary for men to live had worn down men and equipment. The *mantenimiento* was as welcome as a holiday.

"Sergeant Gusman."

The man's head shot up and he jumped to his feet dropping coat and buttons at his feet.

"*Sí, Primero?*"

"Sit down and tend to your work. I just want to know how the morning report went."

"We reported thirty-nine present for duty, four on arrest detail, six in hospital and one missing."

"Change that to one on the penalty platoon. We found Plata in the *"Gouvernail Cassé."* The true name of the alehouse was *Le Pot de Rois*, but "Broken Rudder" was the name the longshoremen called the place and the soldiers adopted the name, sometime shortening it to *"Cassé."*

Gusman returned to the task of replacing buttons.

"Where did you get the buttons? Supply has been out of them for months."

"Brillo bought several from a washerwoman last night." Gusman paused to assess his work. "They look as good as issue buttons."

That is because they are issue, Diego thought. *At least Plata's buttons are back into the ranks.*

"Pardon me, *Primero*." The voice came from the entrance to the tent. Diego turned, stepped to the front of the tent to face the speaker, a man he recognized as one of the headquarters' runners – Gálvez's headquarters. The man proffered a folded paper toward Diego, who accepted it.

"Do I need to sign for it?"

"No, *Primero.*"

"Is a reply expected?"

"No, *Primero.*"

"Then go." Diego waved the man away. He did not like having headquarters people about. They heard too much, talked too much and thought – not at all. The man was gone in seconds.

Diego glanced down at Gusman who quickly returned to his sewing. He looked at the folded paper. The flap was sealed with red wax and impressed with the stylized initials "H-F" which stood for *"Honor et Fidelitas"* the Regimental slogan. *"Sargento Diego deMelilla"* was written in script across the opposite side. Diego recognized the handwriting. It was the hand of Renaldo, the chief regimental clerk. He broke the seal and opened the paper.

Sargento Diego deMelilla is ordered to present himself at the Cabildo at nine in the morning, today 10 December. Report to Colonel Don Jacinto Panis.

Jacinto Panis! The last time Diego had reported to Panis he had been a private solder and Panis a Captain. That was only last April. It was the last time he was with Mézu, his beautiful wife. The lovely and courageous *Doña* Maria "Mézu" Artiles y Ventomo, Diego's wife of ten years and mother to his two children had kissed him goodbye in the courtyard of Fort St. Charles that April morning when Diego, Panis and a scout named T'Chien Dardar left for the Floridas. Mézu had died in July. Yellow Fever, they said. She had been buried in a mass grave along with fifty other victims of the epidemic. Everybody said it had been a small epidemic. He would have a stone set for her in a proper cemetery as soon as he had saved enough. Diego felt his throat tighten.

"Orders, *Primero?*" Gusman could no longer hold his curiosity in check.

"It says there is a good chance you may be acting First Sergeant of Tiger Company for some time, no increase in pay, naturally."

"I would not expect it."

Diego went into his tent, which was so close to the command tent it shared a few anchor stakes, placed his garrison cap on his bedroll and retrieved his tricorn. It would not do to report to the Colonel in anything other than a full dress uniform.

"What time is it?" Diego called from the tent.

"Eight has just struck," Gusman replied.

Enough time for a quick breakfast. Diego retrieved a few coins from his haversack and slipped them into his pocket. The regimental mess would be closed, much too late for breakfast there, but there were a few places on the way to the Cabildo where a man might purchase a cup of coffee, a roll and a slice of fried ham. He tried to remember who had the security detail of the Cabildo and decided it was the Grenadier regiment from Veracruz. There would be no chance of finding out what this was about before nine.

Diego decided to detour to Levee Street on his trip to the Cabildo. It was out of the way, but the possibility of finding a shop or vendor selling coffee and a breakfast was better along the riverfront. He stepped up onto the wooden walkway, called a *banquette* by the locals, not far from the place where he had arrested Plata. He reached the corner of Levee Street and *Calle San Pedro* and turned toward the Cabildo when a voice called out in English.

"Sergeant, please join us for breakfast."

The two British officers Diego and the arrest detail had passed earlier were seated at a table under an awning next to the *banquette*. It was the elder of the two who had called to Diego.

"I am sorry, sir," Diego said. "My English is not good."

"No matter, my Spanish is satisfactory," the officer replied with a perfect Castilian dialect. "Do not worry, sergeant. We will converse loudly enough for our escorts to hear every word." The officer tilted his head toward two civilians loitering at the corner. "We will pay for your breakfast."

Diego was about a block from the Cabildo and the clock had just struck the quarter hour. A free breakfast should not be slighted, so he shrugged and said, "Thank you," in his best English.

"I am Lieutenant Colonel Alexander Dickson of His Britannic Majesty's 16th Foot and this gentleman is my aid, Captain Jeremy Founder." Dickson pushed out a chair and gestured for Diego to sit.

Diego saluted. "Sirs, I am Sergeant Diego deMelilla y Tupinar of the Fixed Regiment of Louisiana." He took his seat.

"What will you have this morning?" Dickson asked.

"Coffee and a roll, please."

Dickson waved toward the innkeeper. "My friend will have a cup of coffee, a slice of that fine ham and a breakfast roll," he said in perfect French. He returned to Diego and Spanish. "A roll is not enough of a breakfast. I believe I recognize you, sergeant. Have we met before?"

"I was at the – your headquarters after the fall of Fort San Carlos."

"You mean Fort New Richmond. It is Fort San Carlos now, I will confess. Yes, you did stand out. I remember you escorted my herald from the lines. Tell me, where in Spain are you from?"

"I am an *Isleño*." Diego said.

Dickson shrugged, not knowing the significance of the word.

"I am from the island of Gran Canaria of the Canary Islands," Diego clarified.

"Ah, I should have known. As it is, I think less than half of His Most Catholic Majesty's army in New Spain has ever seen Europe."

"And half of His Britannic Majesty's army hails from Germany," Diego replied.

"Truly said," Dickson admitted. "War as it is practiced in this modern world is truly worldwide, is it not?" He looked at Founder, but the man's blank face proved he did not speak Spanish. Dickson repeated in English, "I said we are engaged in a worldwide war, Founder."

"Yes, yes. Quite so Colonel, quite so." Founder replied.

The shopkeeper brought Diego his coffee with a fried wedge of ham and a roll on a small plate. Diego, who had not realized he was so hungry, downed both roll and ham in a few bites. The coffee was strong and freshly brewed.

"Who was that unfortunate wretch you had under arrest this morning?"

"A clothier."

"A clothier! The man was in ragged underclothes. A clothier indeed, surely you jest."

"I did not say he was a successful clothier. He cheated the army. Hard labor will set things right." Diego sipped the coffee, enjoying the cool morning.

"I am curious, Sergeant. Have you ever been to Pensacola or Mobile?"

Images of the tiny cell in the fort at Pensacola flooded into Diego's mind: The interrogation by General John Campbell, the lack of food, the want of sleep, the raging storm and the apparition of his beautiful Mézu showing him an escape route.

"No, sir. However, I expect that to change," Diego said.

"Truly? One hears interesting things. Particularly when those about do not believe one understands French or Spanish."

Diego said nothing, so Dickson continued.

"The Fort at Baton Rouge fell easily because we had no hope of support. We were taken by surprise, cut off from the rest of the Floridas by hundreds of miles of wilderness. It seems that General Gálvez had advance notice of our plans so he acted first. Fortunes of war, so to speak. But, we hear that a spy brought this advanced notice to Gálvez. A spy named deMelilla. Was that you Sergeant?"

"Simply a man with the same name, Colonel."

"So you say. Have you ever met General John Campbell, Sergeant?" Dickson paused for a response. Interpreting Diego's blank stare as a denial, he said, "No? He is the commander of all His Majesty's forces in the Floridas. He sent me a letter, the same letter in which he informed me that reinforcements were on the way, advising me that a Spanish spy had escaped Pensacola. He described that spy as tall, wide of shoulders, heavily muscled, with light brown hair and deep blue eyes."

"Many *Isleños* fit that description, Colonel."

"Just so, just so. But, sergeant, I promise you, when we take New Orleans, and we will take New Orleans, we will find that spy and hang him."

The church bell chimed the three-quarter hour.

"Sirs," Diego said, "I thank you for the breakfast, but now duty calls."

Diego stood, saluted and strode up *Calle San Pedro* toward the Cabildo without a backward glance at the two British officers. Once at the Cabildo, he would chat with the guard at the doors until the ninth hour began to toll. At the first stroke of nine he would enter the doors and before the ninth bell had sounded, the headquarters clerk would be announcing him to Colonel *Don* Jacinto Panis.

CHAPTER 2

The grenadiers stationed at the doors of the Cabildo were from the Veracruz regiment. The corporal of the guards, a mestizo with dark, almond-shaped eyes and coal-black hair, recognized Diego from the many bayonet demonstrations he had conducted throughout the growing invasion army.

"You must present your orders to the admissions clerk, Sergeant deMelilla," the guard explained, his huge bearskin hat nearly covering his eyes as he tilted his head toward his left. "If the clerk finds you on the list of today's appointments, I will announce you."

A small awning spanned out from the wall of the Cabildo over a chair and desk on the right side of the front doors. A canvas curtain on the north side of the tiny enclave protected the improvised office and the paper-laden desk from the cold north wind. A harried man, bespectacled and, despite a threadbare white wig, clearly balding, was slouched behind the desk absorbed in a document.

"*Señor* Falcón, Sergeant deMelilla is here with orders," the guard said as Diego positioned himself before the clerk. *This is a new procedure*, Diego thought, *because of the rapid increase in personnel brought on by the preparations for the invasion of Mobile, no doubt.*

The clerk reached out for Diego's order without looking up. He read the order, compared it to a list on his desk and all but tossed it back to Diego.

"Admit him, Corporal. He is to see Colonel *Don* Jacinto Panis," Falcón said.

Diego refolded his order and stepped aside. "Please admit me at the first chime of the hour, Corporal."

As Diego moved from the desk, a black man took his place before the clerk. The man was dressed in a tan tricorn, long black overcoat, tan waistcoat, britches, clean white stockings and brass-buckled shoes, clothing which proclaimed him to be a "*homme de couleur libre*" (freeman of color) in the words of the local people.

The man held a sheaf of papers in his left hand and escorted a black girl of about sixteen years with his right. The girl was quite pretty, barefoot, even though the morning was quite cool. She wore a cotton dress, plain but clean, a shawl and a bandana tied about her head. A small green square of cloth pinned to her shoulder identified her as a domestic slave.

Diego moved back toward the door to stand near the grenadier, but he could not avoid catching snatches of the conversation between the newcomer and Falcón. They spoke in French, but so quickly and in such hushed tones that Diego struggled to understand everything that was said.

The man was *Monsieur* Philippe Barbeaux, a tailor of some reputation in the upper society of New Orleans. The girl was named Douzemé, a domestic slave of the Hodges household. Emmitt Hodges was an English *émigré* from Boston involved in trade along the Mississippi River.

"*Monsieur* Falcón," Barbeaux said as he proffered some documents toward the scheduling clerk. "I have a certified copy of the bill of sale of this Haitian woman, Douzemé, to the Englishman, Hodges. I say this woman has the money and she petitions *coartacíon*."

Slaves were allowed to work for themselves on Sundays or Holy Days of Obligation, of which the Spanish had many, and split the profits with their owners. If a slave earned enough money to equal his purchase price, he could petition the court for the right to buy his freedom at that price. The process was called "*coartacíon*." Owners, faced with a slave wishing to purchase his freedom, might be inclined to exaggerate the original purchase price, so a clerk of the register of sales would write and certify, for a fee, a copy of the bill of sale of an applicant to present to the court.

Spanish law required owners to treat their slaves more as indentured servants than property, particularly if those slaves professed to be Catholics, and harsh treatment of slaves could result in court proceedings against the master.

Many slaves would absent themselves to camps in the wilderness called *Maroons*. Some of these camps, called *Grands Maroons*, were nearly villages and included women and children. Often, a fugitive would grow tired of life in the harsh swamp camps and return to his master with little punishment.

Those plantation owners accustomed to the more severe French laws were much opposed to this aspect of Spanish law which granted too much latitude to slaves for their liking. Owners from the English-controlled colonies considered the French laws too lenient and the Spanish rules absolutely outrageous. These owners pressed to be allowed to import newly enslaved Africans who were ignorant of the law, thus easier to control, and they insisted on the implementation of a new code for Spanish New Orleans which more closely followed the old *Code Noir*. The results of these actions were not entirely what the big land owners had anticipated. Slaves straight from Africa were sometimes agitated into revolt by British agents resulting in the death of many costly slaves and economic loss, or escaped to *maroons* with no intention of returning. The new code adopted by the Cabildo of New Orleans was routinely ignored by the magistrates and functionaries of the courts who considered the Cabildo's actions a usurpation of Madrid's edicts and a corruption of the Law of God. It was no wonder that more than half of the black population of New Orleans were free people.

Barbeaux wanted Falcón to schedule a hearing before Christmas. Falcón examined the copy of the bill of sale. The clerk of registration had signed the document as a true copy and added an embossed seal over the signature.

"It says here this woman was purchased by an agent in Haiti at the direction of Emmitt Hodges for the sum of five hundred twenty three *livre* and three *deriers*." Falcón looked up for a moment as he mentally worked on the conversion from *livre* to *pesos*. The eight-*reale* silver coin was the equal of one peso, but it was called a "dollar" by most in New Orleans. "That would be one hundred fifteen *pesos*."

"And I have here, *Monsieur*, a letter from my bank certifying I have the funds necessary to meet such a payment." Barbeaux clearly knew the law and was fully prepared.

Falcón produced a form and filled in the blanks, muttering as he did so. "*Monsieur* Philippe Barbeaux – Douzemé – one hundred fifteen." He placed the form before Barbeaux. "Sign here. In doing so you pledge to provide the funds to this woman and she will purchase her manumission with those funds. You pledge five *pesos* as court costs and you pledge this woman will not be indebted to you in any way for the funds. The hearing will be at ten in the morning on the twenty-seventh of this month. It will be in *Don* Andular's court. Bring the money in silver."

Barbeaux read the form aloud. It was in Spanish, which he managed. After reading each phrase in Spanish, he translated it into French for Douzemé.

"I did not know such a thing could be done," Douzemé said, her Haitian accent making her words almost unintelligible to Diego. She wrapped her arm around Barbeaux's, as she lovingly looked up at him.

Barbeaux flushed and said, "My father purchased freedom for himself, my mother and me in this very way. Now I do it for you. Once you are free, we can marry." The man and woman walked away, their heads close together and chatting happily as the first chime of nine sounded from the bell at Saint Louis Church.

The Corporal opened the door and announced to someone within, "Sergeant deMelilla for Colonel *Don* Jacinto Panis." He looked at Diego and said, "This way Sergeant."

Diego stepped through the doors and was greeted by Renaldo, chief clerk for the headquarters administration. Because he was wearing his short sword, and therefore armed, Diego did not remove his tricorn.

"Good morning, Sergeant," Renaldo said. "I am happy to see you well. May I take your sword and place it in the armory?"

"Certainly," Diego said as he began to unbuckle the scabbard belt. "Could you tell a friend what this is all about?"

"You will learn soon enough, Sergeant." Renaldo accepted the sword and Diego removed his hat. "May I take your hat as well, Sergeant?" Diego gave Renaldo the hat as well, smoothed his hair back and felt the ribbon holding his hair in a ponytail, insuring nothing had come loose. Renaldo placed the hat on a peg next to the armory door, unlocked the door and stood the scabbarded sword wrapped in its leather belt in a corner just inside the entrance.

"This way, Sergeant," Renaldo said and he led Diego through a short hallway to a closed door. He rapped on the door and waited.

"*Entrar*," said a voice behind the door. Renaldo opened the door then stepped aside for Diego to enter. When Diego had cleared the threshold, Renaldo closed the door.

Diego found himself facing a wide table covered with rolled maps. A twelve-stick chandelier hung over the table, bathing it in a yellow light. The room had no windows and only one other door, opposite the one he had entered. Five men were gathered around the table. Three, he knew. Colonel Jacinto Panis stood at the center of the table and to the Colonel's left was the Houma scout, Pesaofe (Seeing Dog) "T'Chien" Dardar. These were the two men who had led Diego across the Floridas earlier that year. Captain Josef Herrera, the commanding officer of Diego's Tiger Company was to T'Chien's left. The other two men stood to Panis' right. Diego did not know them, but he could see one was a naval officer, an American he thought. The other was another scout or woodsman for he was dressed in deerskin jacket, gaiters and moccasins, but he had the facial features of a European.

Diego came to attention and saluted, "Sergeant Diego deMelilla, reporting as ordered, sir."

"Stand at ease, Sergeant," Panis said. "How are you, my friend?"

"I enjoy good health, sir."

"And your children?"

"Well and in the care of a good friend, sir."

"Fine. Gentlemen, I give you Sergeant Diego deMelilla y Tupinar, *Primero* of Tiger Company, Spain's Fixed Regiment of Louisiana and the finest combatant with lance or bayonet I have ever known." Panis said, addressing the two strangers.

"Sergeant, this gentleman is Captain William Pickles of the Continental Navy."

Pickles nodded. The man was weather-worn. His eyes squinted as if the candlelight were a setting sun. His brown and grey-streaked hair was pulled back into a tight queue bound with a ribbon. He wore a salt-stained coat over a blue jacket with gold trim.

"And this gentleman," Panis indicated the buckskin-clad man, "is Major Toran Segura, my chief of scouts."

"T'Chien has told me much about you, Sergeant," Segura said with a nod of this head.

"And now, the purpose of this meeting," Panis began. "With the exception of Captain Pickles, you all were present for the attack on Baton Rouge. Governor General Gálvez did not blindly initiate that attack. Fully half of the men under his command were spread throughout West Florida gathering information on the enemy. The General knew the British re-enforcements from Pensacola could not arrive in time and had turned back. He knew Captain Pickles had taken control of Lakes Maurepas and Pontchartrain. He knew the British could not send forces down from Natchez because he had eyes everywhere."

Panis tapped his temple as he look into the eyes of each man, one at a time and intently.

"'*Estar enterado antes de actuar* (be informed before acting)' is the General's philosophy. Learn first and then act. And when you act, act hard, act fast and act with determination. The General remembers the disaster at Algiers. It will never be repeated."

Every man present knew the history of the Spanish assault on Algiers. Under the command of General Alejandro O'Reilly, green Spanish troops had been sent ashore without knowledge of the size or strength of the enemy they faced. The enemy, in formation and good order, appeared on the beaches as the Spaniards struggled ashore, and cut them to pieces. Gálvez had led a contingent of this action against the Moors and had been seriously wounded.

"You will be the General's eyes in West Florida. Captain Pickles has already landed nearly two hundred Choctaw at the British trading posts on the north shore of Lake Pontchartrain and seized control of every village this side of the *Rio Perla* (Pearl River). It will be your duty to make the enemy believe that Gálvez is coming by land. If the British are convinced the army is marching over-land, they cannot raise redoubts, garrison villages or station forces at the beaches lest they be cut off from their base at Mobile. They will be forced to decide. Either form up their army, sally into the wilderness to confront us after a hard march and far from their supplies; or retreat to their fort at Mobile and require us to attack them with an army exhausted by two hundred miles of trekking through the wilderness."

Diego remembered how the small march from New Orleans to Baton Rouge had cost the Regiment fully one third of its strength due to illness and fatigue.

Panis continued, "If your deception is successful, a ship-borne army will be able to land, fresh, well supplied and unopposed. The British will be bottled up in their fort, cut off from any help Pensacola might send. If you are not successful in the deception, at the least you would have gained full knowledge of the enemy's dispositions and capabilities."

Panis chose one of the rolled maps, spread it out on the table and anchored the corners with cups. "Major Toran Segura will be in charge of the expedition. *Señor* Dardar will command the scouts. Sergeant deMelilla will command the regular forces. Captain Pickles will ferry our expedition to a location on the West Florida coast just beyond the mouth of the *Rio Perla* and arrange a network of packet boats so there will be constant communication between this advanced force and Gálvez."

Diego could not conceal his surprise at his assignment.

"Do not look so amazed, Sergeant. The regular forces you command will consist of twenty picked men of Tiger Company. You are there to add validity to the story that the army is advancing overland, nothing more. Spies must be allowed a glimpse of uniformed regulars if this ruse is to succeed. T'Chien's scouts will range far inland gathering information and planting rumors throughout the Choctaw villages and trading posts. You and your men will act as if you are the vanguard for a great army. The British must react. If they send troops against you, withdraw and we will come ashore behind them. If they retreat to their fort, we will have them trapped."

Panis rolled up the map. "Gentlemen, General Gálvez will depart with an invasion fleet during the middle of next month. You will have until then to learn the signal codes, memorize your roles, gather the required supplies and exercise your men. When the anchors are weighed in New Orleans for the invasion of Mobile, this false army will be set ashore in West Florida. Dismissed."

The men came to attention until Panis had exited the room.

"*Primero*, walk out with me," Captain Herrera said. He waited until the others had filed out then preceded Diego through the hall. Diego collected his sword and hat from the armory and they exited onto the front steps of the Cabildo. The queue of people jostling for an opportunity to talk with Falcón had grown slightly. The street in front of the Cabildo was a river of wagons, carts, horses and ox sleds plodding along the manure-covered road. Pedestrians crowded the wooden walkways flowing left and right in equal numbers.

"I want a list of the men you select on my desk before the drums roll 'Retire' tonight," Herrera said quietly as he looked around to insure no one was listening. "Pick any nineteen *soldados* (privates) in the company and one corporal. I will also assign to you a wagon, a field gun – a four-pounder – along with a gun crew, a teamster and two horses. Tomorrow we will begin training your people as a vanguard. They will be told they have been selected as the advance troops for an army of three thousand bound for Mobile. They will be given passes every Saturday night, as usual."

"Sir, one cannot expect these men to keep any secrets once they are exposed to rum and the opportunity to brag."

"Warn them not to talk of what they are training for, Sergeant. Of course, they will babble everything into the first female ear. We do not doubt spies will hear of the planned road march and bring the news east. We must convince the British we come by land."

"Yes, sir," Diego said, his mind racing to keep up with the changing circumstances.

"Good! Yes. I will leave you now. Have that list to me tonight." Herrera said. He stepped down into the stream of pedestrians and was gone.

Diego looked across the *Plaza des Armas* toward the forest of masts just beyond the Levee Road. *This is not a plan*, he thought. *This is a hope disguised as a plan.* He remembered his father telling him, "Do not plan based upon what you think your opponent will do, plan only against those things he could do. To do otherwise is to invite surprise." There were too many parts of this plan that could go wrong.

"The surprise will be if it works," he said aloud.

"What was that, Sergeant?" *Señor* Falcón, still seated at his desk next to the doorway, had thought Diego was speaking to him.

"I said, 'it is no surprise that so many want their freedom.' It is only natural."

"Truly said, Sergeant," Falcón's head was bobbing vigorously until the side curls of his powdered wig flapped like wings, "Truly said. Yet, there are many who happily choose the comfortable confinement of domestic servitude over the unfamiliar dangers of true freedom. Otherwise, the Crown would need to place ten clerks in my stead."

Diego remembered the enraged, coal-black renegade slave he had bayoneted on the banks of Bayou Terre Aux Boeufs. Agents from Britain, or so it was said, had agitated two score slaves fresh from Africa into revolt. Instead of fleeing to one of the *grands maroons*, they attacked local farmers and turned into a mob armed with two fowling pieces, axes and knives. Diego had been in the front rank of the ten Spanish infantrymen formed up to oppose them. The mob had advanced into the musketry and bayonets of professional soldiers. The Africans were summarily repulsed. Those not killed in the first two volleys were bayoneted as they threw themselves on the disciplined ranks. Those that had survived ran, only to be pursued and run to ground by dogs and huntsmen hired by the indigo plantation's overseer. Had they been patient and learned of their new situation, they might have contrived a way to gain freedom. Instead they had died, exploited by others for another purpose.

Diego joined the flow of pedestrians going to his left. He arrived at the street corner in only a few steps where he crossed the roadway and headed toward the river. There were several alehouses along the river and one in particular, *El Cuatro Jinetes* (The Four Horsemen), catered to the enlisted men of the Fixed Regiment. The regiment would be taking their noon meal at the bivouac about this time. Knowing he would not be missed, Diego decided a large bowl of seafood stew over rice would be better than the stale bread and boiled fish the regiment was being served. The cook at the *Jinetes* had a way of preparing an oil and flour base that, along with okra, thickened the stew. He wanted the time alone to think of who he would select for the fake vanguard.

"*Buenos días, Sargento,*" *Mamá* Junia greeted Diego the instant he entered the inn. Junia's Spanish was passable, her French tolerable and her native language something from West Africa, Diego knew not what.

"Some of that special *caldo* you make here, *Señora,*" Diego said, thinking of the seafood stew so popular on his home island of Gran Canaria. He worked his way to a table set in a far corner. He pulled out a chair and sat with his back against the corner giving him a clear view of the front door as well as the entrance from the kitchen.

"Is not caldo," Junia said. "My girl uses okra and flour. We call it 'gumbo' because of the okra." *Mamá* Junia was a free woman of color, as were many of the tavern owners along the riverfront. Her white hair was closely cropped and she covered her head with a bandana. She wore cloth slippers, a loose fitting cotton dress, shaped for her ample form, and a canvas apron stained with a sample of everything offered at *El Cuatro Jinetes*.

"I would like a bowl of whatever you wish to call it and a cup of ale, please."

Mamá Junia waved her left hand over her head without looking away from Diego. Beyond Junia, Diego could see a serving girl dip a cup of ale from a barrel. *Left must mean ale. The right must mean rum*, Diego thought. *El Cuatro Jinetes* had no wine to offer.

"You have silver, or do I book this?" Junia frowned disapprovingly when she said "book."

"I have silver."

Junia brightened considerably. "Good. Good. Too many soldiers book their drinks. Drink too much. Then I have to fight the devil come payday."

Mamá Junia drifted into the kitchen and the ale was plopped on his table by the serving girl, a pretty mulatto, who could not have been older than ten. She flashed him a brilliant smile, her dark eyes sparkling. She might have been Junia's daughter or granddaughter. The girl skipped back to the row of ale kegs as the gumbo arrived. Junia had ladled a serving into a wooden bowl from a large iron pot on the oven in the back. The concoction had been brewing all morning. By tonight, it would be as thick as pudding and fantastic.

As Diego enjoyed his meal, his mind evaluated the men of Tiger Company. He could not take Gusman. Gusman was the only sergeant capable of filling the role of *Sargento Primero*. Pook was an easy selection. He would likely be Diego's second in command if Captain Herrera could be persuaded to promote the man to corporal. Plata had to come. Captain Herrera would need to be convinced Plata could come off of the punishment platoon. Not a great task. With the campaign against Mobile building up, every miscreant in the army would be returning to their regular units. Quintero, a hard fighter, would be needed. Olivier could speak English like a native. Diego gave up and decided to have Pook pick the rest when he returned to the company area. Twenty men would leave Tiger Company very short handed, but that could not be helped and was not his problem.

He would have the names for Herrera by nightfall. The next day was a Saturday and Diego was going to be free after morning formation. He had planned to travel down to the village of Concepción, about a three hour trip, to visit his children, Pedro and Maria. Miguel Campo, his wife, Catalina and their daughter Isabella had taken Diego's children in when Mézu died.

Pedro turned eleven just two days ago and little Maria would be eight come this May. Isabella, fifteen years old, could easily be mistaken for a woman five years her senior. *She was a girl*, Diego thought, *who had been forced to grow up quickly and did so courageously*. He had arranged for Isabella to collect a portion of his pay to help support his children. One short visit and then he would be gone into the wilds of the Floridas. Mézu had died the last time he was away and the children had been forced to deal with their grief alone. Almost alone, the Campos became Pedro and Maria's surrogate family.

Diego finished his ale, pulled two small silver coins from his pocket and placed them on the table. He was just about to stand up from the table when the door to the street swung open and two rough-looking men shouldered their way in. The Kentuckians – every woodsman from the English colonies was called a "Kentuckian" in New Orleans without regard to where they actually hailed – searched out a table. Diego lowered his head, pretending to examine his cup of ale.

"Come on," the one called "Hank" said. "Here's a place with a good view of the street." He pushed his friend toward a table near the one window. They sat and waved *Mamá* Junia to tend to them.

"Rum this time," Hank said in French. "None of that swill you call ale. Right, Davy?"

Davy grunted, "Not so much as you can't do your job, Hank."

What were these two doing here? First they seemed to have spent the night at the Cassé, a brothel known to cater to Spanish soldiers and sailors and now, later in the same day, they show up at *El Cuatro Jinetes*, practically the Fixed Regiment's enlisted club. The one called Davy had used English, but Diego caught the drift of what was said. They had pretended to be drunk this morning and evidently wish to remain sober throughout the day. Why?

Diego rose. The movement caught Davy's attention. He watched as Diego emerged from the shadow of the corner, his mouth dropping open when he recognized the sergeant. He gave Hank a nudge.

"What's yer riled about, Davy?" Hank fell silent as well as Diego approached, his route to the doorway passed within a yard of the men.

"*Buenos Días, Sargento*," Davy stuttered, and then he looked back toward Hank, clearly trying to avoid a conversation.

"Good afternoon, I think, Meester Davy and Hank," Diego knew his English was poor and heavily accented. He had no intention of beginning a conversation either, so he pushed through the door, turned right on the *banquette* and headed upriver, away from the window. He went several paces and then stepped into an alley. The place smelled strongly of urine and vomit, as did most alleys along the levee road. He removed his tricorn, held it behind his back and peaked through a gap in the building's corner trim.

Hank leaned out of the alehouse door, looked both ways then eased out onto the *banquette* staring intently in the direction Diego had gone. He gestured vigorously and Davy appeared. Both men turned downriver and walked away briskly, almost at a run.

He thought of following the Kentuckians, but he had duties at the regiment that he could not avoid and there was the matter of compiling the list of Panis' Vanguard, the name he had assigned this detachment of twenty men, one cannon – with *cannoniers* – a wagon, a teamster and two horses. He was to command real men in the advance of a phantom force deep into British territory. He hoped that T'Chien's scouts would be alert enough to prevent an ambush of his tiny force, or give ample warning to retreat if the British, the *godums*, came against them in Force. The British were derisively known as the *"godums"* by soldiers of Spain. During the War of Spanish Succession the Spanish infantry, both those loyal to Charles and those loyal to Philip, noted how often the British sergeants would shout "God damn" at their men during maneuvers, to the Spanish ear it sounded like *"godum."* In this way the British earned the *apodo "godums."*

Only God knew if Panis' Vanguard would be bait to trap the *godums* in the wilderness or beaters to drive them into their forts. He put Hank and Davy out of his mind.

CHAPTER 3

Mézu came out of the door way of their house beneath the *Piedra Perro* (Dog Stone). A silver tiara anchored a silk white and gold veil that cascaded over both shoulders, hiding all but glimpses of her dark brown hair. Her green gown seemed to shimmer in the silver-gray light of the full moon. He could see the tips of her dancing slippers peeking out from beneath the green and gold lace that encircled her at the ground. Her gray eyes appeared to be full of stars as she held out her smooth white hands toward him. He took her hands in his and stepped closer to her.

"My husband," she said. "I could not find you."

"I am here," Diego whispered. He brought her hands to his lips and kissed them, holding them against his lips for a long time. When he lowered her hands he saw that they were no longer the smooth, tender hands of a girl of sixteen, but the calloused, tanned hands of a goat herder's wife. She turned her beautiful face up to him. The tiara was gone, replaced by a flat-crowned hat. The veil had transformed from silk with gold trim into one of white cotton trimmed with an intricate lace. A soft leather eye-patch covered her left eye, but her right looked lovingly into his eyes, into his soul.

"The children are safe, my husband," she said. "Isabella loves our children."

Diego leaned down to kiss her, but a strange noise came from behind him. He turned slightly to see three stones bouncing up and down in concert on a plank table. He thought he recognized the rhythm the stones made. He turned back to Mézu, but she was gone.

~

Diego opened his eyes. First call was being tapped out by the regimental drummer. He could see the silhouette of the boy cast by the breakfast fires against the canvas of his tent, shadow shoulders and hand flowing with the beat. Other shadows began to move about as the bivouac area responded to the beginning of another day.

The dream had been so real. Diego sighed deeply and rubbed away the moisture that was filling his eyes. He tossed back a blanket, for it was a cool morning, and sat up on his bedroll. He found his folded shirt and trousers by feel, pulled them on and struggled to his feet. Gathering his shoes and gaiters, he ducked through the tent flap and sat heavily on a camp chair he kept by the entrance. He slipped on his shoes, put his right foot in the leather stirrup of the right gaiter and did up its dozen buttons from bottom to top. He tightened a black leather strap around his leg between calf and knee to keep the heavy canvas gaiter from sliding down. He buttoned up the second gaiter and stood, stomping his feet to insure the gaiters were properly fastened. *When I unbutton these gaiters,* Diego thought, *I will be somewhere in West Florida.* He strode off between the tents to the long slit latrine. The morning formation would be in a half hour.

Diego stood facing the assembly area before the tents of Tiger Company. He wore a blue waistcoat beneath a white uniform coat with blue lining and cuffs. His tricorn hat had a red cockade on the left side. He was armed with a short sword and a steel-tipped lance. Diego snapped to attention as the drummer boy, who had been watching a half-hour glass, initiated the assembly signal, a series of rolls and taps that lasted thirty seconds. The men of Tiger Company hurriedly formed ranks facing Diego. The boy ended the roll with a loud tap-tap-tap and every man was in his place.

Another day had begun. Today, Panis' Vanguard was to depart. But first, the routine of accounting for the men of the company had to be finished, breakfast taken and duties assigned. Second Sergeant Gusman walked up to Diego and held a wood-framed slate for Diego to read. Gusman had tallied in chalk the number of men in the hospital, those excused from morning formation because of night duty, or absent for other authorized reasons. Plata had been recalled from the penalty platoon.

"Call the roll," Diego said. Gusman consulted a ledger and began to call names. Each man responded with "*Aquí, Sargento.*"

The roll was completed and Gusman closed the roster ledger. "All are present or are accounted for, *Primero*. Forty-one fit for duty."

Forty-one men and he was going to take twenty of those men today. Tiger Company would then have twenty-one men fit for duty. Captain Herrera could not be happy about that.

Diego shook his head, "Take your post, Sergeant." Gusman marched to his post at the rear left of the formation. Diego shouted, "Company, Parade – REST." The men, who had been in the position of attention, went to parade rest. Diego performed an about face and went to parade rest. All were waiting for the commanding officer to officially start the day.

The flap of the command tent was thrown back and Captain Herrera ducked into view followed by Ensign Piernas and a New Orleans militia officer Diego did not recognize.

"Company, Attennn – TION!" Diego barked as he snapped to attention himself. He heard forty-two pairs of heels click together behind him. Herrera marched up to Diego and the moment he stopped Diego saluted and said "Tiger Company, all present or accounted for, SIR. Honor and Fidelity, SIR."

"Honor and Fidelity, Sergeant," Herrera said, returning Diego's salute. "Please take your post."

Diego marched to the front-right of the formation. The men chosen for the vanguard had been notified and directed to fall in as the first five men in each of the four ranks of the formation.

"Men of the Fixed Regiment," accustomed to shouting orders, Herrera's voice carried to the farthest rank. If that were not the case, Sergeant Gusman would have saluted as a signal to the officer addressing the men to speak up. "Today, we begin our advance to Mobile. Our vanguard will depart today. This officer," Herrera gestured at the Militia officer standing to his left, "is Major Jean Demar of the Duplesses Battalion. They will march and deploy with us."

The Duplesses Battalion was a disciplined, meaning well trained and uniformed, militia of New Orleans free men of color. The uniform was a light blue coat with red cuffs and facings. His hat was a bicorn with a red cockade. Gálvez's army consisted of regulars, militia and volunteers that had been collected from three continents. The red cockade was the only uniform feature common to every soldier.

"Sergeant deMelilla, take charge of the vanguard." The deceit had begun. Anyone near the bivouac area would have heard Herrera announce that the invasion was on and the vanguard had been dispatched. New Orleans was a city awash with spies who would be following Diego's detachment and preparing to rush messages of their finds to their respective controllers.

Diego marched his twenty-man detachment to Fort St. Charles along Levee Road past the *Plaza des Armas,* banners flying, to be reviewed by General Gálvez and his staff on their war mounts. The Cabildo and Saint Louis Church were barely visible over the heads of the people who had crowded into the open square. The regimental band had fallen in behind the vanguard to provide marching drums and trumpeted salutes at the appropriate times, which was often.

They turned away from the river at Fort Saint Charles and reached the long, wide and heavily trafficked roadway named by the locals as simply "The Big Road to Bayou Saint John." Most of the freight transferred between the Mississippi River and Bayou Saint John was hauled along this road. Wagons, ox sleds and people had been pushed to the edges of the hard, packed roadway. Planking, ship ballast stones and clamshells provided a crude, uneven surface that had been woven into the hard, packed clay and manure by countless hooves, wheels and feet. The sloop-of-war *West Florida* waited for them, moored where the road ended.

The *West Florida* was armed with two six-pounders, two four-pounders and a single nine-and-a-half pounder. Crewed by thirty, she had been a British ship that dominated Lakes Maurepas and Pontchartrain. Captain William Pickles brought his corvette, the *Morris*, armed with four two-and-a-half pounders and one swivel gun, into Lake Pontchartrain, attacked the larger British ship and took her. The *Morris* was lost in the action so Pickles moved his command to the *West Florida*. Several of the British crew had been impressed Americans, which may have accounted for Pickles' victory. The Americans swore allegiance to the Colonials and stayed aboard.

Diego halted the vanguard and had Pook check each man to insure he was properly armed and equipped while he went aboard the sloop. Major Toran Segura met him at the end of the gangplank.

"Welcome, Sergeant," Segura said as he returned Diego's salute. The Major was dressed as a woodsman. "We have four tents and two iron cooking frames along with assorted pots and utensils loaded in the wagon for you," indicating a wagon lashed to the space just forward of the low quarterdeck. The tents were bell-ended and designed for four men. Five could be made to fit with a little adjustment, but Diego had seen seven men stacked like cordwood into a single bell-tent one night to escape a freezing drizzle.

Cannons mounted on heavy trucks were lashed in place along the decks, three to a side, and a larger cannon was mounted amidships just forward of the foremast where it could be hauled to a starboard or portside firing station as needed. After the great cannon he had slept beside aboard the *San Juan Nepomuceno* during the voyage from Tenerife, these guns appeared no larger than muskets. A long, brass field gun, dismounted from its carriage, was bundled at the foot of the bowsprit. Caisson, carriage and limbers were bound about the gun tube. Five men in the uniform of the Duplesses Battalion were clustered about the foredeck talking quietly.

"Gun captain, to me," Segura called in French toward the gathering of coffee-colored men. One of them, a corporal, separated from the rest and reported to the Major.

"Allow me to introduce you to your artillerymen," Segura continued in French. "Corporal Barbeaux, here is the vanguard commander."

MOBILE MUST FALL: A NOVEL FROM THE DEMELILLA CHRONICLES

"Sergeant Diego deMelilla, I present to you Corporal Philippe Barbeaux of the Duplesses Battalion. Barbeaux will be your artillery. The Corporal, the entire gun crew for that matter, speaks only French."

Diego recognized the man. It was the young tailor who had arranged the manumission of the pretty Haitian girl. Members of the Duplesses Battalion were among the elite of the freemen of color of New Orleans. They were rich and influential. The Battalion functioned as a social club as well as a military unit, though they had the reputation of being a well-trained and effective militia.

"Tell me about your gun, Corporal."

"She is a *galopeur* (galloper), Sergeant," Barbeaux said with obvious pride. "A four-pounder Major Demar purchased with his own money." A galloper was a small gun mounted on a light carriage with tall wheels designed to be rushed about a battlefield and put into action quickly. The horse pulling the gun would be driven at the gallop, hence the name. "We have named her 'Gabriella'."

The center of the deck had an open hatch where the heads of two horses rose above the planking. If a storm should arise and the hatches needed to be secured, the horses would have to be made to lie down. When they disembarked, the horses would be walked up a ramp on deck and made to jump into the sea to swim ashore.

"We will spend one night aboard ship anchored in the lee of an island and land tomorrow afternoon at a place the Choctaw call '*Tuchena bok*.'" Segura said as if reading Diego's mind. "Sudden storms this time of year are not common, so there is little chance we would need to dog the hatches. It will be a cold night, however."

The men of the vanguard filed aboard and were assigned places to stack their packs, which were lashed down by large nets. Their weapons they kept with them. Many sat around the open hatch, dangling their legs into the shallow hold below. The drummers were left on the bank along with those people who had followed the vanguard out of the city. Captain Pickles began to shout a series of commands and sailors scrambled to cast off lines, gather long poles and tend the line that ran to the team of mules that would pull the *West Florida* north along Bayou Saint John to the open waters of Lake Pontchartrain. The wind was brisk and out of the northeast.

The teamster gave his reins a slap and his mules struggled for purchase on the packed clay of *la cordelle*, the local name for the trail along the bank. The sailors pushed the sloop away from the bank until the haul team had them moving fast enough to answer the helm. The haul team would slacken from time to time so men with forked poles could lift the haul rope over small boats and piers or, in the case of taller vessels, a new tow line was played out ahead of the obstruction, made fast and the old line tossed clear.

In about an hour, Diego could see the brick foundation of the small fort at the mouth of the bayou on the left and the end of *la cordelle* on the right. The crew had set a few small triangular sails when the wind from the lake was no longer shielded by the tall trees that lined the haul road. By the time the teamster was preparing to release the tow line the *West Florida* was under sail, close-hauled on a starboard tack. Once they cleared the mouth of the bayou, Pickles ordered the helm up a few points until they were running briskly toward the northwest through a light chop that only occasionally sent a spray of cold, brackish water across the deck.

It was near noon when Pickles changed course to nearly due east, close-hauled on the port. Diego could not see if there were any landmarks to assist the captain and he wondered if they were on schedule. He had the men eat some hard bread and jerked meat from their ration kits and put them to cleaning weapons, checking flints and sharpening bayonets and short swords. Pickles did not seem to mind if sailors idled about when they had nothing pressing, but Diego hated to see soldiers lounging about.

By three in the afternoon, Diego could see they were approaching a narrow pass. He remembered it. He had passed this way last year after his escape from Pensacola. The pass was called the Rigolets. It was seven miles through the Rigolets from Lake Pontchartrain to the island-fringed bays of the Gulf of Mexico.

"Pickles says we will reach our night anchorage just at dusk," Segura said. Diego was slightly startled. He had been staring at the shoreline, lost in thought when the major had come up behind him. "We expect to be disembarking by ten in the morning. *Tuchena bok* is a wide entrance to a bay and we will land on the east side of the entrance. Thirty miles to the east is another bay called Biloxi. We are to determine if the *godums* have rebuilt an old fort there or if they have abandoned it. Knowing this will tell us much about what they are doing to oppose us."

The tide was falling as the *West Florida* entered the Rigolets. She fairly flew along swept by the tide, her sails filled by a stiff breeze and under a full beam tack. A small packet boat appeared and maneuvered around the stern of the *West Florida* until she was pacing them astern and within hailing distance.

"Major Segura," shouted a man in the bow of the packet boat.

Segura stepped forward, cupped his hands to his mouth and shouted, "I am Segura."

"The first is done," the man replied. "The second is not known."

"Understood," Segura shouted and the packet boat sheared off.

Diego looked at Segura expectantly.

"No changes in our plans, sergeant. When we go ashore in the morning, you will lead the vanguard. Remember, you are to appear to be the vanguard for a large army, so don't go rushing east. I will keep in touch by runner or by packet boat, so keep a scout within sight of the sea. T'Chien will be inland from you and he will send runners as well. We must make the *godums* believe the army is marching along the coast."

ᶜ⁄ᵒ

The horse planted his hooves against the deck, refusing to move. Barbeaux had his men pull a blanket across the animal's haunches and pull. With a terrified scream, the horse threw itself into the sea. The teamster rode in a skiff, holding a rope attached to the animal's bridle. Two sailors rowed the skiff as the horse swam, head held high, its breath blowing mist in the cold morning air and eyes wide as dinner plates. They were several yards from the water's edge when the water was shallow enough for the horse to wade ashore. The teamster led the horse up the beach and tethered it with the other.

Diego had been the first ashore. The sandy beach ended at a narrow debris line composed of small sticks and clumps of seaweed. The land inland began as a field of dead grass scattered with twisted, stubby oaks paralleling the beach. Further from the sea, pine trees replaced the oaks. The land between the trees was relatively clear of brush for several hundred yards beyond the shoreline until the sandy soil was replaced by hard, red mud. In a line as distinct as the beach, heavy brush and dense clusters of briars filled the space between tall pines, a wilderness so dense it seemed as if a man could not have pushed a pole through the undergrowth.

Diego and six of his soldiers had been ferried to the beach before the *West Florida* had even settled at anchor. He pushed his men inland for several hundred yards, looking for signs of the enemy. Two small fisherman's huts sat either side of a well-worn trail that terminated at the water's edge inside the mouth of the bay. The trail ran east, parallel to the coast and had been heavily traveled. Diego had posted three sentinels east along the trail and three inland with instructions to send word if they saw anyone. He returned to the beach in time to meet the rest of his men as they landed under the direction of Pook and they all witnessed the horses leap into the sea.

Sailors rowed the equipment to the beach and soldiers carried materials ashore and up the beach to an assembly area. The wagon, caisson and gun carriage arrived in pieces. Barbeaux's men tended to the gun while the teamster directed a few soldiers dealing with the wagon. Once the wagon was fully assembled, it was loaded with supplies. There was no room for twenty backpacks, so the soldiers would have to carry their packs and bedrolls.

Ten men were needed to transfer the four-pounder from the skiff up the beach and onto the carriage under the nervous direction of Barbeaux. When the brass tube was laid in the iron rockers and bolted in place, Barbeaux gave out a great sigh. "Gabriella," he said with loving relief.

Diego sent a runner to tell the men to the north they were moving east. He directed the horse-drawn vehicles onto the road and began marching east with a scouting party five hundred yards ahead. They had moved east about two miles when one of the scouts, Búho, came in from the north escorting T'Chien.

"He gave the correct password, *Primero*," he said. "He said you know him."

"Yes, Thank you. Return to your position."

T'Chien gave a wide smile. "I see you have made it. How was the landing?"

"Uneventful. I am concerned with my inability to scout ahead more than a few *vara* (yards)."

"That is why I am here. I have several groups of scouts well ahead of you to the north and east. We have you well shielded from any large force. If a small reconnaissance force should try to get close, we have been instructed to allow it."

"How small a force would that be?"

"No more than ten men. More than ten may not be inclined to run when they see uniformed soldiers. Continue to send your own scouts, but there will be no need to have them range very far. It does not appear the *godums* have posted anyone on the west side of Biloxi Bay. We have not yet scouted the old fort on the east side of the bay. We think it has been abandoned, but we will not know for a few days. I will send word if anything changes."

Diego turned to the dozen men marching along with him on the road. "This man is T'Chien Dardar," he said. "He is our lead scout."

"I will take my leave of you now. Remember not to make too good a progress. If Biloxi is not defended, we would like to make Mobile Bay in three weeks."

"When will we rejoin the regiment?"

"That depends upon what we find, when we find it, and what happens after we find it."

Diego jogged with T'Chien along the road until they caught up with the lead scouts to make the same introductions. There may come a time when passwords would not suffice and Diego wanted his men to recognized T'Chien.

Diego returned to the main body of the march. The troops were in double file. Fourteen men two abreast did not take up much road. They looked to Diego to be pitifully few. The road was narrow, but well packed. The wagon and caisson moved easily as did the troops. Not so with the ranging scouts, who moved through thick brush and had to be rotated in regularly to be exchanged with fresh men.

Only four hours of daylight remained after they had disembarked and assembled on the trail. They made eight miles in those four hours. From what he had understood from the maps Segura had reviewed with him, Diego calculated they would see Biloxi Bay on the day after tomorrow if they maintained this rate.

The sun was setting when Diego called a halt and the men made camp. Pickets were set, camp fires lit, tents pitched and latrines dug in the sand near the beach. Diego went over the watch rotation with Pook. He took the last camp watch for himself. For reasons he could not explain, Diego loved to be up and about during those two hours just before sunrise. The way the stars would wink out one by one as the sky lightened soothed him.

The sun appearing over the rim of the earth was, to Diego, the most magnificent sight of the day. It made him think of his home in the mountains of Gran Canaria. It made him think of his beautiful Mézu. Sometimes he would talk to her in the quiet pre-dawn hour before the drum beat of first call roused the army. Or should it be called praying?

૭૦

A boot appeared at the bottom gap in the front flap of his tent. The rattle of the soldier's accoutrements had awakened Diego.

"Yes?" He sat up, reaching for his boots. He had slept in his shirt, waistcoat and trousers for the night had been cold.

"Fourth watch, *Primero*," the soldier said. It was Private Pedro Gillama, just coming off the third watch. Winter, with its long nights, required four-two hour watches.

Diego exited the tent, pulled on his boots and began the laborious task of buttoning up his gaiters. Gillama stood watching him. Diego realized he had forgotten to dismiss the soldier.

"Get to bed, man,"

"*Sí, Primero*." Gillama rushed away as if he feared the sergeant would find some chore for him. After all, that is what sergeants did.

Diego stomped his feet to settle his boots and pulled on his coat. He moved about the camp checking the men on watch and debriefing the returning pickets. The shoreline was less than five hundred yards to the south, but he could hear no surf nor smell the sea air. The brisk wind was out of the north and carried the dusky smell of a forest in winter. The beach watch rotated in to report a light on the horizon that did not seem to move. It may be one of the packet boats Major Segura said would be shadowing the vanguard. He moved up the road until he ran into the forward pickets. The men challenged him, even though the moon was well up and they could clearly see the big *Isleño*. If they had not challenged him, he would have given them a severe rebuke.

He moved another hundred yards up the trail. He listened intently, hearing nothing but night noises. A tall stand of trees sheltered the trail from the north wind where he stood. He looked back west toward the camp. The moon was a bright, full disk, yet he could see no sign of the camp. The camp fires had all gone out. He looked east and could see nothing but the narrow trail and starry sky.

"*Doña* Maria Artiles," he said aloud, but softly, the words sending out puffs of mists in the cold still air. "My sweet Mézu, do you see these stars, this beautiful moon? I will have a stone made for you. I will have the mason carve a moon above your name." Mézu was short for Mézucasa. The name meant "Daughter of the Moon" in the language of the Guanche, the people who populated the island of Tenerife before the Spaniards came.

"Our children are doing well," he continued. "Pedro is growing strong and he is learning the ways of a farmer in this land. Maria is the image of you, my dear one. I see you in her eyes."

He heard the crunch of boots coming from the camp.

"*Primero?*"

"Yes."

"The beach watch reports that a light is moving toward us."

CHAPTER 4

D iego stood at the edge of the wash-line facing the approaching light. The sky to his left was beginning to lose its stars and the gray water before him lapped feebly along the wet sandy shore.

"Give them the pass," Diego said.

Plata pulled the canvas screen away from the lantern he had been carrying muttering, "*uno, dos, tres.*" He replaced the cover. "*uno, dos.*" He uncovered and recovered the lamp three times in rapid succession. He left the lamp covered and both men watched the light at sea. It winked out then shone twice, remained dark for the count of four, appeared again, out and stayed lit, twinkling above a black sea.

"Uncover the lamp," Diego said.

Plata removed the cover from the lamp and hung it from a hooked iron staff imbedded in the beach. The black night before them began to lighten as the sun neared the eastern horizon. A speck appeared on the horizon. Occasionally, silver sparkles danced along the eastern side of the speck as oars, dripping with water, rhythmically plunged up and down.

The skiff drew nearer and had begun to take form when the crest of the sun topped the horizon, throwing a yellow-orange light on the boat and a man standing in the bow. A single mast, its sail and gaff tightly furled on the boom, bore a single white pennant with a black stripe. The air was calm, but the pennant flapped open, showing the black center stripe, as the skiff surged with each pull of the oars. The signal meant "dispatches aboard." The skiff slid to a halt a dozen yards from the shore, the water too shallow for it to reach the shore. The man in the bow, dressed in the sailor slops of a common seaman, stepped down, the muddy water reaching as high as his knees. His shoes made a loud squishing sound as he waded out of the gulf and up to Diego.

"*Buenos días, Sargento deMelilla,*" the man said. He handed Diego a folded and sealed parchment. "I am Ojeda, one of Major Segura's runners. I am ordered to wait for a reply."

Diego turned the thick paper over and examined the seal across the fold. It was red wax with the fancy script "HR" of an official regimental document. He broke the seal and opened the paper, turning his body so that the rising sun illuminated the words.

"I have no sick or wounded for you, Ojeda," he said. The first line of the order directed Diego to send any of his party unable to continue back to the ship. The bottom of the message contained a crude map showing a long narrow bay almost paralleling the gulf with three rivers feeding into it from the west, north and east. A dashed line went from the east gulf shore, around the bay and back to the west gulf shore ending at a black square. The script above the map said: *Proceed inland around the bay and take the block house at the west side of bay mouth.*

"Tell the Major we will do as he says. It will take us three days."

"Three days," Ojeda repeated. He waded back to the skiff and pushed it back toward deeper water. The oarsmen helped him by poling with their oars until the boat floated free and Ojeda pulled himself aboard.

Diego turned away from the beach and started back toward the encampment. Plata continued to stare at the receding boat wistfully until Diego snarled at him to "Come along. You are marooned with us." Plata shook himself back to reality, put out the lamp, lowered it from the hook and pulled the rod free from the sand. "I am coming, *Primero*," he said as he glanced back toward the boat.

Diego reached the camp as the security scouts were completing their sweeps of the surrounding land. Pook was getting the camp loaded and prepared to move out.

"Any sign of T'Chien's men?" Diego asked.

"Not yet, *Primero*."

"Tell our scouts to send the man to me if he shows and tell them to report any sign of a trail headed inland." Pook nodded and trotted off.

His orders were to move north. Was he expected to head north now? They had not passed any trails leading away from the beach in the dozen or so miles they had traveled since the landing yesterday. If they headed inland now they would have to cut a trail. Diego guessed it would be about a thirty mile road march to circle the bay, if the maps he had studied were right.

Pook came back from dispatching the scouts. "The wagon is loaded and Gabriella is ready to move, *Primero*."

"East, until noon. Then we will see."

It was well before noon when one of the flank scouts came trotting in with an Indian.

"One of T'Chien's men, *Primero*," the soldier said. "Brought him in, just as Pook said."

"Thank you. Return to your duties."

The Indian was young, perhaps twelve or thirteen years old. He was dressed in deerskin leggings, jerkin and moccasins. He wore a bowl-crowned leather hat with a wide brim that flopped down over his ears and the back of his head until he looked as if his black eyes were staring out of a tunnel. A red and black banded cotton loincloth, his only article of clothing that was not leather, hung to his knees.

"Do you speak Spanish?" Diego asked. He gestured for the Indian to walk along with him. The little column had not stopped.

"Not good Spanish."

"Trade talk?" Diego switched to the version of Choctaw he had learned last summer.

"All people trade talk."

"We must go north, around Biloxi."

"Trail north two hours east," the boy said. He made wide gestures with every word for trade talk was a sign language as much as a verbal one. "Go north. Half day. Cross ford to big trail. Go east one day. I tell T'Chien. He come camp tomorrow night."

"Where are the British?"

"Not near. No see red shirt soldier. See traders going east. Not many. T'Chien say all go Mobile. I go east now. Show trail." The boy trotted east along the shore trail until he disappeared among the brush that bordered the narrow trail.

❧

The trail north was considerably narrower than the coast road. There was just enough room for the wagon to pass. The men marched two abreast and Diego reduced the number of men on flank and lead scout patrols to two each. Before, the beach provided security to his right. Now he was moving through a dense tangle and he had to be concerned with dangers coming from the left, right, front and rear. It required eight men to screen the column of twelve foot soldiers, five artillerymen riding their caisson and one wagon loaded with supplies.

The ford crossing was grueling. The men, six to a side, had to haul on ropes attached to the caisson's tree while the artillery men pulled at the wheels until Gabriella was across. Then the same effort had to be expended for the wagon. By the time they reached the cross trail night was falling and the men were exhausted. They set pickets and made camp on the trail. The cooking fires were screened with a ring of drying clothes and shoes. When the men on the first picket watch rotated into camp, they added fuel to the fires, stripped, hung out everything to dry and huddled around each blaze wrapped in their sleeping blankets.

∼

Morning seemed to arrive quickly, though it was the last week of January and the night should have been long. The new trail east was almost a road. It was wide and the surface packed hard by constant traffic, though they saw none. Diego doubled his forward screen and sent them far ahead. The boy had said it would be one day's travel east before they had to turn south again. Traveling was much easier. Even the small ford they crossed just before the noon meal was no problem. The water was shallow, the riverbed hard-packed sand and the horses managed their loads without any help. The wide road allowed the column to move comfortably and quickly. Diego began to dread the turn south, certain it would prove to be another wilderness trace. Two men were now riding in the wagon, sickened by yesterday's efforts and unable to march.

The light was beginning to fade near the end of day when Diego called a halt. He moved the men and equipment off the road to the north where a small hill offered a camp site relatively clear of brush. Old fire pits dotted the hill top, evidence that others had often camped there in the past. The cooking fires were kept small and Diego posted pickets far to the east and west along the road.

Búho, one of the three forward pickets, jogged into the camp only minutes after he had been sent east.

"*Primero*," he spoke softly, almost in a whisper. "There are people up the road making a camp."

"Pook," Diego touched the man's elbow. "Silence in the camp. Pass the word. Do not stack arms. I will be back in a moment." He turned to Búho. "Show me."

Búho led Diego about seven hundred yards east to a point where the road turned slightly. The other two soldiers of the picket watch were crouched in the brush beside the road watching intently east. One man jumped slightly when Diego crept up to him.

"Holy God, *Primero*," the man whispered. "You nearly scared me to death." It was Quintero. The man had removed his hat and had been peeking through a small gap in the brush. Diego removed his hat as well and crept up beside Quintero to look where the man was pointing.

Five men were building a camp in a small grove near where a trail from the south entered the main road. Diego counted ten horses. Four carried packs, the rest were saddled. Two men were in the process of building a fire while two were pulling gear from the pack animals. One stood in the middle of the road smoking a white pipe and looking west, right at Diego's position. The man must not have seen Diego or any of the other Spaniards, for he seemed content to stare. The brush north of the smoker rustled and he turned to greet someone stepping out onto the trail.

It was a woman dressed in a brown riding skirt and boots with a leather bodice over a tan blouse. A hat, its color matching the blouse, was tilted on her head and cocked to the right side. A small cord ran under her chin and the brim was pinned up with a red and white rosette. She said something to the smoker Diego could not hear. The man removed the pipe and laughed humorlessly. He turned to the others and spoke loudly – in English.

"Little miss says she wishes to have a chamber pot."

The other men guffawed. One handed her a small spade. "Make your pot near a tree and be thankful we give you privacy."

The woman snatched the spade and stomped back into the brush.

"Keep an eye on the camp," Diego told Quintero. He pulled back several paces, signaling Búho and the other soldier, Mina, to join him.

"Búho, you return to our camp. Tell Pook to send six men back with you. Muskets loaded, bayonets fixed and cartridge boxes only. No packs, no haversacks, no canteens. Walk, do not run. Understand?"

Búho nodded. His big, owl-like eyes were wide with excitement. He backed away crouching as if the men in the camp would come storming up the road if he turned his back. Diego watched him recede until the man finally stood and walked quickly west and Diego returned to watch the camp with Quintero.

The saddles were off of the horses now and two men were caring for the animals, rubbing them down and checking their hooves. The woman returned to camp and tossed the spade to the ground near a pile of bedrolls. Two other men were spreading a lean-to near a small fire.

These are careless men, Diego thought. *Camping next to the fire, no one sent to scout around the camp's perimeter. No one set as a watchman.*

The smoker stood and looked east. He hissed the others in the camp into silence. Diego fixed his attention east trying to see what it was that attracted the smoker.

He heard them before he saw them. Four red-coated soldiers led by a Corporal came walking up the road. The redcoats had yellow facings on their uniforms and the men carried their muskets carelessly, balanced across the shoulders, the stocks behind them and holding the bayonet-free barrels with one hand. The new arrivals were greeted warmly. Diego watched for more, fearing these men were but a vanguard for more troops, but none came and those in the camp did not seem to expect more.

Diego gestured for Quintero and Mina to fall back with him. He stopped about a dozen yards from their vantage point. It was growing dark as Búho arrived with the six soldiers armed as Diego had instructed. He formed them into two ranks, five backed by four. He had Quintero and Mina fix their bayonets as quietly as they could, but he dared not have them load, for the sound of a steel ramrod sliding down a steel barrel was too hard to dampen.

"At the guard, forward march," Diego whispered.

The hastily assembled battle line filled the road. The bayonets, glistening in the diming light, tilted forward as the formation of Spaniards rounded a small turn and into full view of the British camp. They had advanced several paces toward the camp before there was any reaction. Then there was screaming and a mad scramble for weapons.

Diego shouted, "Halt. In quickest time, LOCK and LOAD, present when ready."

Nine soldados acting as one, dropped his musket to his waist, placed the lock at half-cock, flipped the frizzen forward, reached back with his right hand, slapped the cartridge box, removed a cartridge, tore it open with a bite, primed the pan, closed the frizzen, dropped the butt of the musket next to his left foot, poured the remaining powder in the cartridge down the musket's barrel followed by the lead ball still wrapped in paper, removed the ram rod from its carrier under the barrel, rammed down the ball, returned the ramrod, put the butt against his shoulder and pointed his musket toward the scrambling redcoats.

Reacting to the sudden appearance of the Spaniards, the British corporal yelled for his men to recover their weapons, which had been stacked in a pyramid at the edge of the camp, and form a line. He pushed his men into line and ordered them to load. The redcoats fumbled with their cartridge boxes and were in the act of ramming down when Diego, seeing that the last of his men had "presented" (pointed his musket in the direction of the enemy), took a deep breath and shouted, "*DISPARAR* (Fire)!"

Orange light filled the space between the two groups, freezing the image of terrified faces in Diego's mind. Two of the *godums* went down, one red coat and one of the original five. The return fire was feeble, ragged and did no harm.

"Lock and Load – Present when ready." Diego ordered. He watched the enemy as his men went through the process of loading a musket. He could hear them as they handled cartridges, primed locks, loaded and rammed down. In only seconds, barrels were being leveled toward the British camp.

Diego's eyes burned from the acrid smoke and swam with blotches of colored lights, the result of the flash of the volley. He could see that the *godums* were fleeing. The redcoats attempted to pull back in some sort of formation while the other men simply fled. Two had mounted their horses bareback and were galloping away. Another of the redcoats swayed and went down, evidently wounded in the first volley. The remaining two, led by their corporal, turned and ran.

Diego hoped the fleeing men had not simply been picketers for a larger force. His mind painted an image of the corporal stumbling up to his brigade commander to report Spaniards ahead on the road. He had attacked without knowing the situation he faced. For all he knew, five hundred infantry would come down the road, six abreast, bayonets at the advance. He moved his men past the remains of the camp and fifty yards or so to the east. There he halted them, and prepared to defend against a counter attack.

The sound of hooves came from behind him. He turned and stepped aside just as Barbeaux arrived with Gabriella. The artilleryman was jogging, leading the caisson's horse by the reins and stopped as he reached Diego.

"Place Gabriella there," Diego pointed toward his men east of the camp. "Send a ball up the road as soon as you can."

The caisson, carriage and a polished brass barrel bounced past Diego. It was full dark now. Everything that moved appeared as mere shadows. The lumps on the road ahead divided and the glint of Gabriella flickered between them as Barbeaux turned the gun and unlimbered it into position.

Pook appeared next to Diego.

"What is happening?"

I have no idea. "We bumped into some travelers and a few redcoats."

The entire road east of Gabriella was washed with a bright orange light as Barbeaux sent a ball crashing up the road.

"What are your orders?"

If I only knew. "Put three men to breaking up camp. It will take a long time in the dark. Tell the pickets we have moved to this location and bring everyone forward. We will stand the night one and one." One man was to stay up, armed and ready to move while one man slept on the ground in a bedroll. "We will put the wagon at the crossroads and be ready to move at first light."

"*Sí, Primero,*" Pook said and he was gone.

"Send a man with a lamp," Diego called toward the shadow that was Pook.

"*Sí, Primero.*"

One of Barbeaux's men returned leading their horse and caisson. Fumbling in the dark, he tied the reins to a tree. Diego touched the man's elbow and he gave a start.

"Come with me," Diego said in French. The man hesitated and Diego assured him they would not go more than a few paces.

In the shadow of the grove that would have been the British camp, they found several bedrolls, two saddles and four pack frames. A string of six horses, snorting and whinnying, pulled against their tethers. Barbeaux's man soothed the frightened animals, stroking the muzzles of the most animated ones until they calmed. A light bobbed into view.

"Go back to your caisson and send the man with the lamp here."

"*Oui, Sergent.*"

A frightened young Private Martin came to Diego, his wide eyes sparkling red in the lamplight.

"Follow me with that light."

Diego went to check the bodies of the two men killed in his initial volley. The redcoat had a gaping hole in the front of his forehead. The man's haversack was provisioned with about four days' worth of hardtack, salted beef and flour. Aside from a tin plate, cup and fork, there was nothing else in the haversack. The man had three canteens strung across his chest, a bedroll and backpack, a bayonet still in its scabbard, a cartridge box and a musket lay at his feet, the ramrod protruding from the mouth of the barrel. The backpack contained a change of clothes, three packets of two dozen musket cartridges tightly wrapped in paper covered with bee's wax and a ground cloth. The cartridge box contained eighteen cartridges in the wooden block and ten spare flints as well as cleaning tools in a pouch under the box.

"We have the other one here," Búho called from near Gabriella's position. Diego held up the light and he could see Búho and another man, Olivier, tending to the wounded redcoat.

"Check him for weapons and keep him there," Diego called.

Olivier was talking to the wounded man in English and Búho went through the redcoat's traps. Diego shifted to the other dead man. He was dressed in buckskin and lay face-down. Two holes gapped through his fringed leather shirt. Diego rolled the corpse over.

"Move that lamp closer to his face."

Martin did so until the body's whiskers sparkled. He had seen this man somewhere, but he could not remember. The man's haversack contained a purse that jingled when Diego hefted it. Tucking the purse into his own haversack, Diego noticed a pistol in the man's hand and pried it free. It had been recently fired, the frizzen was open and the pan was empty. He tucked the pistol in his belt and removed a bag containing materials for the pistol from the corpse.

There was some movement down the slope south of the grove. Martin nervously shifted the lamp to shine in the direction of the noise. Something was struggling in the tight tangle of dead briars.

Diego drew his short sword. "Follow me," he said and stepped down the slope, sliding much of the way. He grabbed an arm and pulled.

"*Vous sont mal me!*"

It was the woman from the camp.

"I do not intend to hurt you," Diego said in his best dock worker's French.

"Then take your hand from my arm!"

"If you go up to the man with the lamp, I will."

"You mean to say the boy with the lamp," the woman snorted.

Diego sheathed his sword, "Go!" He released her arm and she crawled up the slope to Martin who backed away from her as she reached the top.

"She will not bite you," Diego said, switching to Spanish. "Stay where you are." He gained the top of the grove. Behind Martin, Diego could see the rest of the vanguard collecting at the intersection.

Pook came into the light of the lamp. "We have relocated, *Primero*. The wagon is at the crossroad."

"Good. Set pickets three hundred yards east. Tell them to stay off the road when they go to ground. Send two more pickets north a hundred yards and two west a hundred yards. Send three south on the trail three hundred yards from the cross roads. I am expecting someone from T'Chien tonight so remind them of the password. If they see something, challenge first. I do not want one of the pickets to kill a scout. The redcoats were carrying rations and water enough for four days. I do not think there are more nearby. Collect the flints from the captured weapons and cartridge boxes and distribute them to the men." Spanish flints were typically of poorer quality than English or American flints. North American flint from quarries near the Great Lakes was the best and highly prized.

"*Sí, Primero.*" Pook paused to examine the woman before hurrying back to the crossroads.

Diego turned to the woman. She appeared to be about twenty-five or thirty years old and of an average height, five foot tall or so. Her figure was slim and well accentuated by the riding attire. Her hat was gone and her black hair flowed over her left shoulder down to her narrow waist. Her brown eyes reflected red sparkles, tinted by the lamplight. Her expression was one of anger, not fear.

"*Ce que l'on appellee* (what are you called)?" Diego asked.

"A gentleman would ask for my name," she said, tilting her head up slightly until she was looking directly into Diego's eyes, her full mouth in an attractive pout. "My name is Marcelite Gaudet de la Arceneaux of the White River Plantation."

"Tell me, *mademoiselle*, how does it happen I find Marcelite Gaudet de la Arceneaux of the White River Plantation in the Florida wilderness and in the company of British men?"

"You may call me *Mademoiselle* Gaudet," Marcelite said. "To answer your question, I was taken prisoner by an English privateer. I was going to

Paris. I was going to stay with my grandmother. Those men were with the pirates, they were taking me to Mobile, to be held for ransom, I think."

"What was the name of your ship?"

"She was the *Fleur de Mai*. They stole her. I heard them say the ship would be sold in Nassau. They would not allow Dianna, my *chaperonne*, to stay with me. They brought me up that narrow wilderness trail from the coast and now you tried to kill me."

"We did not try to kill you."

"No? No? I am sitting by my saddle and suddenly there is noise all around me. I hear the bullets fly, *monsieur* Sergeant. I hear them! It is like bees, I think, bees. But no, not bees – bullets! How I was not killed, I cannot say." She suddenly touched her head. "I have lost my hat. It cost me twenty *livres*. I expect you to pay me for a new hat." She began to look about in the small circle of lamplight.

"It will turn up in the morning, when we can see." Diego took the lamp from Martin. "Leave the lamp here. Go find Claro. I want the two of you to get a tent from the wagon and pitch it here."

Diego watched Martin leave in search of Claro, sighed and turned back to Marcelite. "*Mademoiselle* Gaudet, my men will set up a tent for you. They will place the opening toward the cook fire. It may prove to be a cold night. Gather those items you may need – "

"I am not spending the night here! Where is your officer? I demand you bring me to your commanding officer!"

The wind had freshened a little and Diego marveled at how wonderful she smelled. Kidnapped at sea and forced to travel up a wilderness trail in the company of brigands and she smelled of flowers. He was certain he smelled like an old goat after several days of hard travel on trails more suited for deer than men.

"I am in command here. You will be safe. I will have guards placed around your tent, you need not fear."

Marcelite placed her hands on her hips, jutted out her chin, "Fear? I do not fear *monsieur* Sergeant. I demand you assign an escort to me. I will be brought to the nearest officer."

"That is impossible. Here is your tent. Step over here with me, so my men can put it up." He touched her elbow to guide her out of the way and she jerked it away as if his hand were on fire.

Once the tent was up, she tossed a bedroll, her saddle and a saddle bag into the tent, went in and pulled the flap closed. He watched as her fingers worked the ties from top to bottom until the flap was laced shut. He posted two guards at the back of the tent. No need for guards at the front, for he opened a camp chair and sat down near the tent flap facing the fire.

Pook came up. "Pickets set, *Primero*. The artillerymen volunteered to stand a watch. It would help, we are shorthanded."

"Have them sleep at their gun. They can do a one and three. (one man on watch, three men sleeping.) I want to be informed the instant T'Chien's man contacts our picket. Tell the teamster to inspect these horses and put them to use if we can."

"*Sí, Primero.*" Pook was gone.

Diego dug in his haversack and pulled out the purse he had taken from the dead man – pirate, according to *Mademoiselle* Gaudet. He loosened the leather binding, opened the purse and poured the contents into his hand. There were twelve silver coins, about the size of a Spanish eight-*reale* piece, but the coins were not Spanish. He turned them over in his hands, positioning each to catch light from the fire. They were all newly minted French *ecu*, a coin he had never seen in New Orleans.

"Quintero!" Diego called out without looking up from the coins in his hand. He had just seen the man spreading a bedroll.

"I will get him, *Primero*," someone said.

Quintero appeared with a blanket over his shoulders. It was getting cold. "What is it, *Primero*?"

"Do you remember who was on the line with us when we fired on the *godums*?"

"*Sí, Primero*. There was me and Mina and Búho and – ."

"I do not need you to name them now. I just wanted to know if you remember who was there."

"*Sí, Primero*, I remember."

"Good. Here is a silver coin for you." Diego placed an *ecu* in Quintero's hand. "Tell each man to report to me when he can. Every man in the fight today will receive a silver coin."

"*Sí, Primero*." Quintero rubbed the coin between his fingers and bit it. "Will we earn eight *reales* for every fight?"

"No. Today was – unusual."

Diego stood and replaced the purse in his haversack. It was time to inspect the camp.

With full half of his men on picket duty, the camp did not occupy much of the trail. Three fires had been set along the edge of the trail around the crossroad created by the trail from the south. The tent was set opposite the center fire. Diego went to the western fire first where the wagon rested with its leads on the ground. The teamster had tethered the horse to a tree and was tending to his animal.

"Grenouille, what do you think of the horses we have obtained?"

The teamster rested his arms on the back of the horse, his wide face distorted with thought. "The four pack horses will do well. I may rig the wagon for a team. We could put pack frames on the riding horses. They will carry freight if it is on their backs. Those horses are fine mounts and would not do to pull a wagon or caisson. We could eat them," the man's hairy face flashed a smile. "I mean if we run out of supplies, that is. Do you ride, *Primero?*"

"No." Diego had never ridden a horse. He doubted if five men in the vanguard could ride, save for the militia. Riding was for rich men. He was willing to bet Corporal Barbeaux and even his gunners could sit a horse. Barbeaux's Duplesses Battalion was a militia unit comprised of the richest and most influential Gentlemen of Color in New Orleans.

The wounded redcoat sat on a bedroll by the eastern cook fire. Private Olivier, who could speak English, was sitting with him.

"How are his wounds?" Diego asked. The redcoat looked up when the sergeant spoke. The man's face was gray and drawn.

"A ball danced along a rib and he has lost a lot of blood. I am no surgeon, but I think he will recover if it doesn't putrefy."

"Wash it with some rum. That was my father's solution," Diego said. "Honey works well too. The wound will not putrefy if it is kept sweet with honey or rum."

"We have no honey, *Primero.*"

"And precious little rum, but it will have to do. Bathe the wound with rum."

"*Sí, Primero.*"

"What does he have to say?"

"He is Private William Dunn of His Majesty's 60th Regiment of Foot."

"Where is his regiment now?"

"He says the full regiment of a thousand men is just up the road, ready to fall on us in the morning."

"He is lying. The redcoats we met were on a long patrol. They carried provisions for several days."

Pook trotted up to the campfire. "I've been looking for you, *Primero*."

"What is it?"

"The man T'Chien just came in through our pickets."

CHAPTER 5

T'Chien squatted by the cooking fire warming his hands. The night had grown cold, though the air was dry. T'Chien glanced at the tent behind Diego.

"Only one tent, *Primero*," he asked. "It is a cold night."

"The tent is for a woman we have – acquired. She says she was captured at sea."

"A woman? Indeed?" He examined the tent, his jaw muscles visibly working on a handful of a mixture of dried meat, fat, honey and grain called *pimîhkân*. "I saw the horses. Good animals." T'Chien pulled another portion of *pimîhkân*, inserted the wad into his mouth and resumed chewing. "We had been following the redcoats you met for two days. We had expected you to be on the coast, at the mouth to the bay, not in the middle of the road to Mobile. The soldiers did not seem to be a problem for you."

"They were no bother."

"I cannot say where the others came from." T'Chien tossed a twig toward the corpse dressed in buckskin where it lay next to the dead redcoat at the edge of the firelight.

"The woman says they came up from the coast. Said those with her were pirates and she was a hostage."

"That may be. The redcoats and their pirate friends have fled east toward Mobile. After you drove them from here, both redcoats and leather shirts stopped where the trail turns sharply, about a half mile east. I thought they were going to rally, but your cannon sent a ball skipping past them and they bolted. One rode a horse. He did not ride as if he were a seaman, I think."

"Is there a regiment nearby?"

"No, nothing from here to the fort at Mobile but those you have met."

Martin came up dragging a trunk. "*Primero*, we were going through the things the *godums* left and this is full of women's clothing."

"Just clothes? No papers? No coins?"

"Nothing but clothes. And I found a hat. There, down the hill." Martin gestured toward the slope where he had found Marcelite.

"Put the trunk and hat at the tent flap and tell *Mademoiselle* Gaudet what you have found."

"I cannot speak French, *Primero*."

"Place it, and the hat, before the tent. I will tell her."

"What pirate allows a hostage to bring her luggage along?" T'Chien asked.

"What woman brings riding clothes on a sea voyage?" Diego answered.

Diego turned toward the sealed tent. "*Mademoiselle* Gaudet. We have found your luggage and your hat. We have placed them before the tent."

Delicate fingers appeared unlacing the tent flap from the bottom until enough was undone to allow the trunk to be pulled into the tent. The hat was brushed off onto the ground when the trunk disappeared. A hand appeared, felt around on the ground, found the hat and pulled it in as well. The tent flap was retied to a chorus of muttering.

T'Chien offered Diego a portion of *pimîhkân*. "What are you going to do with her?"

"She demands to see an officer." Diego placed the food in the corner of his mouth. Experience had taught him to chew *pimîhkân* slowly and thoroughly.

"No problem denying that request." T'Chien chuckled. "The nearest officer is fifty miles away in Mobile and British."

"We are ordered to return to the coast. We will be in a sack, T'Chien. The bay will be to our west, the gulf to our south and Mobile to our north."

"Then go east."

"If the British come down on us they will have us ten to one."

"They dare not come down for fear Gálvez will enter Mobile Bay and cut them off."

"I do not like having to guess what an enemy will do."

"Governor General Gálvez is the one guessing. You will just have to do the dying if he is wrong."

A shriek came from the tent.

"I think she has discovered her things have been handled." T'Chien said, clearly amused.

"*Soldats – cochons, aucune différence* (soldiers – pigs, no difference)!" she muttered, her voice deep and very feminine.

Diego was struck by how Marcelite could sound so attractive even when she spoke in anger. Now that he thought about it, he had never heard her speak, except in anger.

"You have some pack horses now," T'Chien said. "You can lighten the load in the wagons. I will show your men how to make a *travois*. The pack horses can carry a double load with a *travois*."

"Good. I will need the wagons for the sick and injured. The woman will go into the wagon as well, next to the teamster. I dare not allow her on a horse."

"A *travois* will carry a wounded man better than a wagon."

❧

"Cut two long poles, at least twelve foot, for each *travois*. These will be your drag poles." T'Chien had several soldiers gathered around him as he demonstrated. It was still dark and everything was done in the proximity of a cooking fire. Grenouille, the teamster, decided to use two of the best of the pack horses for the wagon and rigged a team yoke for the two new animals. His own, and less fit horse, was consigned to carry a pack. Barbeaux declined to team his small caisson, declaring a team would only hinder him on the narrow trail. That left five horses to act as pack animals, but only four pack frames.

"Cut the butt end of the poles at an angle so they may slide along the ground more easily." T'Chien laid the two poles he had cut on the ground about three feet apart and parallel to each other. "Cut five smaller poles into three foot lengths and lash one across the drag poles in the middle. Lash the rest about a foot apart starting from the middle and going toward the butt. There should be about one foot of drag pole extending beyond the last cross shaft. Tie a rope across the tips of the drag poles. This is the yoke end."

"Bring one of the horses with a pack frame to me." When this was done, T'Chien picked up the tip end of the newly constructed *travois*, positioned the drag poles on either side of the animal and put the rope of the yoke across its withers. "Now you can strap packs onto the pack frame and onto the *travois* behind the horse. This will make room in the wagon for those who cannot march."

"We are one pack frame short," Quintero said.

"Then saddle up a horse and put the yoke of the *travois* beyond the saddle. Lash the poles of the travois to the saddle. You do not need a pack frame."

"We move out at first light," Diego said. T'Chien nodded as he watched Quintero and two other soldiers cut saplings into the pieces needed for four more *travois*. Diego assigned the soldiers who would serve as security scouts and directed them to pass beyond the night picket posts. They would be moving south on the narrow trail T'Chien identified as the one leading to the coast.

Diego walked to the only tent in the camp. He cleared his throat and bellowed in his best sergeant's voice, "*Mademoiselle* Gaudet. We will strike this tent in a quarter hour. It is to be loaded on the wagon."

"Impossible," Marcelite replied drowsily. "I am still sleeping."

"We strike the tent in a quarter hour. It will not matter if you are dressed or not."

"I am dressing, *monsieur* Sergeant." He could hear her moving about. "You must be mad. It is still night."

"Quarter hour and the tent will come down, *mademoiselle.* Breakfast is salted pork and hard biscuits."

"I have my own food."

Diego looked up to see one of the guards he had assigned to the tent grinning at him. "Búho, do you speak French?"

"Only a little, *Primero.*"

"When I send some men to strike this tent, see that it is done without delay." He spoke in French and loudly so Marcelite could hear.

"Oui –" Búho paused and switched to Spanish "I do not know the French word for '*Primero,*' – *Primero.*"

"Neither do I. Just see that it is done."

Diego went around the camp. The scouts had been dispatched, but a dozen chores remained. He verified all had eaten, the cooking fire extinguished, and each man was fully equipped. The five pack animals, each with a *travois*, were loaded with enough baggage from the wagon to make room for the men's back packs. The wounded redcoat was strapped to one of the travois.

"Grenouille, strike the tent and load it on the wagon," Diego said. "Búho is there to help you. Send the woman to me." Grenouille was a native of New Orleans and his Spanish had a distinct French accent. There was no need to ask him if he spoke the language.

"Pook, move out!"

The soldiers moved south in a column of two. With so many scouts ahead, to the flanks, and five men leading the pack animals, the column was only six men long. They marched, muskets slung inverted over their shoulders, ducking under low branches and snaking around ruts in the trail.

"Barbeaux!"

"Yes, sergeant?"

"Move out."

One of the artillerymen rode the horse, Barbeaux and another man rode the caisson and two walked along behind Gabriella.

T'Chien stepped up as the cannon rolled past Diego. "The *travois* are made, loaded and ready. I leave you now. My people have scouted to the east. The only people to be found are a few farmers along the Pascagoula River. No soldiers."

"And how far is it to that river?"

"A dozen miles. No more." T'Chien trotted off to the east without looking back.

Diego remembered the Pascagoula. The river was bordered by wide and nearly impenetrable swamps. If he were ordered east from the coast, he could not imagine crossing such a barrier. He looked at his meager caravan and his heart sank. Perhaps there would be a ship waiting when he reached the coast, or a miracle. He gestured for the string of pack animals to move out behind the cannon.

"*Monsieur* Sergeant!"

Diego turned to see Marcelite dressed in her riding clothes. Her dark hair was rolled into a tight bun that sat beneath her riding hat. Her eyes sparkled and her full lips hinted of the added benefit of some artificial coloring. She carried saddle bags and was pulling the sea chest.

"No one came to get my saddle, *monsieur* Sergeant. Certainly, you cannot expect me to saddle the beast myself?"

"You will ride on the wagon, next to the teamster, *mademoiselle* Gaudet," Diego said, automatically switching to French. He took the saddlebags from Marcelite's hands, opened them and began to shift through the contents. He realized he had failed to have the bags, or the woman, searched last night and the oversight embarrassed him.

"How dare you, *monsieur*! That is my private property."

"Get on the wagon, *mademoiselle* Gaudet. I should search your person as well, but I will take your word that you do not have a weapon hidden on you."

"I will do no such thing!"

Diego tossed the saddlebags onto the wagon seat and moved toward Marcelite.

"You would not dare. My father will have you flogged."

"Grenouille, climb down and hold *mademoiselle* while I search her."

Grenouille, grinning at the possibilities the order offered, wrapped the reins around the break lever and began to climb down.

"You have my word!" Marcelite hissed through clenched teeth.

"I have your word to what, specifically?"

"You have my word that I do not have a weapon of any kind on my person, Sergeant."

"Good. Now get on the wagon."

Marcelite tossed her head back with a sneer. *"Cochon,"* she said and climbed aboard, slapping away any attempt to help her up.

"Fall in behind the pack animals," Diego ordered Grenouille. "Keep up. There are two trail scouts behind you." He had given the order in French so Marcelite would know she was being watched from behind. It was unlikely she would attempt to flee. They were in midst of the belt of wilderness that separated the sandy soils of the gulf coast and the more arable lands found four leagues or more inland. The pirates who had held her captive allowed her to ride, something he would never do. Perhaps she had promised not to try to escape from them. Perhaps he should demand that promise as well, but was she a prisoner? Perhaps she had never been a prisoner. His head swam with so many doubts about her tale.

He forged past the wagon, pack animals and the bouncing polished brass of Gabriella to take his normal station behind the infantry column, such as it was. He had instructed the men to advance at the *"ruta"* which did not require a pace or close formation. For freedom of movement, the men had bundled their uniform coats away in the wagon and wore only vests and gaiters over their cotton shirts and trousers. Their red-cockaded tricorns were slung across the back of their packs tied in place with thin leather strings run through holes at the base of the crowns. Each man had a sweat-stained bandana tied around his head to keep his hair in place. Their muskets were slung over their shoulders muzzle down so both hands would be free to push aside the limbs hanging over the trail. In some places, the overhanging branches were so thick that the lead men had to cut them down with their short swords.

Even though the foliage was denser, their progress was faster than before. The horse-drawn wagon's laborious progress had slowed the entire column. The wagon still set the pace, but the addition of another horse in the traces along with the lightened load allowed the column to move at the speed of a walking man.

Diego searched the ground for signs of hoof prints coming from the gulf, but he saw none. This trail had not been traveled by anything larger than a man in a long time. It was winter, yet brush and twisted vines bordered the narrow path, forcing all traffic to the muddy center of the track. Every bent blade of dead grass, every broken branch indicated travel toward the south, nothing coming north.

In less than two miles they forded a narrow creek. The creek was shallow, its bottom hard-packed sand and the fording went quickly. The water was stained a dark tea color, tasted of dead leaves, but otherwise appeared clean. The men topped off their canteens and the horses drank readily. Pook passed among those who had filled their canteens to remind them they would need to add rum to the water before drinking, lest the water prove "stale."

The dense, brush-choked terrain began to transform into open grasslands interspersed with tall pines. One mile past the ford, the pines were replaced by twisted oaks and they broke out onto a shoreline which ran northwest and southeast. The open gulf was visible toward the southeast and a distant island to the south protected the bay from the open sea. Several fishing cabins and a few ragged piers populated the shoreline. The scouts reported no signs of the inhabitants.

The cabins were built in the fashion of the Choctaw villages Diego had seen in the interior. Logs of four inches or so in diameter had been fashioned into ten-foot lengths. Two logs were lashed together at one end and the free ends spread until they were about five feet apart, and stood on end. Another pair of logs, lashed and spread in the same way was then pushed against the first pair. This was repeated until twenty or more such pairs were packed together forming both wall and roof. Viewed from the end, the huts gave the impression of an inverted "V."

Mud was packed into the chinks between the logs. Overlapping palm fronds were lashed over mud and logs as shingles. The openings at the ends were closed with woven vines, branches, mud and fronds except a small space reserved for a door. Had the fishermen been home, the doorways would have been covered by a blanket or large hide. Each hut had a smoke hole in the center above a clay fire-pit in the floor. Crude as these structures were, they were comfortable and, unlike the canvas tents, had the advantage of permitting a fire within.

Diego sent four men along the shoreline toward the southeast with instructions to scout two miles and return. He sent another four to the northwest with similar instructions, but they returned after a half-hour to report the beach ended in a peninsula that jutted between a reed marsh and the bay. The men sent to the southeast returned to report they had gone two miles, maybe more, and had encountered a bayou bounded by marsh flowing into the gulf.

A five-sided foundation of brick strong-house was found a dozen yards north of the huts. The pattern suggested each side was about twenty feet long. There were no traces of walls. Perhaps the place had been just a forti-fied entrenchment for cannon. Diego decided this was the "block house" indicated on the crude map he had been given. If so, no one had occupied the place as a fighting position for several decades.

"Pook," Diego called.

"*Sí, Primero?*"

"Set our pickets. We will camp here. No open cooking fires. Use the huts and make certain the ends are covered so no light escapes." Two hours or more of daylight remained, but they had nowhere to go. It would be good for the men to have time to rest and repair while they could still see. Moonrise would not be until several hours after nightfall.

"Martin."

"*Sí, Primero?*"

"Get the signal lamp ready. We may see a light out in the gulf come dark. I want to be ready if a signal should come."

No signal light appeared that night.

⁓

Diego was up with the shift of pickets to the dawn watch. He walked the extent of the pickets to the east and north. Their position against the mouth of the bay limited the avenues of approach by land to those two directions, an advantage in one respect; the enemy could not approach undetected from the sea or bay. It was a distinct disadvantage in another; an enemy of superior numbers coming from the north or east would have them trapped against the beach.

He returned from his excursion just as the sky was beginning to lose its stars. The men needed a rest. The march through the wilderness had worn them down, but he could not permit any decrease in vigilance.

"Quintero!" Diego called out once he was back within the crude perim-eter of huts.

"*Sí, Primero.*"

"Get four men and take down three tall pines to fashion a tripod watch tower. I want the sharpest eyes on the sea looking for a sail."

Pook came up as Quintero was receiving his instructions.

"Shall we dig a perimeter, *Primero?*"

"Yes. And cut posts for a palisade. Anchor the center on that old foundation and run the ends to the beach south and west. Take down the huts beyond the perimeter and use the poles in the palisade as well."

"What if the enemy comes from the sea?"

"We will fight from the other side of the wall. If we are overpowered, we run."

"And if the enemy comes from the land in great numbers?"

"Then we die. You are much too inquisitive, Pook."

Pook laughed and trotted off to form his work detail from among those who had not been on picket duty during the midnight watch.

"Barbeaux!"

The artilleryman had been supervising the cleaning of Gabriella and her caisson. He trotted over to Diego.

"*Oui?*"

"I want Gabriella set within that old foundation. Dig it out so she will sit low so she can sweep the land to the north and east with canister, or be turned about to throw balls at any vessels coming from the gulf or bay."

"I will, sergeant. But if a ship of any size approaches, Gabriella may not have the bite we need."

"If a ship of any size comes from the sea, I promise you I will have her limbered-up and racing for the trees. Keep planks for a ramp handy if we must pull her out."

Diego looked around the campsite. Men were cooking breakfast, working on the palisade or digging sand out of the old foundation. In the distance, he could hear the chopping of Quintero's detail as they felled the tall pines needed for the watchtower. It made him feel better when his people were working. *Happiness for a sergeant is every man working.*

"*Monsieur* Sergeant."

Diego turned around and looked down into Marcelite's upturned face. She was wearing a round-crowned, wide brimmed straw hat over a red bandana tied about her head. He could not imagine how she had obtained the hat or protected it from being crushed in her baggage. He had not seen it among her traps. She wore a blue cotton dress. It was high at the neck, flowed to the ground covering her feet and had full length sleeves. She had a shawl draped over her shoulders, for the morning was cold. Even though her face was set in a scowl and she was ready to fight, he thought her quite pretty.

"Yes. *mademoiselle* Gaudet. What is it?"

"I demand you bring me to an officer. I must get word to my family that I am rescued, if that is what has happened, or have I just been captured by a Spanish pirate?"

"Is White River Plantation in Louisiana?"

Marcelite blinked her eyes as if the question were remote to her intended line of conversation.

"What is it you say? Yes, of course the White River Plantation is in Louisiana."

"Then, *Mademoiselle* Gaudet, as a citizen of Louisiana you are a subject of His Most Catholic Majesty, Charles the Third, King of Spain. Governor General Gálvez serves the King, I serve Gálvez and you are under my protection. We are in British territory and at war. When I can, I will see you safely into the care of an officer. Until then, you will accept my instructions."

"I will not. You are no gentleman, a mere sergeant. Before you were a soldier, what did you do; mend shoes or farm?"

"Before I came into the army, I was a goatherd."

"A herder of goats!" Marcelite snorted contemptuously.

"I was the best herder of goats in all of Gran Canaria, and a farmer as well." *I was married to a beautiful woman. We were blessed with beautiful children and I was happy.* "Now I am a sergeant in the King's army and I will be obeyed."

"You cannot compel me to obey you as if I were one of your *soldados!*" She pronounced the Spanish word so well Diego considered the possibility Marcelite spoke the language and he had no needed to struggle with his dockworker French.

"You will obey me," he said in Spanish, "because your life may depend upon it."

Marcelite looked at him blankly, so he repeated the phrase in French.

"Humph!" She said. She stomped a foot, faced about and strode to one of the crude fisherman's piers where she sat, facing the bay.

Diego shook his head slowly. He did not know what to make of the woman. Her story was awash with contradictions.

Quintero returned with his work detail dragging three suitable logs.

"Where do you want us to place the tower, *Primero?*"

"There would be fine," Diego indicated the highest point on the peninsula within the main circle of huts.

Quintero had the men lay two logs, butt ends to the west and one log, butt end to the east, the tip of the eastern log between the tips of the western ones. He lashed the ends together with rope, weaving in and out of the space between the logs. Two pits were dug about five feet apart and three feet deep. The butts of the western logs were placed at the edges of the pits and the tripod pulled upright by a rope. Another pit was dug to anchor the eastern leg of the tower. Rungs of stout branches were lashed to the western pair of logs until a ladder had been created.

"Martin!" Diego called.

"*Sí, Primero?*"

"Go to the top and watch for a sail. Report anything you see that may seem out of place."

"*Sí, Primero.*" Martin ascended the crude rungs.

"Look to landward and east along the beach as well."

Martin arrived at the top and sat comfortably on the center pile as if he were riding a horse.

"Pook, Martin is to be relieved in an hour. Each man shall have a turn, unless you think his eyesight to be poor." It would be nice if they had a glass, but they did not. "And unfurl the regimental flag. Have Martin's replacement bring it up to fly above the watchtower."

The regimental flag, a white square emblazoned with the ragged red cross of *Borgoña*, had been packed away. The trails they had been struggling through were too narrow, overgrown, isolated and primitive to spend the energy required to parade with the tall banner. There would be no smoke-filled wide battle fields in need of a clear rallying point. Any fight they would have on this excursion would be close, quick and deadly. It had been that way with the skirmish at the trail junction two nights ago. *Or was it three?*

"What do we do now, *Primero?*" Pook asked.

I wish I knew. "We will wait for our sea shadow," Diego said with more confidence than he felt. "Our orders were to come to this place. There is a packet boat in the gulf that has been following our progress and reporting what has been found back to Gálvez." He hoped he was telling the truth.

"There was nothing to report until the other night," Pook said. "And nothing to report since."

"Finding nothing is as important as finding something."

"And what about her?" Pook gestured toward Marcelite, who, as if on cue, removed her hat and bandana, shook her hair free until it fell down her shoulders.

"I do not know what to make of that one. She is not what she claims to be, of that I am certain."

"It may be we can send her off on the packet boat, should it ever meet us again," Pook said.

"I think she will contrive a way not to go, even if we offered it." Diego was not certain he might not contrive of a way to keep her with the vanguard, if the opportunity to send her off did arise. He dug into his haversack to retrieve a slice of salted beef. His hand brushed a tightly wrapped bundle of coins, the three remaining French *ecu*. The incident made him think of the dead man and how he was certain he had seen the man before. Once more, he tried to remember where or when, but the memory escaped him. He scanned the shoreline of the barrier island to the south and saw nothing but beach and brush. *It would be nice if one of T'Chien's men or a messenger from the packet boat would appear, or anyone to tell me what to do.*

Diego heard a popping noise and looked up to see the regimental flag streaming out in a freshening east wind. The cold was losing its bite as the day matured and the wind shifted from the north to the east. He watched as the man on the tower, Garza, stiffened, shaded his eyes and stared toward the south.

"I see a sail! *Primero*, a sail!" Garza shouted as he pointed toward the eastern tip of the long island that protected the bay.

"What kind of sail?"

"A sail, *Primero*!"

"What kind of sail, man? Square? Lateen?"

"Pointed at the top. Only one as far as I can tell."

"Can you tell where it is headed?"

"East, *Primero*. It goes east."

That is the problem with an army full of landsmen, Diego thought. *One scrap of canvas on a mast is much the same as any other.* Still, a gaffed top riding above a lateen mainsail would appear "pointed" at the peak. Two of the Spanish packet boats that had been following them east were lateen rigged. If this were one of the packets, they would see the regimental flag, sail east to the end of the barrier island and come up into the bay.

"Can you see any flags?"

"Too far, *Primero*. I cannot tell."

"Watch her. When she clears the eastern end of the island, call out."

"*Ami ou ennemi* (Friend or foe)?" Marcelite was standing only a few feet away. How long she had been there, he did not know.

"We will soon find out, *Mademoiselle* Gaudet. I must insist you go into your tent until we know." He continued in French, "Barbeaux, please train Gabriella on the bay, aim her east as far as she will bear, and make ready to load a solid shot at my command." Gabriella's four pound ball would not do much to a ship, but a single-masted little packet boat was not so formidable.

"Pook, cease all work parties, arm and assemble the men."

Diego strained his eyes toward the barrier island, but the low brush on the island hid the sail from his view. He could hear Pook behind him waking the men who had been on the last watch, supervising the collection of arms. Six men were on picket duty. The artillery men were working Gabriella around. Eighteen, no sixteen men would be in ranks when he turned around. One man was guarding the prisoner and one was sick, sleeping in one of the huts. If he had guessed correctly, and if Garza had reported correctly, it was a packet boat about to come into the bay. Most likely she was a Spanish boat, but if British, she could not be carrying more than a score of men.

"She is turning into the bay!"

"What colors does she fly?"

"I see a white flag with a black stripe up the center!"

Diego sighed in relief. A white pennant with a central black stripe was the Spanish signal for "dispatches on board." He watched as the boat cleared the end of the barrier island less than two miles away. He recognized her. She was the *Alacita* and her master was the contract sailor, Domingo Palmas. The *Alacita* had carried Diego to New Orleans after his escape from Pensacola.

Palmas' deep voice came booming across the water. "Strike all sails!" The main sheet and tiny jib came fluttering down to be bundled up by the two deckhands. Two other men, clearly not civilian sailors, were standing next to Palmas.

"Helm to port!" Palmas sounded as if he were standing at the end of the palisade. An anchor splashed into the bay and the little sloop swung to a stop not fifty yards from the beach. A skiff was pushed into the bay from the low deck of the *Alacita* and held there while the two men with Palmas, both in the uniforms of Spanish Navy officers, struggled aboard. One man sat in the stern while his companion fumbled with the oars. By the time the oarsman managed to get underway, the skiff had nearly drifted ashore.

"Pook, send two men to pull that skiff ashore."

Búho and Plata rushed past Diego, waded to the skiff and pulled it onto the beach. The man in the stern, Diego could see he was a lieutenant, climbed out while the clumsy oarsman, a junior officer, possibly an ensign, struggled to stow his oars. The lieutenant waited until his young companion joined him at the edge of the skiff. Both men strode purposefully up to Diego, who held his salute.

"Sergeant deMelilla, I believe." The lieutenant said as he returned Diego's salute.

"At your service, sir." Diego dropped his hand to his side.

"I am Lieutenant Josef Solano. The *Alacita* has carried me from New Orleans. I was hoping to find General Gálvez."

"He has not arrived."

"Indeed. Palmas learned as much from the other packet boat. Gálvez departed New Orleans with his fleet two weeks ago, but he has not yet been sighted by our watch."

It would take the swift *Alacita* less than two days to sail from New Orleans to Biloxi by way of Bayou Saint John and the coastal lakes and bays. Gálvez's deep water fleet would require the best part of two weeks to sail down the Mississippi River and back up to the West Florida coast. A screen of packet boats had been stationed just beyond the barrier islands ready to relay conditions ashore to Gálvez when he arrived.

"He has been delayed by unfavorable winds, no doubt," Solano said.

"Do doubt, sir."

"Anything to report, sergeant?"

"The *godums* are far inland, sir. We bumped into a few two nights ago, a reconnaissance patrol. We drove them off. The scouts tell us the British are in their fort at Mobile."

"Good." The lieutenant took a deep breath. "The General had anticipated as much. If what you say is true, I have orders for you."

CHAPTER 6

"Are you an officer?" Marcelite strode up. She had been watching the landing from her tent. "I am Marcelite Gaudet de la Arceneaux of White River Plantation and I demand you bring me to an officer. Did you come from a ship? I demand you bring me to your ship immediately!"

Solano looked blankly at Marcelite and then back to Diego. "I do not speak French. What does she say?"

"She is demanding you bring her to your ship."

"Tell her I will not. Tell her to remove herself; we have military matters to discuss."

"*Mademoiselle* Gaudet," Diego switched to French. "I present to you Lieutenant Josef Solano, of His Most Catholic Majesty's Navy, and his young aide, whose name has not been presented to me. The lieutenant is happily ignorant of French."

"Then you tell him I demand to be taken to his ship."

"I did. It is impossible."

Diego ignored the stream of protests from Marcelite and shouted over her head to the formation of soldiers behind her. "Pook, stand down. Direct the men back to their duties and send Martin to me." He turned back to Solano. "Sir, may I present to you *Mademoiselle* Marcelite Gaudet de la Arceneaux of White River Plantation. She does not speak Spanish and does not cease speaking French."

Marcelite stopped protesting when she heard her name. She bowed her head slightly, cast her eyes slightly downward, looked through her long lashes up at Solano and curtsied as she murmured, "*C'est mon plaisir, monsieur.*"

"*Señorita*," Solano said with a tip of his head. "Sergeant, how did this woman come to be here?"

"We rescued her from British pirates, or so she says."

"Pirates!"

"So she says."

"There have been no reports of British privateers along this coast. What do you plan to do with her?"

"Turn her over to the first officer I can find who will take her."

"Private Martin reporting as ordered, *Primero*." Martin had trotted up while Marcelite was being discussed. The presence of Naval Officers had prompted the young soldier's formal speech.

Diego gestured toward Marcelite. "Take the lady to her tent and keep her there. Use force if you must."

Martin's surprised expression suggested he would much prefer not to use force.

"*Mademoiselle* Gaudet, Private Martin will escort you to your tent. If you do not go willingly, he will carry you."

"I will not go!"

"Martin." Before Diego could finish his order, Marcelite tossed her head, spun about and stomped toward her tent, Martin trailing her with his musket at port arms.

"Is there a place where we can sit, Sergeant?"

"Come inspect our gun-pit. We can get out of the wind." Diego showed them the way to Gabriella's emplacement. "I have no wine to offer, perhaps a small tot of rum?"

"Nothing for us, Sergeant. We must not dally." They began to walk briskly up the beach toward the old strong-house foundation. "Forgive me. I have forgotten my manners. This young officer with me is Sub-Lieutenant Jeremy Conden of the Continental Army."

"Pleasure to meet you, Sergeant," Conden said as they hurried up the beach.

"Conden, as you can see, speaks Spanish. He is our liaison with the contingent of Americans who will be joining General Gálvez for the invasion."

"How many would that be?" Diego was hoping for a relief force.

"One ship, the *West Florida*, I think you know her, and two dozen woodsmen."

They arrived at the gun emplacement and found a section of wall out of the wind. Solano took a seat on a powder box and indicated the others to locations on the rim of the brick foundation.

"Gálvez will be arriving very soon. We have not made contact with him since he departed New Orleans. Considering the winds this time of year, we will be in contact once he is a week or more from Mobile. He has with him twelve ships and eight hundred soldiers, about half are militia. Havana has promised to send two regiments. You will be our eyes at the mouth of Mobile Bay. Gálvez will not land his men on a defended beach. Travel east as close to the coast as you can and keep in contact with the packet boats. Do not go to the inland roads."

West Florida was partitioned by several rivers, each bordered by wide marshes and running north to south. The only east and west trails worthy of the name "road" were found several leagues inland where the rivers were more fordable. Closer to the coast, the land was less arable and travelers found it much more convenient to go to the gulf and travel by boat or go north to one of the east and west trails. For land travelers, such as a large army, these geographical conditions divided coastal West Florida into almost isolated segments.

"Once you have established a camp at the entrance to Mobile Bay, make contact with the scouts inland, report their findings and maintain a string of pickets. Here is a log of signals you are to display if you detect British movement." Solano handed Diego a canvas-wrapped packet.

"What if the British come down to the coast?"

"There is a signal for that. Go west and we will take you off with our packet boats. Horses, wagons and other equipment will be abandoned, of course. Any other questions?"

Diego let the crude map of the coast between the blockhouse at Biloxi and west side of Mobile Bay play in his mind. Not much was known except that marshland often extended a mile or more inland in some places. If a trail was not indicated on the map, it was likely the land was nearly impassable. He would have to send men to the coast at night to set the appropriate signals. The biggest challenge would be crossing the Pascagoula River. He did not know enough of what lay ahead to formulate a question.

"I have a wounded prisoner. Could you take him off my hands?"

"I think we can fit him aboard. It will be three days before we could send him to New Orleans. Are his wounds severe?"

"No, sir. We think he will recover."

"Have him sent to the skiff. Any other questions?"

"No questions, sir."

"Good, then young Jeremy and I will be off."

Solano slapped his knees and stood. "Come along, Jeremy."

Solano and Sub-Lieutenant Jeremy Conden climbed out of the gun-pit and began to stride to the beached skiff, Diego following behind. Marcelite saw them from the front of her tent and moved as if to join the procession. Martin nervously barred her way, so she called out to the trio.

"*Monsieur* Solano! Please do not leave me with these ruffians. My father will reward you well if you take me to your ship. Please *monsieur*."

Solano look her way briefly causing Marcelite to jump and wave.

"What does she say now, sergeant?"

"She says she will pay you to bring her to a ship."

"If it were possible I would. Tell her so for me."

Diego was pleased that Marcelite would be traveling with the vanguard. He could not explain to himself why he would, for she was quite a bother. They passed the prisoner and his guard on the way to the beach and

Diego had the man join the procession. They reached the skiff and the prisoner was directed aboard. The soldiers had pushed the skiff off the beach when they saw the officers approaching and held it for them in knee-deep water. Solano stopped at the edge of the beach to formally leave the command to Diego. He turned and Diego came to attention, holding his salute. "May the fortunes attend you, sergeant?"

Solano returned Diego's salute. "See you in Mobile, sergeant, at Fort Condé." Condé was the name the French had given the fort at Mobile. It had fallen into ruins until recently. The British were rebuilding the fort and had renamed it "Fort Charlotte."

"At Mobile, sir," Diego said as he dropped his salute and watched the officers wade to the skiff. In moments they had returned to the *Alacita*. Palmas waved to Diego as the skiff was pulled aboard and secured on deck. Diego waved back and Palmas began to issue a stream of orders. Sails were hoisted, sheets were set and as the swift packet boat ran toward her anchor the slack was taken in and two straining sailors pulled it aboard. In less than fifteen minutes, the *Alacita* rounded the eastern end of the barrier island and disappeared.

Diego looked up to see who was manning the watch tower.

"Cano, can you see any other sail."

"No, *Primero*, no other but the packet boat."

He felt a sinking feeling in the pit of his stomach. They were about to move deeper into British held lands with no other support than what they carried with them.

"*Primero?*" It was Búho. He had been one of the men who had assisted the sailors land their skiff. "This is for you. One of the sailors gave it to me. Said Captain Palmas sends you this." He held out a folded paper – a letter. Officers sent and received letters on a regular basis, but enlisted men had to depend upon a more informal post. Most received nothing from home. Someone who knew the *Alacita*'s routine had entrusted Palmas with a message for Diego. Militia units, being formed of friends and neighbors, provided a regular means of letters to and from home. The men that could not read or write had dictated to those that could. Among the enlisted militia, letters were public, often read aloud at the evening camp fires. Letters to enlisted men of the regular army were rare treasures.

He unfolded the unsealed letter and recognized Isabella's delicate penmanship. The words were written in charcoal. The handwriting reminded him of his late wife, Mézu's, who had been Isabella's teacher on that long voyage from Tenerife. He glanced up to insure everyone was going about their duties, stepped back into the shade of the tower and read.

"*Don Diego, I pray this message finds you in good health. One of the wives who rolls cartridges has saved a few leaves of paper for me. I shall write again soon.*" Diego examined the paper and chuckled. It was indeed the tan, rough paper used to make musket cartridges. "*All here are in good health and the farm is doing well. Pedro and Maria are growing daily. Father says we may even buy an ox next year to pull stumps. The portion of your pay the purser provides me every month has been well spent on supplies and clothes for the children. I write children, but Pedro is as big as a man. We all miss you and pray to the Blessed Mother for your safe and prompt return. Do not fear for us, we prosper.*"

The letter was signed by Isabella, Pedro and Maria.

Diego read the letter again. In his mind he could see Mézu, Isabella, Pedro and little Maria sitting in a circle on the gun deck of the *San Juan Nepomuceno* going through their reading and writing lessons. Isabella was a child of thirteen at the time. Now she would be fifteen, almost a woman.

He would write a reply using the same paper. He would write in soldier's ink, a concoction of finely ground gunpowder mixed with dark wine and using a split reed for a quill. He folded the letter away and glancing up, noticed Marcelite staring at him from the entrance to her tent.

⁓

Diego decided to remain encamped for the next two days preparing for the move east. Men, equipment and animals alike needed time to recuperate. He sent scouts ranging far to the east along several game trails in an effort to appraise the best route to take. The marshes that bordered the narrow strip of beach drove them inland or forced them along a narrow, sandy corridor interrupted by frequent breaks requiring fording, swimming or rafting to cross. While the scouts were afield, Diego assigned six men who claimed some carpentry skills to making crude dugouts. If they moved slightly inland to travel east, he could use the dugouts to send a signal detail south to the coast each evening on one of the innumerable sloughs through the marsh.

Some of the men fished successfully. They waded stealthily in the shallow waters along the beach and speared many wide, flat fish. Diego had never seen such an odd looking fish. It had both eyes on one side of its head and was as thin as a shingle, but the flesh was delicious and enough were caught for everyone to have their fill. It was a pleasant break from hard biscuits and salted beef.

Diego had taken one of the larger huts as his headquarters. The weather had moderated into a comfortable evening with little wind and Pook had set a camp table with a few stools in front of the hut near the cooking fires where the men roasted the day's catch. He invited Diego to sit while Pook played the part of waiter. It was one of those rare occasions on this expedition where a man could sit and enjoy a hot meal eaten from pewter plates and using cutlery.

"Pook," Diego said when he saw the meal that was being served. "Please send for *Mademoiselle* Gaudet and see if she can join us for supper. Perhaps we can prove we are not the ruffians she takes us to be."

"But we are barbarians, *Primero*," Pook replied with a laugh. "Otherwise we would be officers draped in silk and carried about in a *litera*."

"Pook, I am surprised you know of sedan chairs."

"I am a barbarian, *Primero*, of wide experience. I will see if *Mademoiselle* Gaudet will accept your invitation."

"Our invitation, Pook. I expect you to join us."

Pook tilted his head in assent and departed for the only tent in the encampment. Marcelite had refused to occupy a hut, claiming they all smelled of burned fish and filthy savages.

Diego was pleasantly surprised to see Marcelite return with Pook. He had half expected her to decline the offer. He stood as she approached the table, imitating the rituals he had observed when serving as a guard for officers and their ladies at formal dinners.

"I am pleased that *mademoiselle* has decided to join us for our humble meal of fresh fish."

"Thank you, *monsieur* Sergeant," Marcelite said, her face tilted slightly downward so that she looked up at him through a forest of long, black lashes. Her voice was soft, deep and feminine. He could not remember her ever speaking to him in any tone except one of anger. He decided he liked this condition very much. She wore her hair up, bound by a blue bandana under her wide-brimmed straw hat. It may have been the cool evening air, or it may have been something else, but her cheeks were rosy and her full lips were almost red. She wore soft leather riding gloves that extended past the cuffs of her blue cotton dress. Diego mentally compared Marcelite's neat and clean appearance with his own ragged state. How she had managed it, he could not say.

Diego was not certain how a gentleman was supposed to act, so he simply waited until Marcelite claimed one of the places at the table.

Diego motioned to Pook to take the remaining place. "Please join us Corporal Gonzales."

"*Primero*, I beg your leave." Pook's eyes twinkled with an inner laughter. "There are matters I have yet to complete before the day is done." He bowed and was gone.

"We are having fresh fish tonight, *mademoiselle* Gaudet," Diego almost stammered, "and a wine of uncertain vintage."

He placed a tin cup before her and poured a little wine from a skin that had been commandeered after the fight at the junction a few days before, wine he had denied having when he was entertaining Solano. Marcelite tasted the wine and then nodded for Diego to fill the cup.

"Red wine with fish." Marcelite's brown eyes sparkled with the setting sun. "Normally a less than ideal combination, but I find this to be most delightful."

"I am pleased you approve."

"*Monsieur* Sergeant, I must apologize for my behavior. I have been distraught of late. You must know that I am most unaccustomed to being taken for ransom and finding myself in the middle of a battle. Surely, you can understand and forgive me."

"Think no more of it, *mademoiselle* Gaudet."

"Please, call me Marcelite, *monsieur* Sergeant."

"Think no more of it, *mademoiselle* Marcelite."

Marcelite giggled. The sound of her soft laughter stirred a feeling in Diego he thought had died.

"Simply Marcelite, please, at least when we are in private conversation. And may I address you by your Christian name?"

"In private conversation I would be pleased if you would address me as 'Diego', otherwise you may use Sergeant, simply Sergeant."

They ate for a while in silence. The setting sun began to cast long shadows. Men who were not on picket duty or already in their bedrolls were gathered about a few fires, joking. For the first time since departing New Orleans the men of the vanguard could relax. After the scouting reports were in tomorrow, a route would be chosen and the remainder of that day used in preparation for a first light departure on the next day.

"What has you in such deep thought, Diego?"

Marcelite's question startled Diego. He had been thinking about the hundreds of things he had yet to do before he could rest again.

"I was pondering the next few days of travel, Marcelite. I fear it will prove to be an arduous journey."

"I have come to trust your judgment, Diego. We will persevere."

What has caused such a shift in this woman? Not two hours before, she was pleading to be rescued from us— barbarians.

Marcelite moved her cup toward Diego and he poured her more wine.

"Tell me, Diego, are you married? It is difficult to be a married soldier, is it not?"

"I am a widower. My wife died of yellow fever last year while I was away."

"Oh! I am so sorry. I lost my little sister to yellow fever, a terrible thing." He thought he saw a tear of sympathy in the corner of her eye as she sipped on the wine.

"Do you have any children?"

"Yes," Diego felt his mood lighten at the mention of children. "Pedro is eleven and Maria will be nine in April. They are in the care of the Campo family who traveled with us to New Orleans. They live in a settlement called Concepción."

"Good. It is best to be away from New Orleans during the summer. My father will not allow us to go to that city during any month spelled without an 'r'."

Mézu had died in July, Juillet as the French say. Be away before May. Is survival in New Orleans that simple?

"And where does your father send you every spring?"

"Nowhere! That is the problem. We are marooned at White River Plantation for the entire summer, everyday dreaming of September in New Orleans."

"Who is marooned with you?"

"I have an older sister and two cousins. We go everywhere together."

"Except for this latest trip to Paris?"

"What? Oh, yes. Paris was different. I was being sent to meet my fiancé. We were betrothed years ago. We have never met, but I saw a portrait of him. He is most gallant."

They watched the light fade to the west in silence.

"I was very much afraid to leave White River Plantation," Marcelite said as the golden light reflected onto her face. "I had never been away from Louisiana. The furthest I had been from White River was New Orleans, and only then with all of my friends and family. Paris seems to be in another world."

"It is another world, *mademoiselle*. We are in the 'new world' now. Nothing is the same."

"*Primero?*" Búho had come up to the table, unnoticed until he spoke.

"Yes, what is it?"

"A messenger from the scouts, *Primero*."

"Already?" Diego had not expected any reports until tomorrow. "Pardon me, *mademoiselle*, I must attend to this. Please enjoy the rest of your dinner." He ducked into the hut and retrieved the packet of instruction and codes Solano had given him.

"Tell the messenger to meet me at the signal tower," he said and was gone. Marcelite sipped some more of the wine and watched him go.

෴

The news from the scouts had been good. There was a serviceable trail east that was well traveled. The scouts had found a likely campsite not seven miles east near a large lagoon that was connected to the gulf by a wide slough. It would not be difficult to reach the camp in one day. While on the move, scouts could forge ahead to the Pascagoula River and select the next day's campsite.

In less than one hour after first light the vanguard departed the Biloxi blockhouse, flanked on the north by security patrols and following their advance scouts. The trail was enough to allow passage with a minimum amount of clearing for the wagon. They skirted north of the coastal marshland and easily forded a few tendrils of streams flowing down from sandy hills. They made the first campsite two hours before dark. Pook was put in charge of the two freshly-made dugouts and sent south with three others along a slough to find the gulf and set the appropriate signals. One of the dugouts was to return with news of success or failure to post a signal.

Two hours after dark, one of the dugouts returned to report a suitable location had been found not an hour's row down the waterway and the proper signal was being posted. Pook remained at the signal post, but would return as soon as a reply was sighted or dawn broke, whichever occurred first.

Advance scouts from the east reported that the bank of Pascagoula Bay was less than four miles further east. Had they pushed on that day, they could have made camp on the gulf shore. Still, all of the news was good and everything was progressing as planned.

We will reach the Pascagoula by noon tomorrow, Diego thought. *Then what? How am I to transport these people and all this equipment across the Pascagoula?*

That night, Marcelite accompanied Diego as he visited the several campfires spread around the site. When they visited the men camped around Gabriella, she paused to chat with the militiamen while Diego made his round of the pickets. He returned from his rounds to find Marcelite singing to the gathered militia men who sat on caisson, carriage and gun spellbound by her beautiful voice.

Diego waited until she finished the song then said, "Allow me to escort you to your tent, *mademoiselle*. We depart at first light for the Pascagoula River."

"Of course, *monsieur*." Marcelite cast a bright smile toward her audience. "Good night, *messieurs*. Thank you for indulging me, allowing me to sing to you."

Barbeaux and his artillerymen were so profuse and sincere in expressing their appreciation of Marcelite's song it made Diego smile. Soldiers, in truth, are lonely men who love peace, a comfortable home and family. His father would say, *"Negada las cosas son más buscadas"* (things denied are most longed for).

℮ↄ

They reached Pascagoula Bay before noon. Diego's heart sank when he saw how far it was across to the east side. It must be four miles to the nearest shore and he remembered the mouth of the bay was spotted with islands, so it could be even further to the east bank. That could not be helped. It had to be crossed.

"Pook, take both dugouts and cross to that island. Find a way to the opposite mainland and then return here."

"*Primero*, how are we going to cross without boats?" Pook looked at the wagon as he asked the question.

"Scout the shortest water route, Pook. We will find a way." *In truth, my friend, I have no idea how we are going to do it.*

It was another mild day and Diego could not ascertain much of a current coming out of the bay. The tides along the gulf coast were very mild, but still a large bay could generate strong currents if the opening to the gulf were restricted. He watched as Pook's boats moved east. They did not seem to drift significantly as they crossed the wide bay. If the picket boat came, they could ferry everyone across in a dozen trips. Then it came to him. Rafts!

Every man was set to building rafts. Small rafts were lashed together to carry individual arms and backpacks. Larger rafts were built for the wagon and Gabriella. The horses would wade and swim with the help of rafts to keep their heads above water. Each smaller raft would be guided by two swimmers holding onto each side and loaded with muskets and bed rolls. The larger rafts would have to be poled and rowed.

Pook returned with news of the waters ahead. He had identified a route where several wide, shallow sandbars formed a chain broken in only a few places by water deeper than a few feet. There were only two places where the horses would have to swim more than a few yards, and neither of those places was more than a hundred yards across. A fishing village on the far bank of Pascagoula Bay was as deserted as the Biloxi shores had been.

Pook was to take one of the dugouts and guide the string of rafts and swimmers and Plata would take the other dugout and follow to help any that might run into trouble. Diego assigned a man to watch the tide during the rest of the day so he could estimate when the slack would be most likely in the morning.

The sky was clear, the moon was full and the men were able to work on the rafts for most of the night. First light revealed a shore lined with rafts of all sizes and configurations. The men had chosen their places, loaded the rafts and waited for the signal to depart. The men who were to swim stripped to their undergarments and piled their uniforms onto their rafts.

Diego's father had always taught that a leader never sends a man to do that which he is unwilling to do himself. For this reason, Diego assigned himself to the first swimming raft. He eased into the cold water and shouted to Pook to move out.

A string of strange craft followed Pook's dugout across the bay. Diego found himself wading in water that was alternately chest-deep, then waist deep, then chest deep again. He was forced to swim, holding his raft with one arm, for several hundred yards before he was wading again. He looked across to Búho, who was his raft mate and laughed.

"A cold bath, is it not?"

"Very cold, *Primero*." Búho's teeth were chattering. Out of fear or cold, Diego did not know.

He looked behind him and saw his crude fleet following with little trouble. The horses became agitated when transitioning from swimming to wading, but the men assigned to the rafts tethered to the horses were able to control them.

Progress was slow and it was nearing sunset when Diego waded ashore on the east side of Pascagoula Bay. Pook had pulled his dugout ashore and was in the process of starting a fire. As each raft landed the men began to build fires and dry themselves. Those who did not have to swim began unloading the wagon and other equipment. Diego selected several of the dry soldiers to scout inland and establish a picket.

Diego shivered by the fire as he watched the vanguard come ashore. Amazingly, nothing was lost in the crossing. The trail dugout carried Plata in the stern, Martin in the bow and Marcelite seated in the middle. It had fallen somewhat behind the last raft.

Diego stood and was about to call out to Plata to hurry when there was a commotion aboard the dugout. Martin stood, turned around, and went overboard. Diego could see Marcelite clearly now. She pulled out a pistol, cocked it and pointed it at Plata who dropped his paddle and dove into the water. Marcelite grabbed a paddle and began to work furiously guiding the dugout up the Pascagoula River. Plata and Martin could be seen splashing about in the water.

"Pook, take your dugout and get those men!" Diego shouted. He watched helplessly as Pook made his way to the struggling men. When he reached them, each clasped the side of the dugout while Pook brought them to shore. They waded ashore wet, but alive.

The time it took to rescue Plata and Martin provided Marcelite with enough time to paddle around an island and out of sight. Night was falling.

She had an hour's head start and the moon would not be up for five hours. Pursuit would delay the move to Mobile, therefore out of the question.

"What happened?" Diego asked.

"She said she saw a snake come in the boat," Martin squeaked. "When I turned to see, she pushed me into the water."

"And when she pointed that pistol between my eyes, I gave her the boat," Plata said.

"Where did she get a pistol?" Diego asked.

Both men shrugged. Diego suddenly had a sick feeling and hurried to his bedroll which had just been put ashore. He searched for the pistol he had taken from the dead man at the junction. It was gone. He had let his guard down. She batted those dark eyes at him and he allowed her the opportunity to filch his own pistol. How could he have been so stupid! It was not as if she had fooled him. He knew her story of pirates, ransom and White River Plantation was a fabrication. He knew it and still she had taken him in.

Barbeaux came up beside Diego as both men looked west to the spot where Marcelite had disappeared.

"Why did she do that, *Primero*? I thought she enjoyed our company."

No man can know what is truly in a woman's heart. "Nothing can be done now," Diego said, resigned to the situation. *I wager she is laughing right now. Laughing at what a fool I am.*

"We need to dry ourselves and prepare for the move to Mobile Bay tomorrow."

CHAPTER 7

E xcept for a faint trail to the north, the scouts found no useful route away from the remains of a fishing village perched on the narrow spit of land the vanguard now occupied. There were a few standing huts, but most of the fishing village had been flattened either by storms or neglect or both. The land beyond the village was a tangle of wild, low brush and gnarled, stunted oaks for as far as they could see in the fading light.

It had been full dark before the men had been able to dry their clothes, organize their equipment and eat. The crossing had exhausted everyone. During the night, after the cook fires were out, men posted along the beach searched for a light on the water, but reported none. The inland pickets had nothing to report as well. Diego decided to spend one day recuperating and scouting the move to Mobile Bay. If the maps were correct, the west shore of Mobile Bay lay only twenty-five miles or so to the east.

At first light after crossing the bay, Diego had sent men east along the strip of beach to their south, north along a trail paralleling the Pascagoula River and northeast into the scrub brush. He had the men build a small sand redoubt and another three-timber watch platform.

Martin, who proved to be sharp-eyed and quite agile, scurried up the tripod tower with the regimental flag. The sky was cloudless, the air cool and a gentle breeze wafted in from the east-southeast. There was much to do. Equipment and weapons were inspected, cleaned and put in good working order.

Food was prepared in anticipation of a full day of rest and hot meals filling the men before the trek east reduced them to eating dried beef, salt pork, hard biscuits and nuts as they plodded through a wasteland. Their supply of drinking water was getting low and the store of rum, vital to keeping water from turning "stale" was nearly gone. Men sent to search for a source of fresh water reported finding none.

Martin was relieved after two hours and was ordered to report to Diego. He found the big sergeant supervising the re-loading of the vanguard's wagon. The expedition's supply of musket cartridges were tightly wrapped in oil-soaked, wax-sealed leather pouches of one hundred each. These were in turn, crammed into four small wax-sealed wooden barrels, six to a barrel. Including the rounds carried by each infantryman, the total supply of musket ammunition for the vanguard was just over three thousand rounds of ball, not counting the ammunition carried by the artillerymen.

"*Primero*, you sent for me?" Martin asked as he approached the wagon.

"One good fight and we will be committed to cold steel," Diego muttered as he turned around.

"*Primero?*"

"Nothing." Diego jumped down from the wagon. "What did you see from our little *carajo* (crow's nest)?"

"A clean horizon, *Primero*. Not a sail on the water. No smoke or movement inland."

"What about the land?"

"Marshland to the east and along the coast for as far as I could see. Low trees to the north along the river and marshland to the northeast, but I could see tall trees beyond the marshland-hills, perhaps."

"Very well, Martin. Get something to eat and tend to your gear."

"*Sí, Primero.*"

There was no beach along the coast to the east for several miles so the vanguard could not take that route. The trail along the river led inland and his orders were to remain in contact with the packet boats. Diego would wait for the scouting reports before selecting a route.

The decision was made for him by the terrain. Northeast was the only direction comparatively free of deep river crossings or marshland. The previous inhabitants of the fishing village must have relied upon water travel for supplies and fresh water for there were no trails in any direction except for the pitiful trace along the river that ended at a wide tributary from the east.

They pushed northeast using axes and short swords to cut a trail wide enough for the wagon through the dense wilderness of tangled vines, scrub oaks, and brush. Diego did not deploy flanking security because of the nearly impenetrable brush. Winter seemed to have had little effect on the density of the wilderness. The lead scouts could do little more than plunge a few hundred yards ahead and had to be rotated frequently because of the exhausting effort required. Rear security, which did not require any cutting or breaking trail, was considered a "rest" assignment. Those positions were rotated less frequently and then only with men who had been lead scouts. At the end of the day, they made camp where they stopped. They made four miles on the first day.

There were no waterways nearby running toward the gulf as there had been on previous inland detours. Sending signal teams to maintain contact with the packet boats was impossible. Diego could send a rider back to the abandoned fishing village to watch for a night signal, but then that man would have to race back to the vanguard in the morning without sleep. What if the man did not return? Send more to look for him? *No*, he decided. *We know where we are expected to be. We will have to get there quickly.* Unless they were contacted by one of T'Chien's people, the vanguard's location would be unknown to higher command.

They made another four miles the next day. Two days of back-breaking work and they were less than half-way to Mobile Bay. At the rate they were traveling, it would take five more days to reach the bay and when they did, he would have a force of exhausted, thirsty, hungry and demoralized men. God help them if the British were at the mouth of Mobile Bay.

On noon of the third day the lead scouts reported pine trees in the distance over a narrow marsh. Pine trees meant high ground, less underbrush and easier traveling. Diego called a halt and sent his scouts further ahead to find the best route to the high ground. The men fell to the ground and slept. Everywhere Diego looked he saw dirty, exhausted, disheveled men and horses. Three men had taken ill and were huddled on the wagon. *How can I push these men for another three days of this?*

"*Primero?*"

Diego looked up to see, Romano, one of the men he had sent ahead. He had not been gone for two hours.

"What is it? Why are you back so soon?"

"A trail, *Primero*." Romano was breathless. He must have run back with word of what was found. "A proper trail; not a mile ahead, *Primero*. It is on high ground and follows a small stream that is flowing east to west. Plata and Búho have gone toward the east. They sent me back to tell you."

"Pook! Get everyone on their feet and moving," Diego shouted.

"Romano, go back to the trail and wait for us. Look for anything coming from the west."

✎

Romano's idea of a "proper trail" had been distorted by the route they had been forced to take. It was barely wide enough for the wagon, but the axes could be put away. The small stream beside the trail enabled them to refresh their water supply. Diego called another halt so the men could rest and prepare for the push east. If the trail continued, and they had not been detoured too far north, they could be at Mobile Bay in two days.

Plata and Búho returned to report the trail did continue for the four miles they followed it and seemed to continue toward the east. It climbed out of the wooded lowlands onto a crest covered in pines and went east.

"We will spend the rest of the day here," Diego said. "Set cook fires and clean our equipment. Tomorrow at first light we push east." Three days of hard travel and one day of rest had become routine.

Romano and Olivier had been sent west along the trail. They returned escorting an old man. Olivier reported the trail ended in a fishing camp where they had surprised the old man. The camp was at the junction of two streams, the one flowing west next to the trail and another tributary flowing in from the north.

"We tried English, French and Spanish on the old man, *Primero*," Olivier said. "He pretends not to understand anything."

The man had thinning white hair, a wispy beard, hazel eyes and a wrinkled, olive completion. He could have been Choctaw, it was hard to say. Diego tried his "trade Choctaw" and the old man brightened visibly and let flow a stream of words. Diego caught enough of what was said to verify the man was indeed Choctaw or at least fluent in the language.

His name was Cholah. He had remained at the fishing camp while his sons traveled downstream to their village. There had not been enough room for him because of the large quantity of dried venison and deer hides they had collected. One of his sons was going to return for him tomorrow.

He had not seen anyone other than his people for several months. He did not know why or where the British woodsmen had gone. He said the trail they were on went east across a small stream and on to a great sea water, which Diego interpreted to be Mobile Bay. The old man had not gone east to the bay in several months, but the trail was wide, clear and, until this winter, had been well traveled by men on the bay seeking fresh water. No men had come west to get water in the month he and his sons had been hunting in the area.

"What should we do with him, *Primero*?" Romano asked.

"Send him back to meet his son."

"But he could send word of us to the British."

"He probably will. It does not matter. The British know we are here."

Diego sent the old man west and watched as he trotted past the pickets that bracketed the trail and broke into a run.

The next day they traveled seven miles east and descended a slight slope to the ford the old man had described. They camped on the east side of the ford. The land east of the ford was relatively flat and the thick brush that seemed everywhere beyond the pine forests bracketed the trail. They pushed on another seven miles the next day and camped two miles inland from Mobile Bay, stopping only when the scouts reported sighting the bay.

At dawn, Diego ordered the wagon, gun and half his force to remain in camp while he and six men accompanied his team of scouts to the bay. He sent four men with a horse north along the shoreline with orders: if they encountered trouble or sighted any British, one of the men would ride back to report. He sent another four men and a horse south with orders to scout all the way to the gulf.

Mobile Bay was over twelve miles wide where they had emerged onto the beach. The beach was a narrow strip of dirty sand interrupted in places by small sloughs leading back into the brush. From ground level the horizon appeared clear of boat traffic.

Twenty feet in the air and the horizon would be pushed back several miles. He put another detail of men to building an observation tower. Within two hours, Martin was perched in his customary position searching the extended horizon. He saw two small boats far out in the bay being rowed north and nothing else. The bay should have had more traffic. Even in winter, fishing skiffs, small sailing trade boats and other commerce should have been afloat.

"Rider coming from the north," Martin shouted down to Diego.

Soon, Olivier rode into sight.

"We stopped at a wide river, *Primero*. A little over two miles up the coast." Olivier reported without dismounting. "We could see a house and farm on the north bank and some people moving about, looked to be farmers. What do you want us to do?"

Diego thought for a few minutes. He remembered there were two rivers from the west that entered Mobile Bay south of the fort. One was called *Río Perro* and the other *Río Pájaro*.

It has to be the Pájaro, he thought. If they were at the *Pájaro*, the mouth of Mobile Bay was about four or five miles south. If it were the *Perro,* they had emerged less than ten miles from the fort at Mobile. He prayed it was the *Pájaro*. "Pull back and set up a picket in the tree line along the beach where you can see the river and the bay. Ride back with word if anyone tries to cross the river or if anything comes down the bay."

"*Sí, Primero*." The man wheeled his mount around and thundered off.

Diego rubbed his face and moved his hand to the back of his neck. "Plata," he said, "return to the camp and tell Pook to prepare to move east. When I send word, he is to come to the bay and if I am not here, he is to turn south. Martin, come down. We are going south."

They walked south along a sandy shoreline fording the occasional muddy slough or clambering over clumps of debris that storm or tide had stranded here and there. They had walked about two miles when they came to a place where the land to the west changed from heavy brush to saltwater marsh. The beach continued in a narrow neck bordered on the east by Mobile Bay and on the west by marshland.

They could see one of the scouts sent south riding toward them up the narrow ribbon of sand. The man stopped to report. "We have reached the end of a long peninsula, *Primero*. It becomes very narrow with sea on the east and marsh on the west before it widens and ends at the sea."

"Did you see anything on the water?"

"*Nada, Primero*. We could see an island to the south, nothing more."

Diego sent the rider north to Pook with orders to bring the vanguard south. Martin was dispatched south to collect the scouts there and bring them north.

A plan was forming in Diego's mind. He would have the vanguard establish a camp two hundred yards to the west of where he stood, on the last of the firm ground north of the marsh. If he cleared enough land, raised a crude palisade, pitched all of his tents and threw up grass covered huts, someone viewing the place from aboard a ship in the bay might be convinced a large host had landed. He would have Gabriella placed behind a sand berm flanked by tree trunks similarly mounted on berms and pointed toward the bay mimicking iron cannons. He would send scouts west of the camp to reconnoiter a possible route west should they need to abandon the beach. This was as far south as the vanguard would go. Further out on the peninsula they would be unable to conceal their numbers and would be trapped between sea and marsh.

If the truth be told, Diego reflected, *we are already trapped. Any force coming down from the north or landing from the bay would have us pinned.* He pushed that fear aside. *Where were T'Chien or Solano and the packet boats?* More than anything, Diego would like some orders.

He had another tower erected near the beach and Martin was sent aloft with the regimental flag. The scouts found a faint trail west of the camp that snaked west through wild scrub and stunted trees, forded a few small streams and ended at a beach on the gulf. It was seven miles from the camp to the gulf along this trail. This would be an escape route – if they could arrange for boats to meet them.

Diego posted men with horses well north along the beach where the vanguard had first emerged. He withdrew the pickets that had been watching the farm for they would be too far from the vanguard to provide any warning. He had the men cut trails from the camp to locations north of the tower and ending just west of the brush that bordered the beach. If the British came down the beach and formed a battle line to attack Spaniards at the tower, men from the camp could use the trails to take them in the flank. There was nothing to do now but wait, and improve their position.

⁓

Watchers from the tower reported a few boats passing along the east side of Mobile Bay. Nothing large appeared on the bay. In the morning, skiffs and lateen-rigged fishing boats traveled north from a small village on the south end of the bay. Diego was certain it was the same village he had visited during his escape from Pensacola and had robbed of a dugout. In the evening, the same vessels moved south to the village. During the night, no lights were seen except for cooking fires from the village across the bay.

He remembered the matching pair of tall British watch towers and their great semaphore arms ending in lighted lamps. The towers bracketed the pass between barrier islands at the entrance to the bay. Once he climbed up beside Martin to look south at the far entrance to the bay. He thought he could just make out the towers, small black blotches on the horizon but he was not certain. At night, where lights should have appeared, there was nothing. If the towers were still there, they were not signaling.

The days slipped by. No sign of movement from the fort at Mobile. He expected a horde of redcoats to come swarming down the beach, but the scouts reported only regular activity at the farm across the *Pájaro*. He expected the watchman in the tower to shout "sails in sight" and a fleet of British warships would appear to rake his pitiful little sand and post palisade with cannon fire, but every day the only activity on the bay was the little fishing boats going north, then south.

Where were the British? Where was Gálvez? Where was everybody? Diego could do nothing but wait while the vanguard rations were consumed. January faded away.

༄

"*Primero!*"

The shout from the watchman in the tower startled Diego. He had been thinking of Mézu. He often thought of her during the day, but she had not visited his dreams since he had reached Mobile Bay. He missed those dreams. Those times she had appeared to him in his sleep, she was young, beautiful, soft.

"What is it?" He shouted up, his stomach twisting. He could see the man looking north. *This is it. The godums have finally awakened.*

"There is a great storm coming, *Primero!* The northern sky is black all across the horizon!"

A storm! He was almost disappointed. He could see it now, coming south fast; black, boiling, menacing and flashing white hot streaks from clouds to ground. A blast of cold air came sweeping down the beach blowing sand and leaves about in whirlwinds.

"Get down from the tower!" He ran through the gate of the palisade, "Pook, a storm is coming! Cover the wagons, check the tents and call in the pickets!" Diego circled through the encampment ensuring everything of value, particularly the stores of powder and cartridges, was being secured and the men ready. He had every empty bucket set in the center of the camp with a canvas funnel rigged to catch the rain. Sweet, fresh, cool rainwater should not be wasted.

"Is it a hurricane, *Primero?*" one of the men asked.

"No, just a storm." Diego had experience two hurricanes in less than a year since coming to Louisiana.

There was a blinding flash and a deafening crack as a bolt of lightning struck the watch tower, causing it to burst into flame at the base.

"*Mierda!*" said the man standing next to Diego. Just seconds ago, he had been the watchman atop the tower.

"Hurricanes are without lightning," Diego said to the shaking watchman.

"*Mierda,*" the man said again, but quietly.

The rains came pelting down as huge drops the size of a musket ball, which quickly converged into great flooding torrents of water. The wind whipped tents loose forcing the men to scramble about resetting pegs or simply holding the canvas down against the ground. One tent tore away and raced off into the storm. A dark finger of swirling blackness twisted down into a long point that danced about on the water not a hundred yards from the beach.

The rain began to dissipate gradually until it was a fine mist. The sky began to lighten and patches of blue could be seen to the north. After another hour and just before sunset, the sky cleared as a cold wind bore down from the north. The weather had been moderating during the week they had occupied the camp on Mobile Bay. Now it was turning cold and growing dark. The men had managed to keep some wood dry and a cook/drying fire was set in the center of the camp. Clothes, canvas and even some shoes were hung around the fire, but none of it could mask the light from watchers on the bay.

A man was sent up the charred watchtower and instructed to look everywhere but the camp so as not to ruin his night vision. The camp fire was allowed to burn down until it was nothing but hot coals. No lights were seen except for a fire southeast across the bay where the fishing village lay.

Diego was up most of the night supervising storm damage repairs, insuring the stores of powder had not been soaked. The militiamen huddled around their gun emplacement. They had spread canvas over gun carriage and caisson forming a tight and well anchored tent.

"*Ce n'était rien* (this was nothing). I have seen many such storms, *Primero*," Barbeaux said when Diego stepped down into the gun emplacement. "I have seen spring storms worse than this. I have seen it blow until you think the hair will leave your face, rain until fish can swim across the land, and lightning so constant it is never dark. Then the sky clears and a cold north wind will blow for three days, no more."

Diego suddenly remembered his father. They had just finished a sparring exercise with staffs. The seven foot staffs were substitutes for the deadly *magado*, the razor-sharp, needle pointed lance favored by the *Isleños*. He was fifteen, the year his father had died.

"*When is the best time to attack?*" he had asked the old warrior.

"An attack works best when it is not expected," he had said. "The wise will attack where the enemy is weak or when he is distracted. Attack from the unseen quarter. Attack when he is confused."

Confused! Diego looked about the camp. Everyone was working at repairing storm damage or collecting their equipment. *If the British came now*!

"Pook, get that picket back up the beach now."

"*Sí, Primero.*"

Diego walked from tent to tent instructing the men to clean their muskets and other weapons first.

"Make certain all is in working order before dealing with clothes and food," he shouted, angry at himself for allowing the storm to distract him from the fact they were alone in enemy territory.

He had the men not on picket duty or standing watch turn out for a weapons inspection. They numbered sixteen.

How could the godums not fall on us now? We are few, isolated and without escape, he thought as he checked each man's musket by cocking and pulling the trigger to watch sparks dance around in the pan. He pulled bayonets from their scabbards checking for rust or sticking. He tested the edges of short swords and the hatchets some of the men carried. He berated the men with dull blades or bayonets that did not pull easily from their scabbards. A flint that did not throw a ball of sparks into the pan brought a tirade of curses upon the hapless soldier.

When men were sent to relieve the pickets those coming in had to stand the same inspection. The men coming in had been warned that *"Primero was pissing fire"* but, not having time to clean their equipment, they had to suffer through a collective tongue-lashing.

Morning came, cold, bright, clear and free of British troops. The fishing boats headed north and nothing came south.

What can they be doing? Diego could not understand why his little force was tolerated only twenty miles south of the fort at Mobile. A morning's sail or a day's march and the British could be on him, but none came.

Two days after the storm Diego sent scouts to the banks of *Río Pájaro*. The farm across the river showed no signs of life. An uprooted tree, clearly the result of the recent storm, lay across the farm's vegetable garden. If there were people tending the farm, they were not very industrious. No boats could be seen on the river and they had not found any trees suitable for building a dugout.

Tomorrow, he decided, *I will send scouts across the river*. If the British would not come down to him, perhaps he should advance closer to the fort. *We would be small boys poking a hornet's nest*. He changed his mind. Two more days, though, and he would have to forage. They were running low on food and the horses were reduced to eating the course grasses inland from the beach. A month on that kind of fodder and the animals would be worthless.

☙

Four days after the storm the morning broke with blue skies and a slight northerly breeze. The camp had settled into a routine. The men had even named the place "Camp *Lejano* (far away)." Breakfast fires were set, the pickets rotated and the watchman on the tower changed. Life had settled into tedium. They were reduced to eating a gruel flavored with the last of the salted pork, another day of watching and wondering.

Which will arrive first, orders or the British? Today, he would have to begin foraging. There was little game about and no farms this side of the *Río Pájaro*, so he had no choice but to cross the river and find some farms. He would give the farmers, if he found any, some silver for what they took, but if the farms were abandoned they would take all they could find that was edible.

"A sail! I see a sail!" The shout came from the tower watchman.

Diego rushed to the foot of the tower followed by half of the men in the camp.

"Which way?" He shouted up, though the man was only thirty feet above the ground and could have heard Diego if he had simply spoken.

"North, there!" the man pointed.

Diego looked in the direction indicated. He could see a small gray square moving out into the bay. It looked as if the boat was coming from the *Río Pájaro*.

"Barbeaux, man your gun." The order was unnecessary, for the militiamen were even now preparing Gabriella for action.

"Grenouille! Bring the horses into the camp and hobble them." Diego hurried to the cleared area in the center of the camp and shouted, "Draw muskets, full cartridge boxes and form ranks on me. *Honor et Fidelitas.*"

He had ordered the vanguard to fall in many times, but this time the men sensed urgency. This was no parade. This was no barracks inspection. The British were coming down. Two ranks of nine men each. The rest of the vanguard was on picket duty or scouting to the north or up a tower. He quickly inspected the men insuring each man was properly armed.

"Take your posts!"

The small cluster of men broke apart, each going to an assigned place on the palisade.

"Pook, take over here." Diego returned to the watch tower.

"Getting closer, *Primero*." The man said.

"Come down. Draw your weapons and take your post on the wall."

Diego was left alone on the beach at the foot of the scorched watch tower. He could make out a square topsail, billowed fat as the little ship ran before the wind. She was a topsail schooner, two masts, both lateen rigged, but only the foremast had a square topsail. She was small, even for a schooner, not much bigger than a packet boat. He could make out eight guns along the starboard deck. She probably carried a like number on the port side. Sixteen guns, five men to a gun plus a dozen to work the ship, he could be facing ninety or a hundred men.

As the ship grew nearer he noticed few men in the rigging and few on deck. She was too small for a second row of guns. She adjusted sail to a port reach as she began to pass Diego's position. The British ensign clearly whipped from the stern mast. Diego could see every man on the slightly tilted deck. There could not have been more than twenty on the schooner, aloft and on deck. They had not manned the guns.

"Give her a ball!" Diego shouted and Gabriella instantly erupted. Barbeaux had been ready. The four pound ball skipped once and then knocked some splinters off of the schooner's fantail. She adjusted her sail to a port reach and raced away across the bay and out of range.

They acted as if they did not know we were here! How can that be? Surely every man on Mobile Bay knows we are here.

Diego watched as the schooner sailed east. She adjusted sail once more and resumed her southerly course.

Who was it that had been on the tower? He remembered – Tiritar Gillama.

"Tiritar, back up the tower."

"*Sí, Primero.*"

Tiritar ran to the base of the tower and looked around for a place to put his musket. He leaned it against the crude rungs that had been lashed to a pair of tower poles to form a ladder. He hung his cartridge box on a rung and unbuckled his sword belt.

"Up the tower now!"

Tiritar dropped the sword belt in the sand and hurried to the top. He settled into place and began to follow the departing schooner.

"Look around, man. We know the schooner's there. What else do you see?"

"Nothing to the north, *Primero*."

Diego watched the schooner's sails shift as she made her way south, running before a dwindling northerly breeze. Why did she simply run past their position? Was she on a mission to meet a greater force?

Olivier came running to the base of the tower. He had been with the pickets stationed north of the camp.

"Where is your horse?" Diego had been wondering if the distant picket had been cut off and captured. No rider came south to warn them when the ship appeared from near the mouth of *Río Pájaro*.

"*Primero*, my horse went down crossing a slough and broke her leg. I ran to warn you, but the ship sailed past me. I heard you shoot."

"Any men crossing the river or coming from the west?"

"No, *Primero*, nothing, just the little ship. She came down from Mobile, I think. I thought they were going to shoot at me as I ran along the beach. They were so close I could see the sailors laughing at me."

Where were the British troops?

"*Primero*!" Tiritar called down from his perch. "The little ship, her sails are disappearing! *Primero*, the sails, they are all gone!"

The mouth to Mobile Bay was ten or twelve miles away. At that distance, only the uppermost sails of the little ship could have been seen, particularly if she had gone beyond the mouth of the bay. If her sails were furled, they would simply disappear. Naked masts and yard arms would be invisible at such a distance.

"Olivier, get another horse from Grenouille. Ride south until you are close enough to see if the British ship left the bay and return."

"*Sí, Primero*." Olivier turned to go.

"Olivier!"

"*Sí, Primero*?"

"How far north is the crippled horse?"

"About two miles, *Primero*. I had to cut its throat with my short sword."

"Go." Olivier rushed off in the direction of the picketed horses.

I will have to send some men north to butcher the horse, Diego thought. One horse could feed his vanguard for three days.

Olivier rode out of the camp past Diego and thundered south. Diego did not like the idea of sending him alone, but that could not be helped. Diego returned to the camp. He had the men stand down from their posts, but they were to carry their muskets with them at all times. He saw the teamster dawdling about the wagon's tracings.

"Grenouille!"

"*Sí, Primero?*"

"Get some horses teamed to that wagon and go north along the beach with two men. You will find a horse in about two miles. Butcher it and come back."

"It is dead?"

"I cannot fool you, Grenouille." Diego laughed. "Of course it is dead."

The teamster made an expression that turned his face into a wide-mouthed, bug-eyed imitation of a frog. It was clear he deserved the *apodo* "Grenouille" (frog).

"Búho, go north and join our picket. If anyone crosses the river or another ship is sighted, come south, all of you."

"*Sí, Primero.*"

Búho began to help Grenouille with the wagon.

"Do not wait for the wagon. Go now."

"*Sí, Primero.*" Búho ran past Diego on his way to the beach.

"Jog, man, jog. The pickets are four miles up the beach."

Nothing to do now but wait. Diego looked back toward the south. It was four or five miles to the end of the peninsula and that may not bring Olivier close enough to see much beyond the passage between the barrier islands that framed the entrance to the bay.

Olivier should be back in three hours, no more, he decided. Nightfall would be in less than two hours – *Then what?*

Olivier returned to say he could not see the British ship anywhere in the bay, but he thought he could see something near the eastern tip of one of the barrier islands. It was far away and the light had been failing, but something was there.

"Probably the signal tower the British had to help guide ships into the bay," Diego said. "I passed just under it last year." *Was it only last year he had escaped from Pensacola?*

"Could have been a tower, *Primero*," Olivier conceded. "Or it could have been a ship just off the eastern tip of the island. I could not tell."

"In the morning, I want you and two others to go back to the point with a horse," Diego smoothed his moustache as he spoke. "Pook will pick the men to go with you. Ride back with any news, but do not kill your horse when you do."

CHAPTER 8

"Rider coming from the south, *Primero!*" Martin was on watch and his shout brought both Diego and Pook to the foot of the tower. No light had shown during the night, except for a cook fire in the fishing village across the bay. The wind had stiffened and shifted to come out of southwest. Olivier had set out four hours ago, just before sunrise, with two others to set the picket Diego wanted on the tip of the peninsula.

"It is not Olivier!"

"How can you tell at this distance?" Diego stared intently along the beach, but could see nothing beyond a slight bend a half-mile to the south.

"The rider is dressed in blue, *Primero*."

"Pook, get six men and form a line here, fixed bayonets."

Diego could hear the hoof beats of the approaching rider as Pook brought six musketeers and formed a line facing south.

"Should we load, *Primero*?" Pook asked.

"No. It is one man. If he is British, it will be a demand for terms."

The rider rounded a bend and came into view. It was a naval officer – a Spanish naval officer. *Gálvez has arrived*, was all Diego could think.

The officer reined up and dismounted clumsily, nearly falling into Diego. He was a lieutenant, about twenty or so, thin as a string. His eyes were encircled rings so dark and prominent the man might have been mistaken for a raccoon.

"I am Lieutenant Gonzalo delValle of His Most Catholic Majesty's frigate of war *Volante*." DelValle took a deep breath. "Sergeant, do you have any water?"

Diego removed his canteen, pulled the wooden stopper and handed it to delValle, who accepted the gift with both hands. He drank deep, emptying the canteen and wiped his mouth with a sleeve.

"First we were becalmed and then hit by a storm, *lo juro* (I swear) a whirlwind struck us, most of our supplies were lost or spoiled. Now we have run aground."

"Is Gálvez with you, *Señor*?"

"Yes, but he is aground as well, as is half the fleet. Last night we saw an English ship just inside the bay and she was aground as well. Riaño, he commands the galiot *Valenzuela*, investigated. He captured the first mate and five crewmen of the English ship trying to escaping in a skiff. They were bound for the fort at Mobile, *lo juro*, to report on us no doubt."

Diego did not know what a "galiot" was, but supposed it to be a smallish ship. DelValle was a talkative man who provided little real information.

"General Gálvez is aground?" Pook interjected.

DelValle snorted, "The General's ship, you fool – soldiers, *lo juro*. The *Gálvez* is a brig and she is aground, though not as hard as we. My captain will be sending men ashore to lighten the *Volante*. They are in dire need of water."

"There is a stream west of here that has been flowing since the storm a few nights ago, Lieutenant. We have water, for the time being. We lack food."

"Salted pork is not fouled by salt water – Thanks to the Mother – so we have food. Men and gear will be put ashore until the grounded ships are free. Then we will come into the bay."

"A ship is coming from the south!" Martin's shout startled Diego. He had forgotten the man was still on the makeshift tower.

"That would be the *Valenzuela*," delValle muttered. "She draws little water and had no problems coming into the bay."

"Pook, dismiss the guard. Tell Grenouille to fill as many water barrels as he can and haul them south to the point."

"Grenouille is away butchering a horse, *Primero*."

"When he returns, then."

"I will return to the point, Sergeant," delValle said as he struggled back onto the horse. "I will send your men back. Gálvez will use the guns from the *Volante – lo juro –* to build a battery to guard the entrance to this bay. When Riaño comes ashore, he will have instructions for you, *lo juro*."

Pook walked up and both men watched the lieutenant ride south. His efforts to stay mounted were almost comical. The saddles were so light riders could do as well barebacked. "Blankets with stirrups," was how Grenouille described them. They had been taken in the skirmish with the British on the trail to Mobile, the "silver fight" the men called it.

"What are we up to, *Primero?*"

"When that ship arrives, her master will tell us, *lo juro*," Diego said.

ᘓᕽ

So that is a galiot, Diego though as he watched the *Valenzuela* furl her sails and launch a skiff. She was only slightly larger than a packet boat and had two masts. The fore was square rigged and the aft was gaff rigged. Except for the vessel's size, Diego could not discern much difference between a galiot and the packet boat *Alacita*. The *Valenzuela* did not anchor. Running under her jibs alone, she turned away from the shore after the skiff had been launched. The wind was from the southwest and had been rising all day until it threatened to become a gale, so the *Valenzuela* was forced to tack around the vast Mobile Bay rather than attempt to anchor.

The skiff, fighting to hold course against the quartering headwind, appeared to be a great insect as six glistening oars lifted in unison and plunged into the muddy water of the bay, driving the skiff toward the tower to the call of the steersman. A man, a naval officer, was standing in the bow. Diego assumed the man to be Riaño.

The skiff grounded and the man in the bow jumped into the knee-deep water. He waded ashore as the seamen behind him shipped their oars and clambered over the gunnel to steady the skiff.

Diego held his salute as the officer approached. "Sergeant Diego deMelilla, at your service, sir. Welcome to Camp *Lejano*."

"I am Lieutenant Juan Antonio de Riaño, master of the *Valenzuela*." Riaño returned Diego's salute and turned toward the skiff. "Pedro!" he called out, "bring those water casks ashore and have one of these soldiers tell you the way to the nearest fresh water." The men in the skiff rolled two barrels into the water where they floated, clearly empty.

"I will send for some transport for those barrels, Lieutenant. You may wait here and send your men with mine, if it pleases you." Diego said. "Pook, get two horses with *travois* and bring them here for the barrels. Then guide these men to the stream, have them filled and return here."

"*Sí, Primero*." Pook began to wave the wading sailors toward a sandy spit of land.

"You shall have your water soon, Lieutenant," Diego said, wondering why the *Valenzuela* also lacked fresh water.

"We had to distribute a goodly portion of our fresh water to the *Volante* when her casks were broken during a storm," Riaño said as if could read Diego's mind. "None of the fleet carried a full supply of water. We were crammed with men and munitions. Something had to be left out. We were not expecting to be at sea for a month." Riaño gave a wry smile.

The man was short, even by European standards, with a thick, black moustache and goatee. He was wide in the shoulders, solidly built and projected the air of a man who must be obeyed. A jet-black wig poked out from the bottom of his bicorn. Most gentlemen at court wore wigs, white wigs for the most part, but a white-powdered wig was hard to maintain at sea, so many naval officers wore black ones unless they were at court.

Wigs of all types were not as popular in the new world as the old and, excepting for officers, were rarely seen outside of formal gatherings. Diego had never worn a wig. Enlisted men of the Louisiana Regiment cropped their hair short and bound their heads with a bandana or, if they preferred long hair, pulled it back into a tight ponytail. A closely shaven chin and a broad, heavy moustache was as much the uniform of a Spanish soldier as was the blue-cuffed white coat.

"We saw a British ship yesterevening," Diego said as they were waiting for the *travois* to be brought to the beach. "She was sailing south toward the mouth of the bay."

"It must be the one that is aground. No other ship came out. Everything that draws more than a foot of water is going aground. We have a pilot who knows this bay and he says every shoal has shifted about. He has no idea what he is about, if you ask me. Get those barrels filled!"

Pook had arrived with two pack horses rigged with *travois* and soldiers to guide the sailors to the stream.

"We are going to establish a temporary base on the peninsula and offload all we can from the grounded ships. After we pull the ships free and have them inside the bay, we will reload them and come north. This gale will slow things. Can we never start a campaign in this Godless place without a storm confronting our every attempt?" Riaño studied the skies as if the wind were a personal affront.

"What are my orders, Lieutenant?"

"Have you heard from our Choctaw scouts?"

"Not in weeks."

"What do you know of the British activities?"

"Very little, sir. They have not come down toward us and we have not gone north beyond the *Río Pájaro*. We have seen nothing this last ten days save a few farmers and even they have abandoned their farms."

"The General desires you to move north, cross the *Río Pájaro* and camp there. Once we have freed our grounded ships, we will move up the bay with our entire force. You will provide security so that our force can land without opposition."

"How large a force do you bring?"

"A dozen ships with eight hundred infantry, some of which are militia and even a few American rebels. The General is expecting more troops from Havana, but we will attack without them if need be. Spanish ships will fill this bay."

Eight hundred infantry! Diego doubted the British had more than four hundred men at Mobile. Still, two to one against a fortified position was not a certain thing.

"See if you can contact the Choctaw scouts, sergeant," Riaño continued. "Do you need some assistance crossing the *Pájaro*?"

"No, sir." Diego's scouts had reconnoitered the *Río Pájaro* well. They found a trail inland that forded the river. "We will be in place north of the *Pájaro* by tomorrow after noon."

"Excellent! I will return to tell the General. A small launch will call upon you from time to time with instructions. The General expects daily reports. We will take Mobile, Sergeant. Any questions?"

"No, sir."

"Good. What is it your regiment says? Honor and –?"

"*Fidelitas*, sir."

"Right! *Honor et Fidelitas*, Sergeant." Riaño tipped his hat in salute.

"*Honor et Fidelitas*," Diego saluted.

Riaño had timed his departure to match the return of the *travois* loaded with water. He waited until his men had rolled the barrels into the skiff before he stepped aboard. They pushed off and, aided by the southwesterly wind, they made for the *Valenzuela* which had been tacking back and forth in the bay.

"Pook!" Diego felt exhilarated. Finally he had orders and a clear understanding of what was planned. "Prepare the camp to move at first light tomorrow. We are going north."

ᗡᕲ

Clear skies and a late moonset provided enough light for the vanguard to begin the move north before the sun had even risen. The eastern horizon was beginning to turn blue just as the head of the column passed the remains of the butchered horse. Scouts ranged far ahead of the little column reporting on the conditions ahead.

They turned inland and crossed a small tributary of the *Pájaro*, moved north again for three miles along a well-worn trail along the river to a place where it narrowed into another ford where they crossed the river proper. They turned east toward Mobile Bay, cutting across a looping bend in the river. They crossed plowed fields and reached a complex of farm buildings within sight of both bay and river.

It was not yet three in the afternoon and Diego had his people established on the north bank of the *Pájaro*. Pickets were sent north and west while the remainder of the vanguard made camp around the cluster of farm buildings. Barbeaux placed Gabriella in a tangle of fallen trees where she could fire on the road coming into the farm from the north or the beach to the east.

Several hams were found in the smokehouse and were quickly snatched up by men who had been living on boiled oats. The stables were empty as were the corn crib and storehouse. How the hams had been forgotten was a mystery. Diego claimed the main house as his headquarters.

The place was roughly furnished. There were three rooms, two bedrooms and a large parlor with a hearth, long table and several chairs. The windows were shuttered and without panes. Although firing slots in the shutters admitted enough light to examine the place, Diego threw them open. He could see the bay from two of the rooms and the river from the third.

The rope-netted beds were without mattresses, a problem easily remedied. Could he be so lucky as to sleep under a roof?

"*Primero!*"

Diego leaned out of the window to see a soldier escorting a Choctaw toward the farmhouse.

"Bring him in here," Diego said. He returned to the parlor as the men came in.

"Says he is from T'Chien, *Primero*. He gave the password."

"Good. Return to your post."

"*Sí, Primero*." The soldier ducked out of the farmhouse.

"You *Hika Nitah* ?" the Choctaw said. *Hika Nitah* was Diego's Choctaw name. It meant "Flying Bear." A small girl in one of the villages he and T'Chien had visited last year had dreamt of Diego, burly and barrel-chested, flying with a long staff and decided he would be called Flying Bear.

"I am. What is your name?"

The man nodded. "I am called Ferdinando."

Ferdinando reached into the haversack he carried and pulled out a small log book. "T'Chien says you are to give this to the General. He says the British have locked themselves in their fort. Some people would not go into the fort. They stay in the houses in the town." He looked around the room. "This place belongs to a man called Delchamps." Ferdinando's Spanish was very good. He looked every inch a Choctaw, but his Spanish was as good as any *peninsulare*.

"You know Delchamps?"

"Yes. I have visited this farm many times. He would never invite me into his house. Considered me a savage, I guess. He spoke only French and my French is very poor."

"Where did he go?"

"Into town. He has a daughter who lives there. She is married to a smith."

Diego walked to the window facing the bay, opened the logbook and began to read.

"It is written in code," Ferdinando said, "lest the *godums* intercept it."

Diego saw that the pages were filled with nothing but numbers.

"What does it say?" Diego could see a boat with a lateen sail pass the mouth of the *Pájaro* and quarter toward the beach.

Ferdinando shrugged. "Not my place to know. The *godums* might intercept me. One cannot tell what one does not know."

"Go to the cook fire and get something to eat. We managed to find several smoked hams. There might be some left. It will be dark soon. You can return to T'Chien in the morning. I will see this gets to Gálvez."

Ferdinando nodded and ducked out of the room. Diego watched the launch drop her sail and nuzzle up to the beach. A sailor jumped out and said something to one of the soldiers who had gone to meet the boat. The soldier pointed in Diego's direction and the sailor began to run toward the farmhouse, holding his haversack against his side.

Must be orders, Diego thought. He left the room and met the sailor halfway from the beach.

"Riaño wants to know if you have anything to report, sergeant," the sailor said without any introduction.

"Here is a log for the General." Diego offered the little book.

"Riaño wants to know if your people are here."

"Look around. We are here as ordered." This sailor was beginning to irritate him.

"Good. You are to stay here and send scouts up to the *Río Perro*. Tell your man to fire that little gun if the British come down."

That little gun could only mean Barbeaux's Gabriella.

The sailor pulled a roll of paper and some black lead pencils from his haversack. "Make a map of the land between here and the fort – and see if you can capture any prisoners."

Prisoners! The godums are locked up tight in their fort and this man is asking for prisoners?

"I will see what I can do. We may find some civilians to question."

"I will return tomorrow at the same time. Anything I should report to Lieutenant Riaño?"

Diego shook his head. He wanted orders and now he had them. *Poke around an enemy fort and town – draw maps and capture some prisoners while you are at it. The rest of us will be along any time now.*

"Nothing to report."

"Good." The sailor put the log in his haversack and trotted back to the launch.

Diego went to table on the west side of the small house and sat down where the failing light faintly illuminated a small spot. He pulled Isabella's letter from his haversack, unfolded it. Paper was a valued thing to soldiers so letters to and from families were often written on the same scrap until both sides were covered in ink or charcoal. He had been given some pencils, no need to make a batch of soldier's ink. He picked a blank place below Maria's crude signature and wrote.

Isabella, I write today to thank you for your letter. It gives me peace to know those I love are safe. I pray you and all in your house continue in good health. Tell all I am in good health. We are well positioned, provisioned and housed. Do not worry on my account. Diego.

He folded the letter and returned it to his haversack. He would wait until the *Alacita* delivered her dispatches. The letter would be entrusted to Captain Palmas for delivery to the Campo home in Concepción.

❧

Diego had expected the vanguard to be folded back into the Fixed Regiment. Instead, T'Chien sent two dozen Choctaw scouts to be added to Diego's command. A command was created combining twenty infantrymen of the original vanguard, Barbeaux's artillery, and the Choctaw. The unit was also given a new name, *La Cuchilla* (the cutting edge), and ordered to act as the mobile base of a larger scouting effort.

The Choctaw formed small scouting groups of three men and ranged far ahead of Diego's regulars. If the scouts contacted a British force, they were to retreat to Diego's position. Runners would bring the word to the General while Diego fought a delaying action before retreating to a location designated by the General.

La Cuchilla moved north from Delchamps farm on the *Río Pájaro* and ranged inland as much as five miles before looping back out to the bay. Every time they returned to the bay, more Spanish ships were in evidence. *Travois* and pack horses were used to carry supplies for the short one or two day trips inland. Their supplies were replenished when contact with the fleet was renewed.

Farms were becoming more prevalent, particularly inland where the land was more arable, though the soils Diego observed so far were quite poor compared to Louisiana. Tilling for the spring crops was just beginning and, unlike the farms near *Río Pájaro*, occasionally they encountered people working the fields. Most of these farmers were a mixture of Choctaw, Mobile or French. A few were English speakers, but most of these were Scots or Irish. The British and their Loyalist allies were all reported to have collected at Fort Charlotte.

They reached the *Río Perro* near the end of February. The *Perro*, over seven hundred yards wide, was much wider than the *Pájaro* except it necked down to a hundred yards where it entered Mobile Bay. It was a short, meandering river that began just south of the town of Mobile, ran south, then west, then south again and finally back east into Mobile Bay. The river isolated a wide peninsula with a narrow neck bordered on one side by the bay and on two sides by the wide *Río Perro*. Gálvez had decided this isolated terrain created a perfect staging area for his attack on Mobile and *La Cuchilla* had been dispatched to reconnoiter.

Diego drew four day's supplies for his train of *travois* and headed inland along the south bank of the river. At nightfall on the first day they had reached a small tributary that marked the northward turn of the river. The far-ranging Choctaw reported the land west and north of the first camp was well farmed but without any British presence.

They headed north for two days, fording several tributaries and encountering more farmers. At the end of the third day, they were within a league of Fort Charlotte and well inland. Yet, no move was made by the British to intercept them. On the fourth day, they moved east and south until they encountered Mobile Bay. The *Valenzuela* was waiting just off the beach as Diego's lead men came out of the brush. She launched a skiff when the Spaniards were sighted.

Diego was directing his men to make camp a few hundred yards from the beach as Lieutenant Riaño came in escorted by a particularly nervous Martin. Before *La Cuchilla* had departed for this latest scouting foray, Diego was handed his orders by one of *Valenzuela's* boatswains when the sailor mentioned the dangers involved if Riaño were to become disappointed in the performance of *La Cuchilla*. Riaño, the man said, was particularly high placed because he was Governor General Bernardo Gálvez's brother-in-law.

"I thought Antonio Saint Maxent the Younger, of New Orleans, was the General's brother-in-law," Diego had said.

The boatswain laughed. "That man is the brother of Gálvez's wife. Riaño is married to one of the General's sisters. Few families in Spain are as powerful as the Gálvez."

Martin had overheard the exchange, so the proximity of power had unnerved him.

"Lieutenant *Don* Riaño to see you, *Primero*," Martin said, his voice quavering.

"Thank you, Martin. Return to your post." Riaño stepped forward and Diego gestured toward a field table and chairs that had been placed upwind of the cook fires.

"Your reports have been without mention of the British," Riaño said as he eased onto one of the collapsible camp chairs.

"The British have not been found anywhere. They stay in their fort," Diego shrugged. "It makes no sense to me. They remain blind while we move freely."

"There must be a reason for such behavior. That does not matter. I am here to give you your next mission. You are to scout the entire peninsula south of here. I will land fifty men to guard the neck. You will report to me at the mouth of the *Río Perro* in two days. Now tell me about the last four days."

Diego spent two full hours telling Riaño about the lands *La Cuchilla* had traversed, the people encountered and condition of the trails they found.

The slave was digging up a stump. He looked up from his work as Diego approached. *La Cuchilla* scouts had reported a large farm and building complex ahead. The bay was just visible to the east and the *Río Perro* spread out to the south.

"I cannot make out a word he says, *Primero*," Plata said. He had sent word of the encounter with a local and had remained with the man until Diego arrived with an escort of six soldiers.

"Thank you, Plata. Where are the rest of the scouts?"

"Searching along the river bank, *Primero*. There are many places there to hide men or boats."

Diego examined the slave. He was young and healthy. He had several tribal scars, a sign of a man fresh from Africa.

Diego tried to question the man in English, Spanish and Choctaw without response. French produced a response.

"Où est-vous maître? (Where is your master?)"

"Master there," the man said, pointing toward the farm buildings and he returned to his work.

"Plata, after you have scouted the river bank, have the men meet us at the farmhouse," Diego said.

He waved his escorts forward toward the farmhouse. The soldiers fanned out as they neared the main building. Two stopped in clear view of the front porch, two went right beyond the house and two went left until the building was surrounded. Diego strode up to the porch and knocked on the door, though he was certain anyone within had watched their approach.

The man that opened the door was white, about fifty years old. His black hair was pulled into a tight ponytail and streaked with gray. He had a full beard and moustache similarly colored. He wore a fringed cotton frock over a shirt and knee britches. He was bare foot.

"Qui es-tu?" the man said.

"I am Sergeant Diego deMelilla, of the Fixed Louisiana Regiment," Diego said.

"A sergeant? I expected more than a mere sergeant."

"A sergeant is all you have for now. Who are you?"

The man seemed to puff up. "I am *monsieur* Orbane deMouy, master of all the lands between the Dog River and Mobile Bay."

"Where are your people, *monsieur* deMouy?"

"My sons have gone to Mobile to sell to the British. They are filling their stores in the fort. My daughters are with their husbands on their own farms and all of my slaves, except for Stump-puller, have been forced to work on the British fort."

"What can you tell me of the British?"

"Nothing much, but I think I know who can." DeMouy opened his door wider until Diego could see into the room. Huddled against one wall was a boy of fifteen or so in a ragged uniform. He wore his red coat inside out.

"He is a deserter, no?" DeMouy said. "How do you say? A turn-coat. The poor boy has no French."

Diego shouted toward Plata, who was at the edge of the brush along the river bank. "Send Olivier here." Olivier could speak English and they had their prisoner.

CHAPTER 9

The deserter claimed to be Private John Smith. Olivier was certain that was not the man's true name, but that did not matter. Private Smith had joined the army to escape imprisonment and had been assigned to the British 60th Regiment of Foot. If the boy could be believed, only three hundred men defended the fort at Mobile. The majority of the defenders were British regulars augmented by American Loyalists Militia from Maryland and Pennsylvania. A few were local volunteers as well, but not many. Most of the citizens of Mobile and the surrounding farmers were French or Choctaw. The prisoner was turned over to Riaño's care.

The next day Gálvez established deMouy's farmhouse as his headquarters for the assault on Fort Charlotte. The Spanish invasion fleet gradually filled Mobile Bay as additional troops arrived from Havana. Gálvez began the task of moving twelve hundred men into position for the assault on the fort. Some had to be moved up from the mouth of the bay on foot, some were brought into position by ship. The *Volante* could not be freed and was dismantled for her timber. Her full complement of naval guns were brought up and mounted on improvised carriages among the infantry occupying the newly constructed defensive works along a narrow neck of land between a tributary of *Río Perro* and Mobile Bay.

Two days of digging had produced an earthen rampart interspaced with cannon-armed redoubts, converting the mile from river to bay into a formidable defensive work. While the army labored in preparation for the siege of the fort, Diego and *La Cuchilla* were sent to scout the town west of the fort as well as the roadways leading to Mobile.

Half of the farms Diego visited were continuing with their preparations for spring planting, their owners seemingly unconcerned about the impending battle for Fort Charlotte. The town proved to be only partially abandoned. Those houses near the fort had been put to the torch by the British to deny cover to Spanish forces. Gálvez had promised the British commander, an army captain, not to use the town as a shield if it were spared, but the houses close to the fort had been destroyed nevertheless.

The British had carried all of the provisions they could find into the fort. Because of this, many of the citizens who remained on their farms or in the town were short of food. When Diego reported this to Gálvez, the General arranged a truce and had supplies delivered to the docks at Mobile for those who had remained in the town.

"The people of Mobile will soon be citizens of Spanish Florida," Gálvez was reported to have said. "We do not desire His Most Catholic Majesty to gain starved subjects."

Diego's unconventional reconnaissance force managed to establish an operational headquarter of its own in a tavern, *Le Chat Blanc*, on Royal Street at the north end of the town just beyond the sector the British had burned. They had attempted to burn the entire town, but the last few blocks north of town survived. Royal Street was paved with packed manure, interspersed with frequent scum-filled ruts and scattered planks. Fort Charlotte was less than a quarter mile from the tavern's door. If the soldiers of *La Cuchilla* lingered in the street before going into the tavern, the British would send a cannon ball skipping up the street. After a few days, even this harassing fire was suspended and by the last days of February, the Spaniards could come and go as they pleased.

Pook stomped in from the back door of *Le Chat Blanc*. "*Primero*, a runner from the farmhouse wants to see you. Says he has orders." Gálvez's headquarters at deMouy's farmhouse had become known throughout the army as the "farmhouse."

Diego was seated at an upended barrel that served as a table, drinking from a tankard of ale and talking to two Choctaw scouts who had just arrived from the north.

"Show him in, Pook. It must be important if they took the time to write it down." Pook had used the word *órdens*, implying formal written orders instead of the usual *instrucciones*, meaning verbal orders.

The man Pook escorted in was a private from one of the new regiments just arrived out of Havana. They had come ashore less than a week ago. The messenger's uniform was clean, nearly spotless and stood in stark contrast to the ragged, threadbare, filthy condition of the diverse clothes worn by the men of *La Cuchilla*. The man was wide-eyed and appeared to be puzzled at the sight of the big *Isleño* sergeant with two Choctaw warriors crowded around a barrelhead in the dingy room enjoying a tankard of ale. Light drifted in from pane-less windows bracketing a front door. Someone had scrawled the words "If you go out this way – run" in chalk on the door. Diego noticed the man's distraction by the sign.

"The *godums* might send a four-pound ball up your *culo* if you walk on Royal Street."

The man gulped and proffered a leather pouch. "Your orders, Sergeant."

Diego took the pouch. "You thirsty? Hungry?"

"I ran all the way, sergeant."

"Thirsty then." Diego switched to French. "*Madame* Trapenier, another tankard of your best ale. We have a thirsty soldier here."

A woman's voice answered from another room. "We have only one kind of ale. Does your soldier wish to eat?"

"What is your name, Private?"

"Burujón, Sergeant. *Soldado* Julio Burujón."

"We in *La Cuchilla* are not so formal, Julio. You may address me by my first name."

"What is your first name, Sergeant?"

"*Primero.*"

Burujón swallowed again. "*Sí, Primero.*"

"What would you like to eat? *Madame* Trapenier has boiled oats, roasted oats, oat meal, oat cakes and, if you prefer meat, roasted rat."

"I am not hungry, *Primero.*"

"No? Well here comes your ale."

Madame Trapenier waddled in with three tankards of ale. She was a short, round, red-faced woman with equally large breasts and buttocks. She wore a dingy apron over a brown cotton dress and her hair was tucked under a white cotton cap. She gave one tankard to Burujón and the rest to the Choctaw warriors.

"I can understand Spanish, *Primero*," she scolded in French. "We do not serve roasted rats."

"It is good you are not hungry, Burujón" Diego said. "She says she is out of rat."

"Your orders, *Primero*. I am to wait for a reply."

Diego broke the seal on the pouch and withdrew a single sheet of heavy paper. He held it up to the morning light coming in from one of the windows on Royal Street.

"Pook, you need to take over here. Keep running scouts north along the river. I have been summoned to the farmhouse." Diego went into another room to retrieve his uniform coat and tricorn.

☙

"*Primero Sargento* deMelilla to see you, General."

General Gálvez looked up at his clerk. He seemed puzzled for a moment before his face brightened.

"Oh, yes, our commander of *La Cuchilla*. Show him in, Renaldo. Then find Colonel Bouligny and tell him his bodyguard is here." He pronounced the colonel's name "*bowl-in-A.*"

Renaldo walked out of the General's command office. The room had been a northeast corner bedroom in deMouy's farmhouse. The walls were now papered with maps and the bed had been pushed against one wall to make room for a conference table and chairs. An open window on the north wall framed a view of Mobile Bay filled with Spanish ships.

Diego ducked into the room, came to attention and held his salute. "*Sargento* Diego deMelilla reporting as ordered, sir."

"Take a seat, Sergeant." Gálvez gestured at one of the chairs at the table. "I want to ask you a few questions before Colonel Bouligny arrives."

Diego hesitantly took the indicated chair. Enlisted men simply did not sit in the presence of an officer, particularly a general officer. Gálvez seemingly unconcerned with the breach in protocol, took a chair opposite Diego, stuffed a cigar in his mouth and worked it over the chimney of an oil lamp until it ignited.

"I forget my manners, *Primero*," Gálvez said as he blew out a cloud of smoke. "Care for a cigar?"

"No, sir." Diego had never developed a taste for tobacco. "Thank you, sir, but no."

A map of coastal Florida from the Pascagoula River to Pensacola covered the table. Fort Charlotte had several figures scribbled by it as did the several fortifications at Pensacola. A road between the two locations was indicated by a dashed line that halted on the east side of a river identified as the Tensaw and reemerged on the west side of the Mobile River. The map showed eight miles of intermittent rivers and swamp from the east side of the Tensaw to the west side of the Mobile.

"Tell me, Sergeant. If the *godums* were inclined to send a relief force from Pensacola by land, what are the approaches he might use?"

Diego leaned forward. "The most direct route, and the best road, is here." He placed a finger at the symbol for the fort at Pensacola and traced a line that ended at the northeast corner of Mobile Bay. He was suddenly mindful of his rough and dirty hands. "But to get to Fort Charlotte, they would have to ferry across the northern end of the bay. Our fleet would stop any movement as far as half a league north of the bay. The next place is an old trade road here," Diego touched the map at a point about twelve miles north of Fort Charlotte. "It is called *Lokchokhina* by the locals. The old trail crosses a swamp and several rivers. It has been used, but not often, by the Choctaw. They would drag dugouts through the swamp and ride them across the rivers. Very rough going. The next possible road is twenty leagues further north."

"I am told these routes are watched." Gálvez stared intently at Diego.

"Yes, sir. I have my people at *Lokchokhina* and T'Chien has his scouts on the trail at the east bank of the Tensaw. Lieutenant Riaño has a signal skiff on the Tensaw where the road starts. The Americans sent some of their people well north of *Lokchokhina* to guard against Loyalists coming down from Georgia."

Renaldo came into the room. "Sir, Colonel Bouligny is waiting without."

Gálvez held up his hand indicating Renaldo should be silent.

"How many men would it take to stop a regiment from coming to *Lokchokhina*."

"With one hundred infantry, a few field guns and ten flat boats it would be possible to keep two thousand trapped on that trail for a month."

"Renaldo, show the Colonel in, please."

"Yes, General." Renaldo went to the door, opened it and announced, "Colonel Francisco Bouligny."

Diego stood and stepped away from the table to provide room for the colonel to sit if he so desired.

Bouligny entered with his hat under one arm. He did not salute.

"I am here as you requested, General." His tone was almost resentful. He was a paunchy man about ten years Gálvez's senior, with a goatee and mustache that had been dyed black.

"Yes, Colonel. May I introduce you to *Primero Sargento* Diego deMelilla y Tupinar. I am sending you into Fort Charlotte with surrender terms. Sergeant deMelilla will be your guard."

Bouligny attempted to look down his nose at Diego, but because he was a full head shorter than the sergeant, he had to tilt his head back until his powdered wig began to slip.

"Panis' famous spy. The Flying Bear," he said. Diego simply nodded.

"Well, here are the terms." Gálvez pushed a fold of documents into Bouligny's hand. "*Primero* will see you to the gate, accompany you within and escort you back to me."

"Which gate am I to use, General. The British have been free with their powder of late," Bouligny said as he examined the papers.

Gálvez puffed on his cigar. It had nearly gone out. "Which gate do you recommend, Sergeant?"

"I would suggest the north sally port, sir, at the end of Royal Street, sir. The *godums* should have no problem seeing our herald flag well before we are within range."

"There you have it, Colonel. You shall present yourself to the north sally gate."

Bouligny worked his mouth nervously until his dye-stiffened mustache seemed to attempt flight. "These instructions," he proffered two of the six sheets of paper, "are in English. I cannot read English."

"The terms are presented in Spanish, French and English, Colonel. They are identical. I did so to avoid translation errors." In a prior communication with Durnford, Gálvez had promised not to use the houses close to the fort as an avenue of advance if the British did not destroy them. Durnford put most of the homes to the torch anyway and then sent a message of protest when Spaniards were seen moving about in what remained of the town. Durnford claimed that Gálvez had unconditionally promised not to enter the town. The misunderstanding was deemed a "translation error."

Gálvez turned to Diego. "How is your English, Sergeant?"

"Not well, General. I can understand some, but can say little."

"Is there any man in *La Cuchilla* with a command of English?"

"Yes, General. Private Olivier, sir."

"Good. He is to join the escort. Any questions?"

Diego snapped to attention, "No questions, General."

Bouligny simply shook his head slowly and slipped the surrender documents into a leather pouch hanging at his side. "Will that be all, General?"

"Yes, Colonel. You are dismissed."

Diego saluted and followed Colonel Bouligny out of the farmhouse. Bouligny had his horse brought to him and mounted with practiced ease. He was clearly a man accustomed to riding.

"Where is your horse, sergeant?"

"I have no horse, sir. Follow me, please. We must have Private Olivier join us." Diego set off at a trot. Bouligny followed, his horse forced into a very uncomfortable gait.

They passed the siege gun emplacements under construction just southwest of the city. Bouligny reined up to talk to the officer in charge of construction of the siege works, a captain of sappers from a Veracruz regiment.

"*Lo juro*, you soldiers are a chatty bunch." Startled, Diego turned to see Lieutenant delValle, the first mate of the *Volante*. Most of the guns, gun crews and many officers assigned to the siege works had been taken from that abandoned ship. DelValle commanded one of the batteries under the direction of an artillery lieutenant, a fact that chafed him.

"Sir?" Officers simply did not have casual conversations with enlisted men, so Diego was not even certain delValle had been talking to him.

"You are the sergeant who commanded the vanguard, are you not? DeMelilla, is it not? I met you on our first day ashore, *lo juro*."

"Yes, sir." Diego did remember him, particularly the man's verbal tic of adding *lo juro* (I swear) in his sentences. "I am glad to see you well, sir."

"Siege works are new to me, but I have to admire the ingenuity, *lo juro*." DelValle gestured toward the half dozen guns emplaced before him. "There are ten other batteries, some larger than this, scattered about. The sappers have cut lanes through the trees and brush between us and the fort. All of the lanes are directed to one location on the fort. That is where we will bring down the wall. Men in the fort cannot even see our batteries except from that one location of the battlements."

The strategy was very similar to the siege of Baton Rouge. There Gálvez used a screen of trees to hide his artillery emplacements as they were being made. After the guns were set and securely protected by earthworks, he had his sappers clear lines of fire during the night. At daylight, the Spaniards saturated the surprised British with accurate artillery fired from bunkered positions. The fort fell after four hours of constant barrage.

"*Lo juro*, we will send a combined broadside into their wall while they can only answer with a single gun, perhaps two. *Lo juro*, Gálvez is a genius. The British are fools to hide behind their walls, *lo juro*."

Diego remembered his father's advice pertaining to fortified positions. *A determined enemy will always prevail against a castle provided he has time and provisions.* The British lost Fort Charlotte when they failed to oppose Gálvez at the mouth of the bay. Gálvez controlled Mobile Bay and was well supplied by sea. Moreover, the local population was not enamored of British rule. It was only a matter of time, unless the British could send enough reinforcements to challenge the Spaniards in the field.

"Sergeant! Shall we continue?" Bouligny had ended his conversation and, by his tone, was chiding Diego for chatting with delValle.

"This way, sir." Diego jogged to a well-worn path leading to the northeast. A jumble of felled trees, cut brush and piles of lumber seemed to bracket every trail. The *Volante* had been disassembled and her timbers, rigging and planking supported the sides of trench works, gun pits and storage shelters for ammunition. They passed an assembly area for militia from Louisiana where the orders and conversations were in French. Gálvez had brought militia from the plantations above New Orleans, places such as the "German Coast," because these interior settlements, unlike the lands around and below New Orleans, did not need to keep a large garrison at home to counter a possible British attack from the sea.

Diego led the colonel north through the scattered farms just west of the town of Mobile. They turned east at a well-traveled road and stopped at an intersection in a wooded area. Two soldiers, Plata and Serpas, stepped out of the woods. They came to attention and held their muskets at the "salute" position. Bouligny lazily returned their salute, said nothing and, disinterested in the conversation between enlisted men, looked to the south where the tops of Fort Charlotte's corner bastions were just visible over the roof tops of Mobile's few surviving houses.

"Plata, report the conditions." Diego said. This was not a forward picket, but it was important for a commander to inquire of every soldier on guard what had been observed before all other matters, even new orders.

"*Primero*, two Choctaw from *Lokcho* (the Spanish soldiers had shortened the name "*Lokchokhina*" to "*Lokcho*") passed here. They knew the password. They said there has been no sign of the British west of the Tensaw. I sent them on to *Le Chat Blanc* to report to you."

"What time was this?"

"First light, *Primero*."

"I have already gotten their report." The two Choctaw were to spend the night at the tavern and return to *Lokchokhina* on the morrow. "Where is Olivier?"

"Posted east, *Primero*, at the signal tower. He and Búho are watching for signals from the bay." Riaño had a small sailing skiff patrolling the northern end of Mobile Bay communicating orders and receiving reports. Diego had the men erect a three pole tower to provide a clear line of sight to the bay.

"Serpas, run to the tower and replace Olivier. Send him here. *Ahora!*"

"*Sí, Primero*." Serpas ran east, headed for the tower only a mile away.

"Plata, I will send someone up from the tavern to join you here."

"No need, *Primero*. My relief will probably be here before Olivier. Look to the south. Here they come now."

Four soldiers were coming up the road that led north from town. They had distributed themselves on the left and right of the rutted and muddy roadway where the walking was easier. This trail became Royal Street in Mobile. Two were Plata and Serpas' replacements and two were bound for the signal tower.

"Good, then you and Olivier can join the Colonel and me."

"*Sí, Primero.* Join you to do what?"

"We are going to pay the *godums* a visit."

"Sergeant, why are those men walking as if they were on a stroll?" Bouligny had decided to involve himself in the proceedings. "They should be marching in file."

"Colonel, this is not a parade. The center of the road is rutted and muddy, making for poor going. Four men clustered together make a better target than four scattered about."

"There are no British about, Sergeant."

"That appears to be true, sir, for now. It may not be so later. Better to be prepared for an attack that does not come than to be unprepared for one that does."

"Unph!" Bouligny looked south again.

Olivier came trotting up. "You sent for me, *Primero?*"

"Yes. We are going to the fort. Colonel Bouligny has business with the *godums*. You and Plata take the left, I'll be to the right and the Colonel will ride up the center of the road. Is that agreeable, Colonel."

"Yes, yes. Get on with it, sergeant."

They began to move south. The men on foot kept to the edge of the road where the walking was easier and the Colonel, with his horse at a walk, plodded up the center, the animal's hooves splashing down into the churned mud of the heavily traveled road and withdrawing with an audible sucking sound.

The fort was hidden from the travelers by a scattering of shanties and smoldering remains until a slight turn brought the north palisade in full view. Behind the wooden palisade loomed the top of the masonry wall of the main fort. The fort lacked a moat, but a wooden wall of sharpened posts encircled the fort about three hundred feet from the wall itself. This was to prevent a direct rush and escalade. Faces appeared on the wall and Diego could see movement behind the loopholes in the palisade.

Diego signaled a stop about three hundred yards from the palisade gates.

"Plata, Olivier, fix bayonets."

"Fix bayonets, *Primero?*" Plata could not believe he had heard correctly.

"You heard me. Do it now." Diego stared at the cannon that bracketed the main gate. If he were to see a puff of smoke, he decided he would dive to the ground. He listened as the men clattered their bayonets onto the ends of their muskets and brought the weapons to position of shoulder arms.

"Invert your muskets, plant them and come to attention."

The men inverted their weapons and drove the bayoneted tips into the mud. All in the fort could see the gesture. Diego was not carrying a musket or halberd. Of course, this disarming was symbolical for every man, private to colonel, wore a sword. The gate in the palisade swung open. The passage through the fortress walls remained closed. Two redcoats stepped into the opening and similarly stabbed their bayonetted muskets into the dirt.

Colonel Bouligny urged his horse forward at the walk. Diego and his men kept pace with the colonel until they were through the gate. Bouligny dismounted and the redcoats hurriedly closed the palisade entrance and came to attention behind the visitors. No words were spoken.

A noise came from the heavy iron-bound timber sally port of the main fort. A pedestrian door mounted in the gate opened with a squeal of protest. A young British officer, an infantry lieutenant, stepped through the gate followed by a clerk and an orderly. The clerk carried a log book under one arm and a writing kit under the other. The orderly struggled with a collapsible camp table and huntsman's chair. He managed to open the table and place it between Bouligny and the lieutenant. After several attempts, the chair was opened and placed at the table. The clerk placed the log book and writing kit on the table and took the chair.

The British officer cleared his throat. "I am Lieutenant Henry Handleson of His Majesty's 60th Foot. Captain Elias Durnford, commander of Fort Charlotte, has authorized me to speak to this delegation in his name."

Bouligny looked toward Olivier, who translated the introduction into Spanish.

"Tell the lieutenant I am Colonel Francisco Bouligny of His Most Catholic Majesty's army and it is customary for officers of lesser rank to salute officers of superior rank upon introduction. I have dispatches to be delivered in the hands of the commander of this place."

Olivier dutifully translated and waited for the response.

"I will receive the documents for the commander." Handleson offered no salute, a failure that caused Bouligny to redden perceptibly.

"That is not acceptable. I must place the documents in the commander's hands. They contain terms and are written in Spanish, French and English to prevent misinterpretation."

Both men stared across the table while the clerk sat immobile. Diego glanced about out of the corner of his eyes, a skill perfected among rank-and-file soldiers. There were seven redcoats peering down through embrasures behind Handleson to his left and an equal number to his right. Unlike the guards who had opened the palisade gate, these guards carried their muskets at the ready.

Handleson broke the strained silence. "If you could wait here for a moment, Colonel. Pardon me." He turned about sharply and marched back through the pedestrian door.

Diego spoke out of the corner of his mouth to Olivier, who was positioned between Diego and Bouligny. His lips did not move and his voice was so faint that only Olivier could hear him, another skill developed by the rank-and-file. "Do you think any of these *godums* speak Spanish?"

"I don't think so. The *niño* didn't flinch when the colonel mentioned superior rank, but he stiffened when I said it in English." Olivier raised his voice slightly until the men at the table could hear. "There is a large spider on your wig," he said in Spanish. Neither man so much as looked up.

"What are you going on about, Private?" Bouligny asked.

"Nothing, sir. Sorry, sir."

This will be a long afternoon if none of these people can speak Spanish.

Handleson returned. "We are not convinced your English translations correctly reflect your Spanish intent. Is it acceptable if you read the Spanish dispatch to me? I will have them translated and recorded."

Olivier translated.

"None of you has a command of Spanish," Bouligny sneered. "Perhaps I could read the French version to you."

Handleson paused long enough to hear the translation and said. "Peters, prepare to log this meeting."

The clerk opened the log book and writing kit. He selected a quill, tested the tip and, with a satisfied nod, opened a bottle of ink. He dipped the quill and began to write what appeared to be a date on the top of a blank page.

"We will provide our own translator, colonel. A person who's Spanish is Castilian and perfect." Handleson turned slightly and spoke loudly toward the open pedestrian door. "Lady Smythe, would you join us please?"

There was a rustle of skirts behind the door and a lady stepped through. She wore a green dress, which she had to hold up to clear the door sill. Her head was tilted down causing her wide-brimmed and beribboned hat to hide her head and shoulders, as she navigated the opening. She walked gracefully to stand behind the seated clerk and looked up. *Mademoiselle* Marcelite Gaudet de la Arceneaux's eyes met Diego's.

"Gentlemen, may I present Lady Prudence Smythe, wife of Lord Archibald Smythe of Westernton."

To Olivier's credit, he translated as if he had never met Lady Smythe or *Mademoiselle* Gaudet. Plata let out an audible gasp, but that could have been credited to Lady Smythe's beauty. Diego's face remained placid.

Marcelite's eyes registered surprise, then fear and finally she managed a slight frown and almost imperceptible shake of the head. The message was clear – *Do not reveal you know me!*

Diego looked out of the corner of his eye again to see both Olivier and Plata staring at him in wonder. He frowned and shook his head as well. Both men looked to the front again, their faces at parade expression.

"*Doña* Smythe," Bouligny said as he bowed politely. "I am led to believe your Spanish is excellent."

"Yes, my Colonel," Marcelite replied. "My husband Lord Smythe served for several years as envoy to Madrid. I have the good fortune to have a skill with languages. I speak French as well, but I am particularly proud of my Castilian. I can also converse in Catalan, but not nearly as well as Castilian." Her Spanish was indeed perfect, much better than Diego's *Isleño* accented Spanish. Olivier and Plata stood gaped-mouthed.

"Excellent!" exclaimed Bouligny as he opened the leather pouch containing the surrender terms. "I find the arrangement acceptable." He fairly leered at Marcelite. "The Governor General of Louisiana does declare the following to the British Commander of Fort Charlotte at the town of Mobile." He began to read the terms pausing appropriately for Marcelite to translate and the clerk to write her translation into the log book.

CHAPTER 10

arcelite, Handleson, clerk and orderly retreated into the fort with the log book. The Spanish delegation could do nothing but stand before the camp table with the palisade guards behind them and glaring redcoats on the battlements before them while a reply was begin prepared.

Olivier, who was standing next to Bouligny, looked toward Diego as if he were about to speak.

"Silence," Diego hissed through his teeth. "Not a word from you until we are free of here. That goes for you as well, Plata."

Bouligny approved with a nod, then added, "Nothing from anyone unless I request it."

Plata smiled slightly and rolled his eyes. His mischievous expression communicated clearly he understood Diego's true meaning. *Say nothing about Mademoiselle Gaudet or Lady Smythe.* Olivier understood the message as well, but his face lacked Plata's sly understanding.

Their quiet vigil was interrupted by a rousing cheer from inside the fort. It was loud, sustained and must have been two hundred voices or more.

"They must have accepted," Bouligny said. "The troops are relieved that they shall not have to fight."

Diego believed otherwise. *Men do not cheer at defeat. Those were huzzas of defiance.*

Handleson reappeared a quarter hour after the last of the cheers had died away, stepping through the portal with two documents, but without his companions. Diego felt a strange disappointment when Marcelite failed to reappear.

Lieutenant Handleson offered the documents to Bouligny and uttered a rehearsed phrase.

Olivier translated. "The lieutenant says his commander's response is here, written by his own hand. The Lady Smythe has written a perfect Spanish translation which he has also given you. He suggests, sir, you read the Spanish translation aloud and I read the English document so that all are clear as to the subtleties."

Bouligny unfolded the documents, sorted out the English one, which was sealed and signed, and handed it to Olivier. He opened the other written in Lady Smythe's wide, delicate penmanship.

"I, Captain Elias Durnford, Commander of Fort Charlotte by the grace of God and in the service of George III, King of Great Britain and Ireland, confident in the courage and abilities of the forces under my command, do humbly decline the premature offer of terms presented by Governor General Bernardo Gálvez this day, the first of March, in the year of Our Lord one thousand seven hundred and eighty, and of the reign of King George the Third, the twentieth year."

The reply droned on explaining how it was known that the Spanish forces had suffered grievous losses as a result of storms, seven hundred soldiers drowned in the sinking of the frigate *Volante* alone, and the mauling of the galiot, *Valenzuela* when that ship made so bold as to fire on Fort Charlotte. Durnford stated that "This commander, when facing such reduced forces and expecting British reinforcements within a fortnight, was obligated by his duty to hold and defend with his best effort until properly relieved."

Where is he getting this from? Diego thought as the Colonel continued to read Durnford's reply. No men were lost in the storm and Riaño's galiot suffered no damage when he raked the battlements of Fort Charlotte, except for a few holes in canvas. There was also a note of concern for safety and care of the wife and child of a Sergeant Glas, who had been captured when the Spanish encircled the deMouy farm. The lady and child in question were safe and treated with all courtesy, Diego had seen to that himself for it had been *La Cuchilla* that had discovered Mrs. Glas and her little one huddling in the corn crib of a house the sergeant had rented from deMouy. He remembered how terrified she had been, trembling and weeping while holding her wide-eyed and equally terrified youngster tightly. It puzzled him that anyone could think he or his men were such monsters.

Bouligny finished reading the reply and carefully folded it. "Private, is my reading of the document consistent with the version in your hands?"

"Yes, Colonel, it is correct."

"Then our business here is complete. Tell them we are departing."

Olivier complied, though it was clear to all as Bouligny took the reins of his horse and mounted he intended to go. He held out his hand toward Olivier who folded the English copy of the reply and offered it up to the colonel. Bouligny accepted the document and stuffed it along with the Spanish translation into a leather pouch. He wheeled his horse about and shouted to the British guards to open the palisade gates. The two redcoats did not move. Olivier translated the order, but the guards would not budge until Handleson ordered the redcoats to open the gates. Bouligny spurred through the gate; leaving Diego and his men behind.

Feeling all eyes upon him, Diego ordered Plata and Olivier to about face and marched them through the gate at "regular march", a pace slightly slower than simply walking. He was not about to depart quickly and give the impression he was in a hurry. They stopped and retrieved their muskets, ceremoniously removed and sheathed their bayonets, shouldered their weapons and continued up the street as if they were on parade.

Diego could see Bouligny turn off the road and disappear at the north end of Royal Street. *The least the man could do would be to release me from this escort detail.* He guided his brace of *soldados* to the west side of Royal Street, abandoning the morass of mud, scraps of planking and manure that covered the middle of the roadway in favor of the grass-covered shoulders for a more comfortable march.

"*Primero,* I feel an itch between my shoulder blades," Plata muttered out of the corner of his mouth.

"We all do. When we reach the tavern, we will quit the road." *And that fool Colonel be damned.* He would send word to the farmhouse that lacking orders from Bouligny he had returned to his regular duties. They reached the tavern. The door had been opened in anticipation of their arrival and Diego sent his men in first before stepping off of the street himself.

"*Primero*, what was *Mademoiselle* Gaudet doing there?" Plata said.

"I do not know."

"Why did you not say something to the Colonel?"

"*Mademoiselle* Gaudet is our business. You and Olivier keep it to yourselves."

"She pointed a cocked pistol at my face," Plata said. "I had to go into the water and until that very moment, I did not know how to swim."

"Well, now you have acquired a skill that will serve you well in Louisiana."

"Only if I live, *Primero.*"

"Enough, Plata. I will hear no more about the woman. You and Olivier will not say another word about it. Understood?"

"*Sí, Primero.*" Olivier said. Plata simply glared.

"Plata, *entienda* (understand)?" Diego was losing his patience.

Plata's expression faded from angry to compliant. "*Sí, Primero.*"

"Good. Now get to the back, both of you and stand down. You will return to your picket posts in eight hours."

The back room of the tavern had been converted into a guard room where those not manning the several posts north of Mobile could prepare meals, clean their weapons and sleep the eight hours between shifts. Plata and Olivier had been north of Mobile for sixteen hours. The field posts shifted on and off watch after only two hours, but the time between standing guard was used up in reconnaissance patrols and some personal time.

The men would rotate into the tavern in eight hour shifts to eat and sleep. This was known as "standing down."

Diego called to *Madame* Trapenier to bring him a cup of ale and angrily occupied a table. He knew that the men would never keep such a secret and what did it matter to him if they did not? *Marcelite or Lady Smythe or whoever, is nothing to me. Why would it matter if the Governor General was advised she was a spy? And if she is a British spy, why was she so afraid I would say something?* None of this made any sense.

Madame Trapenier arrived with a mug of ale. Diego took it from her hand before she could place it on the table. He brought it to his lips and did not put it down until he had emptied it. She placed her hands on her hips and shook her head slowly saying "Tisk tisk."

"*Madame* Trapenier," he said. "Stop that noise and bring me one I can taste."

He could hear Plata and Olivier in the other room grounding their gear and preparing to go to sleep. Plata muttered, "Must be love," in his practiced barracks complaint tone – loud enough for sergeants to hear, but not so loud as to draw a response.

⁊⁊

The British had begun to bombard the Spanish lines. Fort Charlotte's cannon fire was impressive and ineffectual. The Spanish works were either shielded from view by wooded areas or within deep trenches. The regular heavy thump of the fort's guns became simply background noise. Everyone went about their chores as if the sounds were just distant thunder. Diego had not heard of any casualties among the Spaniards as a result of the constant barrage. His men were far to the north of the siege works and well out of range. The cannon fire directed against those conducting the siege produced smoke, noise, smell and little else. The Spaniards were meticulously, relentlessly moving naval guns into prepared positions and advancing their trench works toward the fort. Two sappers had been killed accidentally when the tree they were felling pitched sideways from the stump and hit them. Those had been the only Spanish casualties during the siege – thus far.

The guns at the fort would fall silent every day about sundown and resume the cannonade at first light. Diego had witnessed Bouligny's return to the palisade gate at the end of Royal Street two nights running. It was said he and Captain Durnford would supper together to discuss the military situation and pursue a peaceful resolution. A safe conduct had even been arranged for two British farmers to quit the fort and return to their farms under a pledge not to take arms against the Spanish. Diego was certain the presence of Marcelite / Lady Smythe as translator was the true reason for the colonel's enthusiasm for diplomacy.

On the night of the fourth day, Martin and Búho returned to the tavern from the signal tower with a prisoner in tow. Martin forced the blindfolded man to kneel facing a corner while *Madame* Trapenier woke Diego.

"Who do you have here?" Diego asked as he came from the temporary guard room buttoning his trousers. He had been an hour into his usual nightly three hours of sleep and looked it.

"This *tonto* came across the mouth of the Mobile River swimming. Hiding between two logs, *Primero*," Martin explained. "I saw him go to ground. He hid under a bush and pulled leaves up to cover himself. So I whispered down to Búho to run to the trail junction, get Quintero and go dig him out. I used hand signals to put him right on top of the man."

Búho picked up the story. "He came out speaking English. I pointed my bayonet at his belly, and he found some Spanish. He had this hidden in the bushes with him." Búho tossed a leather pouch on the table in front of Diego. "Says *'no sé'* when I ask him what it is. Says it is not his, just happened to be there. It has papers in it – there are writings."

Diego was about to ask what was written, but he remembered neither man could read. Diego pulled out the papers. He could see the seal was broken and unfolded the documents. There were two papers, both in English, a language Diego could not read. He had to work to read Spanish, struggle mightily to read French, but English eluded him completely. He was beginning to understand English, a little, when spoken through conversations with the Americans who had joined in the invasion.

He pulled his short sword from its scabbard. The prisoner's back stiffened noticeably at the rasping sound of steel on the brass mouth of the leather scabbard. Diego put the tip of the sword to the back of the prisoner's neck.

"What is your name?" he said in his broken English. The prisoner poured forth a continuous stream of English, some of which Diego actually managed to understand.

The man claimed to be Peter Ocala. Diego recognized the name "Ocala." He remembered it as a tribal or place name. Peter would not be the first Englishman in the Floridas to adopt a tribal name. He looked the part of a woodsman. He wore a dirty and aged deerskin jerkin with a filthy, ragged cotton shirt, leather gaiters, knit cap and moccasins.

"Martin, you and Búho bring Mister Ocala to the back door and wait for me to join you. We are going to bring him and his pouch to the farmhouse."

⁓

Diego and his men waited on the porch of the farmhouse. As soon as it was announced that they had a prisoner with a message pouch, Ocala and the leather purse were taken from them and escorted into Gálvez's office. They were ordered to remain on the porch until called.

It was nearing midnight when Bouligny rode up fresh from his dinner with the British Commander. The officers would swap lies, in the most polite terms, about the size and morale of their respective forces, the likelihood of reinforcement and the abundance of supplies each possessed. Bouligny climbed the steps to the porch unsteadily, the result of too much wine.

The brace of guards at the door to the farmhouse snapped to attention. One dropped his salute to open the door for the Colonel. Diego called his men to attention and held his salute. Bouligny gained the porch and seemed surprised to see the three infantrymen.

"Good evening, sir," Diego said. He waited until Bouligny returned his salute. "Did the Colonel enjoy his evening?"

"None of your business, sergeant. What are you doing here?"

"We await the general's pleasure, sir."

"Did he call you here?"

"No, sir."

Bouligny snorted and went into the farmhouse. The guard closed the door behind him and looked at Diego. "I do not think the colonel likes you, *Primero*," he said.

Diego shrugged.

The door opened and Renaldo, Gálvez's personal clerk, appeared.

"Sergeant deMelilla, have your men stay here and follow me, please."

Diego complied, following Renaldo down a hallway almost at a trot. The clerk opened the door to a bedroom that served as Gálvez's office. Bouligny and a young ensign were seated at a table with Gálvez. The table was covered with maps and the papers taken from Ocala.

"Come in, sergeant," Gálvez was beaming. "You know Colonel Bouligny, of course. May I introduce you to Ensign Josef Castro y Tours of the Havana Grenadiers?"

Ensign Castro half rose out of his chair, uncertain of the protocol concerning introduction to an enlisted man.

"Ensign, Sergeant deMelilla here will guide you and your thirty grenadiers to a tavern on Royal Street. Sergeant deMelilla will familiarize you with the picket, scouting and guard duties of *La Cuchilla*. Sergeant, once the grenadiers have taken over from *La Cuchilla*, you will move your people to the bay and be taken aboard a small schooner, you will be taken up the Tensaw to the swamp road. Position yourself across the road or whatever position you think wise, and prepare to block reinforcements coming from Pensacola using the swamp trail. Send one of your men to get that militia galloper, what is his name? Barbeaux? He will be assigned to you as well. Bring whatever you think wise. The reinforcements must be blocked. Understand? Not slowed – blocked."

"Yes, General," Diego looked down at the map. "I will need a small barge, sir, for the gun and several dugouts. We will place barge and gun here, on the west bank of the Tensaw. When the *godums* appear, sir, we will give them ball and grape until they bring their own guns up. The men will pull the barge, gun and all, along the flooded trail. Then we will fall back to here and give them more as they cross the Tensaw. There will be many small streams to cross, so barge and dugouts alike will ferry us across deep water and act as sleds for our gear when we tow them across the swamp." Diego could not imagine any infantry, forced into column by the narrow trail, maintaining the advance with ball and grape racking them fore to aft. "We will block them, sir."

"Scout east of the Tensaw and send word when the reinforcements appear. We have heard from several sources and confirmed by the documents your men captured with that Englishman. Pensacola is sending two regiments to Fort Charlotte by way of *Lokcho*. See Renaldo. He will tell you where you can get a small barge. Ensign Castro will accompany you back to the tavern on Royal Street."

◦〜◦

It was nearly two in the morning when Diego and his men returned to the tavern. Ensign Castro inspected the tavern and promised to return with his men by noon the next day to begin the task of taking over picket duty. Until then, guards had to be rotated and all other duties had to be conducted without interruption.

Martin and Búho wasted little time getting to sleep. Diego sat alone at one of the tables in the main room, a small lamp flickering on the top of a barrel near the entrance to the storeroom. He was about to rise and draw himself a tankard of ale when *Madame* Trapenier swooped in carrying a tray with a wedge of cheese, a bottle of wine and two cups.

"I thought you would like some wine for a change, *Primero*," she said as she placed the tray on the table.

"Cheese! Have you been hoarding cheese all this time, *Madame?*"

"No, *Primero*. The wine and cheese have just arrived."

"Arrived? From where?"

"I have my secret supply, *Primero*. Now do you want this or no?"

"Join me, *Madame*."

Trapenier wiped her hands on her apron and looked about the room. "Have all the soldiers gone to sleep?"

"Those not posted have, those on post had better not."

She leaned close to Diego and whispered. "*Primero*, you should take this tray next door. You will be able to enjoy your food and drink without interruption."

"There is nothing here that is an interruption." He studied her face. Her expression was unreadable.

"Go next door," she pointed toward the fort. "There is a light on. Go and do not question me so."

This is most strange. Diego shrugged. "If it pleases you, I will go. Send for me if I am needed."

Madame Trapenier waddled over to a side door and opened it. Diego picked up the tray and went through the door into a narrow alley. The neighbor building had been vacant all during Diego's stay at the tavern. Now, there was a light showing in the widow and through the half-open doorway into the alley. He pushed the door open with his foot.

There was a table and several chairs in the center of the room and a mattress against one wall. A wooden candle-keep holding a single, burning candle hung above the table. He placed the tray on the table and took a chair facing the door to the alley. *Except for the lack of snoring from the back room, this is not much different than the tavern. I wonder –.*

There was a creaking sound to his left. Diego jumped to his feet, pulled his short sword and positioned the table between him and the origin of the sound. He watched as an interior door slowly opened. He caught a sweet scent he recognized as *Mademoiselle* Marcelite Gaudet de la Arceneaux stepped into the room.

"I did not intend to startle you, Diego." Her voice was soft, gentle. Her French, as always, was perfect. "*Madame* Trapenier should have told you what to expect."

"I may not have come, Lady Smythe." Diego said, using his heavily accented English.

"We should use Spanish, so there will be no misunderstanding," Marcelite switched to her perfect Castilian. "I am not Lady Smythe. I do not think there is a Lady Smythe. The British Captain is very gullible. A few smiles and he is most malleable."

I know a Spanish sergeant who is no better. "Are you Marcelite Gaudet, or is she also a creation to fool a simple herder of goats?"

"You are not a simple man, Diego. I think you are most complex and intriguing." She moved around the table and pushed the point of Diego's sword aside. "I am Marcelite Gaudet, but I am not from White River Plantation."

"There is no White River Plantation."

"I think not."

"Who are you? Where are you from? For whom do you spy?"

"I told you. My name is Marcelite Gaudet. Do you not believe me?"

"Our brief encounter earlier this year has given me reason to doubt everything you say."

"You wound me!"

She was standing close to Diego now and her scent filled his nostrils. He was suddenly very conscious of his ragged condition. His vest was stained with dirt and sweat. His chin had a week's growth of beard. His hair, pulled into a tight ponytail, was sprinkled with dead leaves and twigs. Months in the field had reduced his shirt to a collection of assorted holes and his gaiters were caked with mud to the knees.

She was staring up at him in the wavering candlelight. Her wide brown eyes flickered with reflected yellow, almost gold, sparkles and he felt his knees go weak.

"You have not answered all of my questions."

"I am from Toulon. I must confess that I have never been to Louisiana."

"And for whom do you spy?"

"I am not a British spy. If I were, would I have urged you to keep my secret? Would I be so grateful to you for keeping my secret? I am in your debt. How should I repay you, *Monsieur* Sergeant?"

Diego did not realize Marcelite had not completely answered his last question.

❧

"*Primero, Primero!*"

Diego recognized *Madame* Trapenier's voice. She was shouting as she scurried across the narrow alley, dreary with predawn light.

"*Dépêchez-vous!* (hurry) An officer is here!"

Diego sat up on the mattress, groggy and disoriented. Marcelite was gone.

"Yes. I hear you. Tell him I am coming!"

Diego struggled to his feet, dressed and crossed to the tavern. Pook, Plata and Martin were waiting along with Ensign Castro.

"Sergeant, we are here to take the guard," Castro said. The young officer's face did not conceal his disgust at Diego's condition. It would be full light in a few minutes. A sergeant should be up, dressed and preparing for the day before the sun appears over the horizon. General Gálvez had bragged that deMelilla was the finest sergeant in His Most Catholic Majesty's service. The disheveled, groggy, half dressed man he saw made him wonder.

"Yes, sir. We will begin changing of the guard immediately." Diego's head was spinning. There was so much to do. He struggled to remember the assignment the General had planned for *La Cuchilla*.

"Corporal Gonzales," Diego gestured toward Pook and realized the man was wearing his uniform coat with the single blue epaulet of a corporal. Plata and Martin were also dressed in their full uniforms. The white coats with blue cuffs and collars had been stored away for months. The men wore much less formal, and more suitable, clothing during their service in the field. The sight of men in proper uniforms made Diego fell even more disheveled. "Corporal Gonzales will bring your first relief to their posts, explain their duties and return with my people. I will have my people here collect their traps and form ranks in the street behind this building."

"That has already been done, *Primero*, as you ordered last night before you retired," Pook said.

Diego was conscious of men moving about in the storeroom converted to sleeping quarters.

"My men – settling in, sergeant," Castor said when Diego glanced toward the open doorway.

"Good. With your permission, sir, Corporal Gonzales with bring the eight men required for the pickets to their posts now."

"The necessary men are already in the street behind this – place. I will bring the Corporal to them. In the meantime, sergeant, I suggest you make yourself presentable."

"Yes, sir." Diego came to attention. He could see Plata and Martin over the Ensign's shoulder. Plata was smirking and Martin looked as if he would cry for shame.

"With me, corporal," Castro said. He and Pook left through the back door.

"*Primero?*" *Madame* Trapenier emerged from a backroom with Diego's uniform and clean trousers, shirt, vest and gaiters. "I have some ham for you and a morning cup of ale. After you change, give me your dirty clothes and I will add them to the wash."

"Thank you, *Madame*." Humiliation overwhelmed him. He turned to Plata and Martin. "Get out. Join the ranks now and send Quintero in." Martin rushed out, happy to be elsewhere. Plata walked behind Martin, paused at the door and looked back at Diego with a bemused expression before he too ducked out.

I will deal with you later, Plata Perez. Diego was angry with himself. Plata would fill every ear with tales of this disgraceful morning.

"*Madame* Trapenier, why did you not wake me earlier?"

"I am not a soldier, *Primero,*" she said as she returned to the backroom.

Quintero ducked into the room. He was in his full uniform as well. "You sent for me, *Primero?*"

"Yes. See that the men are fed and given some private time. I will be out in a moment. The rest of the men will be back from their posts in an hour. Have all of their gear here collected and ready to go. We are going to return to the farmhouse and prepare for the move to the swamp road."

Quintero hesitated.

"That is all. Any questions?"

"No questions, *Primero.*"

"Then go. See to it."

"*Sí, Primero.*" Quintero ducked out. Quintero would be promoted to second corporal before they departed for the Tensaw River, might as well introduce him to responsibilities now.

Finally Diego was alone with his shame. This was a poor beginning to a new mission. Ensign Castro had roused Diego from his bed, unprepared and groggy after a night of what? Carousing with a known spy? He had assigned Plata to the penalty platoon for less. There will be time for self-evaluation later. He stripped off his old clothes and dressed in the clean uniform. When he piled the bundle of worn and dirty garments on the table he caught the scent of Marcelite's flowery perfume among the stench of a week's hard use.

Diego, feeling much more presentable, stepped into the street behind the tavern where rows of equipment marked where the men would form ranks out of sight of the fort. Quintero had directed the men to ground their backpacks and bedrolls in three neat ranks before reporting to the breakfast campfire. After the morning meal and Pook had returned with the eight men from the last watch, he would call for *La Cuchilla* to recover their gear, shrug into backpacks, shoulder their bedrolls and form ranks. They would march, in good order, past the rest of the army to the General's headquarters – the farmhouse. There they would organize for the task of blocking a British relief column.

Moving a military force, even one as small as *La Cuchilla*, required planning and preparation. Weapons, equipment, supplies and a hundred other details had to be considered. Evaluations needed to be reviewed and decisions made.

∽

Diego rode in the bow of the small barge as his men poled it up the Tensaw River from the north end of Mobile Bay. A sloop of war was just ahead; her guns run out and charged with grape. If there were British along the east bank of the river, they did not challenge the little flotilla. Two dugouts were towed behind the sloop. The banks of the river on the east and west were a continuous and seemingly impenetrable cypress swamp bordering the river for the ten miles or so they had traveled from the bay. Although they must have been ten miles or more northeast of Fort Charlotte, they could hear the constant rumble of cannon fire.

Two Choctaw scouts on the sloop must have identified a change in the landscape, for they notified the captain, boarded the dugouts and were cast free. They paddled toward the west bank, waving for the barge to follow. The sloop dropped her sails and, using her sweeps, came about in the river. Before Diego had reached the bank where the scouts waited, the sloop was under full sail and speeding south. The barge slid into the edge of the swamp, the bottom only slightly brushing the mud.

The men had stripped off their uniform coats and stored them, along with their weapons and accoutrements, on raised platforms on the barge. As the barge drifted into the swamp, Diego could see a cleared, winding path heading west. Several men went over the side and hauled the barge further into the swamp by hand. If the water did not fall, ten men could pull the barge along the cleared path through the swamp. If the water fell a foot or more, twenty men would be needed.

Satisfied that the Spaniards were correctly positioned, the Choctaw and four American woodsmen boarded the dugouts and crossed to the east side of the Tensaw. They were to be the pickets assigned to detect the British should the predicted reinforcements attempt to use the swamp trail.

Gabriella, tended by her five militia artillerymen, was mounted in the barge, her muzzle pointing east. All others, including Diego, went into the swamp. Lines were prepared for the time the barge needed to be moved west. There were small mounds barely above the water just north of the anchored barge. Diego had the men clear an area where they could build fires and dry their clothes. It could be days before the reinforcements attempted to cross the Tensaw, maybe never. If the assault on Fort Charlotte succeeded before the British attempted the crossing, *La Cuchilla* would simply withdraw.

By nightfall all had dried their clothes, cleaned their equipment, fed themselves and, lacking tents, built temporary shelters of palm fronds and ground cloths stretched over saplings. Fires were extinguished and watchers set, alert for returning pickets from the east side of the river. The persistent background grumble of cannon fire from the distant fort ceased. Diego was not satisfied to simply wait and had sent scouts up and down stream. These men returned after sundown and reported no activity upstream.

The night was cool, yet mosquitoes appeared in great swarms. Diego showed the men how to smear their face and hands with mud which gave some protection against the insects. Thankfully, two hours after sundown, the air cooled considerably and the mosquitoes retreated.

Plata had covered the front of his over-sized lean-to with a blanket masking the light from a single candle that burned within. He had planted his bayonet in the soft soil and placed a candle in the barrel mount, a soldier's candle stick. So many men used their bayonets this way the regimental slang for bayonet was *candelero* (candlestick).

Five men huddled in a circle gambling, casting cards onto another blanket on the ground. Plata always carried a *baraja*, a deck of cards. The deck consisted of forty cards divided into four suits of ten cards. They played the game called "*pocos pasos*" (few steps). In the game, each player was dealt four cards. A round of bets would be made. Each player, except those who had dropped out, was allowed to discard up to two cards and would be dealt replacements. The remaining players would place additional bets or drop out until, step by step, a large sum of money lay at risk. The soldiers shortened the name of the game to "*poco*." Diego was certain Plata had created the game – and marked the cards.

Diego moved to the northern end of the small mound and found a suitable pair of cypress saplings. He tied a line between the trees, tied two corners of a blanket to the line and anchored the others creating a lean-to, the open end facing east toward the river. He was exhausted, as if he had not slept in a week. It had taken two days to prepare for the move to this place and Diego, conscious of his condition when Ensign Castro came to the tavern, had not slept. He knew Castro had made a report to Gálvez and it seemed as if all eyes were on him as he went about the business of preparing his men.

He lay on the ground and closed his eyes. The distant rumble of guns from Fort Charlotte fell silent, as they did every night. He could hear the voices of the men playing *poco* in Plata's lean-to. "Otra vez!" Plata shouted. *Another win with his marked deck.*

CHAPTER *11*

ézu looked up at Diego. She stood, separated from the circle of students sitting on the gun deck practicing their letters, and walked up to him. Behind Mézu, he could see their children Pedro and little Maria, writing on a slate, their heads touching. Isabella was there as well, standing behind the children, watching over them. Water dripped from Isabella's hair and nightshirt. She held a lance, a traditional Canarian *magado*, in her right hand.

"Diego deMelilla," Mézu said. "See how Isabella is watching over our children? You must help her, Diego. She will need your help."

He tried to wrap his arms around her, but he could not reach her.

Diego opened his eyes. He could see the edges of the canvas lean-to dripping with morning dew. *I was dreaming. Why did she not call me husband?* Before, whenever he had dreamt of Mézu she had always called him "*marido* (husband)." A sudden feeling of guilt washed over him. Mézu – *Doña* Maria Artiles y Ventomo – no longer claimed him as her husband. Was it because he had been unfaithful? Can a man be unfaithful to a ghost?

He rolled out of the lean-to and stood. He could see the guards posted at the edge of the small island. Someone was beginning a breakfast fire and men were beginning to stir. Plata's makeshift gambling tent was quiet. He walked to the edge of the islands and relieved himself. The air was cold and a mist drifted above the waters of the Tensaw River. He returned to his lean-to, belted on his sword and disassembled the lean-to into a bed-roll which he draped over one shoulder. He had armed himself with a sergeant's weapon, an *espontoon*, the short lance which served as a mark of rank. Sergeants were expected to direct their men in battle and not be distracted by having to load and fire a musket. The *espontoon* was very similar to the Canarian *magado*, a weapon Diego had been trained to use since childhood.

The sky across the Tensaw was turning from black to gray when the watch called out that something was coming. All eyes stared at the opening in the swamp where the trail entered the river. Two groups of men were splashing through the mud pushing flat, light dugouts called *pirogues* by the Choctaw, between them. Specifically designed for the shallow waters of the swamp, *pirogues* were ridden like boats when the water was inches deep and pushed as sleds, loaded with gear, when the water turned into mud.

The Choctaw and Americans that had been sent to watch the trail were returning. They paused at the river's edge just long enough to climb in their *pirogues* and begin paddling furiously to cross the river. The distant rumble of cannon fire at Fort Charlotte resumed.

"To arms!" Diego yelled. He looked over to the barge to see Barbeaux and his gunners preparing the brass gun. They had draped a canvas screen across poles to hide the cannon from the view of anyone across the river.

"Gabriella is shy," Barbeaux had said with a wink. "She will stay behind the curtain until she is ready to dance."

Pook came to Diego's elbow. "Should I have the men load, *Primero?*"

"No. Fix bayonets. We will have Gabriella begin the dance."

The Tensaw River was a good three hundred yards across. Muskets were ineffective at such a range. If they ever closed with the enemy in the swamp, muskets would be useless after one volley. Muskets cannot be reloaded in knee-deep water. If it came to close work, it would be cold steel – bayonets, swords and knives.

The *pirogues* reached the west bank of the Tensaw. The men in both *pirogues* jumped out and began to pull the boats inland along the flooded trail. One of the Choctaw separated from the others and splashed up to Diego. He spoke in trade-talk Choctaw.

"*Hika Nitah* (Flying Bear)," the Choctaw all used the name Diego was given by a young Indian girl who had dreamt of Diego in the high mountains of Gran Canaria, a girl who had never seen a mountain. "The redcoats are many. Twenty on horse, Twenty times one hundred on foot. Seven wagons. Five big, black cannons. Twelve wagons and they pull five big skiffs. We go west, to middle river then down to the bay to tell Captain Riaño."

"Go. We will deal with what is coming."

The Choctaw returned to his companions. He and the other Indian began pulling a *pirogue* along the flooded trail. The two Americans pushed their *pirogue* to the barge and climbed aboard. Now that they were able to stand without water to their knees, they began to load their long rifles. The rifles, and Gabriella, had the range to reach across the Tensaw to the east bank.

That was the plan. Diego would harass the British westward march as much as possible. At first contact, messages would be sent back to the Spanish ships on the bay. Riaño would send one of his little sloops up the middle river as a picket. If the British quickly pushed past *La Cuchilla*, Gálvez would need to change his plans. If Diego's people were forced west, the sloop would provide cover for them as they crossed the middle river, and provided an additional obstacle for the British.

Twenty horsemen meant twenty officers. Ten to fifteen commanding the infantry and the rest were likely artillery officers. The boats were intended to serve as ferries for the river crossings. Wagons, cannons, two thousand men and all their equipment, it would take a full day of hard work to cross just one of the several parallel streams that flowed between the east bank of the Tensaw and the west bank of the Mobile, if they were unopposed.

The British lead scouts splashed into view. When they saw the Spanish infantry drawn on the small strip of bank in a battle line with fixed bayonets, they crouched down and scattered into the trees. The scouts would be sending word back to the column now. General Campbell, or whoever was leading the relief force, would soon know the crossing of the Tensaw was going to be opposed.

"The question is," Diego mused as he stood beside Pook, "will he bring his cannon up, take the time to place the guns and drive us off this little spit of land? Or will he place his men in skiffs and rush across?"

"Look!" Pook said unnecessarily as he gestured to the east. Boats, deep, V-bottomed skiffs of the type used to carry men and supplies to and from ships in the bay, were coming. Seemingly moving on their own, several boats came in a column along the center of the swamp trail. As they grew closer, Diego could see the men hauling on the gunnels which were head-high to the struggling infantrymen. Campbell would have been wise to build flat, small barges like the one that held Gabriella. The skiffs, designed for an open bay or the sea, dug into the mud and resisted the efforts of the men struggling to move the boats forward.

"He has decided to rush us, Pook." The tactic was obvious, direct and effective. The British would line the skiffs along the bank, out of musket range. Each boat would load a complement of rowers and infantry. Together, all of the boats would set off for the Spanish position. They would suffer one, maybe two, volleys and then overwhelm the score of men in ragged white uniforms with a red tide of sixty or more.

Diego turned toward the barge and raised his voice. "You may begin when you are ready, Corporal Barbeaux."

The canvas curtain dropped and the little brass cannon roared, sending out a shaft of flame and a solid iron ball across the river. The British skiffs had formed a line along the narrowly cleared trail through the swamp. Gabriella's ball splashed a hundred yards short of the lead boat, skipped over it and plowed into the second, sending splitters high into the air. Every redcoat abandoned the skiffs and broke for the trees. Barbeaux sent another ball as the British filtered into the trees. It grazed off the third boat, caving in its starboard side.

"Pook, get ready to move," Diego said calmly. "Have the men put their weapons in the barge and prepare to haul away."

One of the Americans fired his rifle and a redcoat who had edged up to the river spun back into the trees. The men in the barge were laughing and congratulating the marksman, when Pook whispered, "The *godums* are up to something."

Far to the east, where the trail curved out of the trees a cluster of men came into view laboring away around a squat, black object. They were well beyond the range of Barbeaux's little four-pounder in the barge.

"He is bringing his cannons into action. Let us pray he is slow to mount them," Diego said. "We are moving west, now."

Several heaves were required before the barge broke free and began to slide. Everyone was in the water pulling on ropes or gunnels. The Americans pulled the remaining *pirogue* along, pausing occasionally to climb in the boat, reload and fire their rifles. Their efforts had little effect except to discourage the redcoats from returning to their skiffs. Four hundred yards west of the Tensaw, the trail twisted to the south. If they made the turn before the British managed to mount their cannons, they would be hidden by the thick cypress forest.

Then it would be a race. The redcoats would rush to get their boats to the river and cross a few hundred infantry in pursuit. *La Cuchilla* would have to make one mile to the middle river, cross it and set Gabriella on the west side ready to fire ball and grape. If the redcoats caught them before the middle river, they would be overwhelmed.

The lead men on the tow ropes were at the turn when the swamp not twenty yards north of Diego erupted, spewing up mud, splinters and water. The sound of the big gun's blast followed shortly, drowning out the constant rumble from Fort Charlotte.

"She's a twenty-pounder," Barbeaux muttered.

"Pull away!" Diego urged unnecessarily. Every man was pulling with all of his strength and looking back at the distant guns, watching for the telltale flash of next shot. *How many guns did the godums mount?*

A full minute passed and there was a puff of smoke at the east end of the trail.

"Pull, we are nearly there!" *They have mounted only one gun! We might make it.*

Diego thought he could see the ball pass over their heads and smash into the tree tops beyond them. They had another minute.

"*Primero*, I can see a mast!" Martin shouted back from his lead position on a tow line.

One of Riaño's river schooners had come up the middle river to meet them. Diego hoped the schooner mounted enough guns and grape shot to hold off the infantry that was certainly coming after them.

Those pulling the far end of the tow line were now past the slight turn in the trail and out of sight of the British cannon. Only the men pushing the barge or guiding the leading edge over or around stumps were still exposed to the far gun. Diego watched as another burst of smoke erupted at the head of the trail. The ball was on its way. Men pushed with renewed energy in the hopes they would be out of harm's way before the solid iron, twelve pound ball arrived.

Diego thought he could see a speck against the morning sky. It rose slowly and then fell a hundred yards up the muddy track toward the British. The swampy trail erupted, throwing mud and bits of wood aside, left and right in a wide fan. The image implanted in Diego's mind was one of an angel lifting her wings to fly. Then there was an angry whooshing sound and he felt the air beside his head pulse as if someone had flipped a lady's fan next to his cheek.

A tree to the right of their path split apart. Splinters shot down into the swamp and the soft, light green spring leaves of the cypress rained down onto the barge.

"A close one, that, *Primero!*" Plata said. He was hunkered down next to the barge, pushing up and forward with such effort the veins stood out on his neck like purple strands of yarn.

"We have a minute before the next shot," Diego said. After every shot, the cannon recoiled violently, pulling the carriage back and out of line. The massive combination of wood and iron had to be hauled back into position, and the tube reloaded and aimed before it could be fired again. Apparently, the British had not had time to set aiming stakes, for there was no pattern of improvement in the fall of their shots.

Diego watched as the redcoats pulled their remaining skiffs to the bank of the Tensaw River and clambered aboard. He tried to count how many were making the crossing. Twenty went into one of the skiffs and there were five skiffs in the river as well as several more being pulled up the trail. One hundred British would be across the river soon and racing toward them, unimpeded. He worked over the sequence in his mind. How long would it take for the British to cross the Tensaw, organize themselves after climbing out of the skiffs, and close on the barge. He would have to halt the barge, order his men aboard to recover and load their muskets. Barbeaux would load Gabriella with canister and all had to be ready to fire into the British ranks, if the British advanced in ranks. He did not know what he would do if they dispersed into the cypress forest and descended on the barge from the left and right in a swarm.

The barge suddenly surged forward. Diego almost fell, but managed to hold himself up. The water in the trail was noticeably deeper here and the barge was floating. It was being pulled along at such a pace the men pushing at the gunnels had to jog to keep up. In moments the turn was attained and Diego could no longer see the distant mound where the British cannon was mounted. Another shot skipped by far to the right followed by a deep boom.

"*Primero*, climb into the barge. The sailors are towing,"

It was Martin calling to him. A ship load of sailors, expert and well accustomed to hauling on a line, were now pulling the barge to the ship anchored at the edge of the Middle River.

We may make it. "Everyone onto the barge!" Diego shouted.

The men who had been pushing on the barge clambered aboard. Everyone was dripping water and mud from head to foot. Barbeaux urged his men to Gabriella and ordered them to strip, lest their water soaked clothes wet the powder. The five militiamen, naked to the waist and steaming in the cool morning air, quickly charged the cannon with grapeshot and positioned her toward the bend in the trail. Diego and three infantry men were in the barge as well. The rest of the men had been hauling on the long towropes. If the British appeared now, only four would be available to repel boarders.

"Recover your muskets," Diego said as he selected one for himself. "Lock and load, fix bayonets."

"*Primero*, let us load the other muskets as well," Plata said. There were twenty muskets in the barge.

"Good man, Plata! Load them all and keep them handy." *I should have thought of that.*

Barbeaux looked back to Diego from his position behind Gabriella. He was jamming a brace of pistols into his belt. "She is ready, *Primero*."

Diego nodded. With him were Plata, a good man in a fight, along with Mina and Tiritar. Each man held a bayonet-tipped musket and had four or five loaded muskets leaning on the gunnels nearby. They were as ready as they would be.

"*Primero!*"

The shout was so close it startled Diego.

It was Pook. "The captain says he will have the barge pulled to the stern of the ship. You cover his guns where you are."

They were alongside of the ship in the river! *When did that happen?* He had been so intent upon preparing for the British he had simply forgot they were being hauled to the river. Sailors were fending the barge away from the ship with long poles while others pulled it toward the stern. Diego could see his men collapsed on the ship's deck behind the sailors. They appeared to be piles of muddy, soaked rags.

The ship was the *Valenzuela,* Riaño's little galiot. She carried ten guns, five to a side, six pounders, and seventy sailors. Her deck rode only four feet above the water line, but she had a yard-high gunnel that warded off heavy seas. Her cannons had been run-out through doors in the gunnel and the barrels were chest-high to Diego as the barge was guided to the stern of the *Valenzuela.*

Riaño and Pook were standing at the stern as Diego and his people were pulled aboard. Barbeaux requested he and his artillery men remain on the barge and positioned to add Gabriella's fire to the broadside. Diego reflected that they, in maritime terms, were prepared to send thirty-three pounds of shot toward the enemy.

The *Valenzuela* had not anchored in the Middle River. She had lines attached to trees on the east and west banks. Riaño called them "spring lines," In such a way the ship could be moved around by hauling in or playing out select lines. Riaño barked a series of orders and the *Valenzuela* moved away from the bank a dozen yards. She could now be warped to bring her broadside onto any portion of the shore for a hundred yards up or down stream.

"Welcome aboard, Sergeant deMelilla," Riaño said as he returned Diego's salute. "What can we expect from our friends to the east?"

"A hundred infantry are behind us, sir. The British have heavy guns, but it would require two days to bring such guns forward." *And another two days to mount the guns under the constant fire of five six-pounders and one four-pounder.* Diego glanced toward the clumps of panting men scattered along the deck. Martin was at the river-side gunnel, vomiting into the river.

Riaño noticed his glance. "See to your men, *Primero.* We will confer in a moment."

"Yes, sir. Thank you, sir." Diego turned to Pook. "How have the men faired?"

"They are exhausted, wet, covered in mud and ready to fight, *Primero*."

"Plata, get back onto the barge and hand up the weapons to Mina and Tiritar. After the weapons, put the bundles of coats aboard." The men had taken off their heavy uniform coats and tossed them into the barge before the mad dash west began. Those dry coats would now be most welcomed on this chilly early March day. "Pook, see to it that the weapons and cartridge boxes are distributed to the men. The muskets have been loaded."

Diego walked to each cluster of his soldiers as the weapons were being distributed. He ordered them to strip to the waist and take off their shoes. He had them pull on their dry uniform coats, cartridge boxes and bayonet carriages. As each man dressed and equipped himself, he joined his comrades in three ranks on the deck. A motley force began to form before Diego's eyes. Soldiers dressed in long, blue cuffed and collared wool uniform coats, wet, muddy trousers covered by filthy gaiters, formed neat ranks. Each man stood in a growing puddle of water at his feet. Their bare chests visible under the uniform coats were crisscrossed with whitewashed two inch-wide leather straps holding a cartridge box on the right hip and a bayonet sheathed on the left. Many had a sword belted to their waist.

"Pook, take a dozen men and go to the foredeck. Have the men rest. Quintero, you and the rest of the men come with me to the stern. Be ready to repel boarders, should the British attempt to take the ship."

Diego was now confident they were safe. The hundred that pursued were on foot. If they arrived at the bank, they could not cross the dozen yards of river to reach the ship. They had no cannons with them, nothing but muskets and swords. Both were equally impotent weapons for the situation they would be in.

A shot barked from the foredeck. Diego looked across ranks of sailors hunched over their guns to see one of his American scouts begin the arduous task of reloading his rifle. He could hear men murmuring that a redcoat had appeared and the *Kentuckiano* shot him. There was debate concerning if the *godum* was hit or merely forced back into the trees.

They waited. Two uneventful hours passed. Except for the one redcoat, driven off or killed by a rifle shot, nothing appeared from the swamp to the east. Diego had his men stand down in shifts to eat, sleep and attempt to dry their clothes.

Riaño walked to Diego and sent for the Choctaw scouts to join them.

"What say you, *Primero*. Where are the *godums?*"

"They cannot rush us, sir. I watched them cross the Tensaw, they had no cannon and they left their skiffs in the river to cross the rest of their force. They will have to send for their boats and, if they launch upstream of us, they could try to take the ship."

"I would warp her and send several broadsides onto the boats clustered in the river. Skiffs can take a ship if they can disperse and attack from several directions. It would take days to bring boats across the swamp, weeks to bring cannon."

"Sir, shall I ask our scouts to go east and see if they can tell what the British are about? It is not wise to guess at what an enemy is doing. It is wise to know before acting."

Diego instructed the Choctaw scouts in "trade-talk" to take their *pirogues* and go east to see what the British were doing. The Indians had clearly expected such a mission. They climbed into their boats and paddled east. They did not go directly up the muddy trail, but filtered into the cypress forest and disappeared.

Riaño had several of his sailors launch the ship's jolly boat and row up river inspecting the shoreline and listening for activity in the thick cypress stands along the bank. The boat went up river for two miles and down river for another two. Nothing was reported seen or heard out of the ordinary.

The sun was setting when two *pirogues* materialized from the trees. The Choctaw paddled side by side laughing and chatting as they worked their way to the ship. Riaño and Diego met them at the rail as they came aboard. Sailors pulled the light *pirogues* onto the deck and lashed the little boats beside the jolly boat, which had been returned to its chocks. The two Americans, the *Kentuckianos*, joined the group on the chance that a translator was required, though one of the Choctaw, Josef, had a good command of Spanish.

Josef directed his report to Diego in Spanish, though every man clustered about could hear, "*Hika Nitah*, the British have withdrawn. We went across the Tensaw and watched as they removed the cannon and hauled it east on an ox sled. They left three broken skiffs on the trail. They did not leave a rear guard. I do not think they will come this way."

Diego turned to Riaño. "They were not well equipped to come this way even if we were not here to meet them, sir. They had big skiffs, not flat bottom barges. They had horses, and big siege guns, not mobile field pieces. Had they managed to reach the middle passage, they never would have gotten out. There will be no relief coming for Fort Charlotte for many weeks."

"I think you are right, *Primero*. Let us go tell what we have learned." Riaño began to issue a stream of orders. Grape shot and powder were wormed out of the ship's guns and they were secured. Lines were released and the *Valenzuela* swung around to race downstream. The tall cypress trees blocked the moderate wind out of the east so the great sweeps were run out and sailors began to row the ship downstream, the barge carrying Gabriella in tow.

Muskets were discharged into the swamp, cleaned and stored with all of the infantry's other weapons in the jolly boat. The men stripped naked and hung their clothes from lines stretched into a spider's web across the ship. Each man wrapped his blanket around himself and searched for a place to sleep. The night was cold and the men slept well.

Around midnight the *Valenzuela* emerged into Mobile Bay. Riaño anchored about a mile into the shallow bay to wait for dawn. No need to go sailing about in the dark with a bay full of vessels of every size and description. He sent two men up into the crow's nest with a lamp and a signal log. Before the hour was done, Gálvez would know that the relief column had turned back.

Diego went to the stern where the barge rode lashed closely to the rail. Barbeaux had posted a watch while he and his men slept under a crude awning arranged over the powder stores. The watch was bailing. When first launched, the barge had leaked so profusely two men were required to bail constantly, but, just as the shipwright had advised; the seams had swollen shut as water soaked the raw wood. Only a trickle remained which the single watchman bailed more to keep busy than out of need.

The sailors had posted an ample watch, fore and aft. Satisfied that all was well, Diego did not post a night watch. Every man huddled in his blanket and slept where he could. Diego found a place near the stern with a good view of the distant shoreline and the lights of Fort Charlotte and went to sleep.

CHAPTER 12

Mézu was grinding grain at the tan stone that stood at the entrance to their home. Diego had made the house with his own hands. Built onto the entrance to a grotto under a formation of volcanic rock known as *Piedra Perro*, the house was solid, spacious and had served him, Mézu and their growing family well.

The stone on which she ground the grain had been used by countless generations of *Isleñas* working with smooth stones as pestles until a deep mortar had been worn into the rock. Pedro was on the opposite side of the stone stripping seed husks from long stalks of wheat onto the ground. He had spread a blanket to catch the seeds. Little Maria was thrashing the husks by walking across the blanket on wooden blocks held against her feet by loops of woven cords which crossed beneath the block and were held tightly in her hands.

Diego watched as his children worked intently at their chores. Even at only ten years of age, Pedro's hands were strong and he seemed to work effortlessly as the seeds fell onto the blanket. Maria carefully swept the seeds into thin layers before stepping down to crush the husks. Pedro finished stripping and waited until Maria had crushed the last of the grains. He motioned her off of the blanket. She stepped off, dropping the cords holding the blocks to her feet, and together the children lifted the blanket by the corners and began to toss the contents into the air. The wind coming around the edge of the cliff blew the chaff away as the heavier grains of wheat fell back onto the blanket. Mézu called the children to the stone and scooped fresh grains from the blanket into the stone to be ground into flour.

They were laughing as Mézu plucked bits of chaff from Maria's hair. Diego saw the swell of Mézu's belly. *That is the child she shall lose.* The laughter ceased and Mézu was standing before him, her beautiful but weathered face was turned up to him. One eye was covered with a soft leather patch, the other glistened grey and flecked with gold as she looked into his eyes.

"Our children know how to separate the grain from the chaff, Diego," she said. "It is a thing worth knowing."

ௐ

A gun sounded and Diego's eyes flew open. He was huddled in the stern, wrapped in a blanket. It required a moment for him to remember where he was – remember when it was. His dreams of Mézu were so vivid they seemed real and would always sadden him when he awoke. She had always addressed him as "husband" before. This had been the second dream in which she called him by his name.

Another gun sounded. Fort Charlotte was beginning the daily ritual of bombarding the Spanish trenches that were snaking toward her walls.

Wrapped in his blanket against the cold morning wind, Diego walked toward a line of hanging clothes and found his. The shirt and trousers were reasonably dry and his wool uniform vest was only damp. He dressed, pulling his wool uniform coat on over the vest, adding a bandana to hold his hair in place. He had lost his tricorn during the race through the swamp. He found Pook and Quintero and kicked them awake.

"Get the men up. See that they are dressed, even if their cloths are still damp. Form them up half on either side of the cabin. Pook, you take the starboard half. Quintero, you are now *Interino Cabo* (brevet corporal), take the port half. Put them to cleaning their weapons first, then their gear. Check flints and be certain their cartridges are dry. They can eat from their field rations as they work."

Diego found his haversack and retrieved a blue square of cloth, tore a strip from it and went to the port side of the low mid-cabin where Quintero was forming up a rank of a dozen men. He tied the strip of blue cloth onto the man's shoulder strap in full view of the men. No need for ceremony, all understood Quintero was now a corporal.

Barbeaux clambered over the stern rail. "Good morning, *Primero*. My men are well rested and fed, but we would like to bring Gabriella onto the ship. The barge rides too low for this open water, I think."

"I will ask the Captain," Diego said as he walked to the stern rail to see the barge. It looked tiny in the morning light. *Hard to believe we were going to fight from that little plank.* Barbeaux's gunners smiled up at Diego as they passed a bottle of wine between them. *Wine, cheese and smoked ham for breakfast. The militia did know how to make the best of what they had.*

"Ask the captain what?" Riaño had come on deck and heard Barbeaux's question. His French was heavily accented, but understandable.

"Sir, I ask that our gun be brought onto the ship. If the weather should change, that little barge will be swamped."

"Bring your men onto the ship if you wish, but we are weighing anchor now and towing you to the beach at the General's headquarters. You will all be ashore before the noon meal, and your precious Gabriella as well."

"With your permission, sir, we will stay on the barge."

Riaño shrugged in consent. "Join your men now, Corporal."

Barbeaux saluted smartly and disappeared over the stern rail.

Riaño stared at the file of disheveled soldiers cleaning weapons as they chewed their breakfast of jerked venison. "Are your men sufficiently recovered, Sergeant?"

"Sufficiently recovered for what, sir?"

"I am instructed to put you and your people ashore at the general's headquarters. He wishes to receive a report on yesterday's action directly from you. He also wishes to inspect your troops."

Inspect the troops! "Sir, my men have had a hard time of it. They are dirty and exhausted. It will be days before they will be fit to stand inspection."

"They will stand inspection this very afternoon; full battle dress and all stores as well. The General was not requesting, Sergeant."

"Understood, sir. We will stand inspection, sir."

Most of the equipment had been left at the siege staging area when they departed for the Tensaw River. Tents, kitchen equipment, axes, saws, hammers and the thousand other items that traveled in the wagon were not with them on the swamp road. The wagon carried a change of clothes, spare shoes and garrison caps. At least they would have clean clothes.

The *Valenzuela* began to drift toward the west. A sailor shouted that the anchor was free. Riaño issued a series of commands. Sailors raced about the open deck, pulling down on lines, or releasing others until, with a loud "pop," the mainsail filled and the *Valenzuela* gained speed. Riaño ordered the helm to come to port as the ship listed to the starboard and raced south. Fort Charlotte, its garrison accustomed the Spanish ships passing in the bay, made no effort to engage.

A fleet of ships, large and small, marked the location of Gálvez's headquarters. Barges, skiffs and packet boats moved to and from the beach and about the taller ships. The munitions and supplies to sustain and execute the siege could be seen stockpiled about the land well inland of the beach.

Riaño had all sails lowered and coasted under bare poles while Diego and his men were transferred to skiffs. A line was tossed from Gabriella's barge to one of the skiffs and the militiamen rode ashore under tow. Barbeaux sat on the cannon's carriage smoking a white clay pipe as if on holiday. Two of *La Cuchilla* had become very ill overnight. The exertions of the previous day combined with exposure had overpowered them. They would stay on the *Valenzuela* and be transferred to a hospital ship anchored in the bay.

The skiffs skidded to the beach and listed to one side as men stepped into the knee-deep water. Several hauled on the line to the barge and pulled it onto the shore. The militiamen stepped out without wetting their shoes.

One jogged off to find Grenouille and bring the horse and caisson to the beach so Gabriella could be limbered up and drawn properly.

Diego waded onto the beach wondering if he would ever be dry again. A dragoon rode up, reined his horse to a skittering stop. Diego did not recognize the uniform. *One of the mounted companies from Veracruz, perhaps.*

"Are you *Sargento Primero* deMelilla?"

"I am."

"The General wants to see you now. Follow me." The man wheeled his horse around and trotted inland, forcing Diego to jog in order to keep up. The rider did not turn toward the farmhouse, but veered toward one of the heavily worn trails leading north to the siege trenches. Diego could see a cluster of mounted officers ahead outlined against the almost constant screen of gun smoke that blew across the siege works from Fort Charlotte's ineffectual fire. He recognized Gálvez when the General separated from his entourage.

Diego's escort arrived first, saluted and said, "Sergeant deMelilla, as you ordered, sir."

"Excellent! But did you make the man run all the way from the beach?" Gálvez gave the young dragoon a stern glare.

"Sorry, sir. Thought you wanted him right away, sir."

"You are dismissed." Gálvez dismounted as Diego jogged up, snapped to attention, held a salute, his eyes fixed at some distant point over the General's right shoulder and said, "Sergeant deMelilla reporting as ordered, sir,"

Gálvez returned the salute. "Stand easy, *Primero*. Take a moment to catch your breath."

"Yes, sir. Thank you, sir," Diego uttered breathlessly. "I am fine, sir."

"I was delighted when I received word of your victory yesterday. You must tell me how it went."

Diego's report to General Gálvez consumed the better part of an hour. Gálvez often interrupted with questions and insistence on certain details. There was not a stretch of time greater than five minutes straight during the entire report that was not interrupted by an officer or messenger requiring instructions or reporting siege details. When Diego concluded his report, Gálvez lowered his head, placed his hand on his chin and was lost in thought for a full minute.

The General's head shot up and a enigmatic smile flickered across his face. "We will review *La Cuchilla*. Assemble troops and baggage at the farmhouse in one hour – full dress. Go now."

"Yes, General." Diego saluted and jogged back to the beach. One hour was about two days less than he would need to make his ragged troop presentable.

☙

"Stand down?" Plata said to no one in particular. *"Descanso y recuperación* (Rest and recovery) is not a good thing." Plata was probably the most experienced soldier in the camp. His appetites in drink, gambling and whoring insured he would be a *soldado*, a private, all of his life. But he had served across the Spanish Empire. He, Martin and two others were sitting around the evening fire cleaning their weapons and getting ready for sleep. The army pioneers had constructed a barracks compound using split timbers and canvas. Six men shared a building with wooden floors, a luxury that boosted morale considerably, canvas walls and roof. Plata was skilled at making a "field cot" out of a few sticks, rope and bedroll. Sleeping off the ground was improving the general health of everyone.

"What is bad about getting some rest and new clothes?" Martin asked.

"Look, *Niño*, I enjoy lazing around camp as much as anyone. That is not the part that is bad. It is what comes next that worries me."

"What comes next is we soldier some more."

"What comes next is soldiering, to be certain. The fittest, finest looking troops go into the breach first, *tonto*. The General thinks the *godums* will piss themselves into surrender when fresh, clean, and eager troops climb through the gaping hole in the wall."

"What hole?"

"The hole that the General's cannons are going to make when he gives the order. Have you not been watching? Can you not see? A hundred guns will fire on a ten-yard stretch of wall and we will be the first through the hole. We will go in gleaming white and polished like the pope's chalice. When we come out, those that are left, we will be covered in grime, dust, powder and blood."

"Plata!" Diego had been standing in the shadows, unobserved.

"*Sí, Primero.*"

"Stop telling ghost stories. Everyone is to stack muskets, box a score of cartridges, foot all weapons and turn in now. Dress tomorrow will be full whites." Diego said. He could hear Pook and Quintero giving the same instructions throughout the camp. Stacking muskets required each six-man tent of soldiers to form a pyramid of muskets in the center of their sleeping quarters by interlocking the ramrods of each at the muzzle.

They would draw a packet of twenty cartridges from the supply wagon, remove the oil coated outer wrap and place each individual cartridge into corresponding holes in the wooden block inside the leather cartridge box. Every man's cartridge box, bayonet, sword, knives or other preferred weapon would be stacked at the foot of his cot next to his shoes. His uniform would be draped over all the gear ready to be donned at a moment's notice. No mention was made of pack, bedroll, or other equipment. This meant they would not be going far or that the rest of the equipment would be brought along by others.

Preparations done, Martin slipped under his blanket and lay on his back watching the reflections of some firelight from somewhere dance along the flapping canvas roof.

"There is no doubt about it, *muchachos.*" Plata's voice was soft but very clear in the damp night air. "We are going to the *fiesta* tomorrow."

Martin shivered and closed his eyes.

❧

Martin woke to drums tattooing the "to arms" command. Every man was up and scrambling into his clothes. Fort Charlotte had not begun the daily barrage for it was still dark. Martin had gone to bed in his shirt and trousers so he needed to only struggle into his gaiters, put on his shoes, his vest, coat, sword belt, bayonet sling, cartridge box, haversack and canteen. He retrieved his musket, pushed his hat onto his head and ducked into the assembly area. *La Cuchilla* was forming ranks. Every man was dressed in his parade best. *What a way to go to war.*

"Hurry, hurry," Pook was shouting at the stragglers while the incessant drums created a constant background noise to the shouts of men and the clatter of weapons. Quintero was going from tent to tent insuring everyone was out.

Diego stood in the center of the assembly area facing the gathering ranks. All along the encampment men of other units were gathering as well. Many more were already in the trenches or manning cannons. Diego had heard there would be one thousand two hundred men in the assault. When it was clear everyone had arrived, he took a deep breath and shouted."

"*La Cuchilla*, ATTENTION!"

"*Honor y Fidelitas!*" The men shouted the regimental slogan as they snapped to attention. They had formed two ranks of ten. Pook was at the right end of the first rank, Quintero on the right of the second. Orders to come to attention rippled throughout the siege camp as the other one thousand one hundred and eighty men were formed for the move to the line of departure.

"We are to be the guard for Governor General Gálvez today," Diego announced. "Fix bayonets!" No shots were planned in this assault. It was going to be cannons and cold steel.

"*Mierda*," Plata muttered under his breath. "We are in for it. The General is a madman." Gálvez had been severely wounded several times. From battles with the Apache in California to the beaches of Algiers, Gálvez had been in the thick of it every time.

"We have not had breakfast," Martin complained.

"They do not want us to have full stomachs."

"Why?"

"Less to spill out."

"Quiet!" That last mutter by Plata has been a touch too loud.

"Face right. Carry arms." Diego marched his men to their place on the line of departure. Gálvez and his circle of aides, all mounted, were already at the designated place when Diego brought *La Cuchilla* to the line. Ten soldiers commanded by Pook were to the right of the cluster of mounted officers, ten commanded by Quintero to the left. Diego stood at the right side of General Gálvez's horse ready to move as needed. The sun had not yet risen, but the eastern sky had lost most of its stars.

An aide rode up and leaned across to the General. "The pioneers are ready, sir. On your command."

Gálvez drew his sword and rested it on his shoulder. "The order has already been given. The first shot from the Fort will begin this affair."

A pair of guns fired from the ramparts of Fort Charlotte and their acrid smoke began its westward drift. A sudden common shout came from the forward areas as the trees left standing to shield the Spanish gun emplacements from the view of the fort came down. Over one hundred Spanish cannons fired almost as one. The concussion from the combined discharge caused the coattails of the waiting infantry to flutter.

The smoke cleared just as another Spanish volley was discharged. Diego strained to see the effect of the barrages, but they were still five hundred yards from the wooden palisade around the fort. He looked for the sharp points of the palisade posts, but could only see smoke. He realized the palisade was gone. The first volley had thrown such a weight of steel that the posts were shattered into splinters and stumps.

Smoke obscured Diego's view of the fort again as another volley rocked the ground. Return fire from the fort, if there had been any, was insignificant compared to the Spanish barrage. There was another break in the billowing waves of smoke and Diego could see a section of the brick wall of the fort fall backwards into one of the interior buildings. Another volley roared out. All the shots were concentrated on a small section of the masonry wall and it was quickly reduced to a pile of broken bricks and mortar. The cannons were adjusted to target an adjacent section of wall.

Messengers flowed in and out of the small circle of officers around Gálvez. Sometimes an aide would say something to the General, receive a reply and dispatch a runner who would disappear into the clouds of gun smoke. Officers and enlisted men alike were scurrying about, eyes wide, intent on some task.

Another messenger appeared out of the smoke. He was hatless, powder stained, unarmed and covered in mud. He may have been a grenadier. The man ran to the General who leaned down from his saddle to receive the message. Gálvez nodded, said something to the messenger and straightened in his saddle. The mud-encrusted apparition returned into the smoke.

"Sergeant," Gálvez spoke without looking away from the continuing devastation. "You may feed your men in place and shifts. There will be no assault today."

The General waved an aide over. "Pass the word along the assault line." The General rattled off a list of officers in command of the assaulting units. "We are to stand down today. I have ordered the trench work suspended until dark. Return to the bivouac and see to it the men are fed."

The Spanish guns continued a regular bombardment with a few of their heavy guns until their cannons had been pulled into the safety of prepared bunkers. Many of the British cannons had been dismounted, but those that remained resumed the monotonous, regularly-timed fire of the last several weeks. The Spanish guns and siege workers had gone to ground.

Diego could see that the walls of the fort had collapsed in a few places and there was a breach, but soldiers assaulting that opening would be subjected to murderous fire from the remaining battlements. He suddenly remembered something his father had said about some battle in North Africa. *We won the day, but our General killed more Spaniards than the Moors.* Gálvez was proving to be a different breed of General.

Diego had the men rest in place and told them they could eat. No meal had been planned, but every soldier carried a supply of jerked meat and hard biscuits. Some men sat on the ground, some found a nearby stump or abandoned crate to sit on as they ate. Diego dug in his haversack and pulled out a ball of *pimîhkân* in a tightly wrapped paper roll. The paper had come from a bee's wax coated cartridge packet. Twenty paper cartridges, enough to fill the slots in the leather-covered box each infantryman carried at his side, were issued to the soldier in packets wrapped tightly with waxed paper. Soldiers would save the waxed paper and use it to wrap their jerky, bacon or other foods to keep it reasonably dry.

He ate standing near the General's horse, ready to receive instructions. He could also overhear the messages that continued to come in. The General had called a suspension in the work because a section of the trench had collapsed and exposed the workers to direct fire from the fort. A half dozen men had been killed and nearly as many were wounded. The trenches had to be brought closer to the fort so the assaulting forces did not have to cross several hundred yards of open area to reach the breach. The assault could have continued and the fort taken, but Spanish casualties would have been horrible.

Gálvez dismounted and handed the reins to an aide. He crossed the worn path leading to the siege works to a cluster of stacked brush, as if to relieve himself. Instead, he gestured for Diego to join him.

"Yes, General?"

"I have reports of a British force encamped at the banks of the Tensaw River, perhaps several hundred men. Based upon your reports, I consider them not to be in position to render assistance to this fort. Are you still of the opinion that the swamp road is not usable?"

A General is asking for my opinion? Diego, shocked such a serious question would be put to him, took a moment before answering.

"General, if they do not have barges or *pirogues,* the swamp road is useless. Infantry alone could cross, but heavy guns and provisions needed for even as few as two hundred could not be brought across in less than several days. They may go north and cross, but that would take more than a week."

Gálvez nodded. "That has been the assessment of every officer who has been up the Tensaw River. Still, I will have a sloop-of-war ready on the Middle River should they try to cross. Thank you, Sergeant. Return to your men."

Before crossing the path to return to his post, Diego had to wait for a horse-drawn wagon leaving the trenches. The wagon contained the mangled corpses of the men killed when the British cannon sent grapeshot into the suddenly exposed section of trench. He could see the shattered limbs poking out of mud-encrusted clothing. Someone had covered the heads with a canvas, but the maimed torsos, arms and legs made him think of a butcher's waste pit.

After the wagon trundled by, Diego looked up into the faces of Martin and Plata. Martin's young face paled and aged before Diego's eyes. Plata seemed oblivious and unmoved. One young man was becoming a soldier and one old soldier was reinforcing his mental defenses.

"Someone has already gotten their boots," Diego heard Plata murmur as he crossed to them behind the wagon. He looked at the departing wagon and saw that every foot was indeed bare. Boots and shoes were a precious commodity in this climate of cold rain, swampy land and mud. He could not remember ever being completely dry. *How many times had he prayed for rain when he farmed the high fields of Gran Canaria? How many lifetimes ago had that been?* Now it seemed if water did not fall from the sky, it welled up from the very ground.

Diego looked back toward Fort Charlotte. Already men could be seen working to make repairs to the breach. If six men were killed by a few shots into the siege trenches, how many *godums* died in the tremendous Spanish volleys? *I wonder if Marcelite is safe or is she even within the fort?* She did not seem to have any difficulty visiting the town a few weeks ago. *Has it been a few weeks?* Suddenly, for reasons he could not understand, an image of Isabella appeared in his mind; young, beautiful, honest, faithful and undoubtedly courageous Isabella. His hand went to his haversack where he kept her letter.

It began to rain.

CHAPTER *13*

D iego led Olivier, Plata, Martin and Búho along the edge of the trench closest to the fort. Pook and Quintero each had a small contingent of men, the remainder of *La Cuchilla*. The rest and clean uniforms of two days ago had been long forgotten. One day of rain and one day of crawling through trenches and gun emplacements to reach their assigned sector had negated all. Every man was covered in reddish-tan mud. The siege trench was only four feet deep, so the men had to crouch or crawl to remain protected.

Instead of hats, they wore blue bandanas to keep their hair in place. Each private carried a musket, bayonet, and sword or the small hatchet the *Kentuckianos* called a "tomahawk." Pook and Quintero each carried a large cutlass instead of a musket. It was their job to keep their men fighting, something that is difficult to do if you are also loading and firing a musket. Diego carried an *espontoon,* a short lance very like his Canarian *magado.* The orders were clear. Climb out of the trench, race across three hundred yards of open space, force your way into the breach with cold steel, and only form ranks inside the fort, if possible. Do not stop. A young ensign, Diego had forgotten his name, was stationed between Pook and Quintero. The officers led while sergeants and corporals kept the men moving. When they gained the breach, every man was expected to fight hand-to-hand.

Behind them the trench stretched on, filling with infantry steeling themselves for the order to rush the breach that was being created in the wall of Fort Charlotte. For every shot that came from the ramparts of the fort, the Spanish answered with a score or more. Brickwork turned to dust and shattered timbers flew into the air and the western wall of the fort was slowly transformed into a heap of debris.

"I hope the General is not in a hurry," muttered Plata. Another small barrage was discharged from the fort. "The *godums* are being very frugal."

"What do you mean?" Martin said as he tried to force himself into the earthen wall of the trench.

"Can you not see, Martin? The British do not waste powder and shot. The powder they do burn, but their shot is being returned, with interest."

The top of the trench above their heads exploded, throwing great clots of mud about. The distinct whizzing sound of grapeshot filled the air.

"Just letting us know they see us," Plata said. He gestured Martin and Búho closer to him. "Do not stand up once we are ordered forward. Crouch as low as you can and still run. When the *Primero* says 'go', go fast and low and do not form ranks. He will wait until the guns trained on us have fired; then, it's out the trench and run for the breach. Run fast enough and you will be inside the fort before they can reload."

"Why have we not been ordered to load?" Búho asked.

"Be happy they did not order you to remove your flint. The General does not want us to stop and shoot. It will be cold steel."

Another volley from the Spanish guns drowned all other noises. This last volley was from new positions closer to the fort. The smoke billowed over their heads and cascaded into the trenches along with smoldering bits of canvas from the powder casings. Diego could hear the tinkle of falling bricks and other debris from the battlements even while the booming echo of the guns faded in the distance.

A broken timber discarded on the far lip of the trench exploded sending something growling past Diego's face. He instinctively closed his eyes and tried to turn his face away from the hot air that brushed his moustache, but the earthen wall of the trench prevented him from moving. When he opened his eyes he could see Martin's drawn and horrified face across the stump of a splinter between them. He followed Martin's eyes to his left and the base of the ragged shaft of wood protruding from the wall of the trench and Plata's crushed head. Diego pulled the splinter from the wall releasing Plata's body to slump in the bottom of the trench.

"He was starting to speak to me," Martin stuttered.

"Martin! Martin, pass the word for two *embarrados* to come get Plata," Diego had to shout to get the young soldier's attention."

"What ? What did you say, *Primero?*"

"Pass the word for two of the sappers to come for Plata." The sappers had been working on advancing the siege trenches for over a month. They had become so encrusted with mud the men began to refer to them as the "muddy ones" – *embarrados*.

Martin turned away to pass the message. Diego removed Plata's shoes, cartridge box and sword. Martin turned back, saw what Diego was doing a blurted out "*¿Por qué?*"

"Olivier is wearing leather bags for shoes and Serpas is using a haversack for a cartridge box. Plata will need these things no more. He has willed them to his *camaradas.*"

"The guns have stopped," Búho said. "Listen! The guns have stopped."

Diego realized that a silence had fallen over the battle area. There were no drums, no musketry and no cannon fire. Evening was falling and the world was silent.

Martin started to stand and peek over the edge of the trench.

"Stay down!" Diego hissed. "You will be losing your shoes next." He pushed the shoes and cartridge box to Martin. "Pass these down to Olivier and Serpas. Keep the sword for yourself."

Two *embarrados* arrived with a roll of canvas. They expertly wrapped the body in the canvas after they had stripped it of gaiters and coat. One of the men placed the bayonet on Plata's musket and planted it next to the bloody splinter in the bottom of the trench. It would be gathered later by *los cuervos* (the crows), men who were given the job of collecting bodies, weapons and other equipment from the battle field. Plata would be dressed in nothing but his shirt and trousers by the time he reached the burial area. Diego watched as they folded the body into the canvas and pulled it along the bottom of the trench behind them. Plata would be interred with the rest of the Spanish casualties from battle and disease at some location separate from the camp and latrine. Five years from now there would be no one who could even say where they lay.

Just as it is with my beautiful Mézu. Diego looked back toward the stumps of the deforested landscape and across the hidden gun locations at a sky that was fading into a dark grey. *This land devours people without a trace. I will have a stone made for Mézu.*

The ensign who would have led the assault was getting a message from a runner. Diego suddenly remembered the man's name – "Castro," the young officer that had witnessed Diego's shameful condition the morning after his tryst with Marcelite.

The message made Castro's face break out into a smile of relief. He cupped his hands to his mouth and shouted toward Diego. "Sergeant, get your men out of the trench and form up twenty paces there." He gestured toward the fort. "Do it now."

"Form up on me!" Diego shouted as he scrambled over the top of the trench and turned to face the Spanish siege works twenty paces away. He was half-expecting to be met with grapeshot, but the silence continued as soldiers appeared to rise from the earth and form two ranks of nine men each centered on him. Ensign Castro advanced from the trench and stood behind Diego as the men squared themselves away.

When he saw that the men had satisfactorily collected, Diego shouted, "*La Cuchilla*, attention!"

"*Honor et Fidelitas!*" The men responded in one voice as they came to the position of attention. Diego was filled with pride as he examined the ranks.

The bayonet-tipped muskets were perfectly locked along the right side of each man. Blue, muddy bandanas instead of tricorns adorned each head. Gaiters, mud to the knees, coats torn and crossed with leather belts that had been white-washed in some distant past, were all in alignment. The men before him were soldiers; dirty, disheveled, tired, experienced soldiers.

Diego faced about and saluted Ensign Castro. "*La Cuchilla*, formed and ready as ordered, sir." He fixed his gaze over the young officer's left shoulder and was amazed at the scene behind the ensign. A great gap had been battered into the wall of the fort. The wooden palisade was gone. Nothing but splintered stumps remained as evidence there had even been something there. He could see broken and tumbled down buildings beyond the fallen section of brick wall. Two redcoats stood on the pile of rubble in the breach with a white banner on a tall staff. Fort Charlotte had surrendered.

One shot too late for Plata.

Several other units were emerging from the trench works and forming ranks. Diego dropped his salute and waited for orders. Castro took a deep breath and shouted, "Parade – rest!" Then he turned about as well. It seems they were to wait.

ᶜ⌒ᵒ

Messengers shuttled back and forth between the fort and the Spanish command post somewhere behind the waiting ranks of *La Cuchilla*. Other units had been called from the field one by one until only Diego's eighteen men and Ensign Castro remained. The men had been allowed to eat jerked meat from their haversacks and drink rum-laced water from their canteens as the night wore on. Torches had been lit in the exposed compound of the fort and cook fires were being struck behind the Spanish works, but Diego and his men waited in the dark before the fort.

A messenger summoned Castro sometime around nine o'clock and Diego was left in charge of eighteen forlorn soldiers in the dark. The Ensign returned with a brace of men carrying torches.

Diego had called the men to attention when he saw Castro coming and was awaiting orders.

"Negotiations have been completed, sergeant. We are to enter the fort and supervise the conduct of the enemy. Two companies of grenadiers will enter the fort directly after us. We will all be under the command of Colonel Herrera who will conduct the surrender. Governor General Gálvez will transfer his headquarters to Fort Charlotte once the surrender is completed. Have the men shoulder their muskets and follow me."

"Yes, sir."

Castro headed off toward one of the sally ports in an undamaged section of the wall, bracketed by his torchbearers. Diego had the men face to the left, shoulder their muskets and marched them at the quick on the heels of the ensign. Once inside Diego was assigned to post a guard on the north main gate which opened onto Royal Street and another sally port on the east wall. He was given control of the British guard house for his men to establish the relief rotation. The orders were simple. No men, civilian or soldier, would be allowed to depart the fort. Unlike the occupation of Baton Rouge a year earlier, militiamen and citizen volunteers were not going to be released to their farms. Women and children would be allowed to depart for the town. Guards were posted, instructions given and the rotation established.

The headquarters at the "farmhouse" was transferred to the fort and Diego, a mere sergeant, was summoned to an officer's call in the former British commander's office. Leaving Pook and Quintero to manage the routine, Diego reported to the designated room in the headquarters building to discover he, aside from orderlies, was the only enlisted man there. He found an obscure corner and planted himself there at attention.

Diego listened intently as each officer stood to make a report to Gálvez while Clerk Renaldo scribbled furiously to set the words down in a logbook. The first report was that of casualties suffered by the Spanish. Nine had been killed by hostile action since Gálvez came ashore. *Plata has become one of nine, reported and forgotten.* Deaths from accidents and disease numbered twenty men.

Of the British, those killed within the fort numbered three. Eight had been wounded. Of that number six were expected to survive. Those captured numbered five officers, two surgeons, fifteen sergeants and seventy-eight soldiers of the 60th Regiment of Foot; one sergeant and nineteen members of a Maryland Loyalist militia, sixty sailors (it was not known if the sailors were merchantmen or Royal Navy) and one hundred five male civilians, half of whom were slaves.

The next report covered the relief column from Pensacola that had turned back practically within sight of the fort. After the unsuccessful attempt to cross the Mobile and Tensaw rivers, the British had marched sixty miles north and crossed where the flood plain was much narrower. The force consisted of over twelve hundred infantry and several light field guns. They had left most of their heavy guns behind so as not to slow their movements, but it still required weeks of effort to bring British relief forces into position above Mobile.

American militia newly arrived from New Orleans, both fresh and eager for action, were dispatched to insure the British completed their withdrawal across the Mobile River. If the column had appeared just one day earlier the British could have combined forces with those within the fort to outnumber the Spanish.

"No need to brood about events that did not occur," Gálvez said after this last bit of intelligence was presented. "The British have withdrawn and we have taken Mobile. Now we must keep it while we prepare to take Pensacola."

Officer followed officer as every aspect of consolidating the Spanish position at Mobile was discussed, planned and provided for. British soldiers, sailors and Maryland militiamen were declared prisoners of war and sent to ships in Mobile Bay for transport to the growing population of detainees in New Orleans. Settlers of all nationalities would be extended the opportunity to state an oath of fidelity to the King of Spain and remain in their homes with all of the lands they were recognized to possess under British rule.

The officer's call lasted four hours during which not a minute passed without some matter of importance being discussed and disposed of by the General. Often, Gálvez would ask for suggestions, recommendations and clarifications. Decisions were made, orders given or officers were granted the authority to act as they deemed fit knowing certain goals had been set. The primary goal was – Pensacola.

Sailing orders to select ships in the fleet that crammed Mobile Bay was the last business conducted before Gálvez announced an end to the meeting. Renaldo exhaled audibly as he closed the meeting log. The officers filed out by rank leaving Diego the last to go.

"A moment, Sergeant." Gálvez said. "I want a private word with you."

Diego snapped to attention and waited as Renaldo left, the log book under his arm, and closed the door.

"Your service in command of *La Cuchilla* has been exemplary, Sergeant. Have your men adjusted to their duties here?"

"Yes, General."

"Good. They will need the rest. I have plans for you and *La Cuchilla*. In two days Louisiana Militia will arrive to assume the duties that have been temporarily assigned to *La Cuchilla*. I will send for you when the time is right. See to it your men are well rested and all arms are in good condition."

"Yes, General."

"Good. You are dismissed."

Diego saluted and opened the door to find Renaldo, papers in hand, waiting to enter. Renaldo had to step back to allow the big sergeant to leave. After Diego made his way out of the building, Renaldo entered Gálvez's new office and placed the papers on the General's desk.

"Havana has denied your request, Sir."

"What request, Renaldo?"

"The request to commission deMelilla as an officer."

"You mean Navarro denied it."

Renaldo remained silent. Navarro was the Captain General of Havana. It would be unwise to become involved in a dispute between powerful men, even if one happened to be your commander.

"The man is convinced only *Peninsulare* (men born in Spain) can be granted the privilege of a commission. He may make an exception for a man born in the new world if both parents were *Peninsulare.*"

"General Navarro's own son was born in Havana," Renaldo said.

"That is my point. His own son is a *Criollo*. Until Navarro changes his mind, I will use Sergeant deMelilla as if he were a Lieutenant. Havana cannot stop me there."

❧

Diego returned to discover Pook and Quintero had established a watch roster, inspected all of the men, requisitioned replacement uniforms and scheduled a weapons inspection for the first watch in the morning. Pook was just rotating off watch so Quintero accompanied Diego to inspect the posted guards. It was about four o'clock in the evening and several civilian women and children had collected at the gate begging permission to leave the fort.

"*Primero*, on my own initiative, I had the men keep these people here until we heard from you."

"We can give them leave to go. Our orders are to hold only the men."

"Olivier is posted here, *Primero*. Every woman and child waiting to leave is British. The citizens of Mobile that were not British did not seek refuge in the fort. Every building and room in this fort has been carefully searched by the grenadiers. Women and their children were found hiding here and there. You would have thought an execution awaited, the way they carried on when the grenadiers escorted them to the gate. Olivier was able to settle them and convince them that they were being sent to their homes. He has questioned them all, every one."

Quintero shifted nervously and glanced about to insure there were no listeners. "I think you should speak with Olivier, *Primero*."

"Let us go speak with Olivier now." *What has gotten into Quintero? Our orders are clear; send the women to their homes in the town.* The Louisiana Militiamen assigned to police the residents in the town were trustworthy men and they were well accepted by the French citizens of Mobile. Was Quintero worried that the women would be harmed?

Olivier saw Diego and Quintero approaching and he separated himself from the cluster of civilians crowded about the north gate. He gestured for the men to meet him at the guard enclave next to the gate.

"Primero, Quintero and I thought you should see this," Olivier said as Diego stepped up to the opening of the guard post. He reached in and drew a woman forward by the elbow. She wore a plain cotton dress, heavy shawl and a deep bonnet, clearly a farmer's wife. Olivier touched the woman's chin and she raised her mud-splattered face to look at Diego.

"*Mademoiselle* Gaudet, or is it Lady Smythe?" Diego pushed her back into the enclave. "Quintero, you and Olivier give us some privacy. Have the gates opened and the citizens escorted out by the Louisiana Militia. Those who are from distant farms are to have quarters in what little remains of the town. The General does not want a woman out on the streets alone." The two men walked a dozen steps away and began issuing orders.

"I beg you, Diego. Please let me go with the others." Marcelite's pleading eyes searched his. "You must not reveal me to your officers. The British think I escaped days ago. If they discover who I truly am, it could mean my life."

Splattered with mud and yet, by God, this woman is beautiful. "I do not know who you truly are." Diego felt passions rise in him he believed had died with Mézu. Forcing the unwanted emotions aside, he continued in a rasping whisper. "I do not believe you serve Spain. The French and Americans are with us in this, so you cannot be in their employ. And you say you do not serve the British. What other power is involved here?" *She is using me. That night in the town, now, she is using me.*

"I swear, Diego. I have not – will not betray you or the army you serve. There are more things involved here than this simple fight for Florida. You must let me go. You must believe me."

"I do not believe you. I know when I am being used." He grabbed her roughly by the arm and pulled her toward the gate. "Quintero, see to it this woman is released with the others."

ᐱ❧

"*Primero?*" Pook rapped on the door post to the guard house. "*Primero,* the General has sent for you."

Diego rolled out of the bunk and began to dress. "Thank you Pook. Have the guards been changed?" If the guards have been rotated then the time would be after nine in the morning.

"Yes, *Primero.*"

"What is the hour?"

"Ten less a quarter, *Primero.*" Pook nor Quintero had never openly questioned Diego about the decision to release Marcelite. But their attitude had changed, as if somehow his judgment was questioned. One thing was certain; none of the men had gone to an officer with their doubts. This was *La Cuchilla,* the cutting edge. They had spent the better part of a year together in the midst of British territory with no one to rely upon but each other. Diego knew that among themselves they argued if *Primero* had lost his judgment, or was he just like Plata had been – good in a fight and a fool when it came to women. In a soldier's judgment, being good in a fight overshadowed every other vice.

It was nine forty-five. Ten was the hour Gálvez usually reserved for officer's call, the time when major changes were announced. This summons would dictate a major change. This would be the end of soft garrison duty. In a day or two, Gálvez and a large portion of the army would return to New Orleans or Havana to prepare for the attack on Pensacola. How many would be assigned to holding Mobile was critical. Too few and the British would take back the town. Too many would weaken the forces available against Pensacola.

Renaldo greeted Diego in the anteroom to Gálvez's commandeered office. "I will tell the General you are here, *Primero*. Just a moment please." He gave a single rap on the General's door and entered when he heard "Come" closing the door behind him.

Diego heard murmured voices and Renaldo reappeared, held the door open and stepped aside for Diego to enter. "The General will see you now," with a nod that was nearly a bow.

Diego strode to a spot one pace from and centered on the front of the General's desk. "Sergeant Diego deMelilla reporting as ordered, Sir." He held his saluted until the General, his hands filled with all sorts of papers, returned it.

"Sit down, Sergeant. We have much to discuss. I am about to put La Cuchilla to work again. Have your men rested and rearmed to your satisfaction?"

"Yes, General." It was the only answer Diego could make and it was near the truth.

"Good. Here is what I need from you." Gálvez looked about for a place to put the papers he was holding. He shrugged, stood and placed them in his chair. He moved two other folders from his desk to reveal a map and added them to the pile on his chair. "A General's weapons, *Primero*. Paper and more paper."

Diego studied the map that had been uncovered. It showed Mobile Bay and the Gulf Coast from Mobile Bay to Pensacola. A line from a square marked at the northeast corner of Mobile Bay ran southeast to the symbol for a fort on Pensacola Bay. He looked for a map scale. The distance covered by the line was about fifty miles, no more than sixty.

"And it is a good road, as roads in this place are judged." Gálvez had been watching Diego study the map. "And the road runs well north of Perdido Bay where the rivers are easily forded. There are no wide swamps to slow British movements between here at *Colina Desnuda* (Bare Hill)," Gálvez placed a finger on the penciled square, "and here," his finger touched the symbol for a fort. The map had labeled it "Fort George" in English. There were three other smaller symbols for forts scattered around the bay south of Fort George.

"General Campbell, I believe you have met, is returning with the failed relief column." Images of the stern British general flashed through Diego's mind. "I do not want Campbell to think we are satisfied with Mobile. He would establish an outpost on Bare Hill and be poised to strike the moment we do not have enough ships in the bay or men at the fort. You are going to stop him. I want *La Cuchilla* to cross the bay to Bare Hill and reconnoiter inland. We will build a stockade on Bare Hill that will serve as your base. Do not satisfy yourself with occupying the place once it is built. I want Campbell to receive reports of Spaniards threatening the road to Pensacola so he will worry about being cut off. That will hurry him home. I want him held up in his fortifications so we will be free to act."

"And if Campbell should move against us, General?"

"You will have four guns in the palisade and Bare Hill is a place that lends itself to defense. If he sends a large force, we will land troops here," Gálvez pointed to a place on the eastern shore of Mobile Bay about three miles south of Bare Hill, "and cut him off. If he sends a small force, you will defeat them. Have *La Cuchilla* ready to move at first light. Any questions?"

"No questions, General." The instructions were very clear.

"Good. That will be all. See Renaldo and tell him what you need."

Diego saluted and turned to leave.

"Good luck," the General said as Diego opened the door.

"Thank you, General."

Diego stepped into the anteroom and Renaldo rose from his clerk's desk. "Do you require anything, Sergeant?"

"I will send a list."

Diego arrived at the guardhouse, woke Quintero and sent for Pook. The logistics involved with moving even a small force required detailed planning.

"One of the sailors brought a letter for you while you were away," Quintero said as he sat on the side of the bunk trying to wake up. "I put it under your haversack."

Diego retrieved the letter while they waited for Pook. The letter was from Isabella. She began with the important news first. Everyone was well. Their farm was doing well and both Pedro and Maria were healthy and growing.

She ended with a worried note. A new bishop had been assigned to New Orleans. This bishop was scandalized by the lack of devotion exhibited by the people of New Orleans. Most citizens did not attend daily mass and some even failed to appear for Sunday masses. What is more, many couples lacked marriage certificates and even the army recognized dependents that had no proof of marriage, a practice the good bishop intended to end.

Isabella drew a portion of Diego's monthly pay to help support his children. If this was stopped, she and her parents would have to wait for Diego to return to New Orleans before they could receive any financial help.

Isabella ended her letter with "All will be well. The farm is doing well and we can do without the army money."

Diego folded the letter and tucked it into his coat pocket. When he had the time he would write a return note beneath Isabella's words and send it back to her. Sometimes two or more messages, back and forth, were written on the same scrap of paper.

Pook ducked in. "Are we moving, *Primero?*"

"We are the cutting edge, Pook."

"*Honor et Fidelitas.*" Pook and Quintero replied in unison.

CHAPTER *14*

The Americans who had been dispatched north to hurry Campbell's failed relief force's retreat to Pensacola sent back eighteen prisoners along with word that the British were indeed retiring. The prisoners, all dragoons, were added to the hundred eighty of Fort Charlotte's surrendered garrison and placed aboard ships bound for New Orleans. Mobile citizens were offered the option of being shipped off with the prisoners of war or swearing allegiance to His Most Catholic Majesty and becoming subjects of Spain. Eighty Englishmen and seventy-six Frenchmen accepted the offer and took the oath. The Englishmen also converted to Catholicism.

La Cuchilla was ferried across Mobile Bay and put ashore at the base of Bare Hill where a small trail wound up the steep slope. Meeting no resistance, they advanced quickly up the trail to the crest of the hill. The trail continued along a ridgeline to a small village astride the main road to Pascagoula. There they encountered the trail guard of the retreating British. Diego had the men fix bayonets and form a battle line, but the British rear guard, a dozen mounted men, galloped away.

Another signal tripod was erected on the crest of Bare Hill and Martin was sent aloft to signal to the sloop in the bay that the area was secured. This message was passed quickly to Gálvez who, according to plan, sent construction contractors, along with a security force, with orders to erect a bastion on the hill.

The Duplesess Battalion of Free Men of Color had been assigned as the temporary garrison for Bare Hill post along with Diego's *La Cuchilla*. Gálvez withdrew most of his force to New Orleans and Havana to begin preparations for a siege on Pensacola. Fort Charlotte, now renamed Fort Carlota, was provided a contingent of regulars from Havana and a battalion of Louisiana militia from an area along the Mississippi River known as the German Coast. Maintaining command of Mobile Bay was vital to the attack on Pensacola. The bay, and particularly the eastern side of the bay, provided a staging area with a short overland route into Pensacola.

Overall command of Fort Carlota, Mobile Bay and Bare Hill fell to Colonel José de Ezpeleta. Former Ensign Ramón del Castro, now Lieutenant Castro was given command of Bare Hill. Castro's forty Grenadiers, *La Cuchilla* and the Duplesess Battalion formed a garrison of one hundred eighty. Barbeaux's *Gabriella* was one of four field guns accompanying the Duplesess Battalion. A labor force of men hired from the surrounding community assisted the garrison on building the fortification.

Bare Hill hugged a steep slope at the northeast corner of Mobile Bay that rose rapidly from the mouth of a branch of the Tensaw River to an elevation of one hundred fifty feet within less than a half-mile from the water's edge. Bordered on three sides by steep ravines, the only avenue of approach, except for the road from the beach, was a narrow road along the ridgeline running north and east from the crest of the hill. Flanked by heavily wooded ravines in all other directions, it was an ideal location for a fort.

But Castro did not have the time or the resources to build a fort. Instead he directed the construction of a wall a thousand feet long across the road and ridgeline. Four raised redoubts positioned along the wall served as platforms for the field guns and provided clear lines of fire along the ridgeline. It was about a mile from the wall to the small cluster of buildings at the junction of the main road to Pascagoula the men had simply named "*La Aldea* (the village)."

La Cuchilla assisted very little in the construction of the defensive line. Instead, they manned the picket posts Diego had established along the Pascagoula Road a quarter mile north and south of *La Aldea*. Diego positioned his command post in the village and housed his men in a crude barn next to the road. Foot patrols radiated out from *La Aldea* and past the pickets for several miles. The men on picket duty were ever alert for signs of the British.

The picket posts were only a quarter of a mile or so from the village at locations where another half mile or so of trail could be seen. If an infantry force appeared, the pickets would fire shots to warn *La Aldea* and Bare Hill. Action after that would depend upon actions of the enemy force. If the British force presented mounted troops – dragoons – the signal shots would be followed by a race to the village, lest the dragoons ride down the pickets before escape was possible. Appearance of dragoons was a constant fear, for the fast moving troops could overpower *La Cuchilla* before help could be sent from Bare Hill.

A Frenchman, Antoine Marbone, operated a trading post at the junction and happily provided Diego's men with access to items of which they had long been deprived. Ale, fresh bread, cots, cooked meats and, most welcomed of all, fresh vegetables. A diet of hard biscuits, jerky and salted pork grew tiresome after a month. A hot bath every week or so was also available at a cost of two silver bits.

Diego quickly fell into a regular routine. He directed picket duty rotation and foot patrols, and made daily reports to a nervous Lieutenant Castro at Bare Hill less than a half-mile away. Each day, as Diego approached the wall on his way to make his report he would notice improvements to the position. Brush and trees had been cleared away from the road along the ridgeline until the cannons mounted on their fifteen foot high redoubts had a clear line of fire right up to the edge of *La Aldea*. The wooden palisade first constructed was being replaced by a brick and earthen wall. A gate centered on the road was bracketed by redoubts speckled with loopholes. Anyone attempting to force the gate would have to endure a murderous crossfire.

May 1780 came and went as *La Cuchilla* continued the mind-numbing duty of reconnaissance. Farmers along the Pensacola road, north and south of the village, had returned to their fields. Farm houses scattered here and there were now occupied and the men of *La Cuchilla* began to make friends among the mostly French-speaking population.

Gradually the improvements to the defenses of Bare Hill began to slow until work finally ceased. Diego recognized signs of complacency, the most lethal of all dangers soldiers faced. He decided to broach the subject with Lieutenant Castro after one of his daily reports.

Castro had ordered the construction of a combination officer's quarters, command billet and signal tower on the peak of the hill. Situated at a respectable distance from the garrison's long barracks and other service buildings, Castro rarely ventured more than half a league from his comfortable headquarters. Diego made his reports in the headquarters, locked at attention, front and centered on Castro's desk. Diego had made a poor first impression on Castro and the officer's distain for him was apparent. Diego completed his usual report of no enemy activity observed in the last twenty-four hours, cleared his throat and continued before Castro had the opportunity to dismiss him.

"Sir, can you spare a moment?"

Castro gave a tired sigh. "Continue Sergeant." Castro never addressed Diego as *"Primero."* The term carried an element of respect Castro did not wish to express.

"Sir, I have noticed that the work on the main wall has been finished for some time. I suggest consideration should be given to protecting it from a determined enemy approaching up the steep slopes on the north and south sides of Bare Hill, sir."

"Do you propose we complete a fortress with high walls on all sides? Perhaps we should build a keep as well."

"No, sir. Nothing of the sort, sir." Diego knew there would never be enough resources available to complete a proper fort, particularly since Fort Carlota was still undergoing renovation. "I suggest, sir, the construction of a line of trenches along the north and south crest along with spikes and caltrops scattered on the slopes."

"Trenches which could be used by the enemy to attack the rear of our wall," Castro snorted, clearly unimpressed by the suggestion.

"The trenches, sir, will only be waist-deep. The spoil can be cast up to provide chest-high protection for our defenders to fire down onto any enemy determined enough to attempt crawling up the ravines, sir. If the enemy should gain the summit and occupy the trenches, they will not be sheltered from our garrison. Protection of Bare Hill will be complete, sir. Our ships in the bay to the west, trench works along the northern and southern ridges and finally, your fine wall across the road, the defenses of this position will be formidable."

"We are in a formidable position as it is, Sergeant. Dismissed."

Diego could almost hear his father's words as he exited Castro's headquarters; *Complacency is a self-inflicted and fatal wound.*

As he approached the gate he heard someone call out to him in French. *"Premier Sergent!* Wait a moment and talk with an old comrade."

He turned to see Corporal Barbeaux climbing down from the platform where Gabriella, all sparkling and polished brass, stood ready for an attack from the east.

"Barbeaux, how have you been? Enjoying your duty as emplaced artillery?"

"You know me, *Premier.* Nothing is better than racing Gabriella into position, spraying out some iron and moving away before the *godums* can even think to act. One thing I do like," Barbeaux waved a letter above his head. "Our mail can find us!"

The New Orleans militia enjoyed a very effective mail service. Officers and enlisted alike were from the same neighborhood and, more often than not, were related, if not in blood, certainly by marriage. These were settled men, with businesses or farms and families waiting at home. The men of *La Cuchilla*, the ones that could read and write, rarely had anyone with whom to correspond. Diego's communication arrangement with Captain Palmas of the *Alacita* was uncommon.

"I have a letter from my Douzemé," Barbeaux was beaming with joy. Diego remembered Douzemé. He has seen her only once, but she was not an easy person to forget. He remembered her as small, beautiful and captivating. Douzemé had been a slave girl from Haiti until Barbeaux provided for her manumission – and married her.

"I am a father! My mother writes to say my Douzemé has delivered of a girl. Full of life, she says, and beautiful. Mother and child are free of fever." Often childbirth would be followed by a deadly fever that afflicted the mother and sometimes the child. A birth free of fever was celebrated.

"That is good news, Philippe." The young artillerist's enthusiasm was almost contagious. *It has been over a year since I have seen my son and daughter. I think Pedro will be a head taller when I see him next. Little Maria will be the image of her mother, if I live to see them.*

"Douzemé had predicted a girl. And she says, one day, this little one will be a powerful *mambo*." A mambo was a priestess in the Haiti variant of Voodoo. Although almost all were practicing Catholics, *mambos* were proficient in the healing and spiritual arts of Voodoo.

"What will you name her?"

Barbeaux fell silent.

"Surely, you have settled on a name."

"I have not given it a thought until just now."

"A name is important. You must choose carefully."

"Yes, you are right. But I forget my manners. How are you doing? Is everyone at home well?"

"Last I heard; all were fine." A month had passed since the last brief message from Isabella. The *Alacita* would call at Mobile soon and he was certain there would be a smuggled letter for him.

Diego was about to part with Barbeaux when it struck him that there may be a way to promote a better defense for Bare Hill.

"Tell me, Philippe, who commands the Duplesess Battalion here?" Only a fraction of the Duplesess Battalion had been assigned to the garrison. High-ranking and important officers had long ago returned to New Orleans with the majority of the militia. Sons of influential men had been appointed to command positions at this remote post partly to gain command experience but primarily because back in New Orleans, the young Creoles did no real work.

"Captain Chastane, Chastane the younger. His father gave him command so he would not waste the spring dueling." Rich, young men of New Orleans were often bored, filling their idle time with gambling and dueling.

"I would like to speak with the Captain."

"I will bring you to him! He would be pleased to meet such a known fighter as the sergeant." Diego's skill with the *espontoon* and bayonet was known throughout New Orleans and he was often called upon to assist in training recruits in close combat arts.

Barbeaux led Diego to a walled tent raised on a wooden floor. There being no guard, Barbeaux merely called out, "Captain Chastane. Sergeant deMelilla would have a word with you, sir."

Within the tent, Diego heard the sound of a man getting out of a cot and walking across the plank floor. The tent flap was tossed open and a young man ducked into the fading light. He was tall, rail thin and dressed in a flowing nightshirt. He had the complexion of tea and hazel eyes. His dark hair was bound behind his head.

"Sergeant deMelilla, as I live and breathe, come into my office." The officer stepped aside to allow Diego to pass. "Thank you, Philippe. That will be all." A disappointed Barbeaux withdrew as Chastane closed the tent. Diego was directed to a chair at a table in the center of the tent. Chastane brushed aside a pile of playing cards and an empty rum bottle. He produced a flint kit and expertly struck a light which he transferred to a lamp on the table, as it was growing dark.

"I saw you work the Spanish grenadiers from Havana two months ago," Chastane said as he took a chair opposite Diego. He offered a cigar to Diego, shrugged when it was declined and nipped off the tip, positioned one end over the lamp and puffed away until the cigar was pleasingly producing clouds of smoke. "Magnificent. Tell me, where did you learn to handle the lance and bayonet with such – how can I say it – *dextérité?*"

"In my youth, sir, I was never without my *magado*. It is a kind of lance very like an *espontoon*. My father trained me daily in the use of the *magado* and short sword. The bayonet is nothing more than a lance on the end of a musket."

"And where was this, sergeant, Spain?"

"I am an *Isleño*, sir. I grew up on Gran Canaria."

"One of Gálvez's recruits?"

Diego nodded.

"What did you do before you enlisted?"

"I was a goatherd, sir."

"Truly?" Chastane puffed on the cigar. "What can I do for you, sergeant?"

"Sir, I have some suggestions about improving the defense of this place."

"Why come to me? Castro is in command here."

"The lieutenant is not receptive of suggestions from me, sir. I thought if I discussed them with you, you might present them as your own recommendations."

Chastane had his own arguments with Castro, a mere lieutenant. The man had command of the post and was a regular officer. He directed the militia, and Captain Chastane, as if they were inferior. It would be pleasing to point out needed improvements or, better yet, forward sound recommendations to Colonel de Ezpeleta at Fort Carlota.

"Tell me of your suggestions, Sergeant."

❧

It was well after dark when Diego returned to the trading post at *La Aldea*. Captain Chastane proved to be an eager recipient of Diego's suggestions. He was thoroughly bored with his posting at Bare Hill and the ideas provided a means by which he could exert his influence. He would attempt the construction with his forces alone so Castro would have no reason to halt the efforts.

Antoine Marbone was standing on the low porch of his trading post when Diego entered the intersection. The Frenchman straightened when he recognized Diego in the moonlight.

"*Primero*," Marbone almost whispered as he motioned Diego to come to the porch.

"What is it, Antoine? I have had a long day."

Marbone glanced left and right then spoke in a low, conspiratorial tone. "*Primero*, there is something you must see."

"Well, show me, but be quick."

"Inside, in the back, *Primero*. Follow me.

Diego followed the man through the front area of his store to a door leading to an interior room. Before Marbone reached the door, Diego knew what it was, or rather who. He had detected the trace of a familiar perfume.

Marbone opened the door then nodding to Diego, muttered, "I leave you now."

Diego stepped into the lantern-lit room.

"You could at least pretend to be happy to see me, Diego," Marcelite said.

"I looked for you in Mobile, but no one admitted to ever seeing you, not even *Madame* Trapenier."

"Sweet *Madame* Trapenier," Marcelite said as she floated across the room to Diego. "She is a dear friend and most protective of me. Are you my friend as well, Diego?"

She was standing close to Diego now, looking up into his eyes. "I so want you to be my special friend."

Diego could not think clearly. This beautiful and mysterious woman made his mind race and caused his insides to dance. He would like nothing more than to be her special friend.

"What are you doing here, Marcelite? This is a wilderness outpost. Why are you not in New Orleans or Havana or Paris? A woman of your quality should be in some capital city where there is money and power."

"Unfortunately, my present circumstances prevent me from traveling on the seas. *Monsieur* Marbone has offered me a position here. I can cook, do laundry, soldiers are always in need of that service, and I keep an excellent garden. And I have *La Cuchilla* to keep me safe from the British."

Who do I have to keep me safe from you?

"Is it the British you fear, or do you serve?

"Diego, I swear by the Blessed Mother I serve France and France alone."

"Then why did you not present yourself to Gálvez? France is our ally and Gálvez would have guaranteed you safe passage home."

"Returning to France is not what I must do if I am to serve my King. What I must do is bide here awhile. It is important, and I tell you this because I trust you, all must think I am but a cook and laundress, nothing more."

None of this made any sense at all. Diego was certain she was lying to him – again. Yet she was standing close to him and her scent caused his head to swim. Suddenly, Plata's smirking and knowing face came to mind. Had he become another Plata? He pulled Marcelite against his body and kissed her.

⁓

Plata was laughing as he sat at a field table. A candle burned in a bayonet stabbed into the planking. Playing cards covered the table. Plata looked up and winked. *"Hola, Primero.* It is going to be the punishment platoon for you, my friend."

Diego's eyes flew open. It was still dark, but dawn must be near for he heard signs of an awakening camp outside of the small room. He felt about the bed, but Marcelite was gone. He struggled up and after some searching, found his clothes. He dressed and exited the little room into the lamp-lit main room of the trading post.

"Good morning, *Primero*." Marbone said as he lit another lamp. "Your men will be up soon. For a *peso,* I will have enough oatmeal to feed all who want to eat before they go to the pickets. My new cook has prepared it with pecans and honey."

New cook! Surely the men will recognize Marcelite.

Diego said nothing as he exited the trading post and walked over to the barn. He could hear the men within stirring. Pook's voice rang out. "Move people. The Frenchman has a new cook and if you would like a hot breakfast get going. If not, be ready to move to the pickets in one hour."

Diego entered the barn and almost ran into Pook.

"Good morning, *Primero*," Pook said jovially. "All are present and we will be changing the pickets as scheduled." If Pook was surprised at not finding Diego at his regular quarters, he gave no indication of it. "I am told Marbone has hired a new cook. Did he tell you what had been prepared for breakfast?"

Perhaps Pook has met the new cook. That would explain why he not been concerned with Diego's absence from the barn.

"Oatmeal," Diego muttered, "with pecans and honey."

"Pecans! This time of year? Will the King pay for breakfast, or must the men collect among themselves?" If the men could not pay for the breakfast, they would have to prepare their own from a dwindled store of dried meats.

"Have Marbone put it on my book."

Eight men filed over to the trading post for a breakfast of hot oatmeal. Eight others were serving on pickets north and south. Quintero was with the southern pickets. *La Cuchilla* had been reduced to sixteen privates, two corporals and one sergeant. Keeping the pickets manned while patrolling north and south with such a small force was demanding. Every man had been reduced to six hours of sleep a day, or less.

"Pook, I will go with the southern relief today. You stay here and get some rest."

"Whatever you say, *Primero*."

Diego did know why he wanted to perform a task Pook normally handled. He needed to do something. He needed to clear his mind. He walked into the path at the barn door and waited as the men assigned to the southern post fell in.

Búho appeared. "Where is Pook, *Primero*?"

"I will be taking the walk with you today."

Martin was next, followed by Serpas to make three. Diego tried to remember who else had been assigned. *Plata? No, fool, Plata is dead.* Tiritar appeared, fumbling with his cartridge box.

It was going to be a hot day. None of the men, not even Diego, was in full uniform. They all wore a white cotton shirt, trousers, gaiters, shoes, a light cotton vest, haversack and garrison cap. Their weapons consisted of a musket, bayonet, full cartridge boxes, and a short sword or hatchet – the style called a "tomahawk" by the Americans. None wore a sign of rank, just a red cockade stitched to the right side of the garrison cap denoting them to be soldiers of Spain. Diego was armed with a short sword and an *espontoon*.

As Diego inspected the men and their equipment, he reflected on just how rugged and fierce they appeared. Even young Martin looked to be every inch a battle hardened veteran. In truth, considering the past year or so, every man had been hardened.

"Fix bayonets. Martin and Serpas, take the fore, Búho, Tiritar – trail."

Diego waited as Martin and Serpas advanced south, Serpas on the right side of the wide trail and Martin on the left, muskets at the guard position. After the men had advanced thirty paces, Diego moved along the center of the trail. Thirty paces later, he glanced back to see Búho move to the right side of the trail and Tiritar to the left. It was only a quarter mile to the picket post, but a sharp turn in the trail hid it from view. If they ran into trouble or if the picket had been surprised and taken, someone from this relief would be in position to signal *La Aldea* and the hill.

Diego watched Serpas and Martin for reaction as they approached the turn in the trail. Neither man indicated alarm. Martin gave a hand signal indicating he had one of the picket stations in sight and all was well. The trail curved to the right so the first picket that came into view was on the left side of the trail. This platform also provided a view east along a smaller trail leading to a farm owned by a Choctaw family.

A platform had been fixed to a pine tree about four feet off of the ground. Limbs, brush and smaller trees had been trimmed until a man on the platform could be hidden by the tree and still see more than a half mile to the south. The raised platform extended the line of sight and encouraged vigilance on the part of the soldier. If he nodded off to sleep, he would fall off the platform and be awakened, not an uncommon occurrence even though the post was changed every hour. The platform also prevented a particularly stealthy enemy from sneaking up behind the guard at night and cutting his throat.

Two men were assigned to the right picket and two to the left. One man mounted the platform while the other tended to other things, or slept. Primary among the "other things" was a rapid foot patrol further down the trail lead by the corporal in charge. Today Diego would be leading the rapid foot patrol before leaving the four men at their post and returning to the village.

The men who had been relieved reported nothing unusual occurring except that a covey of small birds suddenly took flight from a point several hundred yards to the south. Cano and Mina, the two men not on the platforms at the time, investigated the edge of the trail where the birds had flushed, but saw nothing. This occurred at dawn.

Diego sent the four relieved soldiers back to *La Aldea*, directed Tiritar to mount the eastern platform and Búho onto the western one. Once on the platform the men loaded their muskets and placed them on half cock.

Diego nodded in approval. He turned to Martin and Serpas. "Tend to your locks and load."

Then each man flipped back the frizzen on his musket lock, dug a cartridge out of his cartridge box, tore it open, primed the pan, and closed the frizzen. Placing the musket butt next to his left foot, each man loaded powder and ball into his musket. They rammed down the charges and shouldered their weapons.

Diego initiated the rapid foot patrol. "Serpas to the fore, move south at a trot."

Serpas instinctively held to the left edge of the trail. A man armed with a bayonet can more quickly fend off a rush from the left than from the right. Following the left edge of the trail would give Serpas more reaction time if danger appeared on his right. It also provided him a better view ahead as the trail continued to curve gradually to the right.

Diego again took the center of the trail. He could hear Martin following twenty paces to his rear. Serpas would scan ahead, to the left and right, then glance back to Diego for any instructions.

When Diego reached the location Cano and Mina had reported as the origin of the flushed birds he signaled Serpas to stop and hold a position where he could watch the trail ahead. He signaled Martin forward to join him.

"We are going into the brush. Keep a watch well forward. I will be concentrating on the ground close to me. It is light now and we might see something Cano could not. If you see something moving, shoot it."

Martin smiled. "Just like *le Pot de Rois*, *Primero*?"

Le Pot de Rois was the name of the alehouse he and Martin had invaded to recover a drunken and technically deserted Plata two years ago.

Again, Plata.

"Just keep looking far ahead so I do not stumble into an ambush."

Diego pushed into the tree line and discovered a steep slope downward not a dozen yards from the trail's edge. Moving down the slope was difficult and required Diego to grab a tree or shrub occasionally to avoid sliding down to the creek far below. He looked back at Martin and was relieved to see the soldier scanning far ahead while following Diego down the slope.

The brush, dense with vines and low growth along the trail, became thinner on the heavily forested slope. Several hundred yards down the slope, Diego could make out a trickle of a stream far below. He found a place where a branch had been broken downward and beneath it a scrape of a boot on the leaf-strewn slope where the man had slipped. He signaled Martin to stop.

Slowly the clues came together. A rub mark on a tree, a bent fern, a pattern in the leaves – someone had been walking along a game path that ran parallel to the road above. Diego tried to estimate how many people were in the group and guessed it to be no more than three. The signs indicated a northerly movement toward *La Aldea*. At some point, the travelers would have to move further down the slope or they would have been detected by the pickets. Or maybe they stopped short of the pickets.

The shot startled Diego so much he slipped a few feet down the slope. He looked up to see Martin furiously reloading his musket while pressed against a tree. Following Martin's eyes Diego could see two men hurrying along the slope toward him. Both were armed with rifles. The man furthest from them stopped to aim at Martin.

Diego shouted, "Martin – Down."

The rifleman fired. Diego heard the wiz of the bullet and looked to see Martin safely tucked behind a tree as bark flew above his head. *That was a mistake! This fight will be over before that rifle can be reloaded.*

It was a two to one fight now. Diego rushed the lead man who was struggling to pull his rifle from his shoulder. The man managed to duck under Diego's lance and caught a knee to his face. Diego passed him and closed with the second man who was in the process of ramming down a charge in his rifle. He stopped and raised his hands when Diego placed the *espontoon's* razor-sharp tip to his throat. Diego glanced back to see Martin disarm the unconscious lead man. After a few gestures from Diego, the shooter placed his weapons on the ground as well.

There was a noise uphill. Martin called out, "This way!" and Serpas appeared. Martin pointed with his musket. "There is another one further down the hill. I think I hit him when I shot."

Both men were dressed as outdoorsmen and could have passed for *Kentuckianos*. "Have this one carry his companion up to the trail, and wait there for me. Make him lie face down in the trail. I am certain Pook heard the shots and he should be along with the off watch. Keep these men on the ground until relieved. I am going to look for the one Martin hit."

After the prisoner shouldered his companion, Martin urged him up the slope with the point of a bayonet. Serpas shadowed the struggling man, alert for any trickery. Diego continued north where the game trail diverted downhill.

He saw the boots first. A swath of bloody leaves documented where the man had fallen, on his back, and slid to a stop against the base of a tree. A gaping hole in the middle of his chest was evidence enough that the man had hit the ground dead. A .69 caliber ball makes a significant wound. Diego pushed back the hat that covered the man's face.

Where have I seen this man before?

Then he remembered. Martin's mention of the day they arrested Plata had reminded him. That day, two English-speaking men at the alehouse had tried to intervene, two men who had also been suspiciously shadowing Spanish troops in the city. The corpse on the ground at his feet was the one called "Hank". Another memory flooded in. The man killed when they captured Marcelite, the one Diego thought he had seen before, was the one called "Davy."

CHAPTER 15

iego sifted through the few things Hank had been carrying. On the ground lay a small bag, called a "possible bag" by the Americans, which carried balls, spare flints and other items for the maintenance of a rifle. The rifle rested on the leaves a few paces uphill where it had slipped off Hank's shoulder as his body slid down the slope. Diego pulled a haversack from under the body and examined the contents. He found five silver coins, all Spanish, some jerked venison, hard biscuits, and a small knife in a leather sheath. These he transferred to his own haversack.

The boots were new and fine leather. Diego pulled them off. He knew of two men in *La Cuchilla* in need of boots. Seeing nothing else of value, Diego started up the hill, picking up the rifle on the way. He could hear shouts from the road. Pook, responding to the sound of gunfire, had arrived with eight men.

Diego stepped out of the tree line just as Martin was recounting to Pook what had happened. Both turned as they heard Diego pushing through the brush.

"What do you think this means, *Primero?*" Pook asked.

"I do not know. How are our prisoners?" Diego handed Pook the boots and rifle. "Have these brought back with you."

Martin gestured over to where one *Kentuckiano* was sprawled face-down on the ground and the other kneeling with his haversack over his head. Each man had been carrying a haversack and their former contents were scattered about. *Except for any silver or jerked meat;* Martin and Serpas would have relieved both men of any valuables.

"Martin, did you search them both for weapons?"

"Yes, *Primero.*" Martin pointed to the kneeling man and then to a pistol tucked into his waistband. "Serpas has obtained a fine knife from the other one."

"Is this one dead?" Diego kicked at the boot of the prostrate *Kentuckiano.*

"No, *Primero.* He breathes."

Diego switched to his version of English. "He will wake when I stab him with my –," he could not remember the English word for *espontoon* and simply poked at the man's back.

"*Espera! Parada!* (Wait, Stop)" the man exclaimed.

Diego switched to Spanish. "He is alive! And speaking Spanish! Pook, you and three men take the kneeling one over to a picket and force him to kneel hugging the tree." Diego wanted to be certain the prisoners had no opportunity to talk among themselves or hear anything said during interrogation.

Diego watched as Pook complied. When he was satisfied the other prisoner could not hear, he kicked the man's boot again.

"Roll over," he said, sticking to Spanish. The man complied.

His face was covered in blood and a clearly broken nose was smashed against his face. Blood poured onto the man's shirt as he struggled up.

"Stay on your knees," Diego commanded and the man complied. "Can we converse in Spanish, or should I call over an English translator?"

"My Spanish is good."

"What is your name?"

"I am Antoine Barnave of Haute Garonne."

Diego thought he had heard of Haute Garonne – somewhere in France, maybe.

"And who is your friend over there?"

"I know him as John Cook. He is from Maryland, I think."

Diego stepped back for a moment. "Martin, arm yourself with that hatchet you carry." Martin stepped forward and pulled the tomahawk from his belt.

"Do not move, Antoine Barnave. Do not make a sound or Private Martin will cave in your skull. *Entienes?*"

"*Entiendo.*"

Diego walked several paces to where the other prisoner knelt, his arms around the trunk of a pine tree. Diego jabbed him with the butt of his *espontoon*.

"What is your name?"

"I do not speak Spanish," the man said slowly in English.

Fortunately, one of the guards was Olivier. Diego waved him over. "Translate for me."

Diego pulled the haversack from the man's head and repeated, "What is your name?"

"I am John Cook."

"Who is your friend over there?"

"He is *Monsieur* Barnave. He is a French nobleman, or so he says. He has papers."

"Where are you from?"

"Manchester, New Hampshire."

'Who is the one we killed?"

"He is dead?"

"What was his name?"

"He was my cousin, William Doone."

"Where were you going?"

"We were bound for Pensacola. The Frenchman had business there. He hired us to bring him there from Mobile."

"Why did you not simply travel on the road? You said the Frenchman had papers. What papers?"

"He did not tell us what the papers were. He just hired us to get him from Mobile to Pensacola."

"Olivier, keep him here," Diego replaced the haversack over Cook's head and returned to Barnave."

"Barnave, what was the name of the man we killed?"

"He was Mister Doone. I had hired them to bring me to Pensacola."

"Why did you not simply use the road?"

"I did not know if you would let us pass."

Diego picked up Barnave's haversack and felt about inside the rough canvas bag. He found nothing so he pulled the haversack over Barnave's head.

"Get to your feet. Take off your coat and put your hands behind you. Serpas, tie his hands."

Serpas expertly lashed the man's wrists together and then his elbows while Diego went through his pockets. He felt along the fringed coat and found where something had been sewn into a hidden pocket.

"Serpas, hand me that new knife you have."

Diego slit the pocket open and pulled out a folded parchment. He opened it to see a very official looking document with a red wax seal. It was in French, a language Diego could speak after a fashion, but not read.

"Pook, have Cook remove his coat and bind him. Take these men to Castro. Keep them hooded all of the way. Wait for me at Bare Hill. Do not stop at *La Aldea*. Do not tell anyone what has happened until you talk to Castro."

"Yes, *Primero.*"

He watched as Pook and the men who had come with him escorted the prisoners north.

So many lies! If the men had left Mobile and were bound for Pensacola, who was it that flushed the covey of birds that morning? Who had left the tracks leading north on the game trail the men were following south? Why was a French aristocrat dressed as a *Kentuckiano* sneaking through the brush when a perfectly good trail held by an ally was available? If the papers were diplomatic or official in any way, Barnave could have simply taken a packet boat under a flag of truce to Pensacola.

They most certainly had not gone through Bare Hill for Castro, a stickler for detail and order, would have alerted the pickets. If these men were out of Mobile, they exhibited a most clandestine attitude toward Spain.

Diego re-established Martin and Serpas at the picket posts with instructions to continue with the scheduled relief rotation. He left the road and returned to the body of the man he knew as Hank but Cook claimed to be his cousin William Doone. He squatted by the body and examined every detail. The trousers were dry and the man's boots had been relatively free of mud.

The stream below flowed north to within a few hundred yards of the village before meandering west to enter Mobile Bay next to the trail leading up to Bare Hill. If they had come from Mobile, they would have had to cross the stream to get to here. The stream between here and Mobile Bay was bordered by a wide mudflat on both sides. They had not come that way. The only place to come ashore on this bank of the stream was at the Bare Hill landing. Castro would have detained them. They had not come from Mobile Bay.

Diego remembered the hidden pocket in Barnave's coat. He pulled the coat off of the body and examined it for any lumps or hidden pockets. He felt something along the bottom of the coat where a strip of fringe had been attached. He slit the sewn end of the strip and shook out ten silver coins – French *ecu*.

Hank and Davy must have been working for the same people.

Finding nothing else on the body, Diego moved north along the trail, back-tracking the last steps of the strangers. The trail dipped down as it neared the picket posts until it just skirted the marsh beside the stream. A few more yards north and it moved up the slope again slightly until the walking was easier. Clearly the trail has been used by animals, or people fearing detection by the Spanish pickets. Suddenly, the path started uphill only to end in a clump of brush.

The trees and brush formed a bower which showed signs of frequent use. Leaves had been pulled together to form three distinct resting places. No sign of a fire. No sign of bedrolls having been used. This was not a camp site for travelers. Diego tried to estimate where he was in relation to *La Aldea*. It had to be nearby. The underbrush thickened noticeably a few yards uphill, indicating a clearing.

He pushed a little uphill until he could see through the brush. He could see the road junction and village. The three men he had backtracked had been waiting here, just out of sight of the village. Except for the trail to this spot, he had crossed no other signs of travelers between Hank's body and here. The three men had come from the direction of Pensacola, stopped here, and were headed back to Pensacola when they encountered Diego and Martin. From the condition of the trail, Diego surmised it was a trip they or others had made many times. Had they been waiting for something or someone? Had they delivered something or received something?

Deciding against pushing out into the clearing, Diego returned to the bower and moved westward searching for any sign of another visitor to the bower. He had gone less than five yards when he came upon a rubbish dump. Debris created in *La Aldea*, including the contents of chamber pots, had been dumped into the wooded perimeter and over the edge of a steep slope where it slid down away from the buildings, out of scent and sight. Anyone from the village emptying a chamber pot or tossing debris would have been within conversational range of the men hiding in the bower.

Diego returned south, following the trail until he estimated he was below the pickets. He pushed uphill and was challenged by Martin after having gone only a few yards.

"*Perro!*" Martin shouted, having heard the sound of someone moving uphill, but unable to see who it was. The challenge was accompanied by the sound of a musket being brought to full cock.

Diego instantly responded with the pass word, "*Rojo!*" The password combination would have to be changed soon, but "red dog" was so difficult for the *godums* to say it was almost perfect.

"*Primero!*" Martin had recognized Diego's voice from only one word. "Come ahead. I nearly shot you."

Diego moved onto the trail. Both pickets were manned and the four men posted here were tense and alert. The brief action had everyone's blood up. There would be no sleeping on downtime today.

"Pook will be back with the change of watch as usual. Any questions?"

"*Primero*, who did I kill today?"

"I do not know, Martin. But trust me, you did the right thing. The man was an enemy. That I do not doubt."

ᴄ∕๏

"The man, Barnave, had diplomatic papers!" Castro had been shouting for a full minute and specks of spittle decorated his thin beard. "The papers carried the seal of the king of France. Did you not see the seal, Sergeant?"

"He had the papers hidden on his person, sir. He did not present them to me."

"That is because the fools you had on picket shot at him. Thank God the only one killed was a hired guide."

Diego decided silence would serve the situation best. Castro had ever held a low opinion of Diego and this incident provided the fledgling officer an opportunity to express the contempt he felt. It would do no good to attempt a conversation with the man.

"You may think you are safe from me, sergeant, because you serve in the General's regiment and are only temporarily assigned to me. But this assault on a courier of France will convince the General his trust in you is mistaken."

Perhaps silence is not the best approach.

"What did the diplomatic papers say, Lieutenant?"

"Say! What did the papers say? That is none of your concern. You are under arrest, Sergeant. You will remove your insignia. I shall place you under guard. You will remain in the barracks until Colonel de Ezpeleta has decided what to do with you."

Diego almost smiled. *So, you cannot read French either.*

The prisoners had been ferried across Mobile Bay to the fort. The incident, along with Castro's report, had been passed to a higher authority. Fortunately, Pook – Corporal Pedro Gonzales – had been sent in command of the escort. Colonel de Ezpeleta would have the opportunity for a more reliable report, if he would think to ask.

Castro was not finished. "You will not send word to *La Cuchilla* or that whore you keep. I have assigned a competent sergeant to take command. A picket is a waste of men. I have half a mind to call your precious *La Cuchilla* into this post and put them to real work."

So he knows about Marcelite. Who does not?

Castro's grenadiers had been the parade guards for his uncle's headquarters in Havana. They had been sent to Mobile because they were not essential to Havana's defense. The commanders in Cuba, ever fearful of a British invasion, were reluctant to send men to support Gálvez.

The seasoned veterans of *La Cuchilla* would devour Castro's parade sergeant.

"I ordered you to remove your insignia of rank! You will do so now!"

Diego unbuttoned the blue epaulets, took them from his shoulders and slipped them into a pocket.

"That will not do, Private." Castro was smiling now, a malevolent crooked smile on a childish face. "Give the epaulets to me," he said as he held out his left hand. Diego noted how smooth and free of callouses it was, clearly not the man's sword hand. Even parade officers practiced daily with the sabre and rapier. One was for war, the other for dueling.

Diego roughly placed the blue epaulets in the lieutenant's hand. His anger was building. A reduction in rank meant a cut in pay and the stipend provided to Isabella for his children would be cut off.

Dismissed from Castro's presence, Diego was escorted to the grenadier's barracks. His personal effects, his haversack and the contents of his pockets were inventoried and placed in a box built into a corner of the barracks. The clerk responsible for listing the things of value in a log book initially neglected to list the ten French *ecu*. Diego quickly corrected the oversight. Had he not, the coins would have disappeared before dawn. His weapons, the short sword and the *espontoon*, were simply added to the grenadier's armory.

He was escorted to an opposite corner of the barracks where he was allowed to remove his uniform coat and shackled to a chain running through a ring in a corner post. As prisons go, it was not an uncomfortable setting. A canvas curtain had been rigged on two sides forming a cell intended to isolate him from the billeted grenadiers. He was told he would be fed twice a day and provided a bench, cot and chamber pot.

Diego examined the ring and was comforted to discover it was not bolted through the corner post but simply screwed into the wood. If the need should arise, he could easily unscrew the ring and be free, though still shackled to a length of chain. The iron cuffs around his wrists were fastened with softer iron rivets and could be easily parted using an ax blade as a wedge. He had done it before when he had escaped from Pensacola. He was a prisoner here only as long as he would allow.

꙳

"Primero. Primero."

Diego shook himself awake. Someone was whispering to him from the other side of the canvas wall of his improvised cell. Lieutenant Castro had addressed the assembled Havana grenadiers the evening of Diego's arrest and admonished all, under penalty of unspecified retribution, to refrain from conversing with the prisoner. But Diego had worked with the men of the grenadiers before. His skill with bayonet and *espontoon* were known by all. His reputation as a fighter superseded the purchased authority of Lieutenant Castro.

By the first night of his confinement soldiers of the grenadiers were already communicating with Diego. They offered him portions of their rations and even collected small contributions of the evening rum ration from each of the nearly forty privates housed in the barracks. Diego was able to enjoy an almost full cup of potent Cuban rum before retiring.

He had requested someone send word to Marcelite and Quintero of what had occurred. Pook was not expected to return from Mobile until the next day and he could only imagine the account Castro had provided to the men of *La Cuchilla*. He recognized the voice whispering to him. It was Corporal Barbeaux of the Duplesses Battalion. The fact that a militiaman had been admitted into the grenadier's barracks was an indication of how widespread the resentment of Diego's treatment was among the troops.

Diego answered in French. "I can hear you."

"Primero, the woman, the one who cooks for Marbone, is gone. She has not been seen since the day you were arrested."

Diego could not explain why such news was not a surprise to him.

"Quintero says that the grenadier sergeant sleeps soundly and does not interfere with *La Cuchilla*. He also says he will post some men along the trail you found. Perhaps others may come seeking the captured spies."

The soldiers of Bare Hill and *La Cuchilla* universally held the opinion that the men called Barnave and Cook were British spies, despite or perhaps because of Castro's declaration that a French diplomatic communication had been disastrously disrupted. Quintero's decision to post a guard on the trail was a good one.

"Has your battalion begun to build the trenches we talked of the other day?"

"Yes. T'Chastane is personally supervising the work. He reads an old book at night about how the Romans built their camps at night and directs work during the day. Everyone has an opinion and we joyfully labor away."

"Men will work hard when they understand and appreciate what they do."

"If you want, *Primero*, I will suggest to T'Chastane you be put to work with us. We would benefit from your knowledge."

"I would like that."

"Consider it done. I go."

Marcelite, gone again. Guards and pickets did not seem to interfere with her movements. After the fall of Mobile, she walked out of the north gate into Mobile and disappeared. Weeks later, she appeared at *La Aldea* as if she had lived there all her life. Part of him feared he would never see her again and part of him feared he would.

He sat on the cot, his head swimming with the decisions he could make. He would join the work parties if for no other reason than to learn every route available off of Bare Hill. Castro had sent the supposed diplomats and a request for Diego's courts martial to Havana where Gálvez was collecting forces for the assault on Pensacola. It would be several weeks before a reply could reach Mobile. He need only wait a week or so until vigilance grew lax and he could easily escape into the wilderness of West Florida. He could speak some Choctaw and he knew the land.

But his children would be lost to him. Isabella was a good woman and she would raise them well, but it would be hard for her without the money his pay provided. Then there was the promise he made to have a stone placed for Mézu. He could escape into the wild country and live with the Choctaw, but there was something in New Orleans, something about New Orleans, he could not explain. He could not go.

He decided to wait for the reply from Havana. He could be sentenced to a reduction in rank. If that happened, he would return to New Orleans after the war and farm with the Campos. If the sentence was something harsher, he would escape to the Choctaw country. Who knows, he might even be vindicated. Gálvez would not be fooled by a forgery, no matter how artful. True diplomats did not sulk about in the wilderness avoiding the frontier guards of their allies.

⁊

In the morning, Diego was permitted to join the work party trenching the southern crest of the hill. He watched as a sloop from Mobile bumped into the landing at the foot of Bare Hill and Pook jumped ashore. He centered himself on a clear section of pier and shouted for the six man escort detail to form ranks on him.

Pook has become a regular sergeant, Diego thought as he watched the escort being inspected. Apparently satisfied with their appearance, Pook marched them single file up the narrow trail to the top of Bare Hill. They trooped past the end of the trench where Diego was shoveling. Pook did not look in Diego's direction, but shifted a leather message pouch from one shoulder to the other with exaggerated movements.

He is telling me he carries orders from de Ezpeleta.

The detail halted at Castro's headquarters and was told to rest in place while Pook carried the message pouch into the building. Ten minutes later, Pook reemerged, called the detail to attention and announced they were to take their noon meal with the grenadiers. In one hour, they were to reform to be marched to the village. "We will go back home," was the words Pook used.

Castro's clerk appeared and rushed past Pook to the smith's shop. He called to the smith, who ducked into his shop and came out with a wedge and a maul. Both men trotted across the compound to Diego.

Panting the clerk said, "*Primero*, I am to take you to the barracks. There you are to retrieve your things, draw your weapons from the armory and take the escort back to *La Aldea*." The clerk extended a shaking hand holding two blue epaulets.

Diego laughed. There had been no time for a message to return from Havana. De Ezpeleta had decided on his own that the men were spies, or at least that the men of *La Cuchilla* had acted correctly. Lieutenant Castro was probably too upset to reinstate Diego personally, so this would be it. No apologies, just a message to return to duty.

"Gentlemen," Diego said in French to the men of the Duplesses Battalion who were working with him in the trench. "I see that I must leave you now. Remember to post pickets far down the slope. This trench will only work if you are in it when the *godums* come."

"Back to being a sergeant, I see." Barbeaux teased. "See that you stay clear of Castro if you want to remain a sergeant."

"Sound advice, my friend." Diego said as he stepped up from the trench. "Take care of Gabriella."

"I will do that, fear it not."

The smith directed Diego to position the clasp of his hand irons on a post, placed the wedge on the riveted joint and struck off the hasps. Diego walked to a laundry maid's tent and rinsed the dirt from his arms and hands before going to the barracks, the clerk trotting behind him.

Once in the barracks, Diego directed the clerk to open the lock box. He retrieved his haversack and all of his personal items. He watched as the clerk counted out ten French *ecu* into the palm of his hand and made the appropriate entries into the log book.

"Get my sword and *espontoon* from the armory and bring them to me."

"Yes, *Primero*." The clerk raced out to comply.

Diego went to the enclosure that has served as his temporary cell. He picked up his uniform coat, which had served as a blanket, and carefully reattached the epaulets. He pulled on the coat just as the clerk returned with his weapons.

"Your hat, *Primero*." The clerk had remembered to get Diego's hat as well.

"Thank you, you are dismissed." The clerk was gone in an instant.

Diego buckled on his sword, squared his hat and placed the butt of the *espontoon* next to his right foot. He felt every inch a sergeant, and he liked the feeling. He stepped out of the barracks into the small parade compound to find Pook and the escort in line and at attention.

Pook was posted front and centered on the small detail. "Escort all present, *Primero*."

"Thank you, corporal. Post."

Pook marched to the end of the six men and stepped into line, an act which formally transferred command of the unit to Diego.

"To the right flank, Face." The line of men became a file facing east.

"Shoulder Arms." Each man shouldered his musket. All were canted at the same angle.

"Forward, March."

Diego had not ordered the quick march so the men stepped off at the slower, lock-step pace, a pace which exuded power and dignity.

CHAPTER 16

Diego stood in the shade of the porch canopy at the entrance to Castro's headquarters. Bare Hill enjoyed a comforting breeze from the east provided one was able to find shade. Dust flowed along the ground like a tan fog in the July heat. His daily picket reports to Castro had transformed from first hand reporting to written briefs handed to a clerk. Castro had not said two words to Diego since the day de Ezpeleta had ordered the sergeant's release and reinstatement. He was waiting for a reply to the report. Castro enjoyed making Diego wait.

The clerk, an old man named Armano who had been the Castro family butler in Havana and would likely be a butler again once the war with Britain was concluded, shuffled out onto the porch. He held two folded papers. One was sealed and the other was not.

"Daily orders for *La Cuchilla, Primero*," he muttered, waving the unsealed papers. "I will have a courier bring them to Corporal Gonzales." He tapped the folded and sealed paper. "These are special orders for you, from Colonel de Ezpeleta. You are to report to him within the hour. I have held the packet boat for you."

Word had finally arrived from Havana. Diego hesitated before accepting the orders. He considered it likely they contained his fate.

"Thank you, Armano."

"It is nothing, *Primero*," a smile appeared on the old man's usually somber face. "You will be back at *La Aldea* by tomorrow, I think."

Seal orders with hot red wax, but clerks know what is written within. Armano was telling him he had nothing to fear.

He accepted the sealed orders and headed west down the wide and well-worn trail to the landing and the waiting packet boat. She was a gaff-rigged double-ended whaler and once had been a British captain's gig. She could accommodate no more than four passengers. Diego passed a shanty town of workers and camp followers that had grown up below the post on Bare Hill. Two score men and a like number of women and children, mostly mestizos from the wilderness of west Florida, had taken advantage of the wages offered for work on Bare Hill and Fort Carlota.

The coxswain impatiently waved Diego to the boat and indicated where he was to sit for the brief trip across the bay to Mobile. The wind was from the east and the men in the boat had been waiting in the lee of tall Bare Hill so they were eager to get out of the stifling heat and underway. It was necessary to row a short distance down the Tensaw River, for the landing was not directly on the bay, to reach open water. It was a trip of less than five hundred yards. The gig had only one bench, a long narrow plank running from nearly stem to stern where four oarsmen sat astride when working the sweeps. Someone had crudely painted the name *"Angarius"* on her side.

"*Angarius?*" Diego asked the coxswain as he clambered aboard.

"The *Padre's* idea – says all vessels of Spain must be named."

"What does it mean?"

"*No sé*," the man said with a shrug.

Diego was directed to the fore end of the bench where he sat and, resting his *espontoon* against one shoulder, he broke the seal on his orders.

"By order of Bernardo de Gálvez, Governor General of Louisiana, and commanding the forces of His Most Catholic Majesty in Florida does hereby order and instruct Sergeant Primero Diego deMelilla y Tupinar of the Fixed Infantry Regiment of Louisiana to present himself to Colonel José de Ezpeleta at Fort Carlota on the twenty-seventh day of July to answer under oath such questions as that officer may present concerning actions occurring on the eighth day of June in La Aldea Mobile Bay."

Diego was impressed. Word had been sent to Havana and returned in less than a month and a half, during hurricane season. Such speed in communication was a wonder, even in wartime. Under oath meant that every word was going to be recorded and analyzed. Colonel de Ezpeleta would be saying the words, but the questions would have most certainly originated from Gálvez and his staff. *Monsieur* Barnave was generating curiosity in some very high places.

Angarius had gone only a few hundred yards past the mouth of the Tensaw when she escaped the lee of Bare Hill. The four sailors joyfully shipped their oars and set the gaff for a full down-wind run. Diego watched as Fort Carlota grew on the horizon. She was much more impressive than last he saw her. The stone walls had been restored to full height and the wooden palisade the British had erected to discourage an escalade had been removed. Colonel de Ezpeleta had apparently surmised that an assault from the beach was unlikely.

Diego saw a small contingent of soldiers trot out onto the pier and form into an escort under the command of a corporal. The corporal called his men to attention as the *Angarius* touched the pier. Sailors held the boat against the dock while Diego climbed up and a message pouch was passed down.

"Dispatches for Mobile Point," the corporal said as the message pouch made its way to the coxswain and a substitute pouch was sent back to him. The *Angarius* pushed off and set sail for a southerly course. Diego did not know where Mobile Point was, but it was clearly south of Mobile.

"Sergeant deMelilla?" the corporal asked. Diego did not recognize the man which meant he had arrived at Mobile after Diego had been stationed at *La Aldea*.

"Yes. Am I to be placed under guard?"

The corporal looked surprised for a moment. "Guard? No. No, we are guards for the dispatches. I was told to watch for you and, if you arrived on the packet boat, I was to bring you to Colonel de Ezpeleta without delay. I am Corporal Rocas, assistant to the Colonel's adjutant, Lieutenant Mazias. Please follow us."

Evidently, Lieutenant Mazias was the officer in charge of communication. Curiously, Rocas did not command the four-man escort from the flank, but situated himself in the middle of the escort, as if he were a prisoner, and clutching the leather message pouch to his chest, ordered the formation forward. Diego followed this unusual formation wondering what could be the cause of such a tactic. *Where dispatches being snatched from couriers between wharf and fort?*

He could see the town of Mobile stretching north of the fort. It seemed to be busy. Traffic moved along the streets and the commercial docks were busy loading and unloading goods. Unlike New Orleans, where the humid summer days were often accompanied by yellow fever or malaria causing the city to almost hibernate, Mobile bustled. He wondered if Marcelite was in Mobile.

They passed through the gates of Fort Carlota into the courtyard and up to the front porch of the headquarters building. An officer, a lieutenant Diego took to be Mazias, waited on the porch. Rocas halted the detail, maneuvered out of the quadrangle of guards and saluted the lieutenant.

"Dispatches from Bare Hill, sir."

The lieutenant accepted the pouch. "That will be all, corporal. You and your men are dismissed for the noon meal."

"Sir, Sergeant deMelilla is here."

Mazias seemed to notice Diego for the first time. "Oh, yes. I see. Please follow me, sergeant."

Mazias led Diego into the front office. "Please place your weapons in the armory and wait here. I will tell the Colonel you are here. The Colonel will send for you when we are ready."

The armory consisted of two racks along one wall that held six muskets, a dozen swords and a brace of pistols. Diego added his sword and *espontoon* to the collection and removed his hat. The door to the courtyard opened and a priest accompanied by two clerks, one with a writing kit, hurried past Diego and disappeared into the next room.

A priest to administer the oath and a scribe!

Diego felt a foreboding sensation crawl through his stomach.

The door to the courtyard opened again. A Captain of artillery and an officer in a French-looking uniform entered. Diego dutifully snapped to attention. The officers ignored him and hustled past into the next room as well. The men were speaking to each other in low tones as they passed. Diego could not understand what they were saying, but he recognized the language. It was English.

The door to the inner office opened by one of the scribes. "Please, come in Sergeant deMelilla."

Diego remembered the room. He and Búho had searched it after the fort had been taken. The room had been in shambles then. Now it was well-furnished. A wide window high on the wall across from the doorway was open allowing a faint breeze to waft through the room. The clerk left the door to the outer office open apparently to assist in the movement of air. An army colonel sat at a massive desk under the window.

The clerks were huddled in one corner surrounding a portable writing desk where they busied themselves with sharpening quills, mixing ink and arranging log books. The priest, studying a book, occupied another corner. Diego thought it might be a prayer book, the kind called a "breviary."

Diego marched to the front center of the colonel's desk, snapped to attention, fixed his eyes on a spot on the brick wall outside of the open window and said, "Sergeant Diego deMelilla reporting as ordered, sir." He held the salute.

De Ezpeleta, engrossed in the papers he was reading, did not look up. Diego patiently accepted the slight – a case of making the underling wait to emphasize who is important. It was a practice some deliberately played and some came by naturally.

The Colonel finished what he was reading and looked up. He returned Diego's salute. "Are you quite ready, Santos?" He said.

One of the clerks, Diego assumed it was the one named Santos stuttered. "Just a moment more, Colonel. We are just now finishing the heading."

"Get on with it, man." He noticed Diego was still stiffly at attention. "Stand at ease, Sergeant. We will proceed directly once my clerks manage to rule their thumbs."

"We are ready, Colonel, sir."

"Fine. Father Dominic, if you please. Administer the oath to Sergeant deMelilla."

The priest ceremoniously closed his breviary, kissed it and slipped it into a hidden pocket in his robe. He fumbled at the cord tied about his waist until he found the crucifix bound to its end. He walked to Diego

"Face me, Diego deMelilla y Tupinar."

Diego complied.

"Are you Diego deMelilla y Tupinar, First Sergeant of the Fixed Regiment of Louisiana?"

"I am he."

"Here, in the presence of these officers, the Holy Mother Church and the Lord God, do you swear, on peril of your immortal soul, that the statements you will provide here will be complete and truthful in both word and intent so help you God's grace?"

Diego was not certain of the meaning of the phrase "word and intent."

"I do so swear."

Father Dominic thrust the crucifix toward Diego and held it there until Diego kissed the figure's feet. He could hear the scratching of the scrivener 's quill behind him.

"Done, *Padre?*" de Ezpeleta said impatiently.

The priest nodded, dropped the crucifix to bob at his knees, fished out his breviary and returned to his corner.

The Colonel cleared his throat. "Sergeant deMelilla, may I introduce the officers here with us. Captain Oeste of Governor General Gálvez staff." The Army Captain seated to Diego's left nodded. Oeste was a name common in Málaga, Gálvez's home town. "And Captain Barrett of the Colonial Army of the United States. I think you know Captain Barrett."

Diego remembered the officer. Over a year ago, on the road to attack Baton Rouge, Captain Barrett had commanded a scouting expedition into a German settlement. Diego was a member of that detail. The mission had concluded in a sharp fight at a British road block.

"Congratulations on your promotion, Sergeant," Barrett said in perfect Spanish.

"Thank you, sir."

"Enough with the introductions, gentlemen." The Colonel made a show of lifting a sheaf of papers from his desk. "We have many questions to ask of the good sergeant."

The first dozen or so questions covered the creation of *La Cuchilla* and Diego's experiences *en route* to Mobile and during the assault on then Fort Charlotte. No mention was made of the fight at the road crossing, the one the men called the "Silver Fight." Diego wondered what all of that had to do with the eighth of June.

"Were you present when Colonel Francisco Bouligny first negotiated for the British surrender of this fort?"

"Yes, sir. We were the truce escorts for the Colonel."

"Aside from the Colonel, who accompanied you?"

"Privates Olivier and –" Diego had to think to remember Plata's surname, "Pérez."

"Where are these men at this time?"

"Private Olivier is at *La Aldea*. Private Pérez was killed, sir."

"Did Colonel Bouligny meet with the British commander in your presence?"

"No, sir. The British commander would not meet with us. He sent one of his lieutenants to review the terms."

"Just the one officer?"

"No, sir. A woman accompanied the lieutenant to serve as a translator." Diego felt a bead of sweat trickle down his back.

"Do you remember the officer's name?"

"No, sir."

"Do you remember the translator's name?"

"It was Lady Smythe, I think, sir."

"Leave it to a soldier to remember only the Lady's name," Oeste quipped. The comment earned him a stern glare from the colonel.

"Do you know what became of Lady Smythe after the fall of this fort?"

"She went into the town when all of the civilians were released, sir." Diego swallowed hard. *The next question will be "have you ever, before or since seen this lady?"* He did not know what he was going to tell them.

"When were you posted to Bare Hill?"

The unexpected change caught Diego off guard and he nearly stuttered. "When we were ordered to fortify the place, sir. I think sometime in April. I am not certain."

"From April until June, what were the duties assigned to you?"

"I was, and still am, in charge of the advanced pickets east of the fortifications at Bare Hill, sir." *Why do they not ask about Marcelite?* Diego suspected a trap, knew there had to be a trap.

"On the morning of the eighth of June, did you command the relief detail for some of the pickets?"

"Yes, sir. I brought the relief for the southern pickets. That is, the men posted south of *La Aldea* along the road to Pensacola."

"Is it customary for the sergeant of the guard to escort the picket relief?"

"No, sir. That is normally done by one of my corporals."

"Why was that not the case on the eighth?"

"I wanted to see the picket posts, sir. See if they were being properly maintained. I had not visited the posts for a few days, sir."

"Who were the men you brought as picket relief?"

"Privates Martin, Serpas," he had to pause again to remember Búho and Tiritar"s proper names, "Franko and Gillama, sir."

The Colonel nodded toward one of the clerks who wrote something on a leaf of paper, folded it and rushed out of the office.

Going to summon those four, no doubt. If any one of them were asked about Marcelite, they would have to tell the truth. Yet, he was not being asked.

"Take us through what transpired once you and the relief detail reached the picket posts."

Diego recounted every step from the report of a flushed covey to Martin's challenge when he returned to the pickets.

"What do you make of it all, sergeant?"

"Sir?"

"Tell us what you think about Barnave, Cook and Doone. How did they get where they were and what were they doing?"

"The three men came from the direction of Pensacola, sir. There is no doubt about that. They crept up to the edge of *La Aldea*, waited there for over an hour or more, and then ran into us on their way back. I do not know what they were doing. There was no sign that they had entered the village. Clearly they were spies."

"Do you think they met someone?"

"I do not know, sir. Possibly."

"Had you seen any one of these men before?"

Where did that question come from? Diego had never mentioned to anyone he had recognized Doone as the man "Hank." How would they know to ask that?

"Yes, sir. The man that was killed, the one they claimed was William Doone. I remember seeing him in New Orleans. He and another man had attempted to interfere in an arrest I was making. Later, I saw them nosing about alehouses frequented by our troops, sir. They gave the impression they were assessing our strength, sir."

"Truly? Had you ever seen the one called Cook before?"

"No, sir."

"The man with Doone in New Orleans, have you ever seen him before or since?"

"Yes, sir. We encountered some Redcoats and civilians on the trail to Mobile Bay. We had a short fight and one of the *godums* killed was the other man in New Orleans."

Captain Barrett interrupted the Colonel. "Did you take any prisoners at that encounter?"

Diego was certain every man in the room could hear him swallow, but before he could respond, Colonel de Ezpeleta said, "Captain Barrett, We have a full account of that action on record. Please, we have enough questions to ask without hunting in the bushes."

"I do beg your pardon, Colonel. Forgive me."

"Yes, of course."

They already have a full report! Diego had forgotten about that. It was all there in the previous reports! Marcelite's capture – her escape at Pascagoula; it was all in the reports. All anyone had to do was read the reports. Did they know Marcelite was Lady Smythe? Did they know the cook at *La Aldea* was also Marcelite? Did they think Marcelite was the one Barnave had tried to visit? Maybe he did speak with her? A trickle of sweat dripped from an eyebrow into Diego's eye, forcing him to blink and rub it away with a finger.

The series of questions that followed concentrated on the evidence Diego found on the trail that convinced him the men came from Pensacola. It was well after noon by the time Diego was dismissed from the hearing. He felt as if he had run a hundred miles. They had not asked about Marcelite, but they knew. They knew everything.

Diego collected his weapons from the armory and walked down to the dock to inquire about the next boat to Bare Hill. One was due in about two hours. It would be the last one until tomorrow. He decided he would visit *Madame* Trapenier's alehouse. Since Bare Hill had been fortified her small inn was no longer the temporary headquarters it had been. He would get something to eat, he suddenly felt famished, and something to drink – definitely something to drink. Perhaps the *Madame* had word of Marcelite. Diego shook his head. The last thing he needed to be concerned about was Marcelite.

Royal Street was bustling with people pushing carts, carrying goods and hawking wares. Two new Spanish ships had landed that day and there were a number of sailors about, fresh from the sea. He pushed through the door to Trapenier's inn and found an empty bench in one corner. The chalk message his troops had scratched on the back of the door "If you go out this way – run" was still there.

A girl Diego did not recognize asked his pleasure in French-accented Spanish. When he responded in French, the girl was visibly relieved she did not have to continue in Spanish.

"We have roasted pork or beef stew. We have ale – very bad, wine – not so bad and excellent rum."

"I will have the stew and rum. Rum first."

"*Primero!*" *Madame* Trapenier called from across the room. She had just pushed her way into the room with several tankards of ale for some sailors who were gathered around an old barrelhead. She distributed the tankards and collected payment before shuffling to Diego.

"*Primero*, how long has it been? Two, no three months. All that time you have been just across the bay and you could not come and visit an old friend?"

"My time is not my own, *Madame*."

"Truly said, truly said, *Primero*. Who can say they own time."

The rum arrived.

"This is my daughter, Evangeline. Say hello to *Primero*, child. The finest soldier in the service of Spain, I think, me."

Evangeline wiped her hands on her apron and curtsied. "Hello, *Monsieur Primero*."

"Go get *Primero* something to eat."

"He has ordered the stew, Mama."

"Then get it for him." Evangeline hurried away.

"Ladle from the bottom of the pot!" Trapenier called after her.

Diego poured some of the rum down his throat. It both burned and felt wonderful. His head was spinning from the events of the day more than from the potent drink. *A soldier of Spain who may very well have been consorting with an enemy spy – and they knew.*

℮∽

The stew was perfect. Evangeline had indeed ladled deep, for there were many bits of beef and potatoes along with the thick stock. Two more cups of strong rum had followed the stew and Diego was only slightly unsteady as he walked down to the pier to catch the last boat bound for Bare Hill. He reached the pier in time to see a packet boat land and disgorge five passengers. Three would have been a tight fit, so it must have been a crowded crossing.

One of the men scrambling onto the dock was the clerk who had rushed out of Diego's hearing. The other four were Martin, Serpas, Búho and Tiritar. Martin saw Diego and said something to the packet boat's coxswain. The clerk ordered the men, all unarmed, into a file and marched them up to the fort. Diego was thankful he had not fabricated anything about the eighth. He hurried unsteadily to catch the packet boat before she shoved off.

Message pouches were being passed between boat and pier when he stepped up. It was a different packet boat, slightly larger, than the one he had arrived in that morning. The coxswain stowed the leather message carriers and waved Diego aboard.

"Are you the one called *Primero?*" He asked.

"I am Diego deMelilla."

"Right! The master of the *Alacita* said you would be at *La Aldea*. This is for you."

The coxswain handed Diego a folded paper. It was a letter from Isabella. Diego stuffed it into a coat pocket and clambered into the boat. He was directed to take a seat on the fore side of the single mast where he would be out of the way of the crew. The trip back across the bay was against the wind and unless the crew wanted to row the seven miles from Mobile to the foot of Bare Hill, the trip would consist of a series of tacks as they beat to the east.

Diego leaned against the mast and put a hand on the pocket holding Isabella's letter to protect it from the sea spray thrown by the packet boat as she beat against the steep chop. It had been a long time since the last letter.

Running close to the wind created a soothing breeze along with the misting bow spray. These conditions obliterated the heat of the day and, when added to the full meal and too much rum, had Diego sound asleep before the second tack.

~

"Poppa! Look what I can do!" Little Maria was walking on wooden blocks held to her feet by cords which she gripped in her hands. Each step was exaggerated by hand movements needed to hold the blocks in place. She was thrashing grain on a wide blanket.

"I can see you." Diego managed to say.

"She can almost run on those blocks." It was Pedro. He was tossing heads of wheat onto the blanket.

Isabella was beside him. "They can separate the grain from the chaff." She looked into his eyes. "Can you?"

"Where is Mézu?" He had dreamed of the children thrashing wheat before. Mézu had always been there.

Isabella pointed. He twisted to see. A wide lake, maybe the sea, was next to them. Isabella's hand gestured toward the water.

"*Primero. Primero*, we are here." The coxswain's leathery face swam into view. It was dark and they were alongside the Bare Hill landing.

Diego sheepishly recovered his *espontoon* from under the center bench where one of the sailors had stowed it as Diego slept and climbed up onto the narrow pier. The boatmen were securing the boat for the night. The little shanties that lined the road up to the top of Bare Hill were home to these sailors. They accompanied Diego up the hill until, one by one, they arrived at their huts and left the trail. Diego reached the top of the hill alone.

He was challenged by a guard, one of the grenadiers from Havana, who recognized him.

"Is Lieutenant Castro still up?" Diego did not know the time. It seemed to be late, nine or maybe even ten. Still, he was expected to report.

"I do not know, *Primero*," the guard said with a shrug.

Diego made his way to Castro's quarters. He noticed that the New Orleans militia battalion command tent was well lit. *T'Chastane reading about the Roman earthworks, perhaps.*

Castro's place did not show a light. Two guards were posted at the front door. One was leaning against the door frame, asleep. The other saw Diego coming and elbowed his partner awake.

"Halt, who goes there?" said the one who had not been asleep.

"Sergeant deMelilla reporting to Lieutenant Castro." Diego stepped up onto the porch and a plank creaked in protest.

"Ah, *Primero*. The Lieutenant said if you returned tonight we were to tell him in the morning. He said you were to report to him after the morning formation."

Diego shrugged. He had no desire to speak to the Lieutenant either. The morning would do. His hand brushed his coat as he stepped down from the porch causing him to remember Isabella's letter. He pulled it out and drifted over to the light that spilled out of Chastane's tent. The lone militia guard saw that Diego was simply finding light and said nothing.

Don Diego Isabella always addressed him as *Don* Diego. She had done so even on the trip from Tenerife when her family and his emigrated to Louisiana together.

I pray that my letter finds you in good health. Maria and Pedro are fine. Yellow fever has visited our village. It was very bad. Many died. My mother and father have died. I am told I cannot keep the farm unless I marry. There are no men here I can marry. All of the unmarried men are at war. The man at Fort St. Charles has been told by the new Bishop not to pay stipend to women who are not married to soldiers or mothers of soldiers. I do not know what we shall do. Do you remember Father Étienne? He has added a message to my letter.

God keep you safe,
Isabella.

Stunned by the news, Diego read the letter twice more. He remembered Father Étienne. He was the Jesuit priest who managed to remain at St. Louis Church even though the Jesuits had been disbanded by the Pope.

Diego looked at the letter where the good Father had added a note and was dismayed to see he had written it in French. The priest had assumed Diego could read French since he could speak it.

"Bad news, *Primero*?" Captain Chastane had come out of his tent.

Diego came to attention. "Yes, sir. The family who are caring for my children, sir. The husband and wife were taken by yellow fever leaving only their daughter and my children to fend for themselves."

"That is bad news. How old is the daughter?"

"Sixteen, sir."

"Perhaps she will wed."

"She may, sir. But she has been collecting the family stipend from my pay, sir. Now the new Bishop has banned stipends to anyone but wives or mothers. They need the money, sir."

"I wish I could help."

"If I may impose, sir. Father Étienne has added something in the letter, sir. But I cannot read French."

"I can read it for you, if you wish."

Diego handed Chastane the letter.

"He says that your children are well cared for. Isabella has some money she has saved from your stipends. He says she refuses to marry any of the widowers in the settlement, but he thinks she will marry you, *Primero*."

"Me? How can she marry me? We are preparing to attack Pensacola."

"Is she not a suitable bride for you?"

"She is better than I deserve, sir." *Marry Isabella? It would work. She and the children would be provided quarters at Fort St. Charles and she could continue to draw the family stipend. She would be a good wife and mother.* "But how can we marry if we are miles apart?"

"The good Father closes with this: *Mézu's good friend will help. If you consent, send word.*"

Mézu's good friend could only mean *Doña* Margarethe Wiltz, wife of Colonel Jacinto Panis. The women had forged a friendship working in the hospital treating yellow fever victims. Work which led to Mézu's contracting yellow fever and her death.

"I have a regular post leaving for New Orleans tomorrow. Shall I add a message for you as well?"

"Yes, Captain. I would be most grateful if you could do that."

CHAPTER 17

D iego watched children playing in the road at the edge of town. They laughed, squealed and ran about shouting to one another in French and English and Choctaw. They had no farm chores, but that would change very soon, once the houses were finished and planting time arrived. Diego thought of his own children and of Isabella. It was not likely his children were carefree and playing.

La Aldea had grown in population by mid-August 1781. Two families, one headed by a Frenchman and the other by an Englishman and both wives Choctaw, had built huts on the northern edge of the town. The huts were but temporary housing as both men worked on proper homes and stockyards. One day they would labor on the Frenchman's house and the next on the Englishman's. There were seven children in the combined families, all cousins for their mothers were sisters.

Marcelite had never returned to the village. No one admitted to seeing her after the day the spies had been captured. She sent no word or letter. It was as if the world had swallowed her up. *She is probably in Pensacola telling all she had learned to General Campbell,* Diego mused.

"*Primero*, the relief is ready for your inspection." Quintero's words brought Diego out of his meditations.

Diego inspected the relief. Each man was armed with a musket and their choice of sidearm such as a sword or tomahawk. None wore a uniform coat and their heads were covered with a cloth garrison cap or simply a bandana. Picket duty at *La Aldea* had become routine, tedious and mind-numbing.

Quintero would bring the picket relief south, collect the men who had spent the night at their posts, patrol to the Choctaw farm to verify all was well and return to report the news of last night's watch. Pook had already departed on a similar mission to the north. After the night reports were made, Diego would walk to Bare Hill and make his report to Castro's clerk. Just as every day had been since mid-July.

He looked in the direction of Bare Hill. The low line of the fortification was bathed in the light of the rising sun. The four-pounders mounted on raised redoubts, the loopholes, the rooftops of Castor's headquarters and barracks beyond the wall were well defined. Nothing but a low-growing grass covered the half-mile between the wall and where he stood. Anyone attempting to take Bare Hill would have to endure a half-mile of shot and canister or begin a siege with trenches.

Or go around and climb the steep slopes north or south of Bare Hill and attack without benefit of cannons or ranked fire.

Diego squinted to see the gate in the wall open slightly and eject a man who scurried toward him. The man's gait betrayed him. It was Armano, Castro's clerk, clutching a folded paper. The message must have been urgent because Armano only needed to wait an hour or so for Diego to come to Bare Hill for his daily report.

"For you, *Primero*," Armano panted when he reached Diego. He held the papers toward Diego as if they were about to burst into flames. "I have held the morning packet boat for you."

It had been sealed orders addressed to the commander of Fort Carlota. The seal had been broken, presumably by Colonel de Ezpeleta. Diego read the orders. After the usual salutations, the Commander of Fort Carlota was ordered to dispatch Sergeant deMelilla of the Fixed Regiment of Louisiana to New Orleans where the sergeant was to report to Colonel Jacinto Panis for assignment. The orders were signed by and carried the official seal of Governor General Bernardo Gálvez.

Diego folded the orders and tucked them into a pocket. He would have to gather his things and transfer command of *La Cuchilla* to Pook.

"Tell Lieutenant Castro that I will report to him within the hour to be dismissed for travel." One simply did not leave a post without reporting to the commander and the clerks in charge of the roster. This procedure was known as "*registro salida* (book out)" throughout the army. Armano scurried off to make his report and Diego ducked into the barn to don his uniform and collect his goods.

"Going somewhere, *Primero?*" Pook had returned with the four men relieved from the north picket just as Diego exited the barn, a sack across one shoulder, haversack bulging and short sword at his side. The *espontoon* he left for Pook.

"I have been ordered to New Orleans, Pook. You are in charge here."

Pook did not ask if Diego was returning or why he was being ordered to New Orleans. The army had taught him not to ask questions that had no answers. You lived with men who became closer than brothers and then they were gone. Maybe your paths would cross again, maybe not.

"Well, watch your back." New Orleans and the intrigue that surrounded the place presented a danger much different than a posting on the front lines.

"And you do the same, Pook. Do not let boredom dull your edge. Remember the *godums* are only fifty miles away and we are *La Cuchilla*." Why the British tolerated the Spanish occupation of *La Aldea* and the fortification of Bare Hill was beyond Diego. Spain could muster an army on the east shore of Mobile Bay in safety and descend on Pensacola in two days. Yet, the *godums* have not ventured near *La Aldea* in months.

"Honor et Fidelitas, Primero."

"Honor et Fidelitas, mi amigo."

Diego reported to Bare Hill and was escorted into Castro's office for the first time in months. Perhaps the young lieutenant had recovered from the embarrassment of having his arrest of Diego reversed by Colonel de Ezpeleta. The clerk in the outer office had a log book open and was preparing a quill. *Someone is in a hurry to be rid of me.*

The door to Castro's office was open and Diego could see the young officer standing near the window. He stepped through the door prepared to salute the lieutenant when he noticed Colonel de Ezpeleta seated at Casrto's desk. Diego centered himself on the desk, came to attention and held his salute. "Sergeant Diego deMelilla reporting as ordered, sir."

De Ezpeleta saluted. "Stand easy, sergeant." Diego dropped his salute, but his eyes continued to be fixed on a spot above and to the left of de Ezpeleta's head.

"I have some instructions for you that will not be found in your papers. We are holding a packet boat at the landing which will take you directly to New Orleans. It is the *Alacita*. I think you know her."

"Yes, sir. Her master is Domingo Palmas."

"Just so. She makes a regular run from Mobile to New Orleans every month. I will accompany you across to Fort Carlota where the *Alacita* will be given the usual dispatches and I will disembark. You are to continue to New Orleans. The documents pouch will remained sealed and in your charge at all times. Do not let it out of your sight. You will personally place the pouch in the hands of Colonel Jacinto Panis and no other. If, for any reason, this is not possible, you will take ship for Havana and report, with the sealed pouch, to Governor General Gálvez."

De Ezpeleta produced another sealed paper. "This is a *Carta de Reguisar*, an authorization to board and direct any ship in New Orleans capable of reaching Havana, if the need arises."

Diego accepted the paper.

"Sir," Castro had been leaning against the wall. He moved to the center of the room as he spoke. "Why do we not entrust an officer with what is obviously such an important message?"

"Because, Lieutenant, an officer leaving this post would draw attention to himself and to the message pouch. A sergeant returning to New Orleans to be married will not."

Married! Diego had not received an answer to his return letter to Father Étienne. He had agreed to marry Isabella only if she freely accepted. He had instructed the priest to assure Isabella that Diego would continue to provide a stipend for her and the children even if she declined to marry. Was this an answer to his offer, or was this just another ruse.

"Lieutenant," de Ezpeleta continued "How do you think it is the Governor General was able to take Fort Bute, Baton Rouge, the entire Mississippi Valley and Mobile, sometimes against superior numbers, and do so bloodlessly? It is because he is a master of information."

Gálvez was well known throughout New Spain for his very aggressive use of reconnaissance and spies. He knew every aspect of the enemy's condition and deployment. Before the Spanish army met the British in battle, Gálvez often knew more of the British numbers and capabilities than the British commanders did themselves. Part of this superiority of intelligence was Gálvez's ability to deny information to the British or supply false information to his advantage.

De Ezpeleta stood. "If you have any questions, sergeant, we can talk while we cross the bay. Lieutenant Castro has many duties. We have taken too much of his time."

Diego collected his goods that had been placed near the door when he came in and followed the Colonel out of the building. Once in the road, he walked to the Colonel's left. They passed guards and other soldiers who snapped to attention and saluted as the Colonel passed. The Colonel absent-mindedly returned the salutes as they descended the steep trail to the landing.

Domingo Palmas was waiting at the small dock. His crewmen held the *Alacita* against the landing by lines from the fore and aft.

"Good morning Colonel," Palmas said as he gestured for the officer to step aboard. There was no gang plank as the deck of the *Alacita* was nearly at the same elevation as the pier. The Colonel stepped over the shallow gunnel and onto the deck. Diego stepped forward. "Good morning, *Primero.*"

Palmas said cheerfully. He touched Diego's arm, leaned closer and whispered, "I have a letter for you from Isabella in my cabin."

Diego stepped aboard and Palmas shouted for his men to cast off and man the sweeps. Palmas took the tiller, a massive contraption, until the *Alacita* cleared the mouth of the river. He shouted for one of the sailors to take the helm and disappeared into the ship's cabin. He reappeared with a letter in his hand and came to where Diego and the Colonel were standing.

"With your permission, Colonel. I have a letter for the sergeant. May I give it to him now?"

De Ezpeleta nodded and stepped to the side slightly so Diego could read in relative privacy.

"Thank you, Domingo." Diego accepted the letter Palmas offered. He could see several exchanges of correspondence written on the paper. He glance through small notes in both his and Isabella's hand writing until he found the most recent paragraph just under his response to Father Étienne.

Don Diego: Father Étienne tells me of your promise to marry me. I pledge to you I will be a good wife. I will work hard to prove myself worthy of you. He also tells me Doña Margarethe Wiltz will arrange for her husband to call you home very soon. I will not sleep until I can see you.

Isabella

He folded the letter and put it in his pocket.

Colonel José de Ezpeleta stepped around the mast of the little packet boat. Her crew consisted of four men and Palmas, the master. This left very little room for passengers. The crew needed room to work the ship and, occasionally, man the long sweeps to row her in calm air. Two passengers stretched her accommodations. The Colonel and Diego had just enough room to huddle about a central hatch cover. The crew, when not scrambling about pulling on ropes or the sweeps, tended to chores or gathered under a small canvas awning rigged near the bow to keep out of the glaring August sun.

Ezpeleta stared ahead at the approaching Fort Carlota. "Tell me, sergeant, how is it a recruit from Gran Canaria has become such a trusted ally of Governor General Gálvez?"

Diego had been lost in his own thoughts about Isabella and his children. *Am I doing the right thing by her?* Startled by the sudden speech, and the fact that a colonel was engaging a lowly sergeant in conversation, Diego fumbled for a reply.

"I am merely a sergeant in the Governor Generals regiment, sir, nothing more."

"You may tell that story to others, Sergeant. You are popular among the enlisted because of your fighting skills. There is something else about you. Your speech tells me you are an *Isleño*. Am I mistaken? Are you originally from Mágala?"

Mágala was Gálvez's home town. As with every powerful man, the people living in his home district served the family in one way or another. Many of the aids and other officers in Gálvez's command had been servants or relatives of the powerful Gálvez family.

"I was born and raised on Gran Canaria, sir."

"Truly? Did you serve *Don* Raphael Arinaga?"

"He was my *Regidore* (lord), sir."

"*Don* Raphael died a few years ago. Is that why you came into the army?"

"Yes, sir." *That and to save my wife and children.*

"What did you do for *Don* Raphael?"

"I did not work in *Don* Raphael's household, sir. I was a farmer, a farmer and a goatherd, sir."

"Truly?"

Ezpeleta returned to watching the fort. Diego noticed that a mention of his earlier status often ended any conversation. He thought this was the case now, but as the *Alacita* gently touched the pier and the Colonel stepped ashore, Ezpeleta turned him and muttered, "I do not believe you, sergeant."

A clerk surrounded by four grenadiers came to the side of the *Alacita* while supplies were being passed aboard.

"This is for you, sergeant." The clerk handed him a leather dispatch pouch. Diego accepted the pouch and hung it across his neck and shoulder over his haversack. The clerk thrust an open log book at Diego and pressed a dainty finger on the bottom of a page. "Sign this. It confirms you have received this message packet from me."

⁓

The light was fading when they drifted into an anchorage at Ship Island. The *Alacita* had made the run from Mobile to New Orleans in a single day under ideal conditions. Late August rarely saw ideal conditions. More often than not, the crew of the *Alacita* would be forced to man the sweeps during the day in a becalmed heat. The sail from Fort Carlota to Ship Island had taken twelve hours. Considering the light air, it was better than Diego had expected.

He remembered the last time he had bordered the *Alacita. Was it two years ago?* She had carried him from one of the Chandeleur Islands to the mouth of Bayou Saint John and New Orleans in a single day. Sailing conditions had been ideal that day and the *Alacita* seemed to fly. Perhaps tomorrow the winds would pick up and he could be in New Orleans before the sun set tomorrow. Or the trip might take a week of back-breaking labor at the sweeps, rowing to the mouth of Bayou Saint John and being towed into the city by a mule.

Two other Spanish ships shared the same anchorage. Both were armed brigs. They were bound for New Orleans as well, but drew too much water to go by way of the shallow pass and Lake Pontchartrain. The brigs would sail south to the mouth of the Mississippi River and were a week away from making the docks at New Orleans. The *Alacita* might be a day away, if the winds cooperated.

The brigs both sent boats commanded by ensigns to the *Alacita* to deliver mail bound for New Orleans and learn what news there was from Palmas. Both ships were from Havana, but because of the light air, they had been at sea for a week and a half. It was the hurricane season and had there not been a war, neither ship would have ventured into the Gulf of Mexico. Both captains were anxious to reach the relative safety of the Mississippi River as soon as they could.

Palmas graciously accepted the gifts delivered in the names of the captains, a jug of rum from each. After all, Palmas was the master of a mere packet boat and a civilian contractor as well. No need to provide elaborate gifts.

Diego listen as Palmas recited the news to the young ensigns hungry for news of their destination. The officers naturally did not direct any questions to *Alacita*'s deck hands or to Diego, a mere sergeant.

Palmas enjoyed the role of reporter and embellished many tales to the point of fabrication. Diego laughed to himself as the wide-eyed ensigns reacted to stories of wild men walking the streets (*Kentuckianos*) and the diversity of the population.

"You will see more officers of the British army than those of Spain," Palmas warned. "If you do not recognize a uniform, salute and say 'good day, sir.'" Palmas recited "good day, sir," in English and had the young officers repeat it. This much of Palmas' report was near to the truth. Gálvez had captured so many British troops and paroled so many officers in New Orleans, the cafés and markets traded in British Crowns as often as the Spanish silver.

The moon had risen by the time Palmas sent the last boat back to her ship. Diego had chosen a spot between mast and hatch, spread his bedroll, and was drifting off to sleep when Palmas, still in a conversational mood, sat on the hatch.

"Congratulations on your marriage, *Primero*."

"Thank you, Domingo."

"I knew you would wed Isabella."

"Did you?"

"Yes. I have been carrying letters back and forth between you both for nearly a year."

"And you read them all?"

"Of course. Everyone who carries a letter must read it. How is a man to know if it is important?"

"How indeed."

"Is it true?"

"Is what true?"

"What the Colonel said this morning. Are you a trusted ally of the Governor General himself?"

"I am a sergeant in the Spanish army assigned to the Fixed Infantry Regiment of Louisiana. I could not be my commander's enemy. You are not making any sense, my friend."

"I believe you must have been born on the moon. Great men have enemies who fight for other kings and they have enemies who are countrymen. More dangerous than foreign soldiers, these men hope to replace those in power with themselves. Great men also have allies, countrymen who work against these *ambiciosos*. So I ask you, *Primero*, are you a valued ally of the Governor General?"

"You think too much, Domingo. I was a happy farmer and herder of goats who turned soldier three years ago. Nothing more. Now let me get some sleep."

Palmas grunted and stood. Clearly unsatisfied with Diego's answers, he walked to the other side of the mast where he had rigged a hammock. Diego heard him muttering as he fell asleep.

☙

The *Alacita* was under way at first light long before the brigs had weighed anchors. Predicting they would likely become becalmed before ten, Palmas wanted to take advantage of the morning breeze and gain as much as they could before resorting to the sweeps.

The predicted calm never came, but the wind dropped off until they were doing well to make two knots. Ten hours of sailing and they had just reached the small chain of islands marking the mouth of Lake Borgne. Palmas decided to pass between the northernmost island, *Isla de San José* and a swampy peninsula jutting south from the mainland.

"More than enough water for our little *Alacita* and the shortest route to the Rigolets," Palmas explained confidently. The Rigolets was the pass into Lake Pontchartrain. "Once we are in the lake and it is a clear night, I can sail her to the fort at Bayou Saint John in the dark."

They cleared the tip of the peninsula by about a half mile and Palmas adjusted sail in the light breeze, intending to run straight to the mouth of the Rigolets. Diego could see a shadow change shape in a inlet behind the peninsula.

"Domingo, something is moving in that cove." Diego pointed to the distant object. The heavy trees that lined the cove made it difficult to see objects on the water.

"It cannot be much. I do not think there is more than two *varas* of water in that cove." Palmas shaded his eyes and concentrated.

"Del, get up the mast to the gaff tree and tell me what you see to our north."

The deckhand scurried up the simple ratlines rigged on the mainstays, wrapped an arm around the mast and peered to the north.

"I see a boat, a long boat. She is moving under oars and coming this way."

"How many oars?"

"I cannot tell. They are yet too far."

"Come down. Prepare to close haul, port side."

Palmas turned the *Alacita* as tight as he dared into the southerly breeze.

"We will see if they can catch us. If they do, I want them to have to work to do it," Palmas said directing a nervous grin at Diego.

"What weapons do you have on board?" Diego asked. He could now make out the flashing of oars in the sunlight.

"We have two *pistolas*, two cutlasses and five knives between us."

Diego had his short sword. "A deck gun would have been nice."

"Do you know how much a little deck gun costs?" Palmas laughed. "I am a poor contractor."

"They do not know what arms we have." Palmas said.

"They know," Diego replied. "They know and are counting on us giving up without a fight. How do you think they will come at us?"

Palmas thought for a moment. "They will work upwind of us, look us over and then come down on us. We cannot run from them in this light air. They will board us by the stern. If there are enough of them, we will not be able to keep them off."

An hour passed and Diego could count the oars now. There were four, two to a side. Four on the oars and the helmsman made five. He watched as the four rowing shifted and four new men took the oars. That made the count nine.

"Del, back up the mast with you and count how many in that skiff." Palmas said softly.

"I see twelve men," Del called down from the mast.

"More than two to one," Palmas muttered.

"Domingo, I suggest we load those pistols now." Diego said.

"See to it, *Primero*. Del will get them for you."

Del brought the two pistols and two cutlasses to Diego, who was standing at the stern of the *Alacita*. He assigned Del and another deckhand called Junco, to positions to his left and right. He gave a pistol to each and some powder cartridges. He watched as both men primed and loaded their pistols. They seemed proficient enough. The other two deckhands were given a cutlass and stationed behind a *pistolero*. Their job would be to hack boarders away from Del and Junco as they reloaded.

The skiff was drawing closer now and beginning to work toward the windward. Diego could see a dozen men crowded into the little boat. There could not have been more than two inches of free board and if there had been any kind of wind, the sea chop would have swamped their boat. *If there were any kind of wind, we would not be running for our lives.*

"More than two to one, *Primero*." Palmas said.

"Yes, Domingo, they have brought too many men."

Palmas turned to Diego. His expression was as if he were examining the insane. "Too many!"

"Can you tack in this wind?" Diego asked.

"The air is too light, *Primero*."

"And if we use all four sweeps on the starboard side?"

"She will tack then. What will it gain? They will be right behind us."

"We can come around until the wind is astern and that overloaded boat is ahead of us."

Palmas recognized the plan instantly. "We can ram them! They will never be able to get out of the way in time, row as they may. Man the sweeps, all sweeps to the starboard."

Palmas pushed the tiller downwind and *Alacita*'s jib began to luff. A cheer could be heard from the pursuers. They evidently thought the *Alacita* was surrendering. Arm-weary men shipped their oars and struggled around to arm themselves for the task of boarding. But the *Alacita* did not stop her turn facing into the wind, a condition seamen called "locked in irons." The sweeps pushed her through the headwind and completely around until the light wind was dead astern.

A young man standing in the bow of the chase boat had been shouting orders concerning the order of boarding until he suddenly realized what the slow turn had created.

"Oars out!" he shouted. "Back water!"

One of the men stood and aimed a rifle at the *Alacita*. Men were moving about desperately in the boat. It rocked wildly, taking on water with every roll. The rifleman fired. His shot passed harmlessly through the top of the *Alacita*'s jib. She was running wing and wing now, jib to starboard and mainsail to port. Palmas calmly adjusted the helm to intercept the chase boat. Diego had called the men forward to repel any enemy who might manage to get a handhold on the bow of the *Alacita* as she slid over the skiff.

The *Alacita* struck with a grinding sound as she slowly slid up and over the gunnels of the skiff. A pair of hands appeared on the forerails and Diego chopped down with his sword. A finger fell to the deck and the hands disappeared. A head appeared and Del shot into the man's face. When the smoke cleared, the man was gone.

The *Alacita* was gliding over the boat now. The bow of the boat was exposed on the port side, but the boat's stern was completely under her keel. Another man attempted to come aboard but Junco put a ball in the man's chest. The men of the *Alacita* walked along the deck, following the progress of the submerging boat until it fell astern. Palmas had to lift the tiller to allow the swamped boat to pass.

Diego counted six men in the water. The swamped skiff held three, including the young man who seemed to have been giving orders. Four of the swimmers returned to the submerged skiff and held onto the gunnels. The other two swimmers flayed about and went under.

"Come about, if you please, Domingo. We can pull some of these people from the water. They can do us no harm now."

"There are seven of them still, *Primero*."

"Then we need to be careful, Domingo."

Palmas maneuvered the *Alacita* until she was drifting about twenty yards from the swamped skiff and her seven survivors. The mild breeze had more influence on the *Alacita* than the skiff, so two seamen had to move the long sweeps occasionally to maintain position.

"Anyone speak Spanish?" Diego did not have to shout.

No answer.

"Anyone speak French?"

The seven men clung to the flooded boat and remained sullenly silent.

"Talk or we will start shooting pistols at you." Diego said in his fractured English.

"I can speak French." The young leader said.

"As can I. We are making progress." Diego laughed. "Are you pirates? You attacked as pirates would."

"We are British soldiers."

"I do not recognize the uniforms. You are spies, I think."

"We are not spies. You knew what our intentions were by our actions."

"Tell me your name."

"I am Sub-Lieutenant Johnathan Dickson of His Majesty's 16th Foot."

Dickson? Where have I heard that name before? Diego remembered the haughty officer in New Orleans.

"Are you related to Lieutenant Colonel Alexander Dickson, former commander at Baton Rouge?"

Cleary surprised, the young man stuttered, "He is my uncle. He will learn of it if we are mistreated."

"Domingo," Diego whispered out of the corner of his mouth. "No one could be half as villainous as the *godums* think we are."

"Except for the *godums* themselves, you forget."

"Truly." Diego returned to his conversation with Dickson. "Your uncle says all spies should be hanged. You think him wrong?"

"We are not spies."

"You are not proper soldiers; that is plain to see."

"Well kill us then or let us be."

Young Dickson is no coward.

"I shall do neither. We will toss a line. Tie every weapon you have left on the line. Once we have every weapon, we will help you float your skiff and take you under tow."

Del tossed a line across the huddle of men and it was reluctantly accepted. Two swords, several sheathed knives and a long rifle were tied to the line. Del pulled the weapons into the *Alacita*.

"That is all, you have my word," Dickson shouted. "All the rest were lost when you rammed us."

"Good. We will send you two buckets. If you all get into the water and level the skiff, her gunnels should float above the water. Bail her out until she raises enough for one to get in. Continue bailing until she is fully afloat. Tie this line to her bow and we will take you under tow as you work."

It was agonizingly slow work. The submerged skiff acted as a great sea anchor until, gradually, she regained her buoyancy. It was full dark by the time they reached the head of the Rigolets pass. The tide was running in invitingly.

"We can run the pass tonight," Palmas said. "It is clear and calm. We need only sweep enough to stay ahead of our tow. We will be in Lake Pontchartrain by the time the moon rises. Then we can run for the fort at Bayou Saint John and be there for breakfast."

Diego thought for a moment. "Agreed. Before we enter the pass, we need to take Dickson aboard. Our friends may attempt to swim to shore when we get in the narrow pass."

"They would be fools to try. The tide is moving at its peak and the current is very strong."

"Just the same, we need to bring Dickson to New Orleans."

The announcement was made to the boat that the tow line was going to be hauled in and Dickson, only Dickson, was going to be taken onto the *Alacita*. This was accomplished with Del and Junco brandishing cocked and primed pistols at the boat. The tow line was played out again once Dickson was aboard.

"Tell your people," Diego told Dickson, "We are going through the pass tonight. Anyone attempting to swim to shore will be shot. Even if they should make it, our shots would awaken Spanish guards ashore and they will be quickly captured and shot as spies. Remember, I know enough English to understand what you say."

Diego did not know if the banks of the pass were patrolled, probably on the west side but unlikely on the east. Shooting a swimming man from the deck of the *Alacita* with a pistol was a skill he suspected neither Del nor Junco possessed. He knew he could never make such a shot.

Dickson shouted the instructions to his men and watched as they settled into the bottom of the skiff to sleep.

"See, sergeant," Dickson said in perfect French. "You need not worry. You have our word."

The *Alacita* and her tow of sullen prisoners arrived at Lake Pontchartrain at moon rise and arrived at the mouth of Bayou Saint John at breakfast, just as Palmas had predicted.

CHAPTER *18*

"Captain du Foreste will curse you for this, sergeant," said Lieutenant Dugas, the militia commander of the fort. "New Orleans is bursting with prisoners of war. Du Foreste cannot parole them off to plantations quickly enough and now you bring us another seven. Seven spies at that. Spies cannot be paroled." The militiamen who garrisoned the fort at the mouth of Bayou Saint John accepted the boatload of prisoners the *Alacita* towed to the small pier after having thoroughly searched each man for weapons and items of value.

"Only six, Lieutenant," Diego responded as he wrote out a note of transfer documenting that Lieutenant Dugas had taken charge of the six prisoners "This one," Diego indicated Dickson, "we are keeping."

"And the boat?" Dugas asked when he saw that it remained tethered to the *Alacita*.

"The boat belongs to Captain Palmas." It did no harm to allow the lieutenant to think Palmas was a naval officer instead of a civilian contractor. The boat was only slightly damaged by the low speed ramming. It was a well-built, British navy skiff and would be worth perhaps one hundred twenty *reales*. Fifteen silver Spanish pieces of eight or, as the *Kentuckianos* in New Orleans would say, "fifteen dollars."

The crew pushed the *Alacita* across to the east bank of Bayou Saint John where a man, a *cordellero*, and mule waited in the early morning heat and stifling calm. Palmas bartered with the man for a *haler á la cordelle* (a tow). A price was settled upon, four *reales*, and a line was rigged from the mule to the bow of the *Alacita*. The plodding mule was able to maintain a minimum momentum for steerage, yet crewmen were still occasionally required to use the long sweeps to fend the packet boat away from the bank as she was pulled to the landing at New Orleans.

Word of the *Alacita*'s arrival had been signaled ahead by militiamen on a rickety tower above the Saint John Fort and there was a reception waiting for her when the mule pulled her into the turning basin at the head of Bayou Saint John. A civilian clerk unfamiliar to Diego was waiting, surrounded by a New Orleans militia guard. The moment the *Alacita* bumped against the pier, the clerk stepped aboard and walked up to Diego.

"Sergeant deMelilla?"

"Yes."

"I am Vinson Chonce, Clerk of the Cabildo. You are to report to Colonel Panis. Please come with me." Chonce's Spanish had a heavy French accent.

"I will. British Sub-Lieutenant Johnathan Dickson will accompany us."

"I was told nothing of a prisoner."

"Sub-Lieutenant Johnathan Dickson of the British 16th Foot is my prisoner and he will accompany us to see Colonel Panis." Diego examined the militia escort. They were members of a "Disciplined" New Orleans unit. Disciplined militia were better trained, equipped and led than were the general militia. "We are escorting a dangerous prisoner," Diego told the militiamen as he stepped onto the pier. "It would be wise if you were to fix bayonets." He used French, for proficiency in Spanish was not common among New Orleans militiamen.

The startled militiamen looked to Chonce for confirmation. The clerk nodded and the four militiamen fixed bayonets to the ends of their muskets. The muskets were, of course, unloaded and unprimed. Diego noticed that one of the muskets even lacked a flint. *So much for disciplined.*

Chonce led the way followed by Dickson and then Diego. The militiamen formed the corners of the formation as they made their way along the well-worn and heavily traveled road from the Saint John basin to New Orleans. They arrived at the edge of the city where *Calle Hospital* met the road along the proposed rampart for the city's defensive wall. The wall had never been constructed, but the street, crudely paved with planks, packed clay and brick debris, had been named *Calle Murallas* (Rampart).

Mézu had been buried very near where Diego now marched. She and fifty other victims of yellow fever had been carried from the hospital near the river to a long, low pit dug along the planned rampart and buried in a mass grave.

My beautiful Mézu. I will have a stone made for you. I promise.

They arrived at the rear entrance to the two-story wooden structure which served as the home for the Cabildo, the Spanish Louisiana ruling body. The building had been the office complex for the colonial French government and had been renamed to "The Cabildo."

The militia guard remained at the rear entrance while Chonce, Diego and Dickson continued into the building.

"Wait here," Chonce said once the three were inside the building. He left them in a small foyer next to an armory. The armory sergeant sitting at a desk next to the iron door was about to ask Diego to place his sword in the armory, as was the custom when enlisted men were called into the commander's office, when he noted that Dickson had his hands tied behind his back.

"Your prisoner?" he asked. "Is he British?"

"A British officer, if you can believe it. The Royal 16th Foot has adapted the uniform of *Kentuckianos*."

"Best you keep your weapon, then."

Diego switched to French. "Anything you would like me to tell your uncle?"

Dickson looked puzzled. "My uncle is paroled in this city. I will tell him myself."

"Spies are not paroled, they are executed."

"You are just trying to frighten me. I am not easily frightened."

A set of doors at the far end of the room burst open and a burly sergeant of grenadiers leading two privates marched into the room.

"Colonel Panis says you have a prisoner for me, deMelilla."

Diego recognized the grenadier sergeant. The man's name was Nieres. He had broken the man's nose once during bayonet training. The big grenadier had challenged Diego's assertion that a well-trained infantryman armed with a bayonet could defeat a man with a short sword.

Diego had substituted a ram from a four-pounder for a bayonetted musket while the grenadier used a short stake as a sword. The grenadier attempted to grab the ram with his left as he attacked with the "sword" in his right. Diego effortlessly disengaged from the attempt and, instead of retreating as Nieres had expected, stepped in to drive the ram into the man's face.

Lesson given and learned.

"His name is Sub-Lieutenant Johnathan Dickson. He claims not to speak Spanish very well."

"He will understand me, deMelilla." Nieres growled as he gestured for Dickson to move between the two privates. "*Vienes con nostros, Señor.*" Nieres ordered and Dickson went without hesitation.

Perhaps his Spanish is not so poor.

Chonce reappeared. "Colonel Panis will see you now." He stepped back to usher Diego into the commander's office. Diego marched in and stood at attention before the desk. Colonel Panis was standing slightly to the right of the desk as Diego announced "Sargent deMelilla reporting, sir."

Panis was the only officer in the room. He was casually smoking a white clay pipe. "Chonce, be so good as to bring the sergeant and me some of that excellent *vino canario*." Canarian wine had the reputation of being both excellent and strong.

"Sir." Chonce must have kept the wine close and open for he was gone only a moment before he returned with two full goblets on a tray.

"Stand at ease, sergeant. Enjoy some wine, please."

"Thank you, sir."

The wine was good, soft and smooth and strong.

"*Don* Pedro Piernas has been so kind as to allow me the use of his office for this – meeting. You have some dispatches for me?"

"Yes, sir." Diego removed the leather pouch and presented it to Panis. He was relieved to be shed of the thing.

"They tell me you had run into some trouble on your trip from Mobile."

Diego recounted the appearance and chase by Dickson and his men. Panis interrupted from time to time to ask questions, but for the most part, Diego was allowed to simply tell the story.

"Do you think Dickson was after these dispatches?"

"Yes, sir. Perhaps not these specific papers, sir, but they clearly intended to intercept messages. Why else would twelve men attempt to seize a packet boat in enemy waters?"

"Yes, why indeed." Panis took a long sip of wine. "Now for the reason I had you bring the dispatches, sergeant. Well, the two reasons. First, we are going to take Pensacola in October. Having been a recent guest of General Campbell, you are likely familiar with the improvements the British have made to the defenses of Pensacola." Diego had been a prisoner at Pensacola and escaped during a hurricane. "And the other reason is personal."

"Personal, sir?"

"Yes, sergeant, a small mater concerning my wife."

"Your wife, sir? I do not understand." Diego had met Panis' wife, the beautiful *Doña* Margarethe Wiltz. The *Doña* had been with Mézu when she died and she had been the one to inform Diego of Mézu's passing the day he returned from West Florida.

"My wife and your late wife had developed a close friendship, of that you know."

"Yes, sir." *Doña* Maria Artiles y Ventomo, Mézu to her family and friends, was of noble birth, well-educated and dignified. She and *Doña* Margarethe had quickly become close friends during the time Diego had been away.

"It seems, sergeant – and this is to remain in this room – Mézu has visited my wife several times in her dreams. At least this is what Margarethe tells me."

Diego was stunned. *Others have been visited too!*

Panis mistook Diego's silence for disbelief. "I do not care if you believe it. I do not believe it, but Margarethe does, and firmly. She would not give me peace until I contrived a way to recall you to New Orleans so you could marry – who is it you have promised to marry?"

"Isabella Campo, sir. She has taken care of my children since Mézu's death."

"Yes, *Señorita* Campo. Holy Mother of God, man, you do intend to marry the girl, do you not?"

"Yes, sir. She has consented by letter, but I have not seen her in months."

"If need be, I would have ordered you to marry her by proxy. As it is, a proxy will not be required. I have sent a coach for Isabella and your children. They should be here before dark. I have also arranged for quarters to be prepared at Fort Saint Charles for you and your family. Father Étienne will be at the enclave of the Virgin Mary in Saint Louis Church at nine tonight. Margarethe and I will attend as witnesses. Any questions?"

Diego swallowed hard. "No questions, sir."

"Thank God. Now finish your wine. I am going to call in some scribes and we are going to talk about Pensacola."

❧

Diego had changed into his full uniform. He stood in front of the Saint Louis Church facing the *Plaza des Armas*, watching militiamen drilling. Beyond the moving ranks of men he could see the tall masts of several ships moored along the river. He was waiting for Panis' carriage to return from Concepción. He had not slept since the fight on Lake Borgne and he was totally exhausted. Panis had questioned him about Pensacola for three hours, dragging out details he had thought forgotten.

Father Étienne, Panis and his wife were inside the church at the altar of the Virgin, waiting for him to enter with Isabella. He had not seen her in months and now they were to wed. She needed a husband, his children needed a mother and so marriage was the logical solution. Several carriages bounced along the brick-paved street between the church and the square, but none stopped and Diego was beginning to wonder if Isabella had found a more promising offer.

A carriage stopped directly before him. The door opened and little Maria jumped down, laughing and squealing. She was nine years old now and thin as a reed.

She must have grown a foot and the very image of her mother.

"Papa!" Maria leapt up into Diego's arms, kissing him on either cheek. Then she grew sullen. "We have lost our home," she said.

The homestead the Campos had begun to settle was not their property. To earn the property, they were required to live and farm it for five years. Another family had been given a chance to make a go of the property.

"We will have another." Diego felt a lump in his throat.

Pedro climbed down from the carriage next. He was twelve years old and already taller than most men. He walked up to Diego, embraced and kissed him on the cheek, as was fitting for a man greeting his father.

"I told the *alcalde* we could work the farm, but he said no. I think I will have to join the army, like you."

"You may join the army when you are seventeen, if you still wish to do so. Until then, I need you to help care for your sister and Isabella."

As he said her name, Isabella appeared in the door of the carriage. She was dressed in a white cotton dress. The sleeves reached to her wrists and the shoulders had large ruffles that framed her face. She wore a veil that covered her head. A comb made from horn held the veil in place and its ends draped down over her shoulders and down to her waist. Her reddish-brown hair seemed to glisten in the lamplight where it escaped the veil. She was not the little girl he remembered. She had grown into a woman, a beautiful woman.

"Hello, *Don* Diego," she said as she stepped down and walked up the wooden steps to him.

"Isabella, you must call me Diego now. I was never a *Don*." He put Maria down. "Go into the church with your brother, Maria. Isabella and I will be along shortly."

"Come, sister," Pedro said as he took her hand. "I know where we are to go."

"Are you certain this is what you want?" Diego asked. "You will be the wife of an army sergeant. It is not an easy life."

"Who has an easy life in this world? Not a farmer's wife, this I know. I will marry you, Diego, because we need each other. Mézu would have wanted this and so do I."

"Then, let us go in. Father Étienne is waiting." Diego placed her hand in the crook of his elbow.

ﾞﾞﾞ

The quarters Panis had arranged for Diego and his family were in Fort Saint Charles, the small redoubt on the Mississippi River standing at the down-stream end of the planned fortification of New Orleans. The redoubt contained some meager apartments for the families of the standing garrison. Because of the war, the regular army garrison was away on campaign. Those standing guard at Fort Saint Charles during the meantime were militia-men. At the end of their shift, these militiamen simply returned home.

Initially, the fort also housed prisoners of war, but the flood of British captives that poured in soon overwhelmed the small post. Officers who were paroled often rented apartments in the city, and reported to the fort every morning for a general roster. Other British officers were provided a simple room at the fort. Enlisted men of the regular British army were dispersed to stockades scattered along the river. More often than not, these men were hired out to local plantations and farms. British militiamen who were captured were simply sent home, with their personal weapons, pro-vided they swore not to take arms against Spain for the duration of the war.

It was after eleven at night when Diego led Isabella and the children into the fort to their new home. One of the guards met them at the gate and guided them to their quarters which were against the far wall from the entrance gate. They were required to walk past the apartment he and Mézu had been assigned when they first arrived. He had never spent more than two nights in that tiny two room apartment. When he left for West Florida, Mézu had been standing in the door, crying. It was the last time he ever laid his eyes upon her. Some paroled British officer now occupied the rooms.

Diego's quarters were next to the post commander's office and were normally reserved for the most senior sergeant of the garrison. It consisted of four rooms. The entrance room had a door and a window opening into the courtyard. There were doors on each interior wall. One opened to a bed-room with a window into the courtyard. One opened into the commander's office and the other to a windowless back room. The other windowless back room was accessible only through the front bedroom. The robust roof beams of both office and quarters served as the platform for three ancient twenty-four pound cannons. Diego was certain if the guns were to ever fire solid twenty-four pound shots the recoil would collapse the roof.

The entrance room had a table, lamp and three chairs. The few posses-sions Isabella and the children had carried from Concepción were stacked in the entrance room along with Diego's bag and a rifle he had confiscated from the British boatmen. The lamp had a flint and steel kit in a compartment in its base which Diego used to strike a flame. He carried the lamp with them as they examined each room.

A bed with a new moss-stuffed mattress occupied the room with a window into the courtyard. The interior room behind it had a small cot. Maria had fallen asleep by the time the carriage had arrived at the fort. Isabella had carried Maria into the fort and she placed her on the cot. Pedro was directed to occupy the other interior room, the one with a door leading to the commander's office. It had a small cot also. Each of the rooms had several wooden pegs along the walls to hang clothes or other items.

It required a few minutes of fumbling around in the light of a single lamp to sort things out. It was a hot night with little breeze, but both windows were covered with a fine netting at Isabella's insistence. Even in the city and close to the Mississippi River, the mosquitoes of New Orleans were merciless. The netting kept most of the insects out of the sleeping quarters.

With the children in bed, Diego and Isabella sat at the table in nervous silence with the flickering lamp between them. Diego was struck by how mature and beautiful Isabella had become in the year he had been gone.

She is clearly no child any longer.

He fished his haversack from the floor and hung it on a peg behind him. He pulled off his uniform coat and put it on the same peg and then his hat. Isabella watched him silently.

"Oh," he said as he dug in his pocket. "This is for you." He pulled out ten silver coins, French *ecu*, and placed them in her hands. "This is for household expenses."

"I have never seen coins like these," she said as she examined them.

"They are French *ecu*. I also have never seen the like before." New Orleans may have been a French colony at one time, but all commerce was conducted in Spanish silver. "They are about the same weight as a piece of eight." Weight of silver was all that mattered. Even chips and bits of silver were traded as coin.

Isabella lifted one of the coins closer to the lamplight. "I will bring them to the bank tomorrow and have them weighed. I – we have an account. I have deposited your stipends, as much of it as I could. It is now nearly forty *pesos*."

She placed the coin down and the room was once again filled with uncomfortable silence. Isabella stood. "I am going to prepare for bed now, my husband."

"I will come along in a few moments, my wife, after you have retired." He did not understand why his heart was racing so. Isabella, for her part, looked quite calm.

He listened as she moved about in the bedroom. Then he could hear the creak of the rope netting of the bed frame and all was quiet. He stood and undressed. He chose the cleanest shirt from his bedroll and put it on. It was long and could serve as a night shirt. He carried the lamp into the bedroom and placed it on the window sill.

Isabella lay on the mattress with the sheet pulled up to her waist. She was wearing a thin cotton chemise that accentuated her beasts. He snuffed out the lamp and felt his way to the bed. He heard her pull the sheet back and slowly slipped in beside her. He lay back and Isabella put her head on his chest. He thought he felt her tremble a little, but she let out a great sigh and he wrapped his arm around her. Gradually his eyes became accustomed to the dim light that filtered in through the window. He could see her eyes now. They seemed to sparkle. She smiled and kissed him, tentatively at first, then firmly.

⁑

"Well, Sergeant," Panis asked. "Are you settled down with your new bride?" They were meeting in the Fort Saint Charles post commander's office. The office was temporarily unused, for the regular army garrison was in Havana with the rest of the invasion force Gálvez was preparing. Until then, the fort was under the command of the local militia colonel, who lived only a few blocks away, and never found a reason to occupy the office. October was the planned date for the attack on Pensacola and it was now the second week in September.

"Yes, sir." Diego said. "Thank you for asking, sir."

Diego had just entered and he moved to stand against one wall of the room. The others, all officers, were seated. Colonel Panis was the ranking member present. Captain Barrett of the Continental Army and a third man Diego knew from reputation, but had never met was there as well. Mr. Oliver Pollock was not a military officer, but he was a close confidant of Gálvez and instrumental to the supply and intelligence network throughout the Mississippi Valley that supported the colonial rebels.

"Sergeant Diego deMelilla," Panis began, "I believe you know Captain Barrett." The men exchanged nods. "This gentleman is *Señor* Oliver Pollock. An 'American,' as they say, and an ally to our cause."

Pollock stood and offered his hand. "It is my pleasure to meet you, Sergeant. I have been hearing much about you."

Diego took the offered hand. "My pleasure, sir. Thank you, sir." He began to say more, but sergeants are not expected to engage their betters in polite conversation. Pollock realized Diego was not going to say anything else, so he resumed his seat.

"I asked Sergeant deMelilla to join us because of his particular knowledge of the defenses at Pensacola and the situation at Mobile. Mr. Pollock, when you depart this meeting it will be with a significant sum of money, all silver, and the good sergeant will be your escort to your office."

Panis picked up a pair of leather saddlebags that had been on the floor near his feet and set it on the table with an audible thud. "You will also need Sergeant deMelilla to help you carry these bags which are but a portion of a contribution by His Most Catholic Majesty to the Continental Army – The army, not the congress. We do regret that the supplies of blankets and arms sent by us did not reach General Washington sooner, but he has them now."

"2,000 muskets have been distributed to our western army," Pollock offered, "and double that number of blankets have reached Washington's army. There will be no repeat of the depredations suffered at Valley Forge."

"We are winning, Colonel Panis," Barrett interjected, "in no small part because of your assistance here in Louisiana. Our new nation owes a debt of gratitude to Governor General Gálvez and Spain."

Panis waved off the complements. "These supplies have been provided in secret, for Madrid has ordered our involvement must remain – clandestine. Our reward will be the expulsion of Britain from this continent. These bags contain five hundred silver eight *reales* coins – *pesos*, what you call 'dollars'. Nine more saddlebags will be delivered to your river schooner by this afternoon."

Diego watched as Pollock placed a ledger on the table and wrote in one of the columns. He first scratched a symbol with the quill and followed it with the numbers "500." He looked up to see Diego watching. "My own device, Sergeant," he said tapping the two vertical lines cut through an

"S." "The coin we call the Spanish dollar has on the reverse two columns entwined with a banner inscribed 'King of Spain and India.' The vertical lines represent the pillars and the 'S' represents the banner. This special symbol tells my clerks that the tally is in Spanish dollars."

Panis redirected the conversation toward Pensacola and the observations Diego made during his imprisonment and escape. Much of the discussion repeated what he had reported before many times, but occasionally a new question arose.

"Did you notice other fortifications aside from the main fort?" Panis asked.

"There were two smaller places with signal towers, and perhaps guns as well. I remember they were working on emplacements near the mouth of the bay."

"What about *La Aldea*?" Barrett asked. "I intended to inspect the place when I was there earlier, but could not."

"The fortifications at *La Aldea* are meager, sir. Fewer than two hundred men are posted there. There are only four guns, all four-pounders. It is more of a wall across the road and trench work." Diego said.

"Then why have the British made no moves against the place?" Barrett asked.

Panis answered before Diego could speak. "It is a mystery to us all. General Campbell does not have the reputation of being shy, yet he has allowed this obvious staging area less than fifty miles to his rear to remain unmolested."

"I am certain he is aware of the forces building in Havana. Perhaps he does not want to commit men to a campaign to regain *La Aldea* when any day Gálvez could appear with three thousand men." Pollock speculated.

"That may be so," Panis said. "One thing is very clear. If the British hope to regain West Florida, Mobile must fall."

The realization of the importance of that little Bare Hill and the ten-score defenders made Diego's head swim. If Campbell sent a thousand infantry to attack *La Aldea*, Fort Carlota, on the other side of a wide bay, would be unable to prevent it. *Why is it the godums do nothing?*

The meeting concluded and Diego discovered the real reason Panis had included him. It was not to guard Pollock and the five hundred dollars in silver. It was to carry the leather saddlebags. The five hundred Spanish dollars weighed well over thirty pounds. Diego felt as if he were a mule.

Pollock led him to a river schooner which served as both office and merchant ship. They trudged up the plank to meet a pair of sentries armed with a brace of pistols each and cutlasses.

"One must take every precaution," Pollock muttered. "Even in a friendly port."

Diego brought the bags below to the captain's cabin and lowered them into a sea chest. Pollock closed the chest and locked it with a great iron padlock.

"Thank you, sergeant. Would you care for a glass of something before you go?"

"No, sir. I thank you. I am expected at home."

"I understand. A soldier must enjoy his family when he can, is that not so? Who knows when you may be off somewhere for months or even years."

"Yes, sir. It is a hard life for a soldier's family when there is a war on."

CHAPTER 19

D iego stood in front of the entrance to the Cabildo. The month of September in New Orleans had been beautiful. It had been a month of cool nights and mild days. His duties at Fort Saint Charles had been as pleasant as the weather. Every militia company had requested, and had been granted, bayonet training sessions conducted by the famous First Sergeant of the Fixed Regiment of Louisiana. The hours were reasonable, especially for a soldier, and Diego made good use of the free time reacquainting himself with his children.

He was beginning to acquire a deeper understanding of Isabella. She was proving to be a particularly able wife. Because her household budgets were always competent, complete and well-reasoned, he had given her complete control of the family finances. The reasons for their marriage may have been practical, necessitated by circumstances of war and need to survive, but Diego realized he was growing to love and respect Isabella.

This morning he received the command to report to the Cabildo for orders. He had been expecting orders. He was a sergeant assigned to the First Regiment of Louisiana and his regiment was in Havana preparing for the invasion of Pensacola. He would have to say goodbye to his wife and children, not knowing when or even if he would return.

The church bell began to chime the hour. Diego nodded to the guard, who opened the door and allowed him to enter the outer office. Most of the clerks, corporals and sergeants of the headquarters staff were all strangers to him. He had been gone nearly a year and the few weeks he had been back were absorbed visiting militia units. Gálvez's command staff was in Havana with the rest of the regular Spanish garrison of New Orleans. He did recognize Vinson Chonce, Clerk of the Cabildo seated at the main desk in the reception area.

"Sergeant deMelilla reporting," Diego said as he showed Chonce the command dispatch he had received. It was very likely Chonce himself had written the dispatch.

"*Don* Pedro Piernas will see you now, Sergeant." Chonce stood and opened the door to the commander's office, stepping aside as he did so for Diego to enter. *Don* Pedro Piernas was the acting military director of Louisiana in the absence of Governor General Gálvez and had the militia rank of colonel.

Diego stepped into the office, centered on the desk and reported. Piernas immediately returned Diego's salute and indicated he was to sit.

"Do you smoke, sergeant?" Piernas said as he offered a cigar.

"No, sir. Thank you, sir." Cigars were expensive and were nearly always crushed if carried in a backpack. Spanish soldiers smoked tobacco in small white clay pipes or rolled pipe tobacco in paper salvaged from ruined cartridges. Diego had never developed the habit, although he did carry a pouch of tobacco in his kit for the purpose of bartering.

Piernas shrugged, bit the tip off the proffered cigar, put it in his mouth and lit it from a lamp's chimney.

"I have dispatches for General Gálvez in Havana," he said around puffs on the cigar. "Sealed dispatches. I am certain you are familiar with the procedure by now. These dispatches are never to leave your possession until you place them in the General's hand. Understood?"

"Yes, sir. I understand, sir."

"Fine. I do have a slight problem, though. The only vessel in New Orleans at this time suitable for a passage to Havana is the *Siderno*. Her Captain, Lorenzo Achille is reluctant to sail into the gulf because it is hurricane season. In truth, I do not blame him. The *Siderno* is a polacca, a type of ship that is of modest size and more suitable for the Mediterranean."

A polacca? How many kinds of ships can there be?

Piernas noticed Diego's questioning expression and continued. "She is a Sicilian ship contracted to the French Ministry of Foreign Affairs and is not subject to the orders of a Spanish militia officer, or so Achille contends."

"I have this, sir," Diego dug in his coat pocket and pulled out the *Carta de Reguisar* de Ezpeleta had given him in Mobile. He handed the document to Piernas who, shaking his head slowly, examined the signature and seal.

"Amazing. Chonce!" he called out without looking up from the letter.

The clerk appeared instantly, "Sir?"

"Send Sergeant Nieres and two grenadiers to find Captain Achille of the *Siderno*. Have him escort the good captain here the instant he can be found."

"Yes, sir. Immediately, sir."

Diego cleared his throat. "If I may suggest, sir, if there are any troops bound for Havana they could accompany me as well. The captain of a commandeered ship may need constant attention, lest he forget his duty."

"A polacca of the size of the *Siderno* carries a crew of perhaps two score, no more. She could accommodate half that number as passengers. I understand your concerns. Sergeant Nieres and two of his hand-picked grenadiers will go with you. The Venezuelan grenadiers are the only regular army people I have."

Four against forty is much better than one against forty.

"Here are the dispatches. Tell Chonce to select two militia guards to accompany you home. Gather the gear you need for the trip, say your goodbyes and go to the *Siderno*. She is moored at the foot of *Calle Hospital*, not two hundred yards from the front gate of Fort Saint Charles. Nieres and his men will meet you there with Achille. You will ensure the ship is provisioned and sufficiently manned. The instant you, Nieres and the other grenadiers are aboard, you will order the captain to make for Havana without delay."

꿍

Isabella carried Maria on her hip as Diego prepared for his trip to Havana. Pedro, too grown to need a hug from his step-mother, busied himself with collecting the items Diego was going to need and stuffing them into a sea bag. Diego was armed with his sword, a dagger and a pistol he had obtained from young Dickson.

"I will write as soon as I arrive in Havana," he said to Isabella. "The paymaster will continue with the monthly stipend. I will not need much where I am going."

"I will pray for your safety, my husband."

"As I will for you, my wife. This war will be over soon."

Isabella kissed Diego quickly on the mouth, other wives were watching. Their husbands had been gone for months and she was conscious of their stares.

"Come, children, kiss your father goodbye."

Little Maria refused to be separated from Isabella and leaned over to kiss Diego on the cheek. Pedro gave his father a manly embrace and a kiss on the cheek, turned away quickly and disappeared into the apartment.

"He does not want you to see him cry," Isabella whispered. Her own eyes were filled with tears.

"I think he does not want to see me cry," Diego joked. "Well, I am off." He hefted the canvas sack over his shoulder and nodded to the two militia escorts that it was time to go.

Isabella waved as the men walked away. *"Vaya con Dios*, my husband," she called after them. "We will all be here when you return, of that, you need not fear."

The last time I waved goodbye to my wife, I returned a widower.

꿍

Diego found the *Siderno* without any trouble. She was indeed moored close to Fort Saint Charles. So close that he could see Isabella and the children watching him from the battlements while he waited for her reluctant captain. The *Siderno* carried three short masts of a single pole each. All were gaff rigged and raked, no square yards at all. Diego guessed she drew little water and, because her masts were no more than thirty feet tall, she was hard to spot at sea.

The first mate, Felipo Danza, was aboard when Diego arrived and reported that Achille had been called away unexpectedly. Diego put the man to work verifying supplies and sending runners to recall crewmembers who had gone ashore. Danza, who's Spanish was serviceable, questioned the Spanish sergeant's authority to order him about and required some convincing. Diego forced the man to the short railing at the stern of the ship and promised to toss him in the river. "This is New Orleans and the alehouses are full of seamen. I can put you in the river and every member of this crew ashore. A visit to a dozen taverns and we will find crew enough to cast off her moorings and be on our way before noon." Danza consented, but promised things would change when Achille returned.

Danza stepped up to the quarter deck to confront Diego. "She has all the supplies we need and she has all her hands, save her master." All hands consisted of sixteen seamen, a carpenter and a cook.

Diego had been watching the sun begin its slow arch down to the western horizon over the city. "She has her master as well, Danza." Diego pointed at a rotund man wearing a blue vest, so small for him it could not be buttoned, over a white cotton shirt and trousers. A straw hat, the kind one would expect a farmer to wear, not a sea captain, was perched squarely on his head. Sergeant Nieres and two grenadiers followed the jovial Achille, who was laughing, gesticulating and bouncing along while the grim-faced soldiers followed.

"Your captain does not seemed distressed by our arrangement."

Danza sputtered and rushed down the gangway, spewing Italian. The captain and first mate conducted an animated but brief conversation before Achille came on board followed by Danza, who had not ceased talking, and the soldiers.

"DeMelilla," Achille thrust out a hand. "I am Lorenzo Achille, Captain of the *Siderno* out of the port of the same name in the Kingdom of Sicily."

"Sergeant Diego deMelilla. You will be sailing under my direction. We are bound for Havana. Cast off as soon as possible."

"You are not a man for formalities, deMelilla. Do you propose we sail downriver at night?"

"It will be a clear night and it is a wide river. We can make Fort Santa Maria at English Turn within the hour and take on a pilot before sundown. If it is too dark to proceed after sundown, we will wait there until the moon comes up before we continue downriver."

"Do you suppose we can run the mouth of the river at night as well?"

"That decision is days away."

Achille shrugged and called out for all shore lines to be slackened and the mainsail gaff to be raised. When the sail filled, the lines were cast off and the *Siderno* slipped into the river channel with an ease that gave the impression she was an extraordinarily nimble craft.

The pilot, Baptiste LaBaure, refused to proceed downriver until full moonrise, which was about nine o'clock. Even then, LaBaure complained loudly and disavowed any responsibility if they should strike something in the river. They kept to the center of the river with just enough way for the *Siderno* to answer the helm. They reached the pilot station at Fort Mardis Gras in the afternoon of the next day. LaBaure, who piloted from Fort Mardi Gras to English Turn, went ashore and another pilot came aboard to make the run through the mouth of the river and into the gulf.

The bar pilot, Lorenzo deLeon, refused to attempt the mouth until first light of the next day. Diego relented, more out of exhaustion than anything else. He had not slept since they left New Orleans. He retired to a small cabin in the stern next to the captain's cabin. The overhead was so low that Diego could not stand anywhere in the room and the space was so small only two men could sleep in it at the same time. It had a single hinged window that overlooked the stern. The window lifted inwardly and was secured by a hook to the overhead. A stout wooden hatch cover which sealed the opening during rough seas was hinged to swing up and outward. The hatch cover was held open by a bar mounted on the sill. The cool air and muddy smell of the flowing river filled the space.

One of the grenadiers was posted as a guard at the entrance to the cabin at all times. The hatchway opened onto the main deck next to the steps leading up to *Siderno*'s slightly elevated quarterdeck. The man on guard had to stand in the open without benefit of a shelter of any kind.

Diego sat on the bunk and slumped onto his side, his feet remaining on the deck. The bunk was a foot too short for him. Private Pober snored enthusiastically in the other bunk. Private Llaños was standing guard and Sergeant Nieres was wandering around the ship making certain there was no mischief afoot. In four hours, Nieres would wake the sleepers, Llaños would switch places with Pober and Diego would walk about while Nieres slept.

The timing of the shift found Diego coming on deck as the eastern sky was turning grey with an overcast dawn. He ascended the three steps to the quarterdeck and walked over to Achille and deLeon who were standing at the fantail watching the weather.

"Good morning, Captain, Pilot," he said, still stretching his body to relieve the aches inflicted by the tiny bunk.

"Good morning, Sergeant," Achille said. "Sergeant Nieres was just telling us how you broke his nose. He seemed almost proud of the fact."

"He talks too much. You know how the Venezuelans are."

"We will attempt to pass the bars this morning," deLeon said, his Spanish was perfect Castilian. "The winds are good and if we get rain, it will not be more than a drizzle. Once we pass the island *Reina Católica* we will be beyond the mud shoals and the pilot boat will meet us to take me off."

"Then we will be bound for Havana." Achille patted the pocket of his sea coat. "And the one hundred fifty Spanish dollars this note in my pocket promises me for my trouble." *Little wonder the man has been so jovial.* "You and your men can go to the foredeck. We are serving a hot stew for breakfast. It may be the last time we can have hot food before Havana."

Diego sent Pober to get the others and waited for them at the hatchway. The sailors had already eaten and the *Siderno* burst into life. Men hoisted the gaff-rigged sails and jibs. The sails snapped open audibly, ballooning out to catch the brisk wind. The ship listed to the starboard and gained speed. Diego could hear the water rolling at her bow and rushing past her sides as the *Siderno* wove through the muddy river under the direction of deLeon.

The foredeck was raised slightly, less than two feet, above the main deck and this created a sort of long bench where men could sit while they ate. The stew was hot, salty and delicious. After eating, the grenadiers found a place forward of the foremast where they could sit out from under foot and Diego returned to the quarter deck.

The banks of the river had changed from a dense forest to an ocean of tall reeds interspaced with clumps of trees.

"We will be able to see a few buildings soon," deLeon said. "Look to port. See those black specks above the reed tops? Those are the pilots' houses on *Isla Reina Católica* (Island of the Catholic Queen)."

"The pilot boat will meet us just beyond the island and we will say goodbye to *Señor* deLeon," Achille added.

The weather continued to deteriorate as they passed two houses on tall piers. One of the houses flew a red pennant signifying a pilot boat had been dispatched. Diego could see it beyond the ends of the reeds, bobbing on the open water far ahead. The little boat seemed to be crowded with figures, eight people or more.

Diego nudged Achille. "Why so many on the pilot boat?"

DeLeon answered, "Sometimes people will become stranded at the pilot house for some reason and they wait for a ship."

"I believe those are agents of the French Ministry of Foreign Affairs," Achille offered. "I had received a message to pick them up when your acting Governor insisted I take you to Havana. I am, after all, under contract to the French."

"Why did you not mention this fact earlier?"

"What difference does it make? Besides, would I have a letter of credit for a hundred fifty Spanish dollars if Piernas knew I was already bound for La Rochelle by way of Havana? I was told to expect five. Nine is the most I can accommodate. No captain likes to sail with half a cargo."

A soft misting rain driven by a strong wind began. The pilot boat drifted out of Diego's line of sight as she passed across the *Siderno's* bow. The boat would come up on the lee side of the ship and Achille ordered a rope ladder lowered. "We will bring my clients up before deLeon disembarks. That little boat is nearly awash," he explained.

Diego nodded toward Nieves who, understanding Diego's intent, took his men to the post rail forward of where the ladder had been dropped to the pilot boat. Diego walked over to join deLeon who was watching the passengers clamber up from the crowded boat. The sailors in the boat below were struggling to keep it from banging against the *Siderno's* hull while the passengers, cloaked against the rain, struggled up the ladder. The first man onto the deck tossed back the hood of his cloak and greeted Achille in French.

"Achille, my friend, we had not expected you so soon. When the signal came to the pilot house that you had been sighted, we had to hurry onto that wretched little boat." He noticed Diego and his thin face darkened into a scowl. "And who is this? A Spanish sergeant, I see."

"This is Sergeant deMelilla. We are bringing him and some others to Havana." Achille led the man toward Diego, "May I introduce *monsieur* Jean Maury, aid to the *Comte de Virieu*."

"The *Comte* was very clear, Achille. This vessel was contracted for his exclusive use," Maury said, ignoring Diego.

"I had no choice, *monsieur* Maury. The Spanish would have seized my ship if I refused. We had always planned to put in at Havana before continuing on."

"The count will be displeased."

"What will I be displeased about, Jean?" said the second man as he reached the deck.

"My dear *monsieur Comte de Virieu*," Achille, fawning, rushed to assist the man onto the deck. "The Spaniards would have seized my ship had I refused. We are to bring these soldiers to Havana. There will be no need to change our plans. My dear *monsieur* Pierre Victor Malouet Barnave, *Comte de Virieu* I present to you Sergeant Diego deMellia, of His Most Catholic Majesty's army."

"We have already met," Barnave sneered. He stepped forward to allow room for the others climbing up from the pilot boat.

"Oh, you know each other!" Achille exclaimed.

"Yes, we are old friends. We met in Mobile," Barnave said as he pulled a pistol from under his cloak. Maury quickly produced a pistol as well and pointed it at Nieres. Diego heard two other pistols cock as the other men from the pilot boat armed themselves as well.

"But, I do not understand!" Achille exclaimed. "The French and the Spanish are allies, is it not so?"

"Barnave is a spy for the British," Diego snarled. "He is a traitor."

The last person to gain the deck, a woman, straightened and tossed back her dripping rain hood. Marcelite's face turned white.

"Sergeant," Barnave said, "may I introduce my niece, *Mademoiselle* Marcelite Gaudet de la Arceneaux, *Comtesse de Tonnerée*."

"Diego! How is it you are here?" Marcelite exclaimed.

"Marcelite, you know this man?" Barnave asked.

"Yes, uncle. We met in Mobile."

"You will have to tell me about it sometime."

"I was a fool she met in Mobile," Diego said. "She convinced me she was loyal to the King of France. You are all spies."

"I do really tire of you, Sergeant. You think you know, but you are *un imbécile*," Barnave seemed to be genuinely angry. "We are loyal subjects of Louis Bourbon, King of France and the sixteenth of that name."

"Then why do you skulk about like spies? France and Spain are allied against Britain yet here you are, pointing a pistol at me because I am a Spanish soldier."

"I could not expect you to understand. Peasants are so simple minded. Advisors to my King have misled him into supporting a revolution against a rightful monarch. If the American revolutionaries win, how long will it be before the rabble of Paris, the enlightened ones, decide to put their king aside? How long before the Spanish crown is toppled? We are the true subjects of our king." Barnave waved deLeon over to the ladder. The man descended and the pilot boat bobbed away.

"Diego," Marcelite continued. "We know that if the Americans win all of the crowns of Europe would be threatened. Civil war would destroy civilized Europe."

"And Mobile was the key," Barnave continued. "Whoever controls Mobile would eventually control New Orleans and the Mississippi River Valley. That fool Campbell did not realize that without Mobile, nothing could move across the Floridas. New Orleans would be isolated and indefensible. But you captured Mobile and I could not convince Campbell to attempt to retake the place. He was paralyzed with the thought of a Spanish fleet appearing at Pensacola while his army was away attacking Mobile. Now Gálvez is poised to take Pensacola as well. Britain will be forced out of Florida and the Americans will be supplied from the south and west. The British blockade will mean nothing."

"I did not lie to you, Diego. I serve France, the true interests of France, not this foolish support of a rebellion against a rightful king," Marcelite said.

"And what do you intend to do with us? Bring us to Havana, or put us in the sea?" Diego glanced at Nieves, but he remembered the man did not speak French and did not know what was being said.

"I promise you I will not put you in the sea—alive. That would be inhuman."

"Then there is just one thing I think you need to consider," Diego said, a smile touched the corner of his mouth.

Barnave sensed Diego was about to attempt something and he pointed the pistol at Diego's chest. "What is it you think I should consider, sergeant?"

"You should consider, *monsieur Comte*, that we have been talking here, in the rain for several minutes. You have had that pistol cocked and pointed at me the entire time. Look at the rain dripping from the barrel. You should consider, perhaps, the powder in the pan might be wet."

Barnave glanced down at the pistol and Diego's hand shot out to grab the weapon by the barrel and pull it from Barnave. He reversed his grip on the pistol and pointed it at Barnave. The men with Barnave reacted by turning their pistols toward Diego, but Nieves and the other grenadiers rushed them. One of the other pistols discharged, splintering the deck. After a brief struggle, the grenadiers held Barnave's men at sword-point.

"Or it may be the powder is not wet after all," Diego said. "Shall we find out?"

"You dare not harm me," Barnave said, thrusting his chin forward. "I am Pierre Victor Malouet Barnave, *Comte de Virieu*. Even if France were at war with Spain, you would not dare to harm me."

"Do not be so certain I have not been infected by the Americans and have lost all respect for nobility," Diego said. He levered the pistol to half-cocked, thrust it into his waistband and drew his sword. "But if I kill you and your servants here, I would have to kill dear Marcelite as well. That, I may not be able to do." He switched to Spanish. "Nieves, bind these men, hand and foot. Make room for them in the forward cargo bay. Search them for weapons or anything that might be used as one. They will be our guests for some weeks until we reach Havana."

What will I do when we reach Havana?

"And what is to become of me, Diego?" Marcelite asked.

Damn! She is beautiful!

"I do not know, my darling. I think I will keep you in my cabin. It is not very big."

"I have not told my uncle about you – about us," she whispered.

"What is there to tell? You did what you did for France. We all serve in our own way."

"That was not my meaning, Diego. I did not tell him of my affection for you."

"I will show you to your quarters," Diego took Marcelite by the arm. He glanced over at Nieves and the other grenadiers. They were doing a proper job of binding the prisoners. "We will have to post our guard carefully. I do not trust our Sicilian seamen."

"I promise you, sergeant," Achille said. "We will bring you safely to Havana."

"And can I trust you to guard the Frenchmen?"

Achille hesitated.

"I thought not."

Diego brought Marcelite down to the small cabin and gently guided her to one of the beds. She sat, smoothing her dress demurely.

"The captain says we must latch down the window if the seas become rough. Watch how it is done."

Diego pulled the window's wooden hatch cover closed and latched it. He then closed the window and latched it as well. "This will keep the waves out, but it may become uncomfortably hot. If water starts coming in, you will need to act quickly." He opened the window and hatch again and went to the door. "I will have food and water sent to you. Call if you need anything. I will ask Captain Achille to post one of his sailors as guard."

"You are not staying here with me?"

"No, I fear that I do not have enough men to post a proper guard on your uncle and his men. I will have to stand my turn with the rest of my men, you understand."

"Yes, of course. But you will be able to see me from time to time? It may be a long trip to Havana."

Diego stepped up onto the deck and closed the hatch behind him. He threw the locking lever in place and exhaled. "Achille, I need to talk to you."

❧

"On deck!" the sailor shouted unnecessarily. It was only twenty feet or so from his perch on the gaff jaws to the deck. "A sail to our stern." Achille raised a small glass to his eye. "She is Spanish," he muttered. "Sergeant, we have company!" he shouted. Diego stepped up onto the quarter deck and joined Achille at the rail.

"She is a Spanish frigate, sergeant, upwind of us and closing fast." Achille said. "My little *Siderno* is fast, but nothing can outrun a frigate running full before the wind. She will catch us within the hour."

The morning had marked their second day at sea. It was becoming difficult guarding the prisoners and avoiding Marcelite. He had an hour to decide what to do.

"Do you have Spanish colors aboard?"

"Of course."

"Fly them now and shorten sail."

⌇

The *El Vizcaino* towered above the little *Siderno*. A man with a speaking trumpet appeared next to the figurehead. "This is His Most Catholic Majesty's ship of war, *El Vizcaino* under the command of Captain *Don* José Borja. Identify yourselves."

"I am Sergeant Diego deMelilla of the Fixed Regiment of Louisiana," Diego shouted before Achille could say anything. "We commandeered this ship. I have dispatches for Havana."

"We are bound for Havana, sergeant. Bring your dispatches aboard. With this wind, we will make Havana by tomorrow. I will send a boat across for you."

"Achille, have your men gather up our gear. We are going to leave you now."

The frigate lowered a gig away and it was alongside the *Siderno* in a matter of minutes. Achille supervised the transfer of the soldiers' sea bags and signaled that it was time for the men to climb down into the gig. The grenadiers climbed down followed by Nieves. Diego looked back toward the cabin holding Marcelite. The hatch cover was closed and latched.

"When we are aboard *El Vizcaino* and out of sight, Achille, you can release the Count and his people. Out of sight, you hear. Not a moment sooner or I will tell Captain Borja you have British spies on board. He is in a hurry, so I think he would simply send you to the bottom."

"I will keep them all below until you are out of sight," Achille promised.

Once aboard *El Vizcaino*, Diego walked to the rail to watch the *Siderno* far below him. It seemed tiny compared to the frigate. Achille waved to him and he waved back. Soon all that could be seen of the *Siderno* was a small triangular sail falling below the horizon. Diego had not seen any of the Frenchmen, or Marcelite, come on deck.

"Sergeant, what are the dispatches you carry?"

Diego turned and saluted Captain Borja. "Dispatches, sir, to be placed in the hands of Governor General Gálvez himself, sir."

CHAPTER 20

Havana reminded Diego a little of the harbor of Gando on Gran Canaria. It was visible from the sea, not hidden behind swamps and forests like New Orleans. Nor was it perched on sandy dunes or hidden away in a shallow bay, as were Mobile and Pensacola. Havana was a city of sloping streets, stone buildings and forts protecting a fine harbor. It lacked the towering mountains of Gran Canaria, but the low hills were enough to bring that distant place to mind. Only two years had passed— *two years and a lifetime* – since he, Mézu and the children had fled their island home for the New World.

El Vizcaino glided between the imposing Castillo de San Salvador de la Punta and the smaller Morro Castle, two forts that bracketed the mouth of the Almendares River. The sun was beginning to set as she dropped anchor and secured for the night. A loud clanking noise echoed in from the river's mouth as a tremendous chain stretching between the citadels was drawn tight, sealing the three hundred yard wide shipping entrance.

Captain Borja insisted Diego accompany him on the Captain's gig for the short ride from *El Vizcaino* to the pier at the Castillo. The gig wove through a fleet of anchored ships of all imaginable types and sizes until the coxswain placed them against a schooner moored at the stone quay below the outer wall of the Castillo. The schooner was in the process of loading supplies. The deck and adjoining quay were a seething crowd of burdened men, carts and material.

Borja climbed aboard the schooner, directed Diego to follow him and dismissed his gig with instructions to return to the ship and wait for his reappearance on the quay. Escorted by the schooner's duty officer, they crossed to the stone landing and joined a line of longshoremen traversing the gangway to the busy pier. The solid stone seemed to pitch slightly and Diego stumbled as they crossed the quay.

"Have you been at sea that long, sergeant," Borja joked.

"Pardon me, sir. I am a soldier who much prefers the land, sir."

They passed through the gate in the low outer curtain wall of the Castillo and crossed the fifty yards or so to the main gatehouse. Both the outer and inner portcullis were raised and the great iron reinforced oak doors were braced open. A constant stream of pedestrians populated the open area between the outer wall and the fortress, an area called the "bray." This jostling crowd ceased at the gatehouse. Every person desiring entrance to the main fortification was subjected to the scrutiny of the Sergeant-of-the-Guard.

Borja presented an impressive document to the sergeant who first examined the paper then snapped to attention, saluted, and said, "Welcome, Captain Borja. You are expected, sir. Please follow Corporal Mamano, sir. He will bring you to General Gálvez."

Gálvez would have been advised of the arrival of *El Vizcaino* when she was first sighted from the watch towers. Watchers noted the events surrounding *El Vizcaino* from the time she entered the harbor to the landing of the captain's gig. Gálvez knew to the minute when Borja would report to him. He would also have been advised that the captain was accompanied by an army sergeant of the Fixed Louisiana Regiment carrying dispatches.

A clerk stood and moved from his desk to meet them in the foyer of the headquarters building.

"The General will see you now, Captain," he said. "Sergeant, you are to wait here."

Borja, his hat under his arm, crossed to a guarded doorway and paused as one of the guards opened the door for him. Diego could see the captain salute and address someone as the guard closed the door. The murmur of voices, barely audible while the door was open, was cut off and Diego stood in the center of a silent room. The clerk returned to his desk and began scribbling on papers while the brace of guards to the inner door stared vacantly at the opposite wall.

The door opened suddenly and a lieutenant Diego did not recognize leaned out. "Sergeant deMelilla, The General wants to see you now," he said.

Diego marched into the room. Governor General Gálvez and Captain Borja were sitting on opposite sides of a desk. A clerk was working away at a writing table in one corner and the lieutenant who had ordered Diego in stood next to an open window. Diego performed the ritual of reporting, removing the documents pouch from his shoulder and offering it to Gálvez.

"Dispatched from Colonel Piernas, sir."

Gálvez gestured toward a vacant spot on the desk and Diego placed the pouch there.

"Sergeant, be at ease, please."

Diego complied by placing his hands behind his back and spreading his feet slightly. It was as close to an attitude of ease as possible for a sergeant in the presence of his commanding general.

"Captain Borja tells me he picked you up from a polacca named '*Siderno*,' a ship of the Kingdom of Sicily."

"Yes, sir."

"Was your old friend Barnave, *Comte de Virieu* aboard?"

"Yes, sir." *Is there anything this General does not know?*

"Barnave was in New Orleans?"

"No, sir. Colonel Piernas commandeered the *Siderno* in New Orleans. Barnave and a few men came aboard at the mouth of the river, sir."

"He must have been upset to see his ship commandeered by a Spanish sergeant."

"He was, sir, outraged."

"Do not keep us in suspense, man. How did you deal with the outraged Count?"

"We disarmed him and his men, sir. They were bound and held in the forecastle, sir."

"I am relieved you did not kill them. He deserves it for meddling in my affairs, mind you. But he is a French noble and diplomacy must be considered. He would have killed you, had he the chance."

"Yes, sir. He did attempt it."

"Indeed? And failed? He must be plotting revenge as we speak." Gálvez seemed genuinely amused. "You never fail to amaze me, Sergeant." He turned to Borja. "The Sergeant here is a man of many skills, Captain. In truth, I find him indispensable."

Diego heard the door open behind him and a clerk's voice. "Captain José Calbo de Irazábal is here as you ordered, sir."

"Excellent! See him in. I am almost done here."

De Irazábal appeared to Diego's right. He was a man of slight build and dyed facial hair. He reported to Gálvez then nodded toward Borja, whom he seemed to know.

"My dear Captain," Gálvez said. "I think you know Captain Borja. You served together in the Algiers campaign, is that not so?"

"Yes, General." De Irazábal's voice did not seem to fit the slight man's build. He had a deep and booming voice developed by a lifetime of shouting orders aboard ship. "*Don* José and I are good friends."

"I was just telling Captain Borja the command council here in Havana has appointed you as the commander of my invasion fleet along with the brevet rank of Admiral."

De Irazábal glanced at Diego and Gálvez added, "This is Sergeant Diego deMelilla of my staff. He commands my special resonance company, *La Cuchilla*."

Diego snapped to attention and de Irazábal inclined his head.

"And who is the officer of this famous band of skirmishers?"

"I assure you, Captain," Gálvez said with some heat, "*La Cuchilla* is much more than a band of skirmishers. Do pardon me for a moment, I must provide the sergeant with some instructions and dismiss him."

Gálvez's angry expression faded. "Sergeant deMelilla, a contingent of the Hibernia Regiment has arrived in Havana, sixteen score in the ranks. The commander is Colonel Arturo O'Neill. I want you to evaluate the rank and file. Provide them with your well known bayonet instructions. Report to me your frank assessment in three days. Colonel O'Neill is expecting you. My clerk will direct you to their billet."

Spain had provided refuge to a large contingent of Irish folk escaping British persecution. The Hibernia Regiment of the Spanish army was composed entirely of Irishmen, officers and enlisted. The Irish could also be found throughout the army and navy, many rising to high rank, as had Governor General Alejandro O'Reilly. The reputation of the Irish Regiments of Spain was excellent.

As Diego withdrew he could hear Gálvez ticking off the list of ships in the fleet for the invasion of Pensacola. Gálvez had named twenty ships, and was still calling out more, by the time Diego was ushered out of hearing.

↜↝

The Irishmen proved to be well prepared and provisioned. The enlisted men were generally older than the rank and file of the regular Spanish army; older and experienced in the use of edged weapons. Spanish recruits tended to be young and drawn from impoverished, lower class families. The army was a way for these men to survive. The Irishmen were of all classes, forced into poverty and out of their homes by British oppression. The Spanish army was a refuge that kept them together and provided them the hope of revenge.

Diego reported his findings to Gálvez and was given a list of additional units to visit and evaluate. The officers of all the units Diego inspected were resentful of the additional scrutiny. After all, they had been examined by commanders of every rank, including Gálvez himself and were provided with a litany of deficiencies that needed to be corrected. Yet they understood that this *Isleño* had the confidence of Gálvez and so most officers cautiously cooperated with Diego.

"A sergeant can see within the rank and file," Gálvez once commented. "Things closed over by officers wishing to make the best impressions are as a false-front, a curtain on a stage. Sergeants can go behind that curtain and see things hidden from a general."

Each day for weeks was consumed with evaluating and reevaluating this regiment or that contingent, regular army and militia as Gálvez continued to build his force for the invasion of Pensacola. Poor units were improved, good units were made better and none was allowed to slacken. The navy was subjected to the same scrutiny and every ship was made as sea worthy as possible.

Diego had been inspecting a regiment, regulars from Aragon, billeted near Morro Castle on the north bank of the Almendares River. His work had dragged on until late in the afternoon and, rather than return to his quarters, he requested permission to spend the night with the Aragon regiment. The commander, Colonel Longoria, granted Diego's request and directed him to the quarters used by his clerks.

The regiment had been assigned to several rooms in the space below the outer walkway of the castle's riverside bray. The area beneath the rampart walk of the bray (called the allure) had been converted into rooms, a practice so common in Spanish fortifications as to be universal. The room included a valued amenity, a loophole in the wall providing a narrow view of the river below. Diego tossed his bedroll on a straw mound to serve as his bed and watched the last of the river traffic coming to harbor before the great barrier chain was hauled up.

A small ship came into view. Its sails were full and painted orange in the setting sunlight. It had three stubby masts each formed from a single tree trunk, not the combined series of spliced poles that drove the tall ships. It passed into and out of view quickly. Something about the ship seemed to register with Diego. He ran from the room into the bray and found a ladder up to the parapet walk.

The view from the top of the wall was spectacular. Across the river stood the Castillo de San Salvador de la Punta bathed in sunlight. To his left was the harbor, a forest of tall masts. A single little ship, guided by the harbormaster's skiff, was working her way between the ships seeking an anchorage. It was the *Siderno*.

Diego watched as several figures climbed down a short ladder from the *Siderno* to the harbormaster's skiff. He counted as four people from the ship crowded into the skiff, four men and one woman. The skiff made for the landing below Castillo de San Salvador where a detail of soldiers awaited them. Were the four to be arrested? Or would diplomacy trump treason, releasing the *Comte de Virieu* and his beautiful niece, the *Comtesse de Tonnerée* to do greater mischief?

Diego tried to follow the skiff to the landing, but the long shadows of the setting sun raced up the harbor and buried the landing in darkness below the gleaming high walls of the Castillo. Suddenly, Diego was thankful he had decided not to return to his quarters this night.

ৎৄ

Diego was in the courtyard of the Morro Castle before sunrise. The high towers of the opposing fortifications were signal stations that carried messages, routine messages, across the river. Every morning the increase in messages caused the signal arms of the flag semaphores to flap in an unending, dizzying blur of colored fabrics.

The message that he would not return to his quarters had been sent, and approved, the day before by semaphore. The message pertaining to his next assignment would arrive this morning woven into the stream of routine communication. He had advised the signalmen he was expecting instructions and did not want to wait for a runner to seek him out, so he stood on the parapet just below the tower and waited.

Hearing footsteps behind him, Diego turned to see the signal clerk approaching with a message.

"For you, sergeant. It is from headquarters." Diego took the scrap and read while the clerk watched..

"Return to Castillo immediately," was all it said.

"Acknowledge I will do so, please."

"Yes, sergeant."

The clerk disappeared into the base of the signal tower. Diego tossed his bedroll across a shoulder and followed the labyrinth of descending steps and landings to the courtyard below. He crossed the bray and onto a pier already busy with commerce. All of the military skiffs and gigs were taken. He found a skiff for hire and for 20 *maravedís* was transported to the Castillo landing.

He half expected to find the same escort for him that had greeted Barnave and Marcelite last night. There was none. *Was the lack of escort a good sign?* Surely Barnave would have made an enthusiastic complaint of the insult to his diplomatic status Diego had delivered when he treated French nobility so roughly, holding them prisoners on their own ship.

The clerk at the headquarters' outer office accepted Diego's written report on the condition of the Aragon regiment and routinely handed him his next assignment without a comment. Diego moved to a corner of the room where the light was better and read the unsealed message. He was to go to the village of Bauta, about sixteen miles west of Havana and inspect the local militia which would be moved to the harbor and serve as part of the garrison left to defend the port after Gálvez departed for Pensacola. He was to remain there for four days before returning. *I am being hidden away.*

Bauta was a small village that served as the supply center for the surrounding farming community. It had a large stone church and an inn. All other structures, except for the government administrative building, were low, one story affairs of brick or stone. Even the most modest of these had long, sloping roofs that extended well beyond their walls to create an encircling gallery. It was not an unpleasant place.

Diego had arrived in time for the noon meal at the inn. The meal was served in a central room which served as a dining room, alehouse and meeting room. A row of doors circled the room as did an open gallery providing access to the second floor rooms. There were large doors on the east and west sides of the room which were kept open to capture a pleasant breeze. The road to Havana bordered the inn to the south, as did most of the dwellings of Bauta. The arrangement had the additional benefit of minimizing the smells associated with a busy street.

He decided to take a room rather than spend four days in a field tent. The business of evaluating so many different units was beginning to wear on him. The inn keeper showed him to a room on the second floor. It was midway along the gallery from the stairs. The door to the room opened onto a space no more than twelve feet square and had a window overlooking the street directly opposite the door. A sagging bed, flattened straw mattress, a table, a chair and a chamber pot were the only furnishings. The inn keeper proudly pointed out that if one would lift the seat of the chair, a large hole was exposed. "For convenience when using the chamber pot," he explained.

Later that day and for the next two days, Diego demonstrated the use of the bayonet to militiamen and then sparred with them. They were all completely ignorant of muskets and bayonets. Having grown up wielding machetes, most showed promise with short swords, but it would be months before they could be used as soldiers. On the last day of evaluation, Diego ate a meal in the general room with the militia sergeants and corporals. Laughter, joking, singing and more than a little rum eased the tedium of the preceding days.

Diego finally managed to separate from the celebration, climbed the stairs and found his way to his room. Once inside, he dropped the wooded latch bar in place, opened the window, stripped off his clothes and fell onto the bed without bothering to pull down the single sheet. He was asleep in an instant.

∽

Isabella worked the plunger smoothly with a practiced ease. Maria stood next to the wash barrel preparing the next batch of dirty clothes. The barrel was as tall as Maria. The plunger handle extended through a hole in the barrel top and occasionally soapy water would slosh out and trickle down the sides. Isabella had contracted to clean clothes for several of the bachelor soldiers. Most of the army wives would do chores, such as laundry, sewing, jerking meats, cutting hair, and any number of things as a way to earn some extra money. She was washing shirts and trousers in the courtyard of Fort Saint Charles. Cleaned clothes hung on lines tied between the eaves of the residence's roof, exposed to the late October setting sun to dry.

Pedro sat next to the door to their apartments with a large leather pad on his lap. He was knapping flint into squares for muskets. The army issued flints, poor grade west European flints. The stone at Pedro's feet was from the upper end of the Mississippi River. He had broken the stone apart and flaked off a long leaf of highly prized black flint and was creating replacements for the government issued flints. Soldiers would buy a few of the more reliable shards to keep in their cartridge boxes on the chance they might find themselves in a real fight. The issued flints were fine for drills, but war demanded a more reliable spark.

Isabella opened the barrel and pulled out a shirt. Satisfied that the clothes were clean, she removed the cover and pulled the wash out. She tossed the dripping clothes into a tub of water for Maria to rinse. After Maria rinsed a shirt or trouser, she handed it to Isabella who hung it on the line. When that batch was on the line, Maria loaded some more clothes in the barrel and Isabella returned to working the plunger.

Diego watched his family working. "Isabella, pause a moment so we can talk."

Isabella continued to work the churn, her smooth, feminine yet strong arms rippling with the effort.

"Isabella, wife, please talk to me."

"She cannot hear you, Diego." It was Mézu standing next to him. *I am dreaming.* Mézu appeared no older than sixteen. She wore a green gown and a silver comb anchoring a veil of white lace to her hair. Her young face was unblemished, her grey eyes alive, sparkling. He had not dreamt of her in months, not since he had married Isabella. He felt a stab of love and loss.

"Isabella is a good mother for our children," Mézu said softly. Diego tried to touch her, but she was just beyond his reach. "And she is now with child herself – another son of yours, Diego."

He looked back at Isabella. She showed no sign of pregnancy.

Mézu's soft and gentle voice came from behind him. "Now there is something you must do, Diego."

He turned to look at Mézu, but she was gone. Her voice drifted in. "You must awaken now, Diego. You must awaken."

❧

Diego's eyes flew open. The room was dark but a shaft of moonlight poured in through the open window onto the door to his room. He heard a creaking noise. A quiet sound yet it conveyed the impression of a large weight being shifted just beyond the door. A glimmer of something moved between the latched door and the frame. A knife blade slid silently under the latch fall and began to slowly push the wooden bar up.

Diego looked for his short sword, unable to remember where it was. He sat up on the bed. When his feet touched the floor he felt his discarded clothes and the scabbarded sword. He slid off of the bed, grasped the sword and while watching the door intently, crept in a low crouch to a position behind the door. He did not pull the sword from the scabbard for fear the noise of the unsheathing would alert the intruder.

The door began to open and the barrel of a pistol slid into view. After a pause, the door opened a bit more and the pistol, the hammer fully cocked, was advanced into the room until Diego could see the hand that wielded it.

Diego reached out with his left, grabbed the pistol around the lock and pulled. A man, unable to release the pistol because Diego's grip had closed around weapon and hand, was hurled into the room. Diego slammed the pommel of his sword against the back of the man's head as hard as he could. Once, twice and the man went limp, releasing the pistol, but not before pulling the trigger. The hammer fell, stabbing the flint into Diego's hand and trapping it against the lock. Pain exploded up Diego's arm as the razor-sharp flint ground into his flesh.

His shoulder was against the door and he felt someone pushing against it from the other side. A second man was attempting to enter the room. Diego slammed into the door sending the other intruder hurling backwards. There was the satisfying sound of breaking wood and a dull thump. Diego had forced the second man back through the gallery railing.

The first intruder lay on the floor, completely motionless, so Diego rushed out the door to pursue the second man. The gallery was less than a dozen feet from the floor of the main room and it was unlikely that the fall had incapacitated the man. Mindless of the fact he was naked, Diego stepped onto the walkway and looked down to see a man struggling to his feet, a pistol in his hand. Diego turned to go down the stairs only to be confronted by a third man.

Fortunately, this one did not have a pistol. Unfortunately, he did have a dirk. He stabbed at Diego, who rolled his body to deflect the thrust away from his chest. The blade skittered across some ribs and stabbed into Diego's left bicep, plunging deep until the tip struck bone. Diego's sword hand had been down when he turned and he brought it up striking his assailant on the chin with the pommel and racking the blade up the man's chest, clipping his face. The man screamed, put both hands to his slashed face, turned and ran.

Diego looked at the man on the ground floor. The second man was on his feet now and aiming a pistol up at Diego. Reflexively, Diego fell back through the open door as the pistol discharged and a splintered hole appeared in the deck of the gallery. *That should bring out the whole inn.* Shouts and running feet sounded from both the main room below and gallery as people awakened by the shot flooded into the main room.

Diego stepped on the intruder as he fell back into the room. The man, no longer unconscious, began to crawl toward the open window. Diego caught the man's collar with his left hand even though the pistol still dangled from the meat of his palm and a dirk was buried in his arm. The pain was blinding, debilitating.

The intruder slipped out of his coat, crawled away from Diego's weak, unbalanced attempt to slash with the sword and jumped out of the window. Diego was left holding the man's discarded coat. A lamp appeared in the door behind him and he turned poised to strike.

"*Primero, Primero*! It is I, Juan. Do not strike. The bandits have fled." The inn keeper, trembling with fear, held the lamp before him, positioned more to shield from a sword strike than to cast light. "Mother of God, *Primero*. But you are hurt! Sit down, please."

Diego sat on the bed. Blood covered his legs and poured onto the floor. He stabbed the sword into the floorboards so it would be within easy reach and began to assess his wounds. He pulled the hammer of the pistol to full cock and managed to work the flint out of his hand. He put the pistol on the bed and looked at the dirk sticking from his bicep. The grip was ornate, the blade, as much as he could see, appeared to be Toledo steel. This was not a cutthroat's weapon. He pulled the knife out and a wave of nausea almost caused him to vomit.

"Somebody, send for *La Anciana* (the Old Woman)," Juan shouted several times. When no one seemed to respond, he grabbed one of the gawkers by the arm. "You, Santo, go get the Old Woman." He turned back to Diego, who was attempting to pull on his trousers. "*Primero*, the old woman is a healer. She will treat your wounds. She is the best."

Diego struggled with the buttons on his trousers but could not fasten even one. His head was spinning and he feared he might faint. People kept coming in and out, peering around Juan and gasping at what they saw.

"Juan, tell the next fool that sticks his head in here will be the one to help me fasten my britches."

Juan pushed the crowd out onto the gallery and posted his son as a guard with instructions to bring the Old Woman in the instant she arrived. Diego lay back on the bed and closed his eyes. Which hurt more, his arm or his hand, he could not say.

"Let her through. Let her through." Juan's angry shouts caused Diego to sit up. The people at the door stepped aside and a shriveled, hunched crone moved into the room. *Old fails to describe this woman.* She had not a hair on her head and a few on her chin. She was clearly toothless and her wrinkled skin was a deep black. She moved close to Diego and inspected his arm, his hand and then the back of his head.

"The cut on the head is nothing," she muttered. Diego had not even realized he had been wounded on his head.

"The hand will heal. None of the bones of the hand have been cut." Though her voice was faint, nearly a whisper, everyone could hear her clearly for all others had fallen silent.

"The arm wound is deep, to the bone. We must wash the spirits of corruption from the wound and burn it closed to keep them out. Bring me rum." The last phrase was so loud in contrast to the preceding words that Juan jumped.

"I go for rum," someone on the gallery shouted.

Old Woman looked into Diego's eyes. He was sitting on the bed and she standing, yet they were eye to eye.

"I will wash the wounds with rum," she announced, "even the scratch on your head. The spirits of corruption may fester anywhere with so much blood about."

Diego had learned from his father that wounds washed with rum or treated with honey rarely festered. He also knew that rum on an open wound burned like fire. His mother would say the burning pain was proof the evil spirits were being driven out.

The rum arrived and Old Woman started by bathing the wound on his head. She recited something as she wiped the rum into the cut. Later, the inn keeper would tell Diego that Old Woman spoke the language of the Devil. That was why she was so successful at driving out infections. Diego thought it might have been her native African language.

The hand wound burned briefly. Though it looked fierce and raw, for some reason the pain in his hand became tolerable. He flexed his fingers and folded his palm. Everything worked, though he doubted he would be demonstrating bayonet techniques for a month or more.

His arm was a different matter. Old Woman washed the wound and, using two small wires, she pushed a rum soaked thread in and out of the deep gash. Diego was certain he was going to vomit and was on the verge of telling Old Woman to get out of his way when she stopped.

She reached into the bag she carried and brought out a jar. The jar contained a foul-smelling jelly which she spread on the entrance wound. Using a flit and steel, she struck sparks onto the jelly which burst into a blue flame. After the jelly had burned away, she gently bandaged his arm and hand using strips of clean cotton to hold linen patches to the wounds. When she finished she stepped back. "You must change the bandages every day for thirteen days. Always use linen against the wounds, never cotton, never wool, only linen. Always soak the linen in rum." She held out her hand, palm up.

Diego understood. "How much do I owe you?"

"Pay what you think is fair," she said.

"You better hope she thinks it is enough," Juan joked. "She will call the spirits back."

Diego picked up the intruder's abandoned coat as he searched for his haversack among the pile of things on the floor. He felt something heavy in an inner pocket. He felt around and retrieved a bandana that was tightly wrapped around a dozen coins or more. He unfolded the bandana and found several silver coins and one tiny gold escudo.

He gave the gold coin and two silver coins to Old Woman. She turned toward the lamplight and inspected each coin. She turned back and returned one of the silver coins to Diego. "Too much," she said and left.

"Juan, here are four silver *peso de ochos* for your trouble." Diego had paid his room and meal charges in advance. "Now find a coach for hire. I must return to Havana today."

"Yes, *Primero*."

"And find someone to help me dress."

"Yes, *Primero*."

Diego shifted through his bedroll until he found clean trousers and a shirt. One of the barmaids appeared at the door.

"I am called Rosa. Juan says I am to help you with your clothes," she said, a smile teasing the corner of her mouth.

Rosa helped Diego into his uniform and repacked his bedroll, except for the blood-soaked trousers. Those he gave to her. She could wash them and then sell them or keep them. The sun was coming up when Diego stepped out onto the street and into a carriage.

"Where do we go?" the driver asked.

"Havana. The Castillo de San Salvador de la Punta, please."

CHAPTER *21*

Diego climbed down from the carriage at the outer gate to the Castillo. The ride had been rough. The driver, seeing Diego's discomfort, offered to slow, but he would not permit it. The jostling had aggravated the wound in his arm until it began to bleed again. He wore his uniform coat with his right arm through the right sleeve and the left draped over his shoulder. The left sleeve of his shirt was bloody from his bicep to his elbow.

The people moving about the market place of the bray gawked at him as he walked through them on his way to the inner portcullis, but they said nothing. The guards at the inner gate asked, respectfully, for Diego's papers. He provided his standing orders as a member of Gálvez's staff and was admitted. He could hear them muttering behind him about his condition as he mounted the stairs leading to the headquarters office.

The clerk on duty accepted Diego's written report on the condition and battle readiness of the Bauta militia. He eyed Diego's arm suspiciously and said, "Please, if you would take a seat, Sergeant, the General would like to see you. I will tell him you are here." The clerk passed a brace of guards at the General's door, knocked and entered when a voice from within announced "Come."

Diego knew the guards from his many visits to this office. One of them swallowed and said, "Mother of God, *Primero*, what happed?"

"Bandits."

"Bandits attacked a sergeant of His Most Catholic Majesty's army?"

"I was out of uniform at the time."

"What did they take?"

"Several slashes, a few cuts, a bad fall and a cracked skull."

"Were they arrested?"

"No. I let them slip through my fingers."

The clerk reappeared. "The General will see you now, Sergeant."

When Diego entered Gálvez was already halfway around his desk and coming to meet him.

"Carlo told me you had been wounded. Come, sit down. Carlo, bring some brandy! When did this happened and how?" Gálvez escorted Diego to a chair and he sat.

Carlo appeared with a bottle of opaque green glass and two silver goblets on a tray.

"Here, Sergeant, drink this and tell me what has occurred." Gálvez poured a golden liquid into one of the goblets. It was unheard of for a General officer to pour for anyone other than a peer or a guest and the action caused Diego to feel slightly uncomfortable

He sipped the brandy, the first he had ever tasted, and thought rum would have been better. Still he politely drank the brandy and told Gálvez everything that had occurred from when he was awakened by a sound at the door to his treatments by Old Woman. He did not mention going to bed drunk or being awakened by a dream.

"It was Barnave's men, General. Of that I am certain. The coat I stripped from one had several newly minted silver coins – French *ecu*, just as was found on his man killed at *Le Aldea*."

"Carlo!" Gálvez shouted toward the closed door.

The clerk rushed in. "Yes, General?"

"Do you know if the *Siderno* has sailed?"

"No, sir."

"Find out. If not, tell the harbor master she is confined until I release her. That is the *Siderno*, Carlo. She is Sicilian."

"Yes, sir." Carlo was gone.

"Your injuries are unfortunate, Sergeant. We sail in two days for Pensacola. I had hoped to have you with the Louisiana Regiment for this attack. That is impossible now. I will have our surgeon inspect the wound and provide an estimate when you will be fit for duty again. Until then, you will be on convalescent leave here in Havana. I will send for you when you have healed sufficiently, or release you to return to New Orleans depending upon the situation at that time."

Carlo reentered. "General, sir. The *Siderno* has not sailed, but the harbor master told me her captain has requested leave to go tomorrow. He will hold her here."

"Good. Thank you, Carlo." The clerk was gone again. Diego sipped at the brandy and decided he was developing a taste for it.

"Evidently, our friend, *le Comte de Virieu* has learned of our intent to depart. How could he not?" Diego knew Gálvez was thinking out loud and did not attempt to reply. "Every man in Havana with eyes knows we are ready. I will leave instructions with the harbor master concerning our diplomatic delinquent. I dare not hold him here longer than two weeks."

Diego was dispatched to El Morro Castle to convalesce and assist the young officer in charge of the garrison troops, Major *Don* Luis Macarty. Macarty was an astute young man of about twenty-five years. Short, stocky and animated, red hair, red beard and green eyes, Macarty was a natural leader, well-schooled in the arts of war, but unseasoned when it came to dealing with enlisted men. He was an aristocrat accustomed to refined company and somewhat ignorant of the baser instincts of the combat infantryman.

The British had taken Havana twenty years ago by landing an overpowering force east of Morro Castle and taking the citadel by escalade. Once Morro Castle fell, the British lowered the barricade chain and sailed into the harbor with fifty men-of-war. Havana happened to be lightly defended at the time and was taken in one day. Macarty fretted the British might come again and he busied his men with spreading caltrops, setting stakes and digging foot traps to impede a rush of infantry.

Diego busied himself with drilling troops, supervising bayonet training exercises. He ordered, or rather he suggested and Macarty ordered, watch and signal towers built along the coast within sight of each other from Morro to *Rio Cojimar*, a distance of about four miles. The entire distance was covered by a continuous beach ideal for landing forces. A cache of twenty light galloper guns, complete with horses, caissons, and copious quantities of grape shot, was quartered back from the beach. Six hundred militiamen had been trained to bring the guns into action at a minute's notice and resist an enemy landing at the beach. The intention was to delay an advance inland long enough to fully organize the remaining forces in Havana. There would be no repeat of the 1762 fiasco.

Diego paced the battlements of Morro Castle flexing his nearly healed arm. Gálvez had departed two weeks ago. He regularly spent his evenings watching the sun set and watching to see if the *Siderno* had sailed. She had not.

A gun boomed from the sea and the signal tower of Castillo de San Salvador came alive in a flurry of flags. Morro Castle's own signal tower burst into frantic activity. The gun must have been a signal from a ship at sea, and now a symphony of semaphores played between the land and the unseen ship.

Diego could decipher none of it. He went to the door at the base of a signal tower and waited until one of the signal clerks came out on his way to report. He did not have to wait long.

A flushed and excited thin man came out gripping a leaf of paper.

"Tell me, what is happening?"

"*Primero*, disastrous news. The fleet has been scattered by a hurricane! Two of the ships, *La Mitilde* and *Santa Rasalia* are returning to the harbor even now. No one knows the fate of Gálvez or the others. I must go, *Primero*." The man flew down the stairs with such abandon Diego expected to see him tumble to the bottom.

The fleet is scattered. Gálvez had standing orders for just such an occurrence. Individual ships would spend two or three days searching for others and then make for the nearest Spanish port. It would be months before the fleet could be assembled again, provided a sufficient number of ships survived the storm.

He returned to the battlements just as the sun was turning the stone walls of the Morro Castle a bright orange. He could see the *Siderno* resting at anchor. There was some movement in the shadow along her side. Her captain's gig pushed off carrying three passengers. One was obviously a woman. Who the two men were, Diego could only guess. When he last saw Barnave, he had three men in his escort. If it was Barnave, he was traveling with only one guard. *Perhaps some are not as quick to heal as others.* Diego smiled at the thought.

A gust of wind caught the gig when it cleared the shadow of the *Siderno* and the woman had to clasp a hand on her hat as it threatened to fly away. Diego's smile faded abruptly. He did not doubt the woman was Marcelite. The gig was making for the pier on the Morro Castle side of the harbor where a cluster of shops and alehouses awaited the newly landed sailor.

He descended to his quarters where he loaded and primed two pistols. He strapped on his short sword, stuffed the pistols into his waistband and donned his best uniform coat. He went to the command office to sign out. The clerk inquired of the reason for his departure and the time of his return.

"I have decided an inspection of the pier-side alehouses is in order. I intend to return before first call tomorrow," Diego said.

෴

Diego approached the third alehouse through the alley. Every establishment had a back door that accessed an alley or privy yard. Had he conducted his search of the half dozen taverns by walking in the front door he could not have escaped notice. Every man watched the front door, but the privy door was often forgotten.

Just as he reached for the pull rope on the door it opened and a slightly drunken soldier stumbled out, fumbling with his trouser buttons.

"Excuse me, *Primero*," he slurred and stepped aside, holding the door for Diego, who stepped into a small alcove to the main room. Three equally spaced sooty lamps hung from the ceiling of the room, casting enough light to make out faces at the tables. There were eight men in the room. Four sailors huddled around one table sharing the contents of an earthenware jug. A soldier, in the same uniform as the man headed to the privy, sat at another table drinking from a flagon. Another flagon was on the table across from the drinker. A bartender was bustling around the room preparing for a busy night. The alehouse had several rooms on a second floor that were accessed by a single stairway and a gallery where a light shone from under one of the doors.

Two men sat at a table in a dark corner. Both were seated with a clear view of the front door. One of the men was Captain Achille of the *Siderno*. Diego thought he recognized the other man as one of Barnave's entourage. A fresh scar ran up the left side of the man's face from his chin to his nose.

The soldier returning from the privy brushed past Diego and joined his friend. He poured his flagon full, sat and leaned over to his friend to say something. The other soldier glanced over toward Diego then returned to his drink. Achille and his companion did not seem to have noticed the exchange.

A door on the second floor, the one that had shone a light, opened. Barnave and Marcelite stepped out. Barnave turned, spoke to someone in the room and closed the door. They came down the stairs to Achille and the other man, who were now both standing. Barnave spoke quietly to Achille. Diego could not hear what was said until Achille answered.

"Yes, my lord. I will bring you across the harbor in my gig. The *Babieca* is an excellent inn," Achille said as the four of them exited the inn. Diego noticed that they paused at the door while the scarred one stepped out and returned. The man nodded, held the door for the other three and gave the room one final scan before exiting. Diego had stepped back into the shadows and, hidden by a post, was certain he had not been seen. He waited for a count of twenty, then walked over to the two soldiers.

"State your names and regiment."

They reported themselves to be *soldados* Taso and Aguilera, privates of the Havana fixed regiment. Both men were regulars and they seemed to have sobered considerably when Diego approached their table.

"Do you know who I am?"

"Yes, *Primero*," they both said in unison.

Diego noticed they were unarmed. He pulled his short sword and gave it to Taso, who seemed to be the more sober of the two. "We are going up to one of the rooms. Aguilera, I want you to stay at the foot of the stairs. Do not allow anyone to come up. Taso, follow me. We are going into a room. I do not know how many are in the room, but if there is a fight, kill any man who is not me."

Taso, now completely sober, swallowed hard and nodded. Diego pulled his pistols, cocked them and the three headed toward the stairs. The bartender was not in the room, but the four sailors stopped their conversations and watched the proceedings.

"Mind your cups," Diego growled, and the sailors pretended to lose interest.

Aguilera posted himself at the foot of the stairs while Diego and Taso ascended.

"You try the latch. If it is unlocked, open the door and step aside. If it is locked, step aside and I will kick the door open. When I go in, follow me and move to my right, if you can. Get in a position where you can use the sword." Diego whispered as they approached the door, light still showing under it. Pistols at the ready, Diego nodded for Taso to try the latch. It was unlocked and lifted easily.

Diego rushed in feeling Taso close behind him.

"Show your hands!" Diego shouted.

A young woman in a chair next to the bed exclaimed, "Mother of God," and complied, a towel falling from her grasp onto the bed. She might have been twenty. Her dark eyes were wide and terrified, but her voice seemed calm.

"What is the meaning of this, Sergeant?" She said.

Diego looked around the tiny room. The woman and an occupant on the bed were the only other people in the room. Whoever was on the bed had not responded to the intrusion in any way and the room had the smell of sickness. Diego set his pistols to half cock and tucked them back into his waistband.

He looked at Taso, who shrugged. "Give me the sword," he said. He returned the weapon to its scabbard and pulling a silver coin from his pocket, gave it to Taso. "You and Aguilera enjoy another jug downstairs." When Taso paused he added, "Now."

Taso stepped out onto the gallery, examining the piece of eight with a puzzled expression.

"What is happening?" Aguilera shouted up from the bottom of the stairs.

"Find the bartender," Taso replied as he descended the stairs.

"Sergeant, why are you here?" The woman asked again.

"Who are you?" Diego asked.

"I am Maria Ybañes," she said. "My father owns this inn. My friends call me Azúcarita."

"I apologize for my rude entry, *Señorita*. Who is it on the bed?"

"A Frenchman, I do not know his name."

"How long has he been here?"

"The *Comte de Virieu* had him brought here two weeks ago." She looked at the motionless form. "He could drink a little when they brought him, but now he takes nothing. He is dying."

"Is he sick?"

"No, wounded. His skull is broken."

Diego walked to the head of the bed where he could see the man's drawn and haggard face. It was the man who had first entered the room in Bauta with a pistol, a pistol Diego now carried in his waist band.

"My lord, the count, has instructed me to send word if he recovers or if he dies," Azúcarita said. "My father has been paid to care for this man for a week I think my father has been over paid."

"How many men does the count have with him?"

"I have only seen one. The one with the fresh cut on his face."

Diego remembered Barnave had three men with him when he came aboard the *Siderno*. He did not recall their faces very well. All were hooded and wet. The man with the cut may have been one, the man on the bed could have been another. The third man, Barnave's aid, had introduced himself. *What was the name? Jean Maury!* He may very well have been the third man in Bauta, the one that fell from the gallery, or Barnave may have hired more men in Havana.

"What is the meaning of this?"

Diego turned to see a portly, greying man in the door way.

"Papa!" Azúcarita exclaimed.

"This is army business Señor Ybañes," Diego said. "How many people know you are tending to this Frenchmen?"

"The French are our allies, No?"

"How many know?" Diego said in his best sergeant's command voice.

Ybañes paled. "Just my daughter and I, no others, I swear."

"Keep it that way. Do not mention my visit to anyone – anyone. Do not speak words about my visit even to Azúcarita lest others overhear. Do you understand?"

"Yes, Sergeant."

Diego worked his way to the door. "I would apologize for this intrusion, but it never happened," he said.

He went down to the main room. The sailors were gone. He did not doubt his visit would be the talk of at least one ship. Taso and Aguilera were enjoying another pot of ale and talking to the bartender.

"Those sailors who were just here, what ship were they from?" Diego asked.

"They were from *La Nuestra Señora del Carmen*, a bilander out of Veracruz," the bartender said. "She sails at first light."

A bilander? How many kinds of ships can there be? Perhaps word of tonight's intrusion could be kept from Barnave, for a while at least. Diego rejected the thought. It is more likely someone posted to watch the alehouse is even now reporting the incident to the Count.

"It is best to strike before the enemy can prepare a defense." Diego could almost hear his father and grandfather discussing combat strategies around a cook fire high in the mountains of Gran Canaria. Doramas deMelilla, the slayer of Moors, was an advocate of quick action while Grandfather Tupinar, the rebellious one, preferred a considered, well-planned action. Both men valued attack over defense.

☙

La Babieca was a stone structure of four floors on a cobblestone street. Close enough to the harbor for a man at a fourth floor window to see every ship at anchor in the harbor and far enough from the dockside shops and warehouses to escape the smell and noise. The stables and service buildings were across a wide courtyard from the inn. As with most inns or alehouses, the main room served as both a dining room and a tavern. Unlike most establishments, the main room was reserved for residents and their guests. The entrance to the inn was guarded by two scowling civilians, armed with staves to discourage visits by the general public.

Diego watched the guards from the corner of a warehouse. He was pondering the best approach to gain entrance and find Barnave's quarters. He did not doubt that the Count had several rooms reserved. How were those rooms arranged? Likely they occupied rooms on the fourth floor.

Scaling the exterior by going from balcony to balcony was possible except he did not know which window would gain entrance to the room he was searching. It was three in the morning and already a few were moving about the streets. Fishermen were headed toward the harbor to ready themselves for a day's work and those who worked the docks were beginning to stir.

What am I doing here?

He had waited one day before crossing the harbor with the intent to do what? Confront Barnave with an accusation of attempted murder by hire? Nobles regularly hired murderers and, unless the victim was also nobility, they knew they could act with impunity. Diego was a sergeant in the Spanish army and a former goatherd from the highlands of Gran Canaria, an unlikely candidate for justice. Barnave was a lord of France, a diplomat and untouchable by the law, but Diego knew that the nobility were not invincible if a man acted prudently.

Diego had decided that accosting Barnave tonight was not prudent. He was about to turn away when a light appeared in one of the fourth floor windows. Three other widows brightened in succession, as if the inhabitants had all been awakened at the same time. Perhaps he should linger for a while and watch.

He did not have to wait very long. Within a half-hour, the guards at the door reacted to someone within, looked up and down the street, and then opened the inn's massive doors. Barnave and Marcelite stepped out onto the street followed by two slaves carrying a trunk. They paused for a moment, looking about before setting off in the direction of the docks, which were only a quarter mile to the north.

Diego sank back into the shadows as they passed his hiding place. The small entourage consisted of a middle-aged man and a young woman strolling toward the harbor followed by two black men struggling with a heavy sea chest. Clearly, two people preparing to board ship and depart Havana. Diego followed at a discreet distance torn by indecision and yet driven by revenge, or was it something else?

Barnave and Marcelite arrived at the harbormaster's station situated on a section of dock reserved for gigs and other small craft servicing the ships anchored in the harbor. A signal tower rose from the center of the building with a pair of large semaphore poles. Paddles were used during the day and lamps at night. Anyone within sight of the tower would be able to see signals from the tower day or night. Barnave spoke to someone within the building and the lamps began to move.

A signal to Achille to send his gig.

Diego moved forward. *"Buenos días, Señor y Señorita."*

Barnave spun around, hand on the hilt of his rapier. Marcelite smiled.

"You! How? You fool, have you been following us!" Barnave responded in French. He did not draw his rapier, but held the grip tightly.

"I should be cross with you, Diego. You did not bid me farewell when last we parted," Marcelite spoke in French as well. Barnave appeared alarmed while Marcelite, eyes sparkling in the lamplight, seemed entertained.

"You should have stayed in your barracks, Sergeant. You have persisted in confounding my plans and escaping my – remedies."

"I would consider it foolish, Count, if I were to ignore your attempts on my life."

Barnave and Marcelite looked at each other with amused expressions as if they held some mysterious secret.

"You should have considered it foolish to follow me without accounting for my loyal servants. Do you think my gentle niece and I would come to the docks at this hour unescorted?"

Diego had been so focused on Barnave – and Marcelite, he had entirely forgotten about Barnave's associates. He heard the blades being drawn behind him. Barnave gestured, unnecessary as Diego turned his head in the direction of the sound. Two men, rapiers draw, stepped into the light spilling from the harbor master's window.

"I think you have met my men, Sergeant. If not, then I present *monsieur* Jean Maury and *monsieur* Jacques Bouillé."

"Monsieur Jean Maury, I remember. We conversed aboard the *Siderno.* Bouillé, I have met as well, but we have never conversed. I remember him as "the disfigured one."

"Jean," Barnave spoke while Diego, regretting he was not carrying his pistols, watched the unsheathed blades. "After Marcelite and I board the *Siderno* I will send the captain's gig back for you and Jacques. Be so kind as to kill this fool before you rejoin us."

"It will be my pleasure, Sir,"

Bouillé moved to block Diego's access to the harbormaster's building and Jean obstructed the way back to the street. Diego, his short sword still in his belt, could go into the alley with just enough time to draw before two men with long rapiers were upon him, or he could rush Barnave.

The Count seemed to read Diego's thoughts, for he drew his rapier as well just as the *Siderno*'s gig bumped at the dock. Six burly rowers and a coxswain were added to the mix. Barnave sheathed his sword and smiled.

"Let me help you into the boat, my dear," he said, offering a hand to Marcelite. "We are finished here."

Marcelite took Barnave's hand as they descended the steps to the gig. Once they were aboard, she turned to look up at Diego. "Goodbye, Diego. See, I have not forgotten my manners."

Diego felt a rush of anger that overpowered his fears and drew.

⁘⁓⁘

Diego had the sudden urge to rush down the pier, throw himself into the boat and kill Barnave even though it would mean his life as well. Maury must have read the thought in Diego's eyes for he moved to intercept any rush toward the gig as it was pushed away from the dock.

Diego spun around the corner of the building into the alley. Bouillé and Maury, unprepared for the move, hesitated slightly before running to the alley in pursuit only to discover a passage so narrow they had to enter one at a time. Bouillé entered first.

"It is a *cul de sac*!" He shouted back to Maury. "We have him trapped!"

Bouillé could see a figure crouching just out of rapier reach. A short sword is an excellent weapon on a congested and confused battle field but in an alley the longer rapier carried all the advantages. Still Bouillé drew a dagger with his left hand and advanced with caution. He had confronted Diego once before and knew the sergeant to be a formidable fighter. There was no need to rush.

The sliver of sky above the alley was beginning to turn grey. Bouillé waited for his eyes to adjust. He felt Maury move up behind him.

"What are you waiting for?" Maury hissed. "Get it over with."

"Not so fast. We will be able to see him clearly soon. Be patient."

Something lunged out of the darkness and blocked out the sliver of sky. Bouillé lunged with his rapier as the dark object fell onto him. The long slender blade met no resistance as Bouillé was engulfed. A net! A net with lead weights around its circular perimeter fell over Bouillé. He instinctively backed away stumbling into Maury, who had crowded in behind him. He felt the net being pulled forward, freeing his head and shoulders, but the webbing was entangled in the cross bar of his rapier.

Off balance, Bouillé was pulled deeper into the alley. He raised the dagger to block a slash from his left, but the stroke came from his pinned right side. Bouillé released the rapier and fell back just as a wide blade crossed where his neck had just been. He turned to run, but Maury hindered his movement.

"What is it?" Maury asked, astonished that Bouillé was scrambling for escape without his rapier. Bouillé seemed to trip and he tried to hold the man up. Maury was looking at Bouillé's face, expecting an answer. Instead of words, blood gushed from Bouillé's open mouth.

Maury backed out of the alley sweeping his rapier from side to side and straining to see Diego. He retreated into the street and stopped, prepared to engage a man armed with a short sword.

"You cannot hide in there, Sergeant."

"I could hide in here, if it pleased me," Diego said as he moved out to confront Maury. "I do not choose to do so." Diego carried Bouillé rapier in his right hand and his own short sword in his left.

Maury lunged, but Diego caught the rapier with a circular movement of his short sword, contemptuously pushing it aside. Reposting with his rapier, Diego cut a slash across Maury's lapel and left arm, then recoiled into a guard position just in time to trap Maury's dagger in his weapon's quillions. Diego gave a quick twist of his rapier and the dagger's thin blade snapped like a dry twig.

Maury moved back, holding the stump of his dagger in his left hand and flicking his rapier from a high threat to a low one. Diego move easily forward, flexing his broad shoulders to loosen the sleeves of his coat, freeing his arms for action.

"What is going on?" The night watch, two militiamen, had been drawn to the sound of sword play. "Sergeant, what is going on here?"

"Two bandits have accosted me," Diego said while circling Maury, looking for an opening.

"Two? Where is the other?"

"Dead. Look in the alley. Go, both of you, examine the body for your report. Then come out and examine the other body as well."

"What other body?"

"There will be one when you return."

"Stay out of the way," Maury snarled in Spanish thick with a French accent. "This is a private affair."

The night watchmen, armed only with halberds, were accustomed to breaking up knife fights between drunken sailors or soldier. This was something closer to a duel, a Spanish sergeant against a French aristocrat.

One of the guards muttered to the other. "Manuel, what do we do?"

"We wait," Manuel said. "We will arrest the winner."

Maury suddenly advanced with a practiced combination of lunges, thrusts and parries forcing Diego back into the alley and causing Diego to trip over Bouillé's body. Diego tumbled backwards and Maury rushed forward, ready to skewer Diego when he rolled to his feet.

Only, Diego did not stand when he regained his feet. Remaining in a crouch, he slapped Maury's blade up with his short sword and pushed his rapier forward. Maury's eyes widened in horror as his momentum carried him onto the thin blade and watched mesmerized, as it disappeared into his coat.

CHAPTER 22

"Do not just stand there," Diego ordered. "Help me check the bodies for stolen goods?"

"Stolen goods?" Manuel asked. "Why would they have stolen things on them?"

"These were two brazen bandits. Did you not see how they attacked a Spanish sergeant here on *Calle de Baratillo*, not fifty paces from the harbor-master's office?"

Diego dug into the purse on Maury's belt and found a roll of coins wrapped in cloth, a common practice to prevent the telltale jingle of money from attracting cutpurses. He tossed the roll to Manuel who reflexively caught the roll.

"No stolen things in that purse. I will see if his friend has anything."

Bouillé's body yielded a similar find which Diego tossed to the other night watchman. Both guards seemed confused by the turn of events, and increasingly reluctant to call for the watch commander.

"Put those away." Diego gestured at the coins. "No need for the *alcalde* to see those." The coin rolls disappeared. "Good. Now one of you fetch the *alcalde* and tell him a Spanish sergeant has killed some bandits. Tell him I will wait until he arrives so we can search the bodies together."

The guard who was not Manuel trotted off.

"Were they really bandits, sergeant?" asked Manuel.

"I think so, yes. Just tell the *alcalde* you witnessed the fight and nothing else."

The sky was beginning to turn gray. A splash came from the direction of the harbor and Manuel glanced toward the pier to see a gig, oars raised and dripping, bump into the landing. Diego, seeing Manuel's distraction, stepped out of the alley and began to walk toward the gig. The coxswain paused for a moment until the realization of what must have happened became clear to him. He shouted an order and the sailors pushed off, dropped oars and pulled away.

"Sergeant, explain what has happened."

Diego turned away from the harbor to see the *alcalde*, *Don* Alexandro Cavallero de Clouet, a gentleman of fifty years or more.

"Josef tells me you have been set upon by bandits! Wait. No need to answer straight away. I have sent for a clerk. Wait until he arrives, then tell me all you know. I must make a record of what has happen."

Everything must be documented and copied in triplicate.

ᥱᦢ

It was noon before the ordeal of compiling a satisfactory report and inventorying the items found on the bodies had been completed. The two fine rapiers and the one remaining dagger were confiscated by the *alcalde*. The weapons were made of the finest Toledo steel and, collectively, worth a year's salary. The *alcalde* offered the opinion that it would have been a shame for such fine steel to go to waste, which meant to anyone other than *Don* Alexandro. Clothes, shoes and all other things found on the two men would be given to a local convent. No one objected to the division of the spoils.

The official report claimed two bandits to have been killed by the *alcalde's* alert night watchmen who had intervened in an attempted robbery. While the incident report was being compiled, a steady stream of the curious drifted by to see the bodies and the two courageous night watchmen. Josef and Manuel were very relieved when no one questioned why two bandits happened to be without coin of any kind.

Diego had managed to search both bodies thoroughly as the *alcalde* admired his newly acquired rapiers and revised certain details of the report with his clerk. Diego found a letter in one of Maury's pockets which he tucked into his coat. Finding nothing else of interest, he stepped back into the street in time to see the *Siderno* shake out her mainsails and get underway. Several figures could be seen on the quarterdeck as she maneuvered to gain a starboard reach.

One of the figures was a woman. A man next to her lowered the telescope he had been holding to his eye and turned to say something to the woman. She waved a white handkerchief above her head in a small circle. Diego turned away. His left arm had begun to ache and he wondered if he had reopened the freshly healed wound.

The *Siderno* was through the harbor mouth and well away before Diego could find a skiff to bring him back to Morro Castle. The news of the attempted robbery had preceded him to the Castle and he had to repeat the story of how two desperate men had attacked him in an alley and how the alert night watch had intervened.

His left arm throbbed and his head swam. After a meal of salt pork and biscuits he bought a bottle of wine from one of the vendors in the bray and climbed to the ramparts to watch the sun set across the harbor mouth. He loved the view of Castillo de San Salvador de la Punta across the Almendares River. In some inexplicable way it reminded him of Gran Canaria.

The booming report of a cannon announced the arrival of a ship. Signal towers on San Salvador communicated with the as yet unseen ship. Diego could see men rushing to the battlements of the Castillo waving their hats and embracing each other.

Diego concentrated on the sliver of sea visible past the walls of San Salvador. A ship of war slid into view. It was Gálvez's ship. The general had survived the storm. Six other ships followed as the small fleet moved into the harbor.

Someone stepped up beside Diego. "Gálvez has returned with two captured British ships, one of them a frigate. The other ships are survivors of the storm." It was one of the signalmen who spoke. "Many other ships found safe harbor in New Orleans and Mobile. The general will reassemble his invasion force."

In matters of war, Governor General Bernardo de Gálvez was nothing if not persistent.

Diego returned to his quarters and opened the letter he had recovered from Maury's body. It was in French, but no more than three simple lines. Perhaps he might be able to make sense of it. After some effort, he concluded that the note said "Joseph Wiggins is the man. He is with the Marylanders. Move when you think best."

☙

The following three months were almost a repeat of the previous six. Diego continued his roving inspections and training of units assigned to the reconstituted invasion force. Only one ship had been lost out of a fleet of fifty, driven ashore near Pensacola where the storm survivors were put to death by native allies of the British.

No mention was made of the incident at *Calle de Baratillo*, as Diego's encounter with Barnave's men had come to be known. Diego did not doubt that Gálvez knew, and knew the truth of it, not the *alcalde's* self-serving report. Gálvez seemed to know everything and had informants everywhere. He was also a master of controlling the things his enemies knew.

It was mid-December when Gálvez summoned Diego to his office. This time the assignment would be very different from the tedious evaluation of this regiment or that contingent of volunteers.

Diego was sent into Gálvez's office while the General was consulting with several ranking members of the Spanish command in New Spain. Acting admiral of the invasion fleet, Captain *Don* José Calbo de Irazábal was seated under an open window flanked by two naval officers. The Captain General of Havana, *Don* Diego Navarro, and merchant Miguel Eduardo were conversing in a corner of the room with two colonels Diego did not recognize. Gálvez's lieutenants, Colonel Esteban Miró and Juan Antonio Gayarré, were crowded around a map on a table in the center of the room. Two recording clerks were seated, each at his own portable writing desk, against the far wall of the room attempting to take notes of the proceedings.

A spirited debate was taking place concerning the actions to be taken in light of the disruption of the invasion attempt. All, except Gálvez and his aides, advocated an increased effort to defend against a British attempt on Havana and urged abandonment of further action on the Florida mainland. Diego expected the debate to cease upon his entry. Mere enlisted men were rarely privy to discussions of higher strategy, so he stepped to his left away from the doorway in anticipation of an exodus of ranking officers.

Gálvez raised his hand for attention. "Gentlemen, I believe you all know my Regimental First Sergeant Diego deMelilla."

Conversation stopped. Diego snapped to attention and held his salute until Gálvez gestured for him to stand at ease.

"Sergeant, we have been debating the importance of seizing Pensacola from the British. I think I would like your opinion."

Good God! A general officer and a nobleman is asking me for my opinion?!

Diego swallowed and wet his lips. "Sir, the General desires my opinion, sir?"

"Yes. You have been closely involved in the reconnaissance of the West Florida. I want your first-hand opinion of the importance of Pensacola to our efforts."

Diego felt dizzy. How could he answer and be taken seriously when many of the men present considered enlisted men to be – inferior? "Sir, I can name two primary reasons for the capture of Pensacola. First, Pensacola is the last outpost of the British in Florida. When we take Pensacola, all of Florida will fall to us."

Gálvez laughed. "Clearly and obviously, but tell me, Sergeant. What is your second reason?"

"The second reason is also the primary reason, in my opinion, sir. A Pensacola in British hands threatens Mobile. Mobile is the key to New Orleans and control of the Mississippi River Valley."

"Interesting," Gálvez said as he looked around the room insuring everyone was listening. "Please continue. Why is Mobile and not New Orleans the key to the Mississippi River Valley?"

"General, New Orleans is an island and can be bypassed. That city can only be reached by ships of any size by way of the river, a route that can be intercepted by a few guns in the right place. Any other route of supply to New Orleans requires off-loading cargo to smaller vessels which must travel a great distance to reach the city. Mobile is accessible to vessels of any draft. Passable roads with fordable rivers connect Baton Rouge and Natchez with Mobile. Both of those villages command the River. Pensacola has no such connection. When Your Excellency attacked Baton Rouge, Campbell sent forces from Pensacola, but the obstacle of the Mobile River swamp delayed them for weeks. The British could not even support Mobile from Pensacola. If Spain is to maintain control of the Mississippi River Valley, we must keep Mobile. If we are to keep Mobile, Pensacola must be taken."

Navarro laughed nervously, "General, the good sergeant is simply parroting what you have instructed him to say."

"Do you think so, *Don* Diego Navarro?" Gálvez responded. "Tell the Captain General of Havana, Sergeant deMelilla. Have I instructed you in any way in this question?"

"No, General."

"See gentlemen, you have it! It is clear that Mobile must remain in our hands." Gálvez turned back to Diego. "Where do you think Barnave may be at this moment?"

The shift in subject startled Diego and Gálvez continued for the benefit of the others present. "Barnave is a French nobleman who is convinced saving the crown of France will require a defeat of the British rebels in America. My *Primero* has had several encounters with Barnave and his people. Some were most unpleasant."

And some were not unpleasant at all.

"Tell me, sergeant. Where do you suppose the Frenchman to be right now?"

"Sir, I do not know where he is, but I think it likely he is at Pensacola, sir."

"Precisely! I know this to be the case." Gálvez was walking around the room looking every man in the eye as he passed him. "And what, sergeant, do you suppose *Le Comte* Barnave is urging General Campbell to do?"

"Sir, he would urge Campbell to take back Mobile."

"This is something you suppose, sergeant, but it is something I know to be the case. I have correspondence from a witness confirming this very thing. Barnave's precise words to General Campbell were 'If the rebels are to be defeated, Mobile must fall.'"

"Who was this witness?" Navarro asked.

"It comes directly from one of my many sources of information, my dear Captain General, and absolutely reliable."

"If the rebels fail, Spain fails," Colonel Esteban Miró muttered absentmindedly.

Gálvez clapped his hands together. "Do we have agreement, gentlemen? There will be no better time than now while the British fleet is preoccupied with the American rebels. Is the invasion of Pensacola to resume?"

Each man presented his consent to Gálvez's proposal, some more enthusiastically than others. Diego, of course, remained silent. The others filed out until only Gálvez and Diego remained.

"I need you to return to Mobile and rejoin *La Cuchilla*. My friend, Colonel José de Ezpeleta will be joining in the assault on Pensacola." Gálvez said. "My scouts have all they can do insuring the British are not moving down from Georgia in an attempt to retake Mobile. I think the rebels have been holding well against Britain, but one must always be alert for the unexpected."

"Colonel Ezpeleta will require *La Cuchilla* to reconnoiter the best route for moving troops, with cannon and horse, to the landside walls of Pensacola. You will examine that route and recommend to the Colonel if any fording, bridging or other arrangements need to be made for crossing the Perdido River or if a route further inland would be best."

Diego had scouted the road to Pensacola many times, but never as far as the Perdido River. The locals insisted that crossing the Perdido was not difficult, but farmers, hunters and tradesmen did not have to make the crossing towing siege cannons.

"I will be sending a young officer with you, Sergeant. A son of one of my wife's friends, he is very bright and eager to learn. He will be an aide to Colonel Ezpeleta. His mother thinks he will be safe as an aide in Mobile." Gálvez smiled humorlessly and called out to his clerk. "Carlo, please ask the Sub-lieutenant to join us."

The office door opened and a slim, very young, beardless youth came in. His uniform was new, spotless and he wore it with obvious discomfort. "Sub-lieutenant *Don* Francisco Grevemberg, I present to you Sergeant Diego deMelilla y Tupinar, First Sergeant, *El Primero*, of the Fixed Regiment of Louisiana. He will accompany you to Mobile and, if you are fortunate, provide you with some military instruction along the way. Be a sponge."

Diego snapped to attention and held a salute. "At your service, Sub-lieutenant *Don* Francisco Grevemberg."

Don Francisco returned the salute smartly. "I look forward to working with you, *Primero*. I have heard so much about you in New Orleans."

Gálvez slapped *Don* Francisco's back. "Now, for your sake, young sir, I will review some military concerns I have pertaining to your new posting. It is possible that the British will not stay cooped up in Pensacola waiting for us to attack."

Diego considered this remark significant. *When Gálvez opines an enemy action is possible it means his spies have detected something.*

Gálvez continued. "General Campbell knows Mobile is the keystone of the Floridas and, by extension, the Mississippi River Valley. As goes Mobile, so goes the war. The colonial rebels will stand if Spain can hold Mobile and keep the Mississippi River open for supplies. The revolution will fail if we lose Mobile. Spain will take Pensacola to keep Mobile and we will keep Mobile to protect New Orleans and the Mississippi River. It is as simple as that. When you report to Colonel Ezpeleta, *Don* Francisco, you will be carrying instructions for a coordination of forces to invest Pensacola. Any questions?"

Don Francisco swallowed visibly, "General, I do not know enough of what I am about to think of a question."

Gálvez laughed. "The first sign of wisdom, *Don* Francisco, is to know your ignorance. Listen to *El Primero* and learn. You have the makings of a fine officer. And you, Sergeant deMelilla, do you have any questions?"

"No, General."

"Fine. Carlo will give you the dispatches on the way out. You are both to leave tomorrow morning at first light, if the wind holds. You will report to the frigate *El Volante* under the command of Navy Lieutenant *Don* Luis Terraza."

~

El Volante, aided by a pilot who came aboard just off the mouth of Mobile Bay, navigated the Pelican Shoals with ease coming to anchor three cables from the fort. A flock of skiffs, barges and other vessels descended upon *El Volante* before she had even set her anchor. It had been a hard crossing that started in late December and, contending with capricious and contrary winds, *El Volante* arrived at Fort Carlota on the fifth of January, 1781.

A packet boat, *Nuestra Señora del Rosario*, came alongside as the frigate settled at anchor to receive dispatches and dignitaries. Sub-lieutenant *Don* Francisco Grevemberg qualified as a dignitary. Diego, though not a dignitary, was summoned aboard the packet boat as well. All were hurried ashore and ushered into the fort's headquarters where Colonel Ezpeleta greeted *Don* Francisco, accepted the dispatches and directed Diego to wait in the outer office until the Colonel was ready to hear any additional instructions Gálvez may have sent.

Diego waited patiently and mentally reviewed the special instructions Gálvez had entrusted to him. He also reflected upon the conditions he had observed thus far at Mobile. The bay lacked any vessels of size whatsoever. A move against Pensacola would require transporting men and material across the bay to *La Aldea*. The largest vessel, aside from the newly arrived *El Volante* was the packet boat. There were several large skiffs fixed with barrel racks used to bring fresh water from a fine well at *La Aldea*. The Colonel would have to have barges constructed. They would need to be large enough to carry siege cannons across the bay but small enough to sledge behind the army and then to be used as ferries to cross the Perdido River.

Ezpeleta was unprepared to move in support of an invasion of Pensacola, but the fort, Fort Carlota, was in excellent condition. If Campbell did move against Mobile, he had better be prepared for an extended siege and the backing of a large portion of the British western fleet, a fleet that was over extended with blockade work along the Atlantic Coast and supporting a major invasion of the rebellious colony of Georgia.

Diego was called into the Colonel's office to report any special instructions. He was not surprised to see *Don* Francisco was to remain for this briefing. Diego had become quite fond of the young officer. *Don* Francisco was almost the same age as Diego's son, Pedro, though slightly smaller. Pedro was tall and broad of shoulders where the Sub-Lieutenant was of average height and slender. Both young men were eager to learn and absorbed Diego's instructions with gusto.

Diego formally reported, dropping his salute only after Ezpeleta recognized him and asked for special instructions.

"Sir, the General requests that you prepare to move a part of your force to the fortifications at Bare Hill and then to *La Aldea*. Assemble such men, guns, animals and equipment the Colonel deems proper to assist in the pending siege on Pensacola. The Colonel will be advised when the fleet is poised to strike at which time the force at *La Aldea* is to move to Pensacola by the route *La Cuchilla* has scouted. The fleet may be able to provide assistance crossing the Perdido River, but the General would prefer if you could manage this river crossing with your own resources."

"I surmised as much from what Sub-Lieutenant Grevemberg had to tell me." Ezpeleta nodded in the direction of *Don* Francisco. "Sergeant, you will cross the bay and resume command of *La Cuchilla* today. As you have seen, we lack vessels of any size at this time. Send me word of any requirements you may have in order to perform your assignments.

"Sir, may I suggest," *Don* Francisco said, "we could build barges with skids. The barges can be large enough to transport men and heavy guns across the bay, but small enough to be pulled by oxen, still loaded with equipment and ready to forge any stream they meet."

Good lad, Diego thought. They had discussed such a possibility during the crossing. Coming from an officer, though young, the proposal would be given consideration.

"Yes, we will consider that option after Sergeant deMelilla has had a chance to scout our route to Pensacola. DeMelilla, I will have one of my clerks escort you to the pier where you will board the packet boat. Captain *Don* Felix Puig has been instructed to bring you to Bare Hill before he sets out for New Orleans."

The acting first mate of the *Señora del Rosario*, a boatswain's mate of considerable years, introduced himself to Diego as soon as they left the pier. He confided that he was a good friend of Captain Palmas of the *Alacita* and was aware of their letter delivery arrangement. He would be happy to bring a letter to Diego's wife, for a fee. Diego readily accepted the offer and had composed a letter for Isabella before they reached the landing at Bare Hill. This would be the first letter he had been able to send since he departed New Orleans in September.

Captain Puig did not have his men moor to the dock. When the packet boat bumped into the pier he directed Diego to step off the ship immediately. His gear, which consisted of a bedroll, backpack and a canvas bag, was handed across to him as the *Señora del Rosario* drifted away. After Diego was safely away, Puig had the sails set for a downwind run.

The landing at Bare Hill was crowded with water barrels waiting for transport to the fort by skiff. The shacks for laborers and fishermen had seemed to multiply during Diego's absence. He slogged up the muddy trail to the crest of the hill and met two men of *La Cuchilla*, Mina and Serpas, on guard duty at the entrance to the military encampment called Bare Hill.

"*Cordero!*" Mina said as soon as Diego was within hearing.

"*Cojo,*" Diego replied. *Cordero – Cojo* were the passwords of the day.

"*Primero*, welcome home!" Serpas exclaimed as Diego stepped up to them.

"What are you doing on guard? Why are you not patrolling the road to Pensacola?"

"Captain Castro has decided *La Cuchilla* was enjoying the countryside too much, so he has pulled everyone back for barracks duty. It is not bad, except we are also expected to work on the defenses along with the hired help."

"Captain? The man was a new Lieutenant not six months ago."

"It seems the militia commander was resentful of taking orders from a mere lieutenant, so Castro was promoted. At least it is a brevet promotion," Mina said.

"I will report to Captain Castro now and speak with you latter."

"Pook and Búho are standing guard at the headquarters." Mina tossed his head and rolled his eyes, indicating he believed the idea of posting guards at the door during the day was unnecessary. Diego had to agree. Patrolling beyond the walls of Bare Hill would do much more for security than stationary guards. He was carrying orders from Ezpeleta that would have his men free of Castro very soon.

Hired laborers returning from their work began to file by, causing Diego to step aside so they could pass through the narrow opening in the compound perimeter. The men spoke as they passed and Diego heard French as well as English conversations. The men were civilians from Mobile. Some of the laborers ducked into trailside huts while others descended to the pier where a small fleet of skiffs and pirogues had began to arrive to take them across the bay to their homes.

"They will return just before sunrise tomorrow," Serpas said. "Castro has decided to extend the trenches beside the wall further down the hill."

"What about cutting away the trees along the slopes?"

"That will be for us to do after the trenches are extended."

Backwards! Clear lines of fire first, trenches next.

The meeting with Castro went well considering Diego was to be given free rein to go as far as the Perdido River, depriving the captain of sixteen good men.

"You will have your men equipped and ready to depart before first light, Sergeant," Castro snarled. "What will you require in the way of rations or transport?"

"We will not require transport, sir. We will draw muskets with sixty cartridges for each man. We will carry rations for ten days and bed rolls, no tents."

"No wagons?"

"No, sir. We will travel light and return to *La Aldea* in six days."

"Just be gone before the sun rises tomorrow."

"Yes, sir," Diego said. "Would that be all, sir?"

"Yes, you are dismissed."

Diego saluted, faced about and exited Castro's office. He stepped out onto the porch to see not only Pook and Búho, but all of *La Cuchilla* gathered to greet him.

"We have just gone off duty, *Primero*," Pook said. "Come to the cook fires and tell us all about New Orleans and your bride."

"I will, Pook, that and much more. I have been wasting my time in Havana for a few months."

"Havana!" Pook exclaimed. "Who could be spending nights in Havana and call it 'wasting time'?"

They relocated to the evening cook fires and mess tent. Diego convinced the mess sergeant to issue an extra rum ration to his men. The fortification at Bare Hill was relatively isolated, so all were eager for news of the world and tomorrow they would be free of this oppressive barracks duty.

CHAPTER 23

Pook stood in the flickering morning campfire and read from a roster. *La Cuchilla* was mobilizing for another long-range reconnaissance foray beyond Spanish lines. Diego watched from the shadows as each man responded to his name with *"Honor et Fidelitas"* in lieu of "Here." It was a cool January morning and every man's words misted at his lips as he responded.

"Quintero."

"Honor et Fidelitas"

"O'Dali."

"Honor et Fidelitas"

"Olivier."

"Honor et Fidelitas"

"Acosta."

"Honor et Fidelitas"

"Godeau."

Diego listened as Pook called out sixteen names. Counting himself and Pook, *La Cuchilla* now numbered eighteen souls. Somewhat fewer than the two score men he had commanded when the campaign began and a third of what would be required to do a proper job.

"Mina."

"Honor et Fidelitas."

Pook closed the ledger and turned about sharply. Diego advanced from the shadows and centered on the formation.

"*Primero*, sixteen men of the ranks present for duty."

"Thank you, Pook. Has every man eaten?"

"Yes, *Primero*."

"Excellent. Post."

Pook stepped to Diego's left rear and prepared to follow him as he inspected each man in the ranks. If a deficiency were noted by Diego, Pook would record it in the ledger.

The uniform for the expedition consisted of the regimental white with blue trim wool uniform coat, blue waist coat, blue trousers, canvas gaiters, and wool garrison cap instead of the felt tricorn hat. Slung to land on the left hip was a haversack with ten day's rations and spare cartridges. On the right hip hung a cartridge box with a score of cartridges. Weapons consisted of musket and bayonet along with a side arm of choice. Most of the men preferred the American tomahawk, though a few carried short swords. They also carried an assortment of knives tucked away in various locations. Additionally, each man carried a backpack, canteens and a bedroll. No tents, no cooking utensils.

"Bounce ramrods!" Diego ordered. Each man withdrew his ramrod from beneath his musket and placed it down the barrel. The steel rods rang as they struck bottom on the empty muskets

"Fix bayonets."

Each man tilted his musket forward slightly and removed his bayonet from its scabbard with his left. If any bayonet stuck or offered resistance to being removed, Pook would note the offending party in his ledger. The men placed their bayonets on the muzzle of their muskets, gave it a twist to lock it in place and returned to the position of attention.

Diego moved to face Corporal Quintero, the first man in the file. The instant Diego was squarely facing Quintero, the corporal began the standard inspection routine that would be performed by each man in turn. He bounced the butt of his musket on the ground so the steel ramrod bounced audibly on the empty chamber. He lifted the weapon to the position of "inspection arms," pulled the hammer to half-cock, tipped the frizzen forward and glanced down into the pan to insure it was empty of powder. Satisfied that the musket was both unloaded and unprimed, Quintero looked straight ahead and waited.

Sometimes the inspecting officer would take the weapon, sometimes he would simply move on. *Primero* never simply moved on.

"Spark," Diego said.

Quintero thumbed the hammer to full cock and pulled the trigger. A roll of sparks glittered brightly in the misty air. Had that not happened, Pook would write in his ledger and Quintero, because he was a corporal, would receive a private lecture on the importance of a reliable spark. One never berated a man in the presence of men of lesser rank. Private soldiers, on the other hand, could expect to hear a litany of profanities, instantly, publicly and colorfully, should their flints fail to spark. The inspection ended without Pook having to open his ledger. The men had been well maintained during Diego's absence.

The inspection done, Pook and Diego assembled their own weapons and packs. The single line of sixteen infantrymen was converted to a column of eight – two abreast. Diego was about to order the men forward to the gate. Once beyond the gate, he intended to convert the tight column of two into a tactical advance with point skirmishers, flank security and a rear security – called "trail" – before they reached *La Aldea*.

Men began to appear out of the mist from the direction of the bay. They were carrying shovels, saws and other tools. There were at least two score of men. None headed for the gate, but walked along the shallow trench works and berm along the south slope that fell steeply away to a stream one hundred feet below. Diego decided to pause and let the men pass as some moved around his formation. The sky was beginning to turn gray.

"Workers for Castro's addition to the wall," Pook said.

The last worker disappeared over the berm and Diego had just ordered "Shoulder arms" when the tree canopy to the east and south erupted in a bright orange. A rattling, ripping noise filled the air.

Musketry!

The men who had just crossed over the berm were streaming back, shouting and screaming incoherently. Other shouts came from the trees and up the slope. Diego recognized some Choctaw words. He stepped up onto the berm to see hundreds of hunched figures running along the slope toward the bay in pursuit of the workers.

"Lock and load in quickest time," Diego shouted.

His men responded with practiced eased. In twenty seconds every man shouldered a primed and loaded musket.

First things first, Diego's mind was racing, "Fix bayonets."

The Choctaw seemed to be fixed on the fleeing men and made no attempt to come up the slope. Behind the Indians came three lines of uniformed men with bayonets at the advanced position. Orders were shouted in German and the lines turned to advance up the slope directly at the berm just east of Diego. In a moment they would cross over the berm.

Diego shouted, "Drop your packs!" His men stripped off their cumbersome backpacks and bed rolls. Instead of drawing his short sword, Diego picked up a shovel dropped by one of the fleeing workers. He did not have his *espontoon* so the shovel would have to serve as a substitute halberd to deliver the close combat signals required of a rank and file battle.

He maneuvered the sixteen men of *La Cuchilla* into a long line across the trench line in position to deliver enfilade fire onto the enemy as they crossed the berm. The enemy appeared in ragged order. The climb up the steep slope disrupted any semblance of military order and the volleys they had delivered out of the dark woods had ruined their night vision.

"Present," Diego shouted and sixteen muskets were pointed toward the men who were beginning to collect themselves in the shallow trench.

"*Disparar* (fire)!" The faces and uniforms of the enemy were exposed, bathed in a bright orange light. Some went down, some turned away, and some froze not knowing what to do.

"Lock and load," Diego shouted. He recognized the uniforms. They were Waldeckers, German mercenaries. There must have been sixty or more. An officer waving a sabre climbed onto the berm screaming orders. Twenty seconds had passed.

"Present," Diego ordered. "Fire. Lock and load."

The officer on the berm disappeared. A few of the Waldeckers had managed to form a line. They lowered their muskets at *La Cuchilla*. Diego was certain several were pointed directly at him. He leaned forward as if to face a great wind and the word turned orange again. He could hear whizzing sounds and the splat of impacts to this left. The Waldeckers, directed by a single officer, began to reload.

"Present," Diego ordered. "Fire. Advance bayonet." They were outnumbered three to one. If Diego simply attempted to trade volleys, *La Cuchilla* would be killed. Their last volley had been particularly effective on the enemy. They had been caught reloading and the officer who had been rallying them was gone.

La Cuchilla advanced in line with bayonets at the ready. A few of the enemy charged with bayonets of their own, but the charge was an undisciplined rush. Diego saw Martin parry a thrust and Búho, who was next to Martin in the file, bayonetted Martin's attacker.

That is how it should be done. Diego thought. Bayonets on line did not engage an enemy in single combat. One man would defend from an attacker and his *compadre* would kill from the left or right. Another officer appeared at the top of the berm and rushed at Diego with his sabre held high. Diego grasped the end of his shovel and lunged forward pushing the shovel before him. The shovel blade struck the German at the bridge of his nose and the man's face collapsed.

La Cuchilla continued to advance on line and in good order. The Waldeckers began to fall away. A formation materialized at the base of the wall to the left of Diego's men. He was about to redirect his men to face a new threat when the formation fired a volley into the retreating Germans. It was Castro and his grenadiers.

About time he joined this fight.

"Several hundred Choctaw passed us," Diego shouted to Castro, who seemed not to hear. "They were headed toward the bay," he added.

Toward the bay and in our rear!

La Cuchilla continued to where the wall met the trenches at the top of the slope. Diego changed the formation to a single column to skirt the edge of the wall and re-formed them into a line on the east side of the barrier. They were outside of the compound.

"Lock and load."

They had been advancing with unloaded muskets. An image of Diego's father flashed though his mind. "*Cold steel, it always reduces to cold steel,*" Doramas deMelilla said.

La Cuchilla had formed a line at right angles to the wall. Three hundred or more British regulars and Maryland militiamen were marching along the road from the village toward the gate. They had anticipated the gate would be opened by the Waldeckers and Choctaw after their surprise attack.

Diego decided he would fire one volley into the column and then retreat behind the wall. If the British pursued, they would have to round the corner of the wall in single file and be cut to pieces.

"Fire."

The volley clearly startled the British. Their officers had assumed the firing from within the compound had been their men routing the Spanish. The column on the road quickly transformed itself into a battle line, three deep, facing *La Cuchilla*. Diego opened his mouth to order a retreat as three hundred muskets were leveled in his direction.

Flame burst forward from the top of the battlements. *Gabriella!* The New Orleans artillery had joined the fight. Canister raked the British. Other shots, rifle fire, came from the top of the wall and mounted officers went down. The British began to draw back in confusion, pushing against the Marylanders who broke and ran.

The little four-pounders on the wall fired again. The canister rounds sounded like a swarm of bees as shot and ragged metal flew into the running men. Diego watched as the artillery sent a third volley up the road toward the village. Round shot this time, for the fleeing enemy was too far away for effective canister fire. Diego watched as the steel balls bounced along the road in the morning light bouncing up from the mist on the road and back down again.

Then the world became a blinding white.

ᘓᕲ

Mézu smiled as her figure consolidated from the whiteness around him. She wore the green dancing gown he remembered from the first day he met her. Only the gown she had worn then was tattered from hard travel. The one she wore now was sparkling, perfect and appropriate for Mézu – *Doña Maria Artiles y Ventomo*. Mézu had been born to aristocracy. The daughter of a wealthy wine merchant. Her grey and perfect eyes glistened.

"Hello, Diego," she said. Her voice was deep, feminine, perfect. He knew he was dreaming. He had dreamed of her before.

"This is no dream, Diego," she answered his thoughts. "There is someone I want you to meet."

A young man of twenty years or so stepped forward. Tall, brown of hair and lightly bearded, he could have been Diego's twin. The young man's eyes were the same haunting grey as his mother's.

"This is your son, Esteban," Mézu said.

"I do not understand. Our only son is Pedro."

"Esteban is the child I miscarried the year we left Gran Canaria." Mézu said as she caressed the lad's light brown hair.

Two more men appeared. Both appeared to be in their twenties. Diego recognized them immediately, despite their youth. One was Diego's father, Doramas deMelilla and the other was Diego's maternal grandfather, Tupinar the Rebellious One.

"What is happening? I do not understand." Diego asked. Suddenly, the back of his head began to ache terribly. "Oh!" he exclaimed.

"What is it, son?" Doramas asked.

"My head hurts terribly. I feel unwell." Diego looked for a place to sit down, but there was nothing but white marble floor everywhere he looked.

"Your head hurts because you must go back," Doramas said, disappointment in his voice.

They all began to recede from him. "Wait! Do not go. I want to stay."

"Isabella is with child," Mézu called out. She was drifting further away. "She is carrying your boy child. You must name him Esteban."

They all faded into the white glare leaving Diego to hold his throbbing head and moan. He turned to look away from the glare. A great bird, an owl, glided silently out of the gloom. It landed in front of Diego and looked at him intently, blinking its enormous eyes.

"*Primero*," it said. "*Primero, Primero.*"

❧

"*Primero, Primero!*"

Diego's eyes began to focus. Búho's round face, contorted with concern, filled his field of view.

"*Primero* lives," Búho exclaimed. "*Primero*, can you stand? Let me help you up."

Diego rose on shaky legs. "What happened?"

"It was one of the Germans, *Primero*. He played dead and after you passed him, he got up and clubbed you from behind with his musket. We thought he had killed you."

He may have.

"Martin did for him though. Hacked him to pieces with his tomahawk."

Diego looked around. Bodies were strewn along the road where Gabriella and the other cannons had sprayed the British with grape. Some wore red coats and others the tan with red trim of the Marylanders. Castro was directing men searching for wounded among the litter of bodies. Some prisoners were being escorted back through the gates.

"Pook," Diego called out as he looked about for his first corporal.

"Pook is dead, *Primero*," Búho said.

"Dead?" Diego blinked his eyes. "Quintero!"

"Here *Primero*!"

"You are first corporal. Get the men into formation and move them back to where we dropped our packs. Look for any wounded and tend to them and keep an eye out for those Choctaw that passed us earlier. I will join you after I talk to Castro."

"Yes, *Primero*."

"Olivier!"

"Yes, *Primero*."

"You are second corporal. Get the roster and be ready with a report when I join you."

"Yes, *Primero*."

"Well, move!"

Quintero called out, *"La Cuchilla.* Fall in on me."

Diego turned away muttering, "Pook dead? *Mierda!"* He found Castro standing next to the road supervising the examination of the fallen.

"Captain Castro. I must talk to you."

"Ah, deMelilla. Excellent work, Sergeant. Your men were stupendous!" Castro's face was flush with excitement. His blood was still up and he had difficulty standing still.

"Sir, two or three hundred Choctaw raced past us on the slope headed toward the bay."

"Yes, I know. They killed several unarmed workers, but fled to the south and across the stream when the Germans retreated."

"Why? They had us outnumbered and they were in our compound. Why quit the field?"

"Who can say, Sergeant, just thank God."

"Truly, sir. With your permission, I will see to my men."

"Yes, yes. Do so. This may have changed plans."

Diego returned to *La Cuchilla* and was dismayed to see how few were waiting for him.

"Quintero, please have the men stand for a roster call."

"La Cuchilla, attention." The men formed a single line.

Diego took the roster and read. "Martin."

"Honor et Fidelitas."

"Corporal Gonzales."

"Dead, *Primero,"* Quintero responded. As first corporal it was his duty to respond for those who could not answer for themselves.

Diego made a mark in the ledger. "Corporal Pedro Gonzales – killed." His hand shook.

"Franco."

"Honor et Fidelitas." Búho answered to his given name.

"Godeau."

"Dead, *Primero."*

Diego made another mark in the ledger.

"Serpas."

"Wounded, *Primero*. He is at the aid tent."

Diego made another mark in the ledger. He finished the roster call. Four had been killed. Corporal Pedro "Pook" Gonzales, Privates Francisco Godeau, Tomás Fuzmorin and Salvador Roquerols. Two had been seriously wounded, Privates Josef Serpas and Pedro "Tiritar" Gillama. They were in the aid tent. Several had received minor wounds but had refused treatment.

La Cuchilla had been reduced to ten men at arms and one sergeant. Diego had the men stack arms and released them to tend to the dead. He tried to help, but quick movements caused the world to spin about and blood kept trickling from his ears. He left Quintero in charge and went to see the wounded.

⤴

The next morning, January 8th,1781, *La Cuchilla*, ten men at arms and a sergeant, marched out of Bare Hill compound and passed through *La Aldea*. Diego sent Olivier with two skirmishers ahead and dropped two into trail. Two provided flank security, one to the left and one to the right. They were so few.

Castro had suggested the scouting mission be scrapped, but Diego pointed out that the orders came from General Gálvez and he intended to carry them out. It would be important to know if the British had abandoned an assault on Bare Hill or if they were marshalling their forces for another try. Only one hundred sixty defenders remained. Castro had sent for reinforcements, but Ezpeleta lacked transport and could only send a few men across the bay in squad-sized units and no cannons at all.

La Cuchilla advanced through the wooded margin on a line parallel to the road to Pensacola. The man providing right flank security was responsible for insuring they did not wander far from the road. In war, one never traveled down a road unless it was known to be secure. Diego did not have the men necessary to provide adequate advance security, so he directed *La Cuchilla* to work though the wilderness, ever alert for a trap.

The road was littered with the cast-offs of a defeated force. Torn uniform coats, broken equipment, bloody bandages and other debris lined the road. The margin of the roadway was more telling. At every location where the British had called a temporary halt, clusters of discarded items had been left behind.

The road to Pensacola turned sharply north about five miles east of *La Aldea*. It continued north for another five or six miles before changing to an almost direct southeast track for Pensacola. The detour was necessary to avoid having to ford several small streams. Diego was very familiar with this terrain.

Instead of following the road on the northern detour, he directed his men east along a foot path. He planned to ford a small river and intercept the Pensacola Road after only three miles of wilderness march. If they continued to follow the main road, they would have to cover twelve miles to reach the same point.

Diego would be in unfamiliar territory once they rejoined the main road and, worse yet, he had no way of knowing if the British retreat had progressed enough to pass where *La Cuchilla* would emerge. Olivier and the advance scouts would have to be particularly alert after they forded the river and began to climb up the ridgeline.

They forded the river with little effort. It was shallow, sandy and cold. As they climbed the gentle slope, Diego would signal for a pause every few minutes to listen for movement ahead and to smell. Four hundred men, horses and mules smell. Camp fires, cook fires, animal dung and human waste marked the passage of an army more clearly than the rattle of equipment, the creak of leather harnesses, the squeak of wagon wheels or the murmur of voices. Smell lingered.

The day was beginning to fade when Olivier stepped out onto the trail and signaled Diego to halt. Everyone stopped stock still, straining to see, hear or smell a reason for the pause. Diego could not detect anything unusual. He could only see fifty yards to the east and he could ascertain nothing indicating they had reached the road, though they ought to be getting near it. Olivier signaled again for Diego to come forward.

Diego approached Oliver as quickly and as quietly as he could. When he reached the man, he caught a whiff of horse manure mixed with wood smoke. The road must be just ahead. Diego looked at the tree tops and thought he saw a break in the canopy another hundred yards or so east. They had reached the road.

"Acosta signaled me," Olivier whispered. "He saw two men, hiding in the brush. I have him watching those two while Cano circles around to see if there are more lurking about."

"Can he tell if they are British?" Diego asked.

"Tan coats with red trim, from what I could see." Olivier said. "Mary-landers."

Diego knew the majority of the force that attacked Bare Hill had been Maryland militia. The German mercenaries had suffered great losses. Castro's interrogation of the prisoners produced a less-than reliable conclusion. Captain von Hanxleden, the Waldecker commander and expedition leader, had been killed along with two other German officers. The lone British officer was also killed. The officer now in command of the expedition was a militia captain named Key and he seemed keen on getting back to Pensecola.

Cano appeared. *"Primero,"* was all he said in way of greeting as he approached.

"See anybody else?" Diego asked.

"Not a soul. The *godums* stopped here not four hours ago. Cook fires are still smoldering."

"What do you think, *Primero*," Olivier asked.

"Deserters, I think. They are hiding, not watching the road behind?"

"Never looked once to the northwest, but they continually watched the road in the direction of Pensacola." Olivier said.

"We will surround them. I want Cano on the south and Acosta on the north, Tomahawks at the ready. If they run, cut them down. No musketry. The *godums* may hear." Diego said. He turned to Olivier. "When Cano and Acosta are in position I want you to call out to them in English. Ask what they are doing here. Stay out of sight until we can determine if they are armed. If they are deserters, tell them who we are and see if we can get them to surrender."

⁊

Privates William Hall and Thomas Tilghman responded to Olivier's hail by leaping to their feet and thrusting their hands into the air. When Olivier announced they were surrounded by Spaniards and prisoners, the men slumped in relief.

"Thank God," Tilghman muttered when Diego walked up to the pair. "We was hope'n you Spaniards would be along."

Diego did not trust his command of English so he waved Olivier in. He had the prisoners sit and wait. It was dark and security matters had to be addressed. Guards were posted, relief scheduled and a cold camp was prepared. Scouts sent down the road toward Pensacola returned after having traveled a mile, reporting no sign of a British force.

When things were settled, Diego began his questioning of the prisoners. He spoke in Spanish and Olivier acted as translator. Diego found that he could follow much of what was said, but his command of English would not permit him to conduct the interrogation in that language. The men were both Catholics forced into the Maryland Loyalist Militia by circumstances. Neither man cared who ruled Maryland, they just wanted to farm their land in peace.

"It is hard to be a Catholic posted with the British in this wilderness," Hall said. "They sent us here on account they do not trust us none. Got us here with a bunch of Germans."

"That is because the bloody king of England is a German. I hear he does not speak English, even." Tilghman added.

Hall nodded in agreement. "Thinks we are all rebel spies. Got us here fighting mosquitoes, yellow fever, and hurricanes just to get us out of Maryland, I say."

"It is true," Tilghman continued. "We are from Fells Point. Just before we left on this little walk, they hung one of our mates for treason, they said. And not a proper hang'n neither. They just tied a loop around his neck and hauled him up a beam. Did not tie his hands, did not give him a proper drop to break his neck. No, just pulled him up in the air by a rope around his neck and him trying to hold the loop so as not to choke and kicking his feet. It took him a quarter hour to give out. Him being an officer and all and from our town we figured we might be next."

"Why did they think this officer was a traitor?"

"Why? I cannot say why," Hall said. "He was a decent fellow far as I could tell. From Fells Point, like I said. Newly made widower and all. Did not figure him to be no spy."

"Looked to me like he was gettin' on well," Tilghman said. "He was getting to know that lady what showed up some weeks ago."

"Gettin' to know," Hall scoffed. "She had him following her around like a lap dog. Gettin' to know. Piff!"

"What lady," Diego asked in English, startling both prisoners.

"Fancy lady, Sergeant. Name of Smythe. Prudence Smythe. So pretty as to be a sin."

"He did not have a chance," Tilghman added. "What with being a lonely widower and all and her batting them big eyes at him."

"What was this officers' name?"

"Wiggins, Sergeant. Lieutenant Joseph Wiggins of Fells Point."

Joseph Wiggins was the name on the note Diego found in Maury's pocket. Barnave had gone to Pensacola knowing to look for Wiggins. The lieutenant was a lonely widower in a posting far from home. Marcelite must have laughed at how easily she seduced Wiggins and pried secrets out of him. He remembered how easily, jokingly she had departed from him on that dock in Havana when everyone, him included, believed he was about to die. Did she watch Joseph Wiggins struggle at the end of a rope as easily and with as much humor?

Diego had the men provide food for the deserters, had them trussed about a tree and placed under guard. In the morning, he would send the prisoners back with Olivier and two others while he and the rest, all seven of them, would continue to the Perdido River.

⁓

La Cuchilla, seven men at arms and one sergeant, reached the Perdido River at noon on the second day after parting with the prisoners. Eight men free of encumbrances travel much faster than an army of four hundred, even a retreating army, and *La Cuchilla* had caught up with the British force. Diego, concealed by foliage, watched as the last of the British were ferried across the Perdido River by five skiffs. It must have required eight crossings to move so many across the river. The skiffs, small enough to be hauled by men, must have been why the British attacked without artillery.

The river was wide and too deep to ford. Ezpeleta would have to drag barges with him or arrange for boats to come up from the gulf when he moved down from Mobile to support Gálvez at Pensacola. The road from Bare Hill to the banks of the Perdido was sufficient to support a thousand troops with wagons, cannons, horses and siege equipment. If Ezpeleta could arrange it, the heavy gear could be transported from Mobile to this location on the Perdido and join his army on the east side of the river.

Diego stepped out of concealment and walked down the center of the road to the edge of the Perdido River. The last of the troops to cross, Redcoats all, were still trying to gather themselves on the opposite bank when one of them saw Diego. The appearance of a single Spanish soldier should not have created much of a stir, but these were tired men who were on edge.

Two battle lines were quickly formed and skirmishers rushed into the woods on either side of the road. Diego hoped none of the British had a rifle. He took a deep breath and cupped his hands about his mouth.

"Hello, Sixtieth Foot," he yelled.

A sergeant separated from one of the lines of Redcoats.

"Hello, Dago," the man answered.

Diego was momentarily surprised the man addressed him by name until he remembered "Dago" was a derisive British slang for "Spaniard" much as "*Godum*" was for British.

"Just come to see you safely away," Diego said. He noticed the Redcoats; evidently satisfied one Spanish sergeant did not portend an attack, were breaking formation and beginning to withdraw.

"You will do well to keep to that side of the Perdido, Dago."

"I have a message for someone at Pensacola. Can you deliver it?"

"That would depend upon the message and the recipient."

"Please tell the Lady Smythe she is not forgotten."

I hope to be a witness, my lady, when you are tried as a spy. A pity Gálvez will not have you hung.

"Who shall I say sends such word?"

"She will know."

The sergeant made s dismissive gesture and turned away.

"Perhaps, she may not know," Diego said to no one. He turned and walked up the road and shouted, "Quintero, fall the men in on the road. We are going back to Bare Hill marching down the center of the road as if we had not a care."

Although Pensacola will be a fight, it will fall, Diego thought. Mobile was the key. Spain had already won Florida and guaranteed free passage on the Mississippi River when Mobile was held. Two hundred men, Spaniards and New Orleans militiamen, repulsed four times their number in a fight for their lives.

They could not have known their desperate battle assured the creation of a nation – the United States.

Historical Note

The involvement of Spain in support of and as an ally of the American Revolutionaries has been a well-kept secret. This novel focuses on one of the pivotal aspects of that support, Spain's siege of Mobile and subsequent desperate fight to maintain control of that vital port. The strategic importance of Mobile to the vulnerability of New Orleans, Baton Rouge and ultimately, control of the Mississippi River, has been recognized by military planners from Iberville to Andrew Jackson.

Mr. Thomas E. Chávez in his fine work "Spain and the Independence of the United States – An Intrinsic Gift," University of New Mexico Press, 2002, documents very well the depth, financial and military of that support. Mr. John Walton Caughey's "Bernard de Gálvez in Louisiana 1776 – 1783" Pelican Publishing Company, 1998 is an excellent work addressing Gálvez and the Spanish commitment to the American cause. José Montero de Pedro, Marqués de Casa Mena's "The Spanish in New Orleans and Louisiana" Pelican Publishing Company, 2000 and translated by Richard E, Chandler is another excellent reference. There are hosts of other scholarly historical works addressing this almost forgotten aspect of Spanish Colonial Louisiana.

The Canary Islander settlers, the *Isleños*, transported here between the years of 1778 and 1781, were recruited as soldiers in the Spanish army for the purpose of driving the British out of East and West Florida, an area that today encompasses parts of Louisiana, Mississippi, Alabama and all of present-day Florida.

My protagonist, Diego deMelilla y Tupinar, is a compilation of many actual *Isleños*. The reader would have noticed names I assigned to many of the Spanish soldiers may not seem "Spanish." Spain had taken control of Louisiana in 1764. In the decade and a half preceding the Spanish war with Britain, citizens of Louisiana were enlisting in the militia and the Spanish regular army. The people in Louisiana came from all over Europe, Africa, Asia and the Americas. Even in Europe, Spain accepted hoards of Irish émigrés escaping the oppression of Protestant Britain, enough to form Hibernian Regiments within the Spanish army.

With few exceptions, the names of ships and individuals I have chosen for my story were taken from the actual rosters of the army Gálvez assembled for the attack on the British outposts or from the passenger manifests of the *Isleños* settlers. The names of the British defenders, with some exceptions, were also drawn from the historical record. Of course, the actual involvement and activities of all these characters is fictitious. The names of the Spaniards killed were drawn from casualty reports of the entire campaign. I have taken little license with the timing of events. The condition of the land, weapons and tactics are as true to history as my research would allow. Some things will always be lost to history.

Some histories report the village of Mobile was completely burned to the ground by the British before the Spanish siege. Other reports imply only that a portion of the town nearest the fort was reduced. In either case, the citizens of Mobile suffered more at the hands of the British defenders than the invading Spanish. The British failure to hold Mobile sealed the fate of that nation's diminishing influence in the southeast and freed the Mississippi River as a conduit of supplies for the rebels' western front.

Historians have concentrated on battles within the former British Colonies when researching and documenting the American Revolution. The French alliance provided ships and even some troops in the Atlantic theater of the Revolutionary War.

Spain's alliance provided arms and supplies to Washington's army, but Spain's ships and troops battled the British on the southern front. Subsequent conflicts, the push of Manifest Destiny and the propaganda campaign known as the "Black Legend" has obscured Spain's vital role in the establishment of the United States of America.

England in particular propagated stories of Spanish atrocities in an effort to widen the divide between Protestant Western Europe and Catholic Spain. Stories of torture and religious persecution by the Spanish were exaggerated, embellished or created from whole cloth. The Spanish were particularly characterized as bloodthirsty, cruel and heartless during the rule of Henry VIII, a king who perpetrated outrages far beyond those his propagandists attributed to the Spanish.

The Black Legend developed a life of its own during the American period of "Manifest Destiny" as proponents of the expansion of the United States sought to justify military action against the only remaining European influence in the Western Hemisphere, Spain. Because of these influences, American history books and historians fail to properly report Spain's contribution to the creation of the United States.

The men who, in the service of Spain, fought and were killed driving the British from what would become American soil have all but been forgotten. The deMelilla Chronicles are a series of novels intended to uncover the deep, but often hidden, influence of Spain in general and the *Isleños* in particular on Louisiana customs and genealogy.

About The Author

Stephen Estopinal grew up in the swamps and bayous of Saint Bernard and Plaquemines Parishes. He is a graduate of Louisiana State University (class of 1968), a US Army veteran (Combat Engineers 1969-1971) and is a Land Surveyor and Civil Engineer employed by the SJB Group, LLC, in the Baton Rouge area.

Mr. Estopinal was a living history volunteer at the Chalmette Battle Field National Park and a black powder expert. His love of history, particularly the history of colonial Louisiana has prompted him to write a series of novels to bring that history to life. A descendent of Canary Islanders (*Isleños*) transported to Louisiana by the Spanish during the American Revolution, he draws on extensive research as well as family oral history to tell his stories of Colonial Louisiana from a Spanish point of view.

Mr. Estopinal began writing books in 1986 when John Wiley & Sons published his textbook, *A Guide to Understanding Land Surveys,* now in its 3rd edition and required reading at LSU's engineering survey course. His second textbook, *Professional Surveyors and Real Property Descriptions* was co-authored with Wendy Lathrop and also published by John Wiley has just been released.

The first of his novels was *El Tigre de Nueva Orleáns* published in 2010 and has been approved for sale by the National Park Service at the Chalmette National Park Visitor's Center. It has been followed by a novel every year. *Incident at Blood River* was published in 2011, *Anna* in 2012, *Escape to New Orleans* in 2013, and now *Mobile Must Fall* in 2014. Collectively, the novels are known as the **deMelilla Chronicles.** These novels are all historical fictions of 18th and 19th Century. They tell the story of the *Isleños* settlers in Louisiana and their struggle for survival. Writing historical fiction has provided Stephen Estopinal with a means of keeping alive the diverse and nearly forgotten history of Spanish Colonial Louisiana.

Made in the USA
San Bernardino, CA
13 August 2014